OF GOLD AND IRON

OF DREAMS AND NIGHTMARES TRILOGY

NICKI CHAPELWAY

BOO'S BOOKS PUBLISHING

Copyright © 2020 by Nicki Chapelway

All rights reserved.

No portion of this book may be reproduced in any form without written permission from the publisher or author, except as permitted by U.S. copyright law.

Cover by Cover by **MiblArt**

Edited by Deborah

Formatted by Jes Drew

To Mama and Grandpa Tom.
Love you guys.

CONTENTS

Chapter		1
		2
1. Chapter 1		3
		8
2. Chapter 2		9
		14
3. Chapter 3		15
		20
4. Chapter 4		21
		28
5. Chapter 5		29
		34
6. Chapter 6		35
		42
7. Chapter 7		43
		48
8. Chapter 8		49
		54

9.	Chapter 9	55
		62
10.	Chapter 10	63
		70
11.	Chapter 11	71
		80
12.	Chapter 12	81
		94
13.	Chapter 13	95
		102
14.	Chapter 14	103
		110
15.	Chapter 15	111
		120
16.	Chapter 16	121
		128
17.	Chapter 17	129
		136
18.	Chapter 18	137
		146
19.	Chapter 19	147
		156
20.	Chapter 20	157
		164

21.	Chapter 21	165
		176
22.	Chapter 22	177
		182
23.	Chapter 23	183
		192
24.	Chapter 24	193
		198
25.	Chapter 25	199
		206
26.	Chapter 26	207
		212
27.	Chapter 27	213
		218
28.	Chapter 28	219
		226
29.	Chapter 29	227
		232
30.	Chapter 30	233
		246
31.	Chapter 31	247
		254
32.	Chapter 32	255
		262

33. Chapter 33 — 263
34. Chapter 34 — 271
35. Chapter 35 — 283
36. Chapter 36 — 289
37. Chapter 37 — 301
38. Chapter 38 — 307
39. Chapter 39 — 315
40. Chapter 40 — 325

Afterword — 328

About the Author — 329

Acknowledgments — 330

CHAPTER ONE

We have three fundamental rules when dealing with the faeries. Never trust a faerie. Don't make bargains with faeries. And never go anywhere near a faerie without wearing a charm of protection. But I think, in all honesty, that there should be a fourth rule.

Don't fall in love with a faerie.

I know in theory it seems so simple and easy—of course I would never fall in love with a faerie. What an idea. Only an idiot would do that, right? Faeries are dangerous, conniving creatures that have no care for any soul other than their own twisted rotten ones. But like outside of theory... I mean, have you seen a faerie?

I have spent my life knowing of their existence, bracing myself for their terrible beauty and their cunning charms. Not all faeries are beautiful, mind you, but the ones that are... Well, those are the sorts that might just make you reconsider being smart and keeping your distance from the foul creatures. Those are the sorts that remind you that you are only human, and humans have more than their fair share of weaknesses.

People are like birds in a way. Constantly drawn to pretty things.

I shake my head, causing my braid to flop off of my shoulder. Not me of course, I'm too smart to ever have such a thing happen to me. In all honesty smarts may be the only thing I have going for me. But there are the people, my brother included, who rely on other things like brawn. It's people like that who the rules were made for anyway.

Who in their right mind would make a bargain with a faerie, or near them without a protective charm? It's like asking to be turned into a toad. And I don't care how persuasive a faerie can be, the history of the Guardians has more than its fair share of stories proving that no faerie can be trusted. No matter what they say.

I know all of this, and I don't need any old rules to make sure that I don't do them.

I'm not even sure why I'm thinking about this at this particular moment when I have much bigger issues to occupy my mind. Like my first actual mission as a Guardian. My fingers tap against the hilt of the iron blade strapped to my waistband, hidden from view by my plaid shirt.

By all intents and purposes, I look like a regular human, out for a lovely evening hike, who wandered too far. Straight into the faerie world.

The cover shouldn't technically work, a human can't just wander into the faerie world. The only way that my family and other Guardians have managed to pass through has been through using technology—a little disk in my satchel invented by Great Grandad McCullagh. Before that, we were forced to rely on unpredictable faerie allies. If you could in any honesty call a faerie an ally. But fortunately for us, as little as we know of the faerie's travel between worlds, it seems that the faeries know even less about ours.

As a general rule, faeries care nothing for the coming and going of mortals through the years unless it directly pertains to them and their games.

I find it hard to believe that we haven't been spied on by our own fair share of the Fair Folk. But it seems as if only we humans truly remember the ancient war between our kind and theirs. I don't know if they would even consider it a war. We are so far below their notice, more like inanimate objects existing only for their pleasure to be used and forgotten and thrown out at their leisure. One does not wage war against a couch.

But we humans don't see it that way.

One of these days we will strike a crippling blow against the Fair Folk, and maybe they will finally get it through their thick sculls that we aren't to be messed with. But until then we really just got to try to hold our own.

I inhale deeply, breathing in the crisp air. We are near the Autumn Court, home of the Solitary faeries. But technically according to faerie geography it isn't the Autumn Court until the leaves start to glow, fueled by their inhabitant's chaotic magic. I don't know where the faeries would consider this point of their world, maybe they don't even have a name for it. They tend to stick to their courts and ignore all else.

Which is why it was suspicious that the cameras we set up around my family's faerie ring, which we use as a gateway between our worlds, picked up two faeries in the area. Even more suspicious, at least one of the faeries was a Solitary faerie. And yeah, I know that these woods are pretty close to their home, but Solitary faeries are more hermitlike than my homeschooled antisocial self, and trust me when I say they don't stray from their home at all.

Without a cause.

And seeing as Dad positively identified the faerie, we got a good look at as a Far Darrin, that cause is trouble. Quite literally. Far Darrig's are one of the more malignant Solitary faeries, they thrive off of chaos and trickery. They live to play pranks. Magical, dangerous pranks that could quite possibly end in death, but pranks all the same.

Although, even if it is the most malignant of the Solitary faeries, at least it isn't a member of the Winter Court, which I've heard only tolerates humans when they are either dead or enslaved.

It's just a Far Darrig, out for a bit of fun. Of course, their form of fun tends to run along the lines of dismemberment and bloody chaos.

Unfortunately, Mom and Dad didn't think that this new development was enough to cancel their meeting with my uncles, which is how I find myself on my first actual mission.

I press my hand against my chest, feeling the rapid thrum of my anxious heart beating away as a gust of wind blows, rustling the leaves around me. I peer around and swallow when I see that I am still alone. I press my back against a tree and squeeze my eyes shut. I need to calm down. Dad wouldn't have sent us on this mission if he didn't think we couldn't handle it. We aren't even in a faerie court. Just out in the woods. With two Solitary faeries to deal with.

It's practically a training mission. It is so easy.

Just get in, figure out what it is they are doing, and get out.

No interactions even necessary.

I breathe in again and clench my fist. I am going to be doing these sorts of things all my life. Someday Thomas and I will take over for our parents. I need to get over this irrational fear. Unfortunately, faeries, knowing that they are real and that they are truly evil, have always frightened me. I read everything I could, learned everything anyone else knew about faeries in the hopes of feeling like I am in control when it comes to faeries. But I definitely don't feel like I am in control right now, despite the vast amounts of ancient Irish history I memorized in the sixth grade. Great...

I wish I could talk to a human being just for one second so I don't feel so isolated, but my parents are on Earth waiting for our report and my brother isn't currently a human. He is off romping on all fours in the forest somewhere making the best use of his faerie given gifts and not dressed up as a hiker hoping that the faeries really don't know the exact way humans can come and go between their world.

I push away from the tree, the dead leaves crunching under the heel of my custom-made leather boot. It's certainly not a hiking boot, yet another thing that we are hoping the faeries don't know. My eyes dart across the trees which are becoming nothing more than dark inhuman forms in the quickly approaching dusk.

A sharp, chill wind blows, slicing right through my plaid shirt. I wrap my arms around myself and shudder. A sound like flapping echoes through the still air. At first, I had thought the silence was unsettling. Now that I hear something, I actually miss it.

Something crunches behind me.

My breath stalls somewhere between my lungs and my nostrils as my whole body goes still. Fight or flight flees, leaving me with some sort of weird statue instinct. Like somehow if I stand still enough no one will see me, despite being out in the middle of the trees in full view of whoever is behind me.

Because there is something standing behind me. I know it. I can feel all of my hairs stand on end, hyper aware of the added presence. And yet I still can't turn around, the statue instinct saying that if I can't see them, they can't see me either.

A foolish sentiment I know. I *know* it is, and yet I somehow can't move. It's like I have been ensorcelled, but that isn't possible because the protective pendant on my wrist is still in place. It's familiar weight my only comfort right now.

More leaves crackle as something draws closer to me. Something much larger than the bird that I thought I heard earlier.

Please be Thomas, please be Thomas.

I want to draw my dagger, but I force myself to remain rational. I still have my senses no matter who is here with me. Once that dagger is out then that's it, my status as a Guardian will be known to all. I will have no other wild cards. To deal with faeries you need to think like a faerie. Act like a faerie thinks humans truly act. My number one weapon right now isn't my dagger but the faerie's hubris and tendency to underestimate humans. Play dumb at first, keep all your cards close to your chest, and play strategically.

The creature behind me huffs a laugh, a short, humorless, almost mocking sound. A voice that is equally gravelly and silky follows. "Enjoying the scenery, are we? I can assure you; the more lovely view is behind you. Truly."

Nope, not Thomas.

I lick my suddenly dry lips and inhale a short breath. Well, I came to find out what the faeries were up to in these woods. I just hadn't wanted such a front row seat. The statue instinct finally releases me from its stony hold and my heart pounds faster, demanding that I turn *right now*. My mind racing with images of some sort of ferocious, vicious creature reaching bony fingers and claws toward my exposed back.

I whirl around, but that's as far as I get before I freeze again. For all of my talk about how I wouldn't fall in love with a faerie, I will admit that I have never been faced with such a beautiful being before. And while I will gather my senses well enough, it does take a second to desensitize yourself.

Jutting cheekbones and glowing bronze skin signifying the underlying magic contained within, classify him as a faerie. I don't even need his pointed ears or overly graceful tall form to do that. I would mistake him for the Sidhe race, known in legends for their beauty, except he does not have the telltale blonde hair. No, his hair is so black that it puts the growing shadows to shame. What he does have is the telltale red vest of the Solitary faeries over his slim chest.

They say that the Solitary faeries are not as beautiful as the rest of the Fair Folk, and suddenly I am absolutely terrified to see one of these more beautiful Fair Folk.

Because this faerie is enough to knock my custom-made leather shoes right off.

The faerie seems almost as surprised as I feel. The smug smile slips off his face and his eyes start to widen. For a second, I think that they are a dazzling purple and try to remember if purple eyes are a key defining trait for a certain type of faerie, but then I blink and when I open my eyes again, I see that his eyes are actually a dull black.

"By every court there ever was, and the dead queen's head, you are without a doubt the most *hideous* creature I have ever—and I do mean ever in the entire existence of my rather impressive life—had the misfortune to lay my eyes upon." His face twists as if he is in great pain, and he spits out each word deliberately, as if to further enunciate his already crystal-clear meaning.

I will admit, I don't fully think on what I do next, I just sort of act on instinct. And that instinct told me to pull back my leg and kick him as hard as I could in the shins.

CHAPTER TWO

There is a reason we have our rules.

Never trust a faerie because no matter how sincere they may seem, no matter that you are both working to a similar goal, faeries are only, *only* ever out for their own skin. Any time that you do not coincide with their plans, they will drop you in a heartbeat, not caring about any sort of shared history you may have had. Faeries don't suffer from sentimentality.

Never make a bargain with a faerie. You cannot beat a master at their own game. They will always end up on top. And you. Will. Lose.

Never go anywhere near a faerie without a protective charm. Faerie's magic is in manipulation, they can use it to control anything around them. Humans as well as inanimate beings. Such a charm protects humans from their magic, saving them from being cursed. Which means that I don't have to worry about being enchanted, ensorcelled, or enthralled into oblivion.

A very angry faerie can however use any sort of nearby object to swiftly end my life. That tree for instance? Its roots could come alive and drag me underground where I'd suffocate. Or the branches could lash out and snap me like I'm the twig. Or perhaps the leaves would become razor sharp and flit through the air straight toward my exposed flesh. All possibilities.

And all seeming somewhat likely as the faerie jumps back with a startled howl. My hands fly up to cover my mouth as I stare wide eyed. I can't believe I just did that. I mean, I know I have a quick temper that has always gotten the better of me, but I must say this has to be the most dangerous display of anger I've ever had.

The faerie pulls to his full height which is at least a foot above my head. A bit too tall and a bit too thin to look natural on a human, but somehow faeries pull off the look very gracefully. His eyes flick over me and I consider making a break for it, but I hold my ground because I don't actually think I would get too far. Plus, I haven't finished my mission yet.

If I'm to die I shall do it as a Guardian in service. Not as a teenage girl fleeing like a coward.

He sneers, it should mar his handsome face just a little bit, but instead it slides into place. Like that was the position his face was made to be in. Maybe the coward's way has more of an upside than I had previously considered. In one fluid motion he steps forward and grabs my arm. I yelp and try to pull back, but his grip is like iron. Except not iron, because one of the few weaknesses a faerie has is actually iron.

My free hand shoots to my belt just as the faerie starts talking again. "Disgusting. Loathsome. Ungrateful. Tactless—"

I pause and look up into his face. This close I actually see that his eyes are yellow, I don't know how I could confuse that for purple or even black, but stranger things have happened in the Otherworld. "What are you doing?" I'm surprised by how strong my voice actually is. I would have thought that it would have long abandoned me just like my common sense apparently has.

"Describing you," the faerie spits out.

I jam my free hand into his chest, forgetting momentarily about my knife. "Watch it or I'll kick you even harder and in a more strategic place next time." I never knew a faerie to be so petty. They never cared enough about humans to insult them. Abuse them? Use them as helpless pawns in their crafty games? Enslave them? All yes.

But insult them?

To them our entire existence is an insult to us in and of itself and there isn't anything that they need to say or do on the matter.

I don't know how it happened but somehow the faerie and I end up staring at each other for a long and very pregnant moment. Neither of us saying anything, just sort of staring. It's kind of awkward actually, but somehow I can't force myself to look away. A hint of purple flickers in his yellow eyes, it must have been what I spotted earlier. Not that it matters.

I don't actually care what his eye color is.

I finally pry my mouth open ready to ask him what the heck he is even doing when suddenly he yanks me forward. I stumble into him and he turns into it effortlessly, holding me in his arms in what can only be described as a dip. Like what the dancers do.

I snap my head up and elbow him at the same time. He releases me with a grunt and I fall to the side, gaining my footing at the last second. "What is going on here and why did none of my books warn me about this?"

The last half of the question is less directed to the faerie and more at the world in general.

He folds his arms and glares at me. "I just saved your life, the least you could do is show some gratitude."

"Excuse me, but what the..." I trail off as I notice the ground right where I had been standing... well it isn't ground anymore. Instead it is a pit in the ground, slowly the ground closes, the circle falling into itself until the hole is filled. "What was that? What is happening?"

My voice is hysterical to my own ears, but at this point I am beyond caring.

Words cannot express it enough. What. The. Heck. Is. Happening.

In a very short window, I have gone from just a normal day in the life of Jaye MacCullagh to... I don't even know how to describe this, and it's quite unreal.

The faerie tosses his head, causing the single perfect curl to fall further into his eyes. "I understand this must be difficult for your mortal mind to comprehend but I, the great and the majestic Ravven Crowe, just saved your life. To think, not long ago you hadn't even met me. Now you have two grand honors in such a short span of time. Your feeble mind must be reeling."

My mind is reeling, but not from awe of this *Ravven Crowe*. Which isn't even his real name. Faeries don't go by their real names but rather an adopted name because knowing a faerie's real name gives that person power over them. Power to make that faerie do anything they want. And if there is anything a faerie can't stand, it's to be powerless. Out of tradition, Guardians also don't go by their real names, but most of the time I forget that my name isn't actually Jaye.

See, as much as I don't want to trust him, here's the thing. When a faerie says that they saved your life. That means that they saved your life. As unbelievable as that fact is.

The Fair Folk cannot lie. It is one of their very few weaknesses.

No, I think the question now is. Why did he save my life? Because I can assure you that he didn't do it from the goodness of his heart. Faeries don't have goodness of their hearts. My eyes dart to where his immortal heart is doubtlessly beating under that crimson vest. All faeries are by nature selfish—perhaps it is a trait gained from living thousands of years in your own company. By far, the faeries that are the kindest to humans are the Tuatha De Danan of the Seelie Court, and that is because they have fond memories of when they ruled over my Irish ancestors as gods.

Although now that I reconsider the specific meaning of his words, a good habit to be in when dealing with faeries, I realize that he didn't specifically state that he wasn't the one who endangered my life in the first place. Just because a faerie can't lie, doesn't mean that their truths cannot paint a deceiving picture.

Ravven frowns. "This is where I believe your kind thinks it is appropriate to thank their savior."

I pull back, crossing my arms, my eyes darting across the trees looking for any other threats to my safety. "I'm not thanking the likes of you." For all I know he might take it to mean that I owe him now. But I'm not bound to the same law of honor as the Fair Folk, he can't turn me into his life servant. "Why did you save me? For all I know you were the one trying to kill me in the first place."

Ravven places one hand against his chest, a gold ring on his middle finger glinting even though there is no significant light source for it to catch off of. His fingers are long and around the fingernails, his skin shimmers a type of gold. He has a similar patch of the gold glow on his upper cheekbones. "Rude on top of hideous, how can you even stand to exist?"

I snort. "You're avoiding answering my questions."

"Am I now?"

"Stop playing games with me," I say flatly. I'm not sure where I'm getting my bravado from. Perhaps it is a fake bravado. Or maybe it's just my temper kicking back in. Because I don't take too well to being insulted. I don't have much in the way of self-confidence, and I hate when people mess with what little I have. It doesn't matter if the person insulting me could snuff out my life with a flick of his wrist, technically I could snuff out his life with a flick of my own wrist and my iron dagger. I trained extensively with it, since it's my only true advantage on the faeries, and one Thomas doesn't have. At this distance I could easily kill Ravven.

Of course, faeries don't take very well to humans killing them. They even issued a law banning humans from using iron on one of their kind. If I were to use my iron dagger on this Crowe, I would be on every faerie's hit list. No, my daggers are for emergency situations, not to eliminate rude jerks.

"Oh, but I dearly love games," he says with a smile that chills me to my very core.

"I'm losing patience," I grit out. His smile grows as if he can't think of anything more enjoyable than to see me lose patience.

"Breathe, mortal, you're in the Otherworld. You are no longer decomposing around your own bones. You have time to actually be civil."

I blow out a breath, causing a strand of hair that had fallen out of my braid to lift off my cheek. Well, he certainly has a way with words. But it is true. In the Otherworld, even humans don't age. It has to be something to do with the pervasive magic around us, though we don't have any true scientific explanation for it. There are a lot of things we don't have a scientific explanation for when it comes to the faeries.

"Although this isn't news to you, now is it, Guardian?"

My hand flies to my side, but Ravven doesn't make any move to attack me. Instead he continues talking like him knowing that I am a Guardian isn't an important fact. Maybe to him it isn't. The Solitary faeries never had any part in the war.

"If you simply must know, my fellow Far Darrig and I had a bet. We wished to see who could cause the most mischief and mayhem this evening. Killing a mortal would have been quite a bit of mischief, so naturally I had to intervene. Otherwise Acheanid would have won. But all is better now, I have saved your life. So off you go, on your way, and try to continue with your life the best that you can in my absence."

"You're awfully full of yourself, you know that?" I say. Mom always says that I don't have a right to have such a temper since my hair is only strawberry blonde, but that never stopped me from breaking Thomas's nose when I was eight and it never stopped me from losing my temper every time before and after that.

But my questions have been answered and technically my mission is over. I have it straight from the faerie's lips. This has nothing to do with the war or the Winter Court. Just two Solitary faeries playing a game. In fact, best to get out of here before Ravven Crowe decides that he should win by killing a human. Or I run into this *Acheanid* who already tried to kill me, face to face.

"Of course I am," Ravven replies as if that is the simplest thing in the world. Like every conclusion should lead back to that statement that was supposed to be an insult. "How could I not be? How could anyone not be?"

"I can think of a few reasons," I mutter to myself.

Ravven suddenly stills and I grimace. Me and my big mouth.

Instead of flying into a fury all he says is, "It's amazing how mortals can lie." He drops into a quick bow and the chill wind returns blowing directly into my face and stinging my eyes. "Farewell, mortal Jaye, though I feel this farewell may be unnecessary considering we shall be seeing each other again very soon."

I stumble back like his words actually were a physical blow. How does this faerie know my name and what does he mean by—

A rustle fills the air and when I blink away the tears, I find that he is gone.

"Wait!" I cry, but only silence answers me. "*What*???"

CHAPTER THREE

"Oh my gosh, Thomas!"

I stumble to a stop, just barely tripping over my brother as he slinks out of the shadows in front of me. I'm already on edge, I don't need to be snuck up on or I might just jump right out of my skin. If I wasn't so used to seeing my brother in his wolfish form, he probably would have given me a heart attack. Long black fur, a snout and paws and a tail, really the only human feature about him are his eyes. Brown and intelligent.

Though I would never admit it out loud, no need for him to get airs.

He tilts his head as if to say that he could hear me for miles. It's crazy how he can make mocking faces even as a wolf. And I know what my overprotective perfectionist brother would think of the way I crashed through the trees alerting the whole Otherworld to my presence. But what does it matter if I'm stealthy or not? The faeries already know I'm here.

Everything else is basically a moot point at that point.

"There you are," I say, glancing around to make sure that we are still alone. "Come on, I figured out about the faeries. I'll tell you on the way."

Thomas tilts his head, but as a wolf, he can't actually pose a real question. One of the many things I enjoy about his wolf form. I move past him. With a little growl he plods after me.

I know that he will start nipping at me if I don't elaborate so I explain about the Far Darrig's game. I leave out all the important details, like how I found out about it, or nearly ended up as a pawn in that game.

If he knew about that he would probably turn right around and attack a faerie or two.

Impetuousness runs in the family.

Finally, we make it to the clearing where the faerie circle is situated. I breathe the first real breath that I think I have since getting here.

Thomas plods over to the pile of clothes he left out back when he turned into a wolf. As he moves, black tendrils snake off of his form which is growing slightly taller as his paws lift off the ground.

"Oh gosh, Thomas!" I cry again, whirling around just avoiding seeing him morph back into a human. "Give a girl some warning."

"Hey," he says. "I'm changing back."

I hold my hand up with my fingers only an inch apart. "You know, pretty close, but maybe next time you should try doing that *before* you change back."

"Now where would be the fun in that?"

I roll my eyes.

"You can look now. I'm decent."

I turn, but find that he lied because Thomas still had his shirt off.

I roll my eyes, but honestly, a shirtless Thomas is not something I can escape. He works out a lot and I guess that means he thinks he deserves to show off his muscles. It's my humble opinion that he believes that the ladies would all find him completely irresistible. Call it my inner sister speaking, but I just find it annoying. Like who wants to see that much skin on anyone?

Personally, I think a man looks good in a nice long coat and vest with polished boots and maybe gloves. And I'm talking about Period Drama style, not what Ravven Crowe was wearing. In case anyone was wondering. Which of course no one was because I didn't say it out loud but still you can never be too safe when it comes to stoking that fiend's ego.

"Ugh, put your shirt on," I say, crossing my arms. "You're not doing anyone any favors. You're just giving the mosquitoes a larger target to attack."

Thomas rolls his eyes but pulls his shirt on. "There aren't even any mosquitoes here."

Of course not, the faerie realm doesn't have animals and bugs like our world does. Not normal animals and bugs that you would find on Earth, anyway. Which makes me wonder what that bird I heard actually was.

"We're heading home soon," I argue. "And there will be plenty of mosquitoes out then. Especially at this hour. You know that when the sun goes down the bloodsucking monsters like to come out and play."

Thomas snorts. "Honestly, Jaye, you're weird."

"Says the werewolf."

"I'm not a werewolf," Thomas says defensively. I smirk. He gets so uppity about this point. I don't even care except that he does which means that I, of course, can't resist.

"You are a man, *were*, who turns into a wolf, *wolf*. By the very definition of the word you are a werewolf." I move my hands in front of me like I'm putting an object into two boxes. "Therefore, you are a werewolf."

"I'm not a werewolf. I transform because of faerie magic, not a full moon. Thus, I'm gifted."

That he is. On Thomas's first birthday, as one of the next generation of Guardians, he was given a gift by the fae of the Seelie court: the ability to turn into a wolf at whim. He was cursed too, by the fae of the Unseelie court, so it seems a little one sided to call him gifted when he is also cursed. We don't talk about the curses much, though. Kind of a sore subject and all that.

As his sister of the same lineage and bloodline, I should also be gifted and cursed, but I suppose the faeries didn't see the second child as all that important. Either that or they had the day off when I turned one. Or they didn't care, but either way, I was passed up on my first birthday and now I'm just as human as everyone else.

Thomas is a good sport though so he doesn't bring up my lack of gift or even curse despite the fact that it would be an easy way to one-up me in an argument. For that I'm grateful.

Honestly, everyone tells me that I'm lucky because without a gift, I don't have a curse either. The favored curses bestowed on the members of my family are a weakness to iron and an inability to lie, though my dad's sister Aunt Clara was cursed to fall into a slumber on her sixteenth birthday. A slumber that would last a hundred years. Dad and my uncles hid her away somewhere here in the Otherworld, so that she would not age, but still when she wakes up, everyone she knows will be dead. Which is kind of a bummer.

There's a large possibility that I'll even be dead by that time and I never even had a chance to meet her. One less person for her to mourn, I guess.

My grandfather was cursed to be a frog, and so the blessing he got was so that he could shape-shift back into a human, canceling out his blessings and curses seeing as the only thing he could turn into was a frog, but at least he can also be a human. He was lucky.

Many members of our family were not.

"So, Jaye, you didn't actually tell me how you figured this all out about the faerie's game? Or why you were running through the woods earlier? What exactly happened?"

I glance over my shoulder toward the trees. I'll tell Thomas all about my odd encounter with Ravven Crowe. Heck, I'll tell Mom and Dad too—I could use a second opinion or two or three because quite frankly I don't even know what to begin to think of it. But not here, with Ravven's ominous promise that he will be seeing me again very soon still echoing through my head.

"Jaye?" Thomas asks, stepping forward and grasping my arm.

I shake him off and reach into my satchel, pulling out the disk. "I'll tell you in a sec, but let's at least get to Earth. This place is creeping me out."

By now the sun has almost completely disappeared and all-natural light with it. Of course, in the faerie world due to the magic it is very common for a random grass blade or tree to glow. The grass and stones all around the faerie ring are illuminated like someone's collection of forgotten glow sticks.

Wait no.

That analogy sounded better before I made it.

Thomas snorts. "My poor baby sis. I knew this mission was too much for you."

I kick his ankle's but much more lightly than I kicked Ravven. This is just a warning kick, not a war kick. "Don't forget who accomplished this mission."

Although the way I accomplished my mission still bothers me.

Ravven Crowe acted in a way completely unbefitting a faerie. He should have murdered me at least six times back there, but instead he saved my life and then just... walked away. With the promise that he would be seeing me again. Honestly that part bothers me the most. The last thing I want to see ever again is his smug face and mocking eyes.

The light on the screen blinks, blinks, blinks, as it boots up. Other than the electronic whirl, there is absolutely no sound. Then suddenly a sharp wind blows straight through me. Like I'm nothing more than straw.

Darn, that analogy doesn't fit either.

Something isn't right.

"Thomas—" I begin, the words barely leave my lips before they are snatched away by a thundering gust of wind.

Thomas glances back at me, his eyes still crinkled and amused. He still thinks that this is fun and games. I open my mouth to warn him, but before I can, the ground around the faerie ring erupts into the sky, sending rocks and dirt flying into the air, before landing all around me in a torrent of very deadly rain.

CHAPTER FOUR

Dirt and stones fill my vision as I blink my eyes open. I groan as I try to figure out what exactly happened. I'm lying on the hard ground, with dirt chunks all around me. I sit up, spitting a small clod of earth out of my mouth and rub my forehead.

I glance over my shoulder and my heart stills. The area where the faerie ring had previously been is nothing but a jagged crater.

Panic seeps up through my very core, but I stuff it down, reminding myself that this isn't the only faerie ring. As long as we have the disk for transportation, we will be able to pass through the next faerie circle we find.

I look down at my hands, half expecting to find it still there, but it's gone.

My breath hitches in my throat and I glance around wildly. My eyes land on a small bronze glint half buried under a pile of dirt. I lunge across the distance and with shaking hands, brush off the dirt. I lift the disk and my stomach plummets. One of the stones that made up the faerie circle is embedded in the center of the circuitry.

My stomach twists queasily. I was holding that disk in my hand. If I hadn't been, I would have a rock embedded in the palm of my hand instead.

"What the devil was that?" Thomas asks. My gaze flies to where he's sitting only a few feet from me. He rubs at the side of his head where a small gash sits above his temple.

"I think someone just tried to kill us," I say, but as soon as the words are out of my mouth, I doubt them. If someone tried to kill us then why aren't we dead? The rocks were flying all around us, some even hitting their marks and yet we are still alive.

Faeries don't tend to make sloppy mistakes like that.

But if they did not want us dead, then what did they want from us?

Thomas glances around, but freezes when he sees the pit where the faerie ring once was. "Holy—it's-it's gone. Jaye, what are we going to do?"

I don't have an answer to give. I don't know why he is suddenly expecting me to have the answer. He is the older sibling here, the one with a magical power. Sure, I have spent my life studying faeries, but it's not like folklore was lacking from his school schedule either.

And folklore doesn't have a whole lot of answers of what to do when your technology fails us.

Thomas wipes some dirt off his forehead and turns to me. "You have the disk, right?"

I press my lips together and hold it up. "Is it too much to hope that you packed a spare?"

Now would be the perfect time for Thomas's excessive worrying and overbearing nature to pay off. But instead he blanches which is really all the answer I needed.

"That was quite impressive." I whirl to see Ravven step out of the trees toward us as if the faerie ring did not just shoot up into the sky a few minutes ago and then rain down on us. No stray dirt clods are anywhere near him, he's completely unharmed and of course spotless. "You certainly have a knack for bringing destruction in your wake, pest."

I scramble to my feet, grimacing as my ankle threatens to give out underneath me. Naturally it is twisted, I don't even know when that happened, but I figure it was somewhere in the course of throwing myself to the ground to avoid death by flying stones. I slide my knife out of its sheath on my thigh and step toward Ravven. I don't bother with civility and caution, those exploded with the faerie ring. "You did this didn't you?"

Ravven holds up his hands and steps back, his gaze flicking to my dagger then back at me with some surprise. He hadn't been expecting me to be armed with an actually deadly weapon. To a faerie that is. Most anything can be a deadly weapon to humans, even rocks. "Why would you suggest that? I never had anything personally against that faerie ring and besides, stray dirt could have landed on me."

I laugh, maybe it sounds a little maniacal, but I'm feeling a little maniacal right now. "You didn't directly answer my question, faerie." Even though they can't lie, it won't stop them from talking around in circles for all eternity.

He dusts at the front of his black coat that he is wearing over his scarlet vest as if there are invisible specks of dirt on it. "Ravven, if you will recall."

"I know who you are," I grind out. "And you are going to tell me what you want from me and why you destroyed that faerie ring or I'm going to cut off each and every one of your fingers."

Ravven slowly curls his fingers into a fist. "How unnecessarily and unethically violent of you."

I let out a growl and stalk toward him, but Thomas stops me by grasping my arm from behind. "Jaye, stop! Leave it alone, we'll just find another faerie ring to go home by."

I whirl on Thomas, holding up the disk to remind him of just how dire our situation is. As if he could have forgotten. "We can't just get home now, we're—" I cut myself off, unable to be able to say it.

We're trapped in the Otherworld.

Thomas swallows, although the action appears to take some difficulty. "We need to keep our heads here, Jaye."

"I just want to know why he did it," I say, turning back to Ravven.

Even by faerie standards, this is twisted. Why would Ravven save my life only to trap us here? Surely this isn't revenge because I didn't thank him properly or profusely enough. Even he couldn't have been that petty, could he?

"I didn't," Ravven says simply, grimacing slightly as if he is just now wishing that he had thought of the idea first. His eyes are as black as the shadows of the trees behind him. As black as the sky should be, as it would be if we were back on Earth, but here it is a murky red.

I'm about to tell him that I don't believe him, but then I realize I can't. Ravven is a faerie. He can't lie, so if he says that he didn't do it then he... he couldn't have. Even though I know faeries can't lie, there's a part of me that doesn't want to believe him. Who else would have destroyed the faerie ring? That other Solitary faerie Arachnid or whatever his name was?

I reach up pressing my palm against my mouth as I try to keep a cool head. I need to think of something, anything. But as I stand there with Ravven and Thomas both staring at me I realize I have absolutely nothing. No answers, no plan, and no clue.

Thomas drapes an arm over my shoulder, guiding me farther from Ravven. "Jaye, it will be all right, we'll figure it out."

Yeah, just as soon as a faerie lies.

There are just so many unknowns. *Someone* destroyed the faerie ring, last I checked stuff didn't explode all on its own. But that someone wasn't Ravven, and even knowing who did it and why they did it, didn't solve our problem of how we were going to get home.

"Who are you anyway?" Thomas demands, turning his attention to Ravven Crowe.

"As if you didn't know. I am certain your sister could not speak of anything else but our meeting."

"What?" Thomas asks, glancing at me, but my attention is on Ravven.

I narrow my eyes. "How do you know we are siblings?"

Ravven waves his hand. "As if two humans could be so hideous and not share blood."

"Excuse me what?" Thomas recoils as if Ravven suddenly grew horns. Which could still happen to be fair, I don't know what kind of faerie he is or if he is using any glamor to hide his appearance and make himself more pretty. Somehow though it seems I am standing here with the two most vain men in both the worlds and quite frankly I don't have time for it.

"Ladies, I think you are both pretty. But seriously, Ravven, if you want me to believe that you had no part in this then tell me what you are doing here?"

Ravven glances behind him as if he is wondering who I am talking to. He turns back to us and arches a brow. "This is the Otherworld," Ravven replies smoothly, running his hand through his hair. "It's my home. I think the better question would be, what are you doing here?"

"I don't have to answer you."

"But I am expected to answer you?" Ravven asks, tilting his head and tapping his chin. "You seem to forget who is the faerie and who is the human in this relationship, pest."

"There is no relationship between us, just a really hot-tempered human and an idiotic faerie who thinks he can cross her. Do not test me, Crowe, I am having a terrible day and I will kick you in the shins again. So, I will ask one last time, what part do you play in stranding us here?"

"I'm so confused," Thomas mutters, pressing the heel of his hand against his eye.

Ravven clucks his tongue. "You miserable being, I believe you are being played for the fool. Why would I want you to remain in my world? You're short, angry, and ugly." He grimaces as if just thinking about my physical appearance causes him pain.

And he's tall, annoying, and far too pretty, but who's keeping track? "I'm not ugly," I mutter under my breath, though I can't put much force into it. Faeries can't lie. Humans can.

"Wait, hold on," Thomas says, stepping between us, now pinching the bridge of his nose. "Why are we going on about Jaye's appearance? This has nothing to do with the current issue."

I cross my arms tightly and glare at Ravven. True. I need to find a way to get us home. I can buy some beauty treatment creams and lotions later back on Earth.

There has to be some trick in here. Ravven very clearly has a large part in what just happened. And he is just finding some way to talk himself around it, but that's the beautiful thing about rule number two. It doesn't say, *never trust a faerie unless he is telling the truth*. It says, never trust a faerie. Never as in not ever. "You said that we would be seeing each other again. What was that supposed to mean?"

"I did say that," he replies, an amused smile pulling at the corner of those perfect lips. "But I was simply stating a fact as I knew that you would never be able to resist me. Sooner or later you would go mad from the longing and come seeking me out again."

I snort so hard that I nearly give myself a nosebleed. "Oh please."

"No amount of pleading will change my mind. You are beneath me in every way." Ravven's eyes dart back to me and he presses his lips together. "But I suppose that faerie ring is destroyed which, I'm afraid, means that someone wants you two rotting mortals here, and that can mean nothing good. The already murky waters of the faerie courts are always muddied up when mortals are involved."

I bite my tongue to keep from saying that Thomas and I are technically not rotting while we are in the Otherworld. He knows that, he was the one who brought up my temporary immortality earlier.

It's weird to think that we could stand in this field for a hundred years and nothing would change. It was the reason that Aunt Clara was hidden in this world after her curse took over, because in the very least she would not age.

Such thoughts offer a modicum of comfort. *We have time.*

But then I remind myself that we really don't.

Immortality has a way of offering a false sense of security. Because even if Thomas and I never age another day, the seconds, minutes, and hours in the human world continue to tick by, taking everyone that we love with them.

This would all be so much easier if Mom and Dad weren't out of town for the whole week. We would just have to wave our hands in front of the camera for a few hours and they would come and rescue us. But no one is watching that camera while they are gone. Thomas and I were left in charge of monitoring everything.

I wrap my arms around myself, trying to stave off the chill that wants to take over my body. I'm pretty sure that it's shock, but I don't have time to deal with me going into shock on top of everything else.

Thomas stares at Ravven then at me. He steps back, rubbing at his temples. "I'm so confused right now. Jaye, please tell me who this faerie even is. This is the Far Darrig who was playing the game?"

Ravven dusts off his spotless red vest. "Of course, I am. What else would you think I was?"

Thomas shakes his head. "No one I guess, it's just, I thought Far Darrigs were ugly."

"You are mistaking them with your own kind, mortal," Ravven replies, his eyes flashing in the dim light of the night.

I resist the urge to roll my eyes again. I turn back to the crater, my mind churning. "Would you have any idea who would want us here?" I ask, turning back to Ravven.

He arches a brow. "How could I know? As a Solitary faerie, it is not as if I spend much time with other faeries, even my own kind."

"What about Arachnid? Isn't he a buddy of yours?"

"I do not know anyone by the name of Arachnid."

"You know what I am talking about," I say, glaring at him. I have barely even met Ravven and already I am sick of him and his condescending behavior. I guess we don't need a rule about not falling in love with faeries after all. No one in their right mind would fall for one of *them*.

Ravven rolls his eyes. "That romp with Acheanid was hardly a common occurrence. We had simply come across each other earlier today and decided to play a small game. Nothing more."

Well, Ravven is less than forthcoming about faerie politics. Although who wants us trapped here is less of an issue. What truly matters in the long run of my life is just getting back home in one piece. I rub my chin as I consider Ravven. "Humans have entered into the faerie realm before we invented a way to pass through on our own."

I hold up the bronze disk to look at it and Ravven sneers in disgust. "Surely you have doors other than the faerie circles that humans can pass through without needing this disk."

"Of course, we do," he replies, his eyes full of disinterest as he glances around as if bored.

I glance back at the faerie ring. Mom and Dad, even Dad's brothers all have spare disks, but there's no knowing when they will come looking for us. And with this faerie ring destroyed they shall have to use another.

The faerie world isn't exactly small and I think the next nearest faerie ring on Earth is somewhere in Kentucky.

We could be waiting for them for quite some time.

So, we could try the human way and possibly fail in a hundred thousand ways. Or we could go the faerie way. Find our own way home. As much as I hate the thought of traveling further into the Otherworld, it seems to be the best chance we have of getting home in the next century.

But two humans in the faerie world, even if one can transform into a wolf and the other can wield iron, would hardly be able to get far. Especially since we have no idea where these special faerie doors are.

But if we had a guide...

My eyes dart to Ravven. "You say that it's so bad for us to remain here and be used as pawns. Clearly we need someone to help us escape the Otherworld."

He snorts unimpressed. "I think that you will find it difficult to locate a faerie who is willing to help you. But I could point you in the direction of the Summer Court; perhaps one of the Seelies are feeling generous, seeing as they claim to be so fond of your kind."

"Actually..." I say slowly as I reach into my satchel, glad that I still have that on me. It has a good deal of emergency supplies in it. I try to recall what exactly it is seeing as it is all the earthly supplies that I have to get home. In that retrospect it isn't actually much, but it was more than Thomas had thought we needed for this scouting mission. I have a spare dagger, a little baggy of some herbs that work as salve against some of the more deadly plant life in the faerie court, a PB&J sandwich in case I got hungry, and a pair of iron bound handcuffs in case I needed to detain any faeries. I wrap my fingers around cool metal. I whip out a pair of handcuffs and slap them on Ravven's wrist.

He stares down at them, blinking in surprise and I smile widely. "I thought you would do it. Thank you in advance for volunteering your time, but you're a faerie so you shouldn't miss it too much."

CHAPTER FIVE

"Jaye, what are you doing?" Thomas demands.

"What does it look like I'm doing? I'm recruiting a guide."

"Seems more like kidnapping to me," Ravven drawled.

Thomas makes a strangled sound in the back of his throat. "I hate to agree with the faerie, but that is what it looks like. And I can't believe that I have to say this but *you can't just kidnap people.*"

"Too late I already did."

Ravven tugs at the cuffs now linking his wrists and looks back up at me. "Listen to the slightly less annoying mortal, pest. Did you even stop to consider your foolhardy actions?"

"Oh, I considered them," I reply, crossing my arms. For like two seconds but it counts. "And it's no use trying to escape, this particular pair of handcuffs consists mostly of iron."

They were made specially for detaining faeries, though as far as I know, they've never actually been tested, so I don't know how well they work outside of theory. They are made of iron which weakens the faerie so that they cannot use their magic, but to keep the faerie from becoming incapacitated, the interior of the cuffs where the metal touches the faerie's flesh is coated in bronze.

I only brought them in case of an emergency and well... I guess this is a certifiable emergency.

"Jaye, are you crazy?" Thomas demands, pressing a hand on my shoulder.

"I believe she is," Ravven says, before I can form a response.

I shove a strand of my strawberry blonde hair that fell out of my braid behind my ear and glare at both of them. "I'm not crazy. Slightly ruthless, admittedly yes, but not crazy."

Ravven's eyebrows rise and something akin to admiration flashes in his eyes. I shake my head. I must have read his expression incorrectly. He would never admire the likes of me. Although maybe he is impressed to meet a human willing to think like a faerie, who knows what goes on in that twisted mind of his.

"I'm serious here, Jaye, we can't just kidnap someone."

I clamp my hands on my hips. "Says who?"

"How about common decency?"

I roll my eyes and stifle the urge to laugh. "Thomas, relax. He's just a faerie."

"That doesn't make it any better. It just makes it more dangerous. You should know better, there is no way we can trust him."

"We're not trusting him!" I cry, waving my hand to Ravven. "Why do you think he's in handcuffs?"

"Because you are a fiend," Ravven offers unhelpfully as he tests his wrists in the handcuffs. He grimaces, but that expression is quickly gone as he drops his hand. It's less in defeat and more like he's done trying to pretend. If anything, he looks smug rather than upset. But then again smug seems to be his default expression. I'm pretty sure that if I pushed him off a cliff, he would still be smug about it.

He turns his attention to Thomas. "A word of warning from a timeless immortal to one whose life is like a blink of an eye. Never save a girl's life." He holds up his chained hands for us all to see. "This is all the thanks you will ever get."

Thomas inhales sharply and looks at me. "He saved your life?"

"Ish?" I still don't know that he wasn't somehow involved in the endangering of it in the first place. And quite frankly I don't want to even consider that he is somehow innocent in all of this because that would hardly aid my argument that it's all right to use him.

Thomas turns back to Ravven, shoving his hand through his thick auburn locks. "You saved her life?"

"I'm regretting it now," Ravven says dryly. He glances back down at the handcuffs and frowns.

"Why would you save her life?" Thomas demands, but before waiting for a response he turns back to me. "He saved you and you still intend to use him?"

Ravven adjusts his weight on his feet, looking more amused than upset. "This is why faeries are not noble. It never pays."

I heave a sigh and roll my eyes. Faeries are such drama queens. "Look, we need to get home and this faerie is our only chance of making it through the Otherworld without getting torn to pieces. Because he saved my life means that he's really the only one that I would *let* lead us around the faerie world."

Thomas steps forward. "That isn't how this works, Jayebird. What is wrong with you, why can't you see that this isn't right? We can't use him like this. Let him go."

Ravven nods. "I heartily concur with the mortal boy."

"No," I tell them both. Why can't Thomas see that this is a necessary evil? Does he want to die here on his first mission? Honestly, it is good that I'm here with him because I don't know what my brother would do if he were here on his own. Give up, throw in the towel, and make friends with the faeries? They are the enemies, we are in the middle of a war between humans and the Fair Folk, albeit a cold war. But a war all the same and all's fair in war, you know.

He grunts and reaches up to pinch the bridge of his nose. "Fine, where is the key? I'll do it myself."

I clear my throat and scuff my foot against the ground. I hate to have to do this, but not enough that I would give up what is possibly our only chance of returning home. "It's made of iron, Thomas. You can't touch it."

Thomas flinches and recoils and I feel even worse for using his curse against him. Especially since he has never once mocked me for not having a gift or anything else.

But this is for his good, I remind myself. I straighten to my full height which, while not short for a girl, still feels tiny compared to my lanky brother and the gracefully tall faerie. "I'm the only one who can unlock those cuffs and I will not do it until Ravven brings us to the doorway that will lead us home."

Thomas's shoulders slump and he bows his head. "Is there really no convincing you to do the decent thing?"

"You'll thank me when you are safely home."

"This just doesn't sit right with me; the ends don't justify the means."

"It does if the means is a faerie. Need I remind you that faeries are evil."

Ravven clears his throat. "Need I remind you that I am standing right here. Your argument for morality is admirable, mortal, but that is all it is. You are in the Otherworld now, there is no morality."

Thomas shoots Ravven an incredulous look. "Are you seriously taking her side in this."

"No, but I am tired of this back and forth arguing. It certainly isn't getting me out of these accursed cuffs. If bringing you two to a faerie door will get me out of them then I shall do what is necessary to get *these* off. The sooner the better. You two make eternity seem unbearable if I have to spend one more second in your company."

Thomas shakes his head as he steps back. "Go on Jaye, ask me what it is like to be the only person here with a smidgen of decency. Cause it's kind of crazy. Fine. Let's get this over with then and let's do it fast before my common sense catches up with us and wants to know exactly what we're doing."

I shove his shoulder playfully, trying to lighten the tension between us. I hate it when Thomas and I argue. "You don't have any common sense."

Thomas huffs a small laugh and shakes his head wearily. "Well that explains a lot. Like why I spend so much time with you."

I kick his shin. "I'm your sister."

"Family ties certainly are strange; humans pretend that shared blood equals loyalty."

Thomas looks at Ravven like he grew another head, but I just shove him. "Shut up and get leading."

He heaves a heavy sigh. "I'd forgotten that you mortals have so little time to waste." Actually, he probably didn't. He probably thought it every second which was why he keeps making comments like this.

But I'm not going to lose my temper on him. Again. He isn't worth that kind of effort and the headache I always get afterward. "Just tell us where to go. Where is the nearest door to the human world?"

"It doesn't matter where the nearest one is. Each of the courts have their own doors into the human world. And the nearest door is in the Winter Court. But since you would not survive such a journey, not to mention that I am not eager to see the Winter Queen, I would suggest that we travel through the Autumn Court."

And this is why I cuffed Ravven, because now he has every reason to keep us alive. If I hadn't, he could have tried to lead us to our certain death. That iron key is a gamechanger.

But the Autumn Court isn't too bad. We have long considered it the least deadly court.

As long as we stay out of any faerie's way we might just get out of this alive.

"So, we go to the Autumn Court," I say, forcing bravado as Thomas pales. Neither of us have ever entered a court. Whenever we came to the Otherworld to train, we always avoided it and the possibility of seeing faeries like the plague.

But now we are going deeper into the faerie's world than we have ever gone before. I had hoped that there was a rabbit hole or something nearby where we could jump down and appear in the human world, but unfortunately it isn't that simple. Nothing ever seems to be. Or Ravven could be leading us into a trap and not to any doors at all. Either one is a possibility.

In order to have Ravven as our guide, I have to trust him. If I want to get out of here alive, I can't trust him. There is a fine line I have to walk between trust and mistrust called discernment and I'm not sure if I have it in me. I'm relying on the fact that he desires his freedom more than revenge. But I could always be wrong. We might just end up destroyed, body and soul, and left for dead in the faerie world.

Especially since I still can't shake the feeling that we're actually doing exactly as Ravven wants. He doesn't seem as upset as he should be about being kidnapped.

"There is no need to look so wan. The Autumn Court is quite the sight, not so much as me, but it is my home you know."

Shoving aside my discomfort before it has too much of a chance to show, I nod to Ravven. "Then stop wasting our time and lead the way."

He smiles before turning away. "As you wish. Follow me, little mortals, and try not to die."

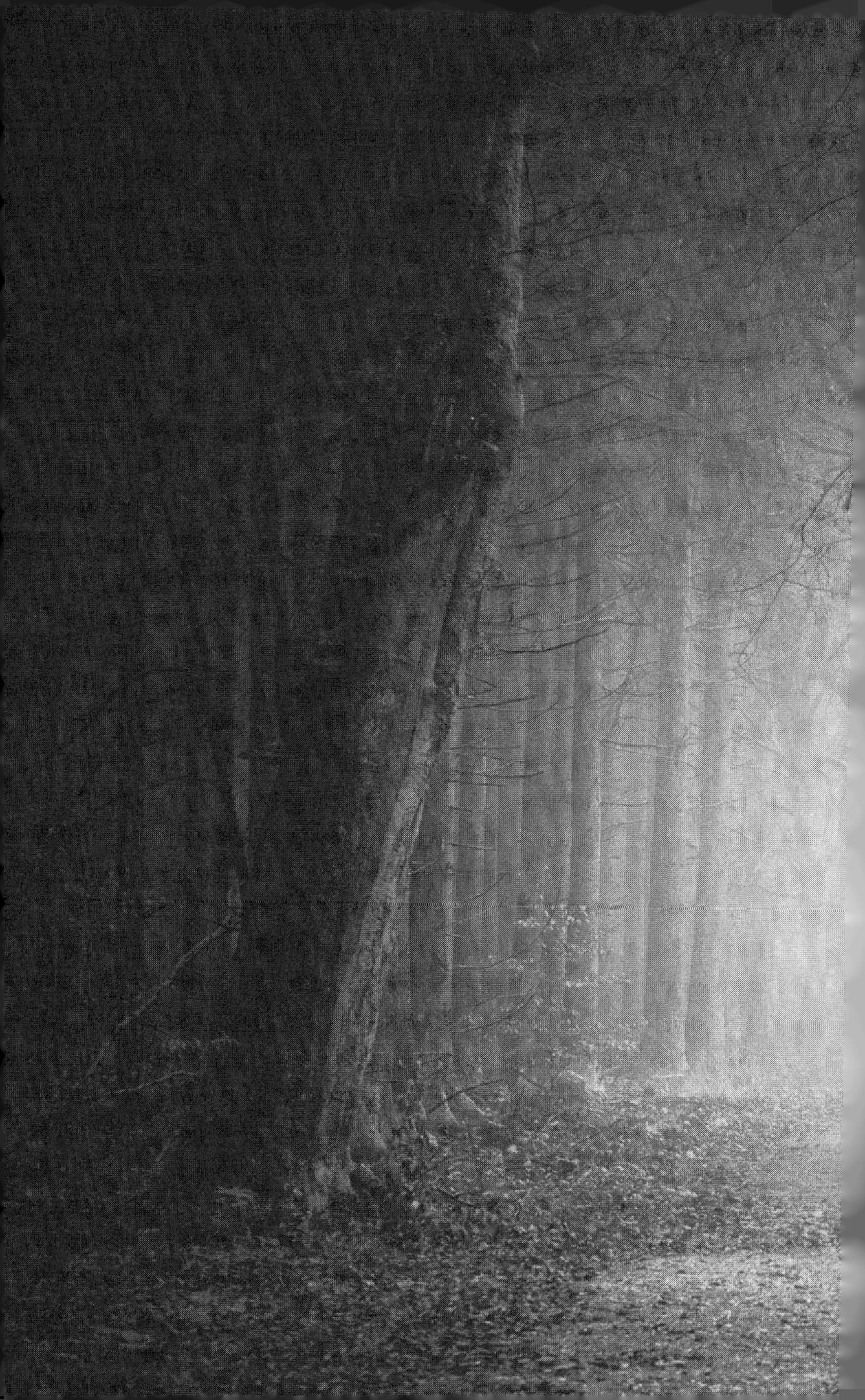

CHAPTER SIX

The Autumn Court is unlike any of the other courts. That much I know from my studies of Irish mythology and the stories that we have of the other Guardians before us.

The Autumn Court is not made of stone or ice, it is not hidden off in some cave, or underneath a hill, or at the bottom of a lake. It is not a building at all, but rather a forest. This probably has to do with the fact that the occupants of the Autumn Court do not like to spend time around each other. Since the Autumn Court consists solely of Solitary faeries, they probably much prefer to roam in the open woodlands where their chances of running into each other are significantly less than if they were in, say, a confining palace.

Another thing that makes the Autumn Court unlike the other courts is that it does not have a ruler. Not that the Solitary faeries would listen to anyone trying to give them orders anyway. Most find themselves all the world they ever need. Others just don't care. It depends on the faerie.

Ravven is probably the kind who needs no one else because he is perfect in and of himself.

He inhales deeply as we step under the multicolored leaves. Even though it is the height of summer, it looks like the dead of fall here. I've heard that the seasonal courts are only ever the seasons they represent. So here it is perpetually autumn.

The golden and red leaves over our head and under our feet glow faintly, the same way that Ravven does, giving light to the forest.

"Ah, home sweet lonely home," he murmurs.

"It doesn't look like much," Thomas says, peering up at the trees.

"Oh, but looks can be deceiving. Everything is deceiving in my world." His lips curls over his straight white teeth as he looks us over. "I would be careful if I were you."

As if we aren't currently being as cautious as we can possibly be.

Thomas moves forward. "Let's just get this over with. The sooner we are home and you are freed the better."

Ravven steps after him. "Now, I do not usually advise traveling through the Autumn Court during the night. That is usually an invitation to your own funeral. There are many faeries that roam the Autumn Court at night and not all of them are as generous as I."

"Oh, so you're generous now, too?" I ask impatiently. Ravven saying that he is generous is like me saying that I am good natured. "Does the list of your wonderful qualities ever end?"

"I have yet to find the end, but you are welcome to search for it. You are fortunate that I've always had a soft spot for humans. Disgusting, rotting corpses."

Thomas coughs. "Wow, you must really like humans."

"Isn't he such a catch?" I ask sarcastically. Thomas coughs again, this time to cover up a laugh. "How are you still possibly single?"

Assuming he is single—actually now that I have said that I have no idea. Because he is a Solitary faerie, I'd just assumed that he didn't have anyone. But now I'm not sure. For someone as beautiful as Ravven Crowe... well, odds were some idiotic faerie chick or the other had staked her claim. I don't even know why I am thinking about this at all. I don't care about his love life.

"Well, unfortunately, I have yet to meet anyone who is worthy of me," Ravven replies airily. "I fear such a faerie most likely doesn't exist."

I roll my eyes. "If you fall any more in love with yourself, you'll probably die of desire just from seeing your own reflection."

Ravven releases a heavy breath as if he actually considered this option. "I know that I would want my life to go on. So, I must persist in my lonely existence."

I glance at him, but I can't tell if he's teasing or dead serious. His facial expression hasn't shifted at all, it's still just as smug and superior as it always is. Well, all right then, I think I may have found someone even more vain than Narcissus. Welcome to the Otherworld, I guess. Even our myths pale in comparison to what the faeries are truly capable of.

Well, I am no Echo, and I certainly don't plan on sticking around here long enough to become one.

He looks down at me and raises his eyebrows. "If you rest your eyes on me much longer, I shall have to require you to pay rent."

I shove him and he stumbles to the side, holding up both his arms to try to steady himself. "You wish. I would rather gouge out my own eyes."

He grimaces as he looks me over, his eyes going black. "I do wish that you would gouge out your eyes. Perhaps that would somehow lessen the hideousness of your deformity."

"Are you going to keep bringing up how I look?" I ask sharply.

"How can I not when I keep having to look at you?"

I clench my teeth sharply and glance away. I fall back several steps, shoving Thomas in the shoulder. "You watch him."

"Why do I have to?" Thomas asks. "I didn't even want him as a prisoner."

"You could always let me go," Ravven suggests, as if I would change my mind so suddenly. As if I could even change my mind. The second I release him he will turn his magic against us. It's a dangerous game to anger a faerie.

"Now that's an idea," Thomas says.

"A terrible idea," I say, shooting Thomas a look.

"Do you truly need me?"

"No," Thomas says at the same time I say, "Yes."

Ravven's eyes turn to me, glinting oddly in the glow of the leaves overhead. "One of you is lying."

I roll my eyes. "Okay, maybe it isn't *needed*, but it is the easiest course of action at this point so shut up."

"Ease? That is reason enough to kidnap me?"

"Maybe not, but I could kidnap you, so I did."

Ravven leans closer, too close, he smells of Autumn wind and flowers. Of the outdoors before a storm and after it. Blasted faeries, can they not be a contradiction for just one second? "So that is the madness that drives you? You do what you do because you can."

I shrug. "No one has stopped me yet."

"Perhaps you are more faerie than you think."

It takes everything in me not to punch Ravven in his perfect nose. "Just watch the prisoner, Thomas, because I'm liable to kill him if I have to hear one more thing from his mouth."

"Why would you want to kill me?" Ravven demands, turning to look at me, his eyebrows raised incredulously. His dark hair ruffles in the light breeze. "I'm lovely."

I slow my pace, allowing some much-needed distance to form between me and Ravven. I'm wondering which will last longer—my sanity or my patience. Both seem to be running very thin, and even thinner each word that leaves that faerie's mouth.

The wind is chilly, not icy, but still nips at my nose and the tips of my ears. I wrap my arms around myself thankful that I am dressed relatively warmly, though my warmest summer clothes still aren't warm enough for fall weather.

Something snaps to my left and I whip my head around at the sound, my hand automatically drifting toward my dagger. I scan the forest warily, my eyes landing on a blue form floating through the trees right toward us. I catch the glimpse of something white moving through the trees. "What's that?"

The white figure, whatever it is, continues moving through the woods, going farther away. It pauses and glances back as if it is waiting for me and I finally get a good look at it. Large antlers crisscrossing from its head, so pale they almost glow crystalline, and dark eyes that ooze the wisdom of the ages.

A white stag.

I thought they were just a legend.

I mean, I know how crazy that sounds. Faeries, pixies, sprites? Those blighters exist. But one single white stag shows up and suddenly I'm questioning everything I know? It's insane, yes, welcome to my life.

But the thing about the white stag is that only one Guardian in the history of ever has seen one. Adair McCullagh, the first Guardian. Legend has it that the white stag led him to the faerie world where he met the Tuatha De Danan and helped them win their faerie war. For aiding them, the Tuatha De Danan agreed to bless his descendants and agreed to not enslave humans any longer. The Winter Court—who lost—well, they cursed all the McCullagh's after that.

Well, except for me it seems, seeing as I never developed a gift. Or a curse.

That's how the Guardians came to be. That's where the gifts and the curses came from. But over the years the Guardians have come to wonder how true that tale was, since no white stag was spotted in the literal thousands of years since. Somehow Adair came to the faerie world, that much was true.

But other than that, there was absolutely no evidence of an ethereal white beast that led a soul to their fates. Until today, that is.

I take a step forward, but someone grabs my arm and yanks me back. I startle and blink, glancing back to see Thomas.

"Where are you going? Tell me you don't intend to talk with every faerie we come across here."

I haven't the faintest idea what he is talking about. "Thomas, I saw a—" the words die on my lips as I glance back to find that standing in the white stag's place isn't a white stag. It is a ghostly woman, with rags hanging off of her thin frame and hair hanging limply around her gaunt face. She glows a pale blue, with a faint greenish hue, and is floating about an inch above the ground.

Ravven mutters something that isn't familiar to me, but I take it to be a faerie swear word. "Mvtalach, do you court your own demise, mortal? That is a Banshee. Do not—whatever you do—*do not* listen to the Banshee's proclamation. If you do your fates will be sealed."

Thomas tightens his hold on my arm as if I would go near the creepy floating lady. Which I wouldn't, although I am admittedly curious about the Banshee. Can she truly see people's deaths to come? The stories say that is why she weeps, because of the horrors she has seen. She cannot meet a new person without knowing how they will die. It sounds like a horrible way to live—it's no wonder that she would be a Solitary faerie and avoid everyone. But does she see my death?

"Doom!" the Banshee wails. Then she starts floating toward us. "Doom!"

"We should get going," Thomas says, his voice high pitched and strained.

I nod and turn away. Supposedly Banshees aren't deadly but actually some of the more friendly of the Solitary faeries, actually caring about the fates of mortals. But she looks like something straight out of a horror movie complete with claws and white sightless eyes that have an endless stream of tears pouring from them.

Besides, curious as I am, I'm not actually sure if I want to know how I die.

"Let's make it quick," Ravven says. He actually looks unsettled which scares me just a bit.

"Too late for that," a gravelly voice pronounces directly behind us.

I'm not sure which of us yelled louder, but it might have been Ravven.

I turn as the Banshee opens her mouth and her exhale is like that of the last breath leaving a dying body.

"Do not listen to her!" Ravven cries, stumbling back.

"I see your death," the Banshee says. Her voice is husky, but also oddly comforting, like the soft whisper of wind on a summer's night.

With a start, I realize that she isn't talking to me. Her eyes are on Thomas. "I see a thousand possible deaths for you, mortal. You love your own demise and the only way you live is for another to die."

Thomas blanches, but before any of us can respond she turns toward me. She reaches out, almost longingly. Like she wishes to wrap me in her spindly arms and protect me from my own future.

"And your death will come soon by your own hands."

I clench my suddenly trembling fingers into fists. How could my death come from my own hands? I would never kill myself. I couldn't do that to Thomas or Mom or Dad. I have too much to live for. But then another terrible thought comes to me. If I am ensorcelled, I would not be able to help it. Is she saying that a faerie will kill me like they did to my grandmother?

She inhales and it's like the hungry gasp of someone who has not been able to breathe for too long. Her milky white eyes hold mine, piercing my core, freezing my soul. "Your only hope of cheating this death is for you to be betrayed."

I blink, stunned and stumble back, bumping into Ravven. No wonder he had wanted to leave. Nothing good can ever come from a Banshee's mouth. And now I am left with the pronouncement of a fate I cannot escape. I will probably go mad from trying to prevent it. I could go mad from just trying to figure out what it means.

"We—" I begin, but my tone is weak. I pause and clear my throat, trying not to make it look like the Banshee's words rattled me as much as they did. Thomas hasn't moved since she declared his thousand possible deaths, I don't think he has so much as breathed either. Maybe this is one of those thousand possible deaths. "We should go."

"For once, I shall not argue," Ravven says, but then the Banshee snaps her gaze to him and lets out a wail so loud and sudden that I jump. My knees are trembling. I don't know if I have ever been so scared in my life, I half expect for her to snatch those long terrible claws at me even though there has never been a reported Banshee mauling in the long and mixed history of humans and faeries.

"I see your death as well. In all of the years that you have roamed these woods, I have never seen your death, oh troubled faerie prince. But I see it now."

I turn to Ravven, stunned. All these years that he's roamed these woods and she's never seen his death until now? There is no possible way that can mean anything good for Thomas and me. His words from earlier echo in my mind. If he listens then it will become true.

"Stop, don't listen!" I cry, stepping toward him.

But he doesn't heed to his own advice. Instead, he watches the Banshee with a shocked expression on his beautiful face.

A sob bursts from her lips. "You thought you had thousands of years, but death is stalking your every breath. Oh, doomed immortal, you taught your heart not to love and yet it is love that will be your downfall. And yet, if your slayer is strong enough, you may yet live."

The Banshee's eyes flick between us. She reaches up to clutch her hair, tears streaming down her face, dripping off her cheeks and soaking into the rags wrapped around her. Her heart is breaking over our sad twisted fate. "Heed my warning," she says, her eyes imploring but also hopeless as she stares straight at Ravven and me. "Your fates are entwined now. The death of one will be the death of another."

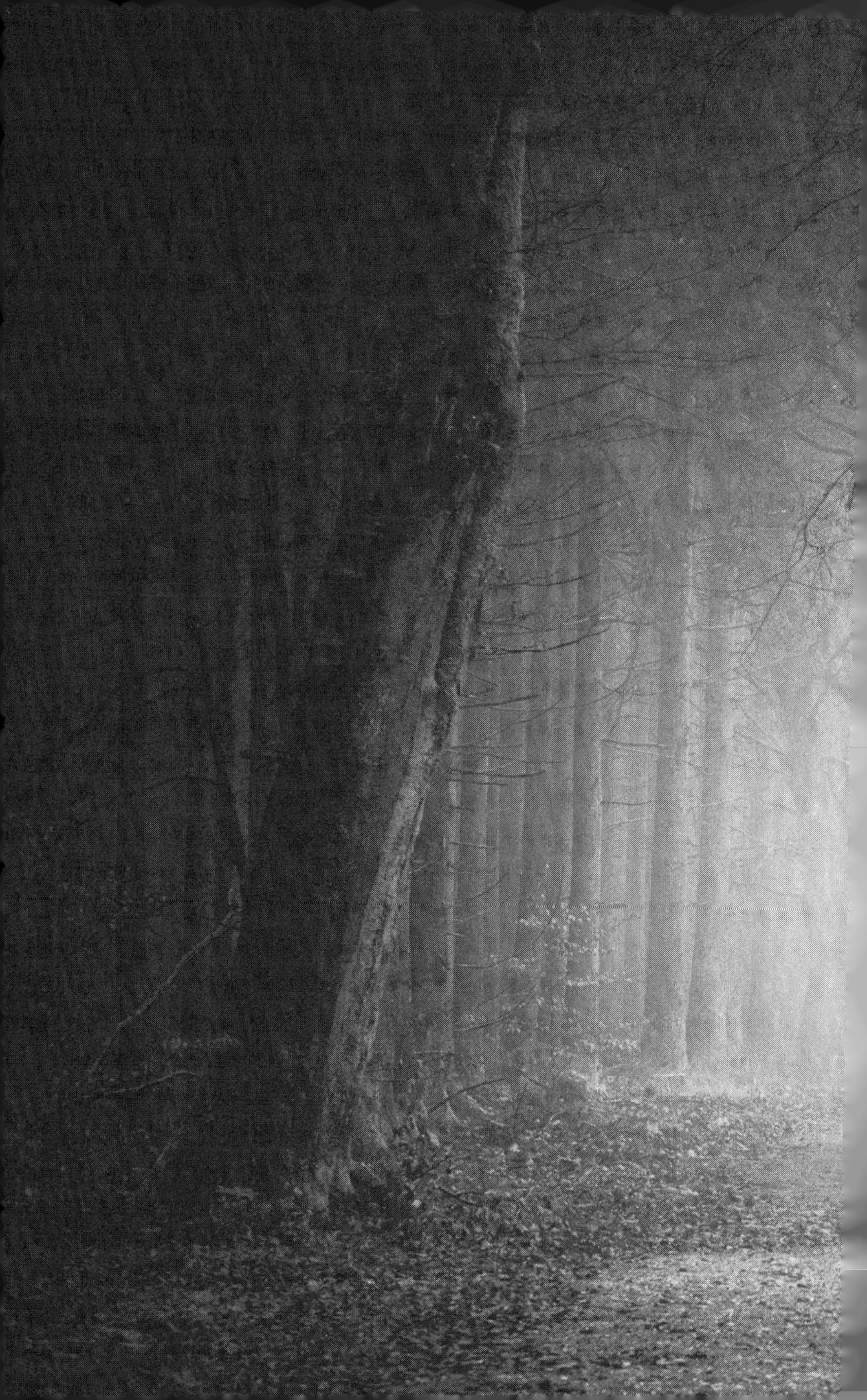

CHAPTER SEVEN

As soon as those horrible pronunciations of our deaths have passed her lips, the Banshee screams, nearly scaring the living daylights out of me, before vanishing into thin air.

"Wait, no!" I cry, but it's too late. She's gone and I'm left brimming with unasked questions. My eyes dart down to my hands. They look so inconspicuous. They're so pale, devoid of any scars, or blood. There's a smear of dirt on the back of my knuckles and my left thumbnail is broken. These hands—*these hands?*—right here, attached to my wrist are going to be the cause of my death? I throw my head back and laugh from the sheer absurdity of it all.

"Why are you laughing?" Ravven asks, looking at me as if I might try to bite him next. "I don't see anything about this situation that is humorous. What is wrong with you mortals? Do you really find your coming doom as something that is amusing?"

"What do you have to be freaked out about, man?" Thomas cries, whirling on him. "At least you only have the possibility of dying once. I've got a thousand of them."

"Sounds to me like you are an extremely careless individual," Ravven says.

"I don't think Ravven is too concerned," I mutter dryly. "In order to get your heart broken, you would first have to have a heart."

Ravven tilts his chin toward me. "Precisely, my pest."

Thomas shakes his head. "I can't believe this. No one is that unfeeling."

"Welcome to the faerie world, corpse," Ravven says with a wicked smile. "I believe that you shall be forced to change your opinion soon. No one loves here."

I reach up and rub at my forehead. Yup, I definitely have a headache. Wish I would have thrown some pain medicine into my satchel. I can't believe I considered what would happen if I had to take a faerie captive but not if I got a headache along the way. "Let's just... let's just forget this whole thing ever happened."

Ravven turns to me, arching his brow. "Do you think that will somehow make it so that it has not?"

Chills race up and down my spine, but I struggle to ignore them. I don't plan on staying in the faerie world very long so it's not like ominous foretellings of my doom even matter right now. Tomorrow I will be safely back home, getting ready for my senior year and trying to figure out if I was going to go to college after graduation or not.

Until then, my rune bracelet will protect me from any ensorcellments. I'm not saying that I am going to defy fate, I'm just saying I'm way too smart to let myself die in any way that it is actually my fault.

Someone inhales a rattling breath just behind me. "Well, isn't this just a merry little gathering."

Okay, my nerves are already frayed, but the fact that neither Thomas or Ravven just spoke has me about to lose my last little grasp of courage.

A scream clogs in my throat and comes out as an awful choked sound. I whirl and stumble back as I take in the creature that seems to have appeared out of nowhere. I know he wasn't standing there a few minutes ago even if I might have been distracted by the Banshee, I couldn't have missed that freaky son of a gun. Even if he is kind of short. He's so stooped over that he only reaches my elbow in height. His skin is drawn so tightly across his cheekbones that I almost imagine the white skeleton peeking through. He could possibly be mistaken for an old man with his shock of white hair and wrinkles, if not for his tiny pointy teeth and how utterly unnaturally thin he is. The creature before me looks as if it has already starved to death, but was so hungry that it dragged itself out of the grave in search of food.

"What the heck is that thing?" Thomas demands, grasping my arm, as if he is about to make a run for it and wants to make sure that he drags me along with him.

Ravven looks us over with an amused expression "Oh, don't mind him. It's simply a Fear Gorta."

"A Fear—*what*?" Thomas demands. I stare at the creature as my mind races through all of the different types of faeries, trying to place this one.

Ravven clicks his tongue, glancing between us and the emaciated faerie. "A Fear Gorta, they're really one of the most harmless of the Solitary fae, but I suppose you can panic if it makes you feel better."

Oh, the Fear Gorta. Now I recall, I had been intrigued by their name thinking that they must be some sort of terrifying creature, only to learn that they are nothing more than emaciated fae that beg for alms. Essentially that is all they do.

The Fear Gorta extends a thin arm that looks like it could snap from just the weight of my gaze and makes a gurgling, "Ahem," sound.

"What does it want?" Thomas asks, his grip on my arm tightening. I resist the urge to wince.

Ravven chuckles, he really is enjoying this way too much. "It is a he, don't be rude. And he wants your pocket change."

"What?" Thomas demands.

"I said that he wants your pocket change."

"Oh, if that's all," Thomas says, his shoulders slumping. He stuffs his hand in his pocket. "I think I have a few pennies I can spare."

"Good, because if you don't give him anything, he will probably curse you."

The Fear Gorta smiles, poking its darkly colored tongue through the gaps in its spiky teeth.

"*What?*" Thomas squeaks, desperately digging into his pockets.

"By my wings, you certainly are a dense one. I said that if you do not give him any alms then he will most likely curse you. But if you pay him, he will bless you."

"You don't have any wings," I mutter, glaring at Ravven's decidedly wingless back.

Thomas finally fishes out his wallet. He opens it up and dumps the coins into the cup of the Fear Gorta's hand. There had to be ten buck's worth of quarters but he just nods and says. "Keep it."

The Fear Gorta bows deeply. "Thank you, kind sir. I will not forget this service that you have paid me and I shall pay you back in kind. I give you a boon." The coins in his hand vanish, replaced by a dark jagged shard of glass wrapped in a brittle black string. "When you require my aid, simply shatter this glass and I shall come and give you an act of service." With those words he turns around and hobbles through the forest, disappearing from sight back into the darkness.

I frown and rub at the goosebumps on my arm as Thomas pockets his shard. I don't know if they are there because of the Banshee's words, the Fear Gorta's appearance, or the chill air. In one day, I have gone from never having ever seen a faerie to having seen three. Plus, a white stag.

Ravven lets out a disgusted sound. "You two are ill omens. In all the time that I have roamed these woods, I have rarely come across so many faeries in such a short amount of time. Do you realize how inconvenient it is for me to have to deal with other faeries?" He releases a heavy breath and turns away, muttering something that I probably am glad that I can't hear.

"We're terribly sorry for inconveniencing you by forcing you to *socialize*." I can barely keep from rolling my eyes. "But it's not like we're trying to draw the faeries' attention."

Thomas snorts. He shakes his head looking incredibly tired. "Jaye, don't make fun of him for being antisocial. You know that saying about rocks and glass houses. Well, you are in a glass house."

Okay, I may not be the most social human being but I'm not as bad as a Solitary faerie. Thomas really needs to stop taking Ravven's side; this is getting tedious.

By now the tip of my nose is numb in the crisp, cold air. I rub at my fingers, trying to bring some feeling back to them. I would hate for one of my fingers to fall off in the night without my realizing it.

Ravven shakes his head, and reaches his two bound hands to knock a lock of hair from his forehead, it flops right back into place another second later in a far too attractive way. I think he did that on purpose just to bring attention to his dark curls.

I quickly look away so I'm not accused of staring again. Something tells me that his dark curls get far too much attention as is.

He holds up a single finger, apparently not finished with his rant. "If seeing them weren't bad enough, at least most faeries that I come across ignore me just as thoroughly as I ignore them. But *no*. When I am with you two, they have to stay and interact with us!"

"I would think that you and Jaye would get along what with you both being unfriendly grumps," Thomas whispers to Ravven as if they are chums suddenly and I'm not standing in easy hearing range.

I elbow him. "I'm sorry some of us like a little quiet now and again."

"Why would I require anyone else?" Ravven asks, he sounds genuinely curious about the answer to that. "I provide myself excellent company."

Good grief. "Whatever happened to lonely existence?"

"You say that as if loneliness is a bad thing. If what your brother says is true then, I would think you understand exactly what I mean."

I frown. The last thing I want is to have anything in common with that self-satisfied, smug, little—

"That frown does nothing to improve your already horrid features, just so you know."

If I strangle Ravven to death with my own two hands then technically I haven't used iron as a weapon and technically that means the faeries don't have to hunt me down and execute me.

"Will you two stop—"

"Be quiet!" Ravven hisses, holding up both his bound hands.

"Don't tell us what to do," I mutter. Ravven seems to have forgotten who is the captive and who is the captor in this situation.

"I can do whatever I want," Ravven says haughtily. "And at the moment I don't want to die, so for the sake of the five courts, do be quiet."

Thomas rests a hand on my shoulder. "What do you mean, die?"

"I mean to have my magic robbed from me, and my lungs no longer draw in breaths, my heart stops beating, and I cease to exist in this particular body. *Death*," Ravven snaps. "What did you think I meant?"

"But what do you think is trying to kill us?" I whisper, glancing around at the still forest. There is no movement whatsoever. For once. No sign of the Banshee, Fear Gorta, white stag or anything else.

"How should I know? They haven't tried to kill us yet," as he speaks, an icy gust of wind washes over me nearly knocking me to my knees. It is so cold that it pierces my very core.

"What the heck?" I breathe as a shudder rips through my frame just as swiftly as the frigid air slices through the thin cotton of my shirt.

Ravven turns gray. Which may be the most alarming thing that has happened yet. "But, no, we are in the Autumn Court—"

"What is happening?" I demand as an icy gust blows over us. I look down to see a sheet of ice traveling across the ground at a freakishly unnatural speed.

"Mvtalach. It's the Winter Queen—" Ravven begins, but just then spikes of ice shoot up between us. Some spikes start interweaving like some sort of prison cell. Others shoot out toward us, jagged spears of ice.

I hear Thomas cry out.

"Thomas!" I shout, whipping my head around. I can't see more than two feet thanks to the sudden blizzard and bits of ice and snow tearing at my face and causing my eyes to blur. I just barely catch sight of something shooting toward me and I stumble to the side, managing to avoid impalement. But not by much.

My foot lands on a patch of ice that I swear hadn't been there a second ago. The sole of my custom-made leather boot loses traction and flies out from under me and I fall backward. I feel a sharp snap of my head hitting the ice and then everything goes black. The last thing I see are large white fluffy snowflakes drifting down toward me.

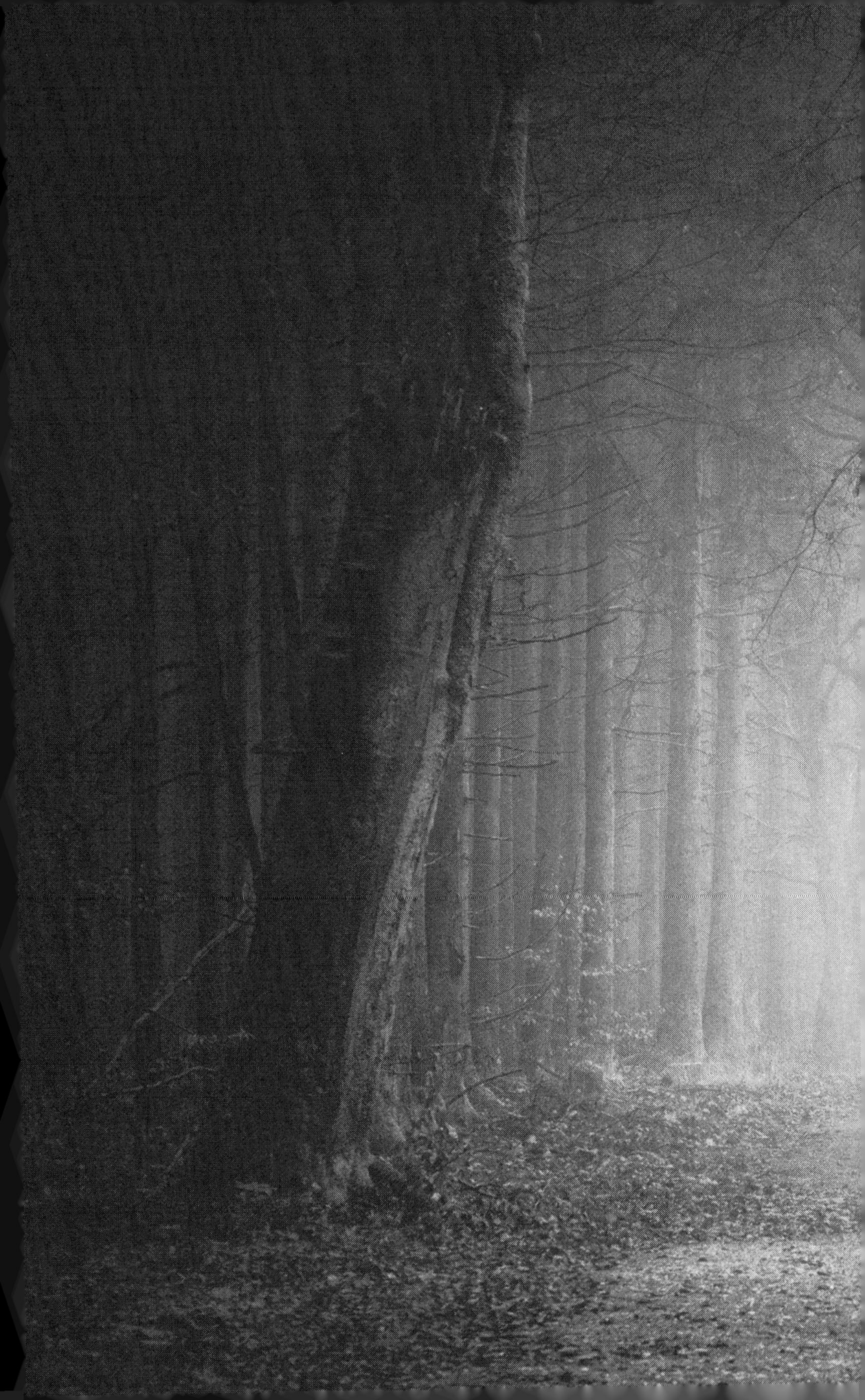

CHAPTER EIGHT

It is a struggle to even open my eyes. My eyelids are too heavy, my eyesight too blurry, and everything's too fuzzy for me to face the world. In other words, it is a usual morning for me, except for the headache piercing through different portions of my skull all at once.

I move my hand and press it against my forehead, resisting the urge to groan.

I force myself to take stock of my situation. I'm lying in a room that is some sort of cavern. Jagged clumps of rocks arching over my head and everything in the room appears to be cut out of obsidian black stone. Across from me appears to be a wardrobe, protruding from the wall, with engravings adorning its uneven surface. It is also made of black rock.

I sit up, grimacing at the pain. I am sitting on a flat slab which could be mistaken for a bed—a very uncomfortable bed. A blanket of white linen lies across the bottom. To my right appears to be the only door in the room, almost invisible because it too is made of the same rock as the rest of the room. It would be practically invisible if not for the fact that it is also engraved like the doors to the wardrobe.

I brace my arm against the bed and freeze when I see for the first time what I am wearing. It is a silver tunic with long sleeves that dangle in a way that is bound to get in the way. The ends of the sleeves are lined in some sort of soft white fur, though I have no idea what animal it could be from. The scoop neckline is a little too low for my taste, leaving my shoulders bare to the chill of the air. The edges of the neckline are also lined with fur. The tunic extends to my mid-thigh and under it I am wearing warm black leggings.

What happened to my old clothes? Who changed me? Where the heck even am I?

Then a new terrifyingly awful realization comes upon me. My rune bracelet—it's gone.

I am defenseless.

The Banshee's threat hangs ominously over my consciousness. I'm fated to destroy myself with my own hands, and now I'm defenseless to stop it.

The air is bitterly cold and stings the interiors of my nostrils as I breathe in. Other than the heavy mildew scent that fills my nose, it also smells almost crisp. Clear. Like the kind of weather, you would have on a winter day. Like the cold has removed all signs of impurifications from the air.

My socked feet touch the cold stone floor and I resist the urge to yelp as the cold nearly immediately makes my toes go numb.

I rub at my forearms which are exposed by the billowy sleeves of the odd tunic that I am wearing. Goosebumps cover my flesh and my fingers are cold, even when I touch them to my own skin. It's a miracle that I don't have frostbite, then again, I can't see my ears or nose so I don't really know for sure.

I spot my boots lying near the foot of the rock slab bed and nearly slump off of it in my relief. At least some part of my old ensemble remains. I quickly pull them on, stopping to inspect the pockets that line the top of both the boots. They still have my lock picks in them and the hidden compartment sewn into the side of my boot still has my spare iron knife.

I smile to myself. The iron should be able to protect me at least a little bit from any curses. Of course, I still can't actually use it without becoming public enemy number one. But things are escalating enough that might not end up being the worst thing to happen to me.

I step toward the door and try the handle. It stings my flesh, growing more painful each second that I hold it. It's like trying to hold onto a block of ice. I grit my teeth and force myself to keep a hold of it as I pull the handle, but it doesn't budge. Locked. Of course, I shouldn't be too surprised.

"Dang it!" I hiss, shaking out my hand as I step away. I blow my warm breath on it as I try to rub the shooting pain of the cold away. I step back and study the room for another escape. There is no window, I might be underground from the way that the walls look like they've been cut out of sheer rock.

I kick at one of the walls, but I hear no hollow thump.

I turn back to the door. It looks like it's my only hope to get out of here. But if I can't open it from in here, I'll need to wait until someone else opens it. If I can hide somewhere then perhaps I can jump out and get the jump on them.

I've seen this in movies. Maybe not the wisest course of action, but I'm a tad desperate here. I glance at the wardrobe, considering it for jump-getting potential.

I reach up to scratch my head which is when I realize that my semi-curly strawberry blonde hair has also been washed and styled. Gone is my braid, but now my hair hangs loosely down my shoulders in crimson waves. Like the sea when the sun is setting.

I am so disturbed on so many levels. What all did these faeries do while I was unconscious. Who were the faeries that did this to me?

As if summoned by my thoughts, the door swings open.

I straighten and immediately try to look like I hadn't just been plotting my escape from my strange prison. But since I blush crimson straight up to my hairline, I'm not entirely sure that I succeed.

Standing on the other side of the door is probably one of the single most beautiful individuals I have ever seen. I've lived in the human world and I already know that human beauty cannot compare to the ethereal appearances of the faeries. I shouldn't even compare them. The faeries achieve a form of beauty that is inhuman and unfair.

I've also not seen that many faeries for all of my bravado. I haven't actually seen a Sidhe faerie with their rumored enchanting golden hair and always laughing eyes. I have never seen a majestic Tuatha De Danan. My limited experience with faeries extends to a small grouping of Solitary faeries, and they aren't all that attractive actually. With the exception being Ravven.

But even with Ravven... he's handsome, don't get me wrong. He's really quite attractive for all his flaws. But this faerie—this faerie isn't just attractive. To call him handsome would be an insult. He is beautiful. Every part of him is so perfect that it looks like he's actually a runaway Michelangelo statue come to life.

He is pale as freshly fallen snow, with piercing blue eyes that I could possibly mistake for a body of water in the Caribbean Sea, because there is no way any other area in nature exists where blue could be so *blue*. He has soft curling hair of every varying shade of blonde. It's almost white down by his ears but darkens the higher it gets until there is a streak of hair on the top of his head that is almost a chestnut brown that curls gently against his forehead.

He smiles at me, revealing cruelly placed dimples, and I feel my knees go weak even though I sternly command them not to. "How wonderful, I was just coming to check on you. I am so glad to see that you are finally awake. I was concerned. It had appeared that you had been injured and I know mortals to be such fragile things."

He steps forward, his body moving fluidly as his ice blue tunic clings to the muscles in his chest and tight-fitted sleeves circle his forearms.

This faerie, my friends, is a perfect physical specimen. He reaches out, fluidly, not an ounce of hesitation as he grasps my hand and lifts it up. "But you must be hardier than you appear." He smiles at me over my hand before pressing a long kiss to the back of my hand.

The fear melts into nicely warmed goo.

I blush and pull back, catching a whiff of something that smells like lavender only somehow better. "I actually hit my head a lot. I have an extremely thick skull."

Oh my gosh, what am I saying?

I want to die of embarrassment, but the faerie chuckles like what I said actually amused him. I smile back at him hesitantly.

"I can imagine that you must have. I am Iorwerth, chamberlain of the Winter Court. And what is your name, human maid?"

My heart freezes over with the very ice that I would have expected to find here. I am in the court of the Unseelie faeries? The faeries of the Winter Court have never been quiet about their distaste of humans. They fought in the faerie wars for the side that wished to conquer and enslave us. It is their queen who curses our line of Guardians when the ruler of the Tuatha De Danan blesses them.

I need to snap out of whatever spell this Iorwerth has me under because if he serves the Winter Court then he can only have ill intent toward me.

"Jaye," I say, pulling back my hand. I wipe it on my dress at the reminder of everything that I've been through. Suddenly, I feel dirty for having let his lips touch me when I don't even know who he could be. "Why am I in the Winter Court?"

He chuckles. "Because that is where we brought you, little bird."

I hate his vague answer, the truth, but not answering my question at all. My heart is beating like a humming bird's wing and it takes a concerted effort for me not to freak out. "Where are my companions?"

Thomas had been hurt; I remember that much. Ravven... well, I care less about him but it would certainly be a pain to find a new guide. Plus, he still has my handcuffs. Although without my satchel I don't have a key to bargain with.

He released a breath as if he is somehow angry with me for even bothering to ask. "The other mortal is recovering in the best care he can receive. I can imagine he is extremely happy where he is," he says with a chuckle as if he is in on some sort of private joke. "And Ravven Crowe was summoned before the queen. She wishes an audience with you as well—that was why I came. To retrieve you." He extends his arm toward me and arches one brow. "May I?"

I stare at his arm with reluctance; he could be trying to lead me anywhere. But if there's even a chance that he is taking me to see Ravven, I have to take it. A neutral Solitary faerie is better than an Unseelie faerie. Ravven himself admitted to having a soft spot for us humans—he called us rotting corpses afterward, but I can only hope that he meant it as a term of endearment. Whatever his feelings, they are more sympathetic than anything the Winter Court must be planning.

With a deep breath, I slide my arm through Iorwerth's and try my best to ignore his perfect lavender scent. "Then take me to see your queen," I say with forced bravado, dearly hoping that I will not come to regret those words.

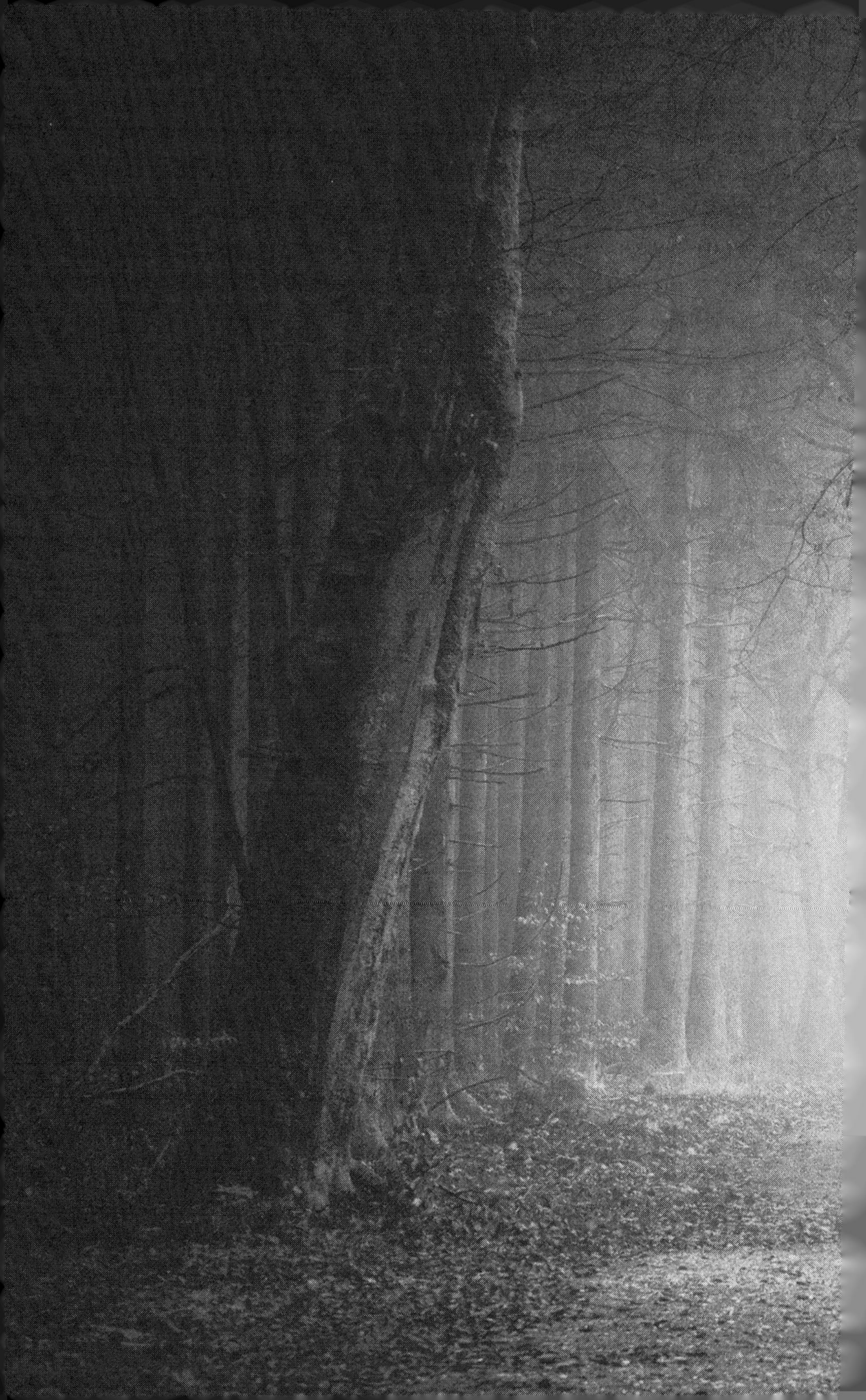

CHAPTER NINE

The hallway outside is even more frigid than the chamber I had woken up in. It is as if my entire core is frozen. I can almost feel the skin of my hands drying up and becoming chapped as the harsh breeze kisses my cheeks and claims the feeling from my nose.

I'm not even sure if we're in a hallway or outdoors. Clumps of trees grow on either side of me in the vast cavernous expanse, but stone echoes under my booted feet and I can see the stalactites hanging from the ceiling above.

The trees that line either side of the hall are dead with bare branches which interlace above our heads, creating some sort of passage within the larger hallway. A faint blue light that seems to be emanating from everywhere and yet nowhere at the same time is the only light source and it seems to only make the hall seem colder.

And here I stand in the middle of it all, alone, defenseless, and completely at the faeries' mercy. Too bad they don't have any.

I inhale a shaky breath and turn to Iorwerth. "Why does the faerie queen want to see me?" For some reason I feel better asking him questions because I know that at least when he answers he is not lying to me.

"She wishes to meet you."

"Why?" I ask, pulling back. I can think of only a few utterly horrible reasons why the queen of the Unseelie faeries will want to meet a mortal.

"I shall allow her to tell you that."

I press my lips together in frustration. Riddles and half answers and no answers at all. That's all I seem to get from these faeries. I try not to even let my mind wander to the Banshee's predictions. She may possibly be the most maddening faerie of them all.

My hand moves to fondle my charm bracelet before I remember that it is gone. My stomach twists uncomfortably.

"I have grown fond of you, little bird," Iorwerth says suddenly.

"You have?" I ask, pulling back. "But you barely know me."

"Perhaps... but I would very much like the opportunity to get to know you better." He tugs me toward him and smiles in a way that makes my heart physically ache because I know that it isn't real. I always considered façades to be full of deceit, I didn't realize they could be painful too. That I would ever want a façade to be true, not when it came from a faerie. But I do wish Iorwerth weren't a faerie with a rotten soul and a black heart. "For a mortal, you are exquisitely beautiful."

I force myself to keep my eyes off of him. If I don't look at him then I don't have as much of a desire to do something stupid like kiss him. I don't have time to flirt or fall in love. Especially not with a faerie. Especially not with a Unseelie faerie. I force my gaze straight ahead as we stroll under the skeletal trees. They sway softly as we pass as if acknowledging our presence. "You said that my brother is being cared for. Is he safe?"

Iorwerth laughs; it's a rich tinkling sound that echoes to the trees and back with just as much force as if it were coming straight from his mouth. "His only danger is himself."

Somehow Iorwerth's words don't comfort me. Especially since my rune is gone; that probably means that Thomas's is too. They could make him do anything and he wouldn't even know.

"Who is caring for him?" I demand.

"The queen's own sister. Aoibheann. I imagine he is very happy."

I betray myself and glance at Iorwerth out of the corner of my eye. Even though I know he is telling me the truth, I also know that he is not telling me the whole truth. He seems oddly smug at the thought of this Aoibheann tending to my brother. It makes me nervous.

Iorwerth must sense my distrust because he looks down at me and smiles reassuringly. I quickly pull my gaze away, my pulse racketing in my ears. "Aoibheann has always had a soft spot for mortal heroes. In the olden days when we still walked the Earth, she was called the Muse by you mortals. She inspired your bards to sing such beautiful songs."

A breath slithers its way out from between my slightly parted lips. Surely... surely that must mean that she is not too bad. Iorwerth could not be lying about any of the facts. She has a soft spot for mortal heroes and used to inspire bards. I can live with that.

What I'm not sure I can live with is what he obviously isn't telling me.

He smiles again; this one is also stupendously beautiful, but it's also secretive and untrustworthy. "Ah, the queen's chambers."

I look up and gasp as I take in two double doors. They're huge, making up maybe three Iorwerths in height and he is not a short faerie, he stands well over six feet. Actually, most faeries are extremely tall which is probably why they have such high doors. The edges are jagged and swoops and swirls protrude from them, making them look almost like a butterfly's wing. A butterfly's wing that has been turned entirely into ice. The doors creak open seemingly of their own volition because the guards standing just inside don't even bother turning around. The swirls disappear into cuts in the wall that appear made just for the purpose of not blocking the doors when they move on their hinges.

It's really impractical for a set of doors, but dang does it make an impression.

Iorwerth ushers me inside to a room that is almost too dazzling for my eyes. I resist the urge to squint like some pathetic human as I glance around. Everything from the walls, to the ceiling, to the giant chandelier hanging overhead, to the floors… all made of cut ice and shimmering like crystals. Light bounces everywhere. The walls are covered in sharp corners, designed best to reflect the light, which appears to be shining straight through them from some sort of light source on the other side.

It hurts my eyes, but not as much as the pale woman sitting directly in the middle of the room on an ice throne. She is so pale that she almost looks like she is carved from ice as well. Little blue veins line underneath her skin. Her lips and her eyes both are the palest blue I have almost ever seen.

Her hair is corn silk blond and is pulled up at the nape of her head with loops dangling around her pointed ears and framing her face. She wears a crown that appears to be made entirely of cut crystals, with a band made of white gold that is so thin that I have to do a double take to make sure it was there at all. She is wearing a silver blue dress that cascades from her bare shoulders and pools at the foot of her throne as if it is water instead of fabric.

She is sitting stiffly, inhumanly so. Like she truly is an ice sculpture.

She looks otherworldly, beautiful, unreachable. Sharp to the touch. And unimpressed.

I finally manage to turn my gaze away from her to the rest of the room. Besides the two guards at the door, Iorwerth, and the queen, there are only two other faeries. A dark-haired faerie who is handsome, but his beauty seems pale in comparison to the others in the room and Ravven Crowe.

The breath is punched out of my lungs when I take him in. I don't know why I'm surprised by how beautiful he is—I've seen him before. But I had begun to think him not quite so beautiful because surely nothing could hold a candle to Iorwerth's beauty. However, when I look at him, I think how he could compare.

He looks a little more—dare I say?—human, whereas Iorwerth is so beautiful it's unnatural.

I feel like I've been dunked into cold water and jolted awake. I sneak a peek at Iorwerth and frown. Faeries do not usually reveal their true forms, but often use their magic to amplify their outward appearances. Somehow Iorwerth's glamour works so well that it tried to make me forget all things beautiful when I looked upon him? It seems ridiculous, but then I am in the faerie world.

Ravven looks up at our entrance into the room. He remains perfectly still apart from his fist clenching slightly. But his eyes flash a murderous yellow.

His appearance surprises me almost as much as being jolted from that glamour or whatever it was that Iorwerth had me under. His clothes are torn and crumbled and a single trickle of silver, crimson, and gold blood runs down the corner of his lip. His hands are still bound, which I suppose is because I'm probably the only person here even capable of touching the iron key. I don't know where my satchel is, but my key is still inside it.

I take an unbidden step forward, feeling concern for him before I remind myself that he's just a faerie. That I only met him today. That I can't trust him anymore than the other faeries in this court.

With everything that is going on, I want to feel safe around him. I want to feel like I have one ally. One single person to watch my back. But that is not a healthy thing to want. Not when the person I wish were my ally will very likely stab me in the back that I want watched.

But still, I feel somewhat guilty. I am directly responsible for getting him wrapped up in this mess. I mean I kidnapped him, weakened his magic with my iron traps. He probably wouldn't be standing there if it weren't for me. Instead he would be freely roaming the woods of the Autumn Court to his Solitary heart's content.

"So, you are the mortal companion of Ravven Crowe?" the queen says. Her voice is musical but flat. She appears to be bored out of her mind as she looks me over.

I cross my arms as I briefly debate whether intimidation or overestimation is the key to surviving this situation. But before I can fully make up my mind, my smart mouth decides for me. "His captor actually."

The queen arches a single brow that is so thin and pale that it is almost invisible against her porcelain complexion. "Oh?" She turns to Ravven. "Is this true? Is she the one who I have to thank for incapacitating you?"

Ravven rolls his eyes, looking completely at ease in the situation. Like he isn't even a captive. The only flaws to the mask he wears are his crumpled clothes, his bloodied lip, and his eyes that flash yellow when they land on me. "You know how mortals can be, always lying. She exaggerates."

Bold of him to say while his hands are currently bound in my handcuffs.

I bite the inside of my lip hard. And faeries are incapable of lying, but somehow, he still exaggerates. I am his captor. He must have found some loophole, maybe he really thinks I exaggerated when I kidnapped him.

Faeries are bound to speak the truth. But that does not mean that they have to speak the whole truth.

In fact, faeries rarely do.

"I don't know," Iorwerth, of all people, says coming to my defense. He slinks up to me and looks me over in an almost predatory way. It makes me feel cold and slimy rather than warm and fuzzy. "She seems capable of it. Tell me Ravven, you always did have a weakness for beauty. Did she draw you in with her charms?"

Iorwerth once again lifts my hand again, but instead of kissing it, he simply sniffs it. Loudly. It's more than a little weird. And more than a lot creepy.

I pull my arm back as soon as he loosens his grip.

"You forget who I am, Iorwerth," Ravven says dismissively. "If you think that I am so easily charmed."

Two faeries, neither can lie, both saying opposite things about my appearance. Sheesh, these faeries are going to give me a major complex.

Iorwerth looks up at Ravven and smiles slowly, showing all of his teeth. His incisors are surprisingly sharp, like fangs. "Your eyes are yellow," he says at last.

Ravven stiffens. "And your eyes are blue. May I ask why we are stating the obvious?"

Iorwerth tilts his head, but he says nothing. He raises both his hands to either side of my face. Fingering my hair, he trails it between us as he steps back, until he finally reaches the end and it flutters down to my shoulders. I shudder and take an unbidden step toward Ravven.

He steps toward me as well, but freezes when the Winter Queen begins speaking again. "Is this human your little pet, Crowe?" she asks, obviously sounding amused.

"Am I not allowed to have one?" Ravven said, raising his chin. "You have many, Cliodnha."

"Why is she your pet?" Cliodnha asks, shifting in her seat, ignoring his statement. "Why *her*? Why not a different mortal?"

"Because she was handy," Ravven said.

It's like they are speaking another language because I don't know what they are saying exactly. But I think it pertains to me and that makes me uncomfortable.

It's never good when faeries show a mortal too much attention. "She is also right here so if we could stop talking about her—I mean, *me*—like I'm not here, that would be great."

The faeries ignore me. Go figure. I am just a mortal to them, a pawn to be played with and then discarded when they tire of me.

The Winter Queen pushes to her feet. "I would like to see how much this little pet of yours actually means to you."

My breath shudders in my throat and my heart turns to a block of ice when she looks at me. I resist the urge to look away despite how much holding her gaze hurts my eyes.

She strides toward me, walking around me in a small circle as if contemplating me for a long moment. I swallow hard. "Actually, I can assure you that I mean nothing to him," I squeak. "So, there's really no need to do whatever you were intending to do."

I dart a quick look at Ravven, but he won't meet my gaze, his face impassive.

The other faerie standing in the back of the room, so quiet that I almost forgot he was there, pulls a face so twisted that it draws my attention. But when he catches me looking at him, he quickly wipes that look from his face.

"Is this truly necessary, my queen?" Iorwerth asks, once again being the one to come to my aid. I look at him over my shoulder to see him looking at me in a way a dog would a treat that was being held over the garbage disposal.

The queen wiggles her fingers. "Of course, it is. But even if it weren't... I'm not one to deny myself of amusement."

Iorwerth heaves a heavy sigh. "Do not scar her too badly, please. I would rather if she were to remain in one piece."

One piece? I can't help the whimper that escapes my lips. My wrist feels naked. I am defenseless against anything that they might do with me. I consider lunging for my knife, but I only have one and I can't risk them taking it from me.

Where I stand, they seem to be planning on keeping me alive. That would change awful quickly if I tried to use iron against the Winter Queen.

"Never fear, young one," the queen says in almost a soothing voice. She raises her hand as if to stroke my face, but her hand hovers above it instead. "Your pain is necessary. Ravven owes me; he belongs to me, and I must teach him that." She smiles coldly. "I'm sure that you can understand. Being a possession yourself."

I feel like she's actually trying to soothe me. She looks at me as if her words are supposed to have a calming effect, and while her voice is honeyed, I do not feel calm at all. And I am seriously getting ticked by everyone saying that I am Ravven Crowe's when *I* was the one who had kidnapped *him*.

"I come from a long line of Guardians," I say, stumbling back, tripping over my own feet in my fear. "If you harm me, I will be avenged."

Cliodnha seems startled at first by my words, but then she smiles at me, a cold unfeeling gesture. "I fear no mortals." Then she reaches her hand out to snag my forearm. I brace myself for pain, but I only find myself standing there, breathing hard and grimacing over nothing.

I straighten and stare down at my arm. I'm about to say, "Is that it?" when I realize that my forearm is cold. The cold is emanating from where her skin is touching my bare flesh. At first, it's bearable, almost numbing, but every second the cold intensifies until I realize all at once that this is the coldest thing I have ever felt. Even colder than the door to the room that I woke up in.

It is excruciating. My breath puffs out in hard gasps, the fog of it blinding me, but then I realize that it is actually the tears welling in my eyes that mar my vision.

Every second that her hand is on my arm, it hurts more, until I can't take the pain anymore. I try to pull back, but she will not yield. It's so cold, I have to get away—but I can't. I grunt and raise my other hand to hers but the second my fingers touch hers I have to pull back as the cold pierces that hand as well.

A cracking sound reaches my ears and then I realize that it is my skin freezing over.

I don't know when I start screaming, I can't even feel or control my body anymore. All I can comprehend is the pain shooting up my arm, plaguing my shoulder. Causing my right hand to spasm. I drop to my knees, tears streaming down my face and I'm screaming. Begging her to let go. The pain is so numbing and yet so intense, like the cold cannot truly numb me like it usually would, but instead it can only stab me with a thousand small daggers.

Suddenly my ringing ears notice another voice mixed with my own, begging for the torture to cease.

"Stop!" Ravven cries. "Stop! You have your answer now. You can release her."

Through my tears, I see the queen smile again. This time there is actually feeling in it. She actually looks pleased as she releases my arm.

My breath catches in my throat and I find myself unable to breathe from the relief. My arm still aches, but now the blessed numbness covers it. I collapse to the ground and look down to see that she has left a blue and red handprint in the skin of my forearm. I faintly wonder if the mark will ever go away.

"So, you do care for her," the queen replies. She smiles again and looks at me dotingly like she hadn't just been torturing me two minutes ago. "Good."

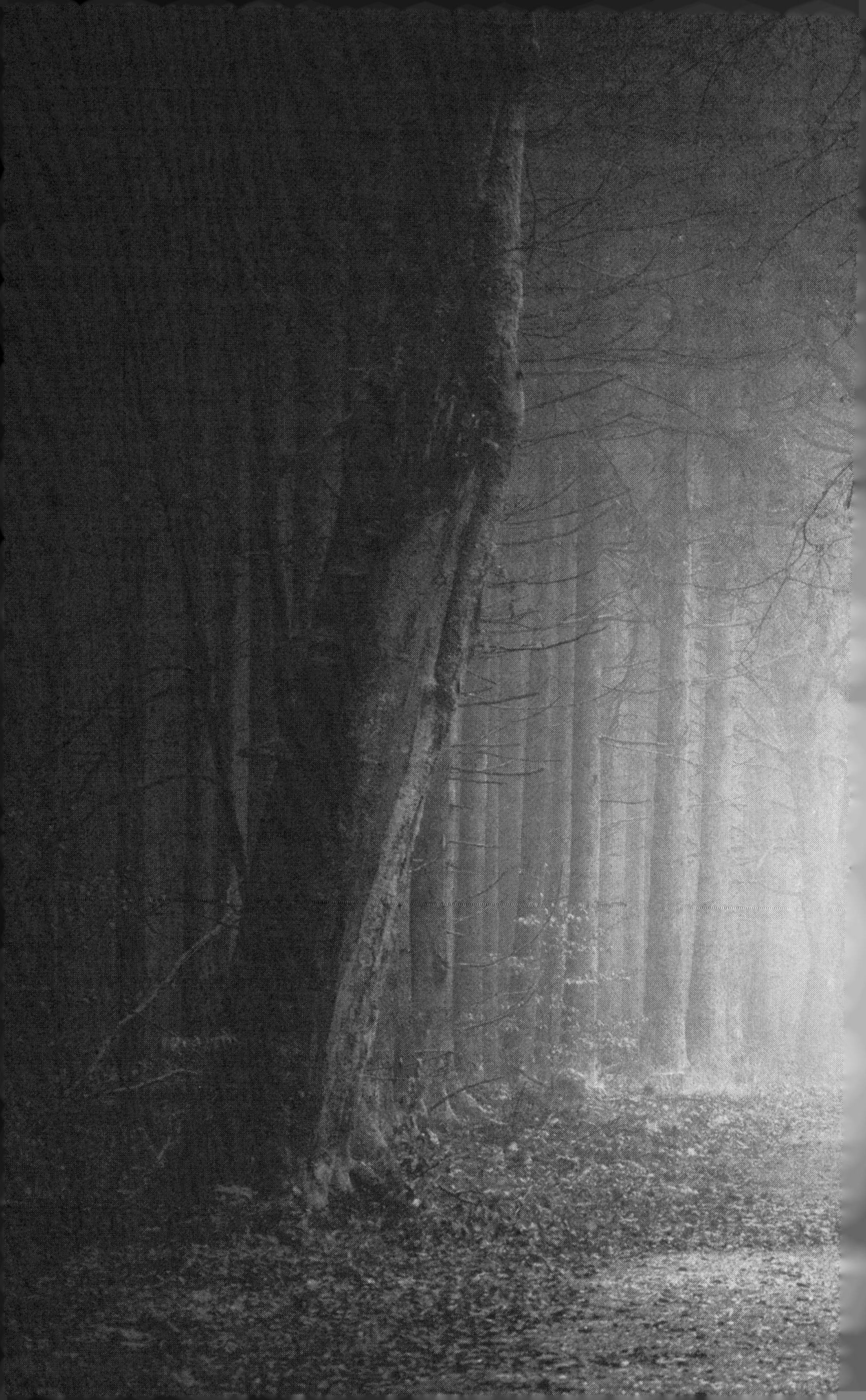

CHAPTER TEN

Iorwerth steps forward and I don't know what he intends to do. I want nothing more than to leave the presence of this wicked, wicked queen. But I can't move. My bones and muscles feel like they have frozen into ice sculptures, locked together with pain. I am incapable of moving, and I can only lie there gasping for breath and trying not to cry as the numbness fades replaced by the pain again.

Why did she do this to me? What did she gain from this? The pleasure of seeing me scream or something else and possibly more sinister?

Whatever happened, Ravven of all people is the one who told her to stop. Why would he do that, why the heck does he care?

But my brain refuses to process anything at this point. It's dull and useless, crippled by a pounding headache.

And then Ravven is at my side, his hands gently cupping my shoulders, and in that second, I forget that he is a faerie and that just earlier tonight I had been holding him hostage. In that second it is just nice to have a gentle touch and a little comfort.

"Jaye," he whispers, jostling me. "Come now, pest, you must get up."

I nod weakly and try to force my weak legs to work. But every movement is like being stabbed with ice.

"I can't—" I rasp, surprised by how hoarse my throat is, but then, I must have been screaming more than I'd thought I was. I brace my good hand against the cold marble floor and try to steady my breathing.

Ravven releases a heavy breath beside me then whispers. "I want to remind you that this would be much less uncomfortable if you hadn't had the gall to handcuff me. The use of both my hands would be very handy right now."

I frown. "What—"

My question lodges in my throat, only a gasp managing to escape as he grasps my good arm and yanks me to my feet. It hurts so bad that I want to cry. I squeeze my eyes shut to keep from doing just that in front of all the faeries.

Ravven braces my hip with his hands the best he can with them still bound.

"Wrap your arm around my shoulder, corpse, I cannot help you if you continue being this stubborn." I turn my head and pry my eyes open just enough to glare at him, but his words do the trick and my anger spurs me with the strength to move my arm to his shoulder. The one that the queen actually froze lies limply at my side.

"Follow me," Iorwerth says, his eyes lingering on me as if enjoying seeing me so helpless.

"Lead away," Ravven says airily as if nothing is the matter. As if he isn't currently stooped over to help support my weight. As if everything about this isn't wrong.

Iorwerth turns and with a gesture leads us out the door, which once again opens by itself. He strides through the trees, but doesn't stop in the area that used to be my room. The faerie guards don't follow us; neither does the queen and whoever that other faerie had been. I wonder why Ravven doesn't make a break for it. Then I realize that I am sort of a dead weight—he's carrying me more than I am walking—and that there are probably a thousand guards positioned throughout this palace.

And Thomas is somewhere, so I couldn't even leave without him anyway.

The farther we go down the hall, the darker it gets until Iorwerth is leading us down a metal spiral staircase and I can barely see anything at all. The faeries seem to have no problem, however. Their eyesight is better than humans, though I don't know by how much. Apparently good enough to see in the almost pitch dark. It's a good thing that Ravven is supporting me because I think I miss more than half the steps. One arm is still throbbing from whatever the Winter Queen did to it and the other will probably be wrenched out of socket by the end of this flight of stairs. I'd ask how this day could get worse but quite frankly I don't want to jinx myself.

A steady dripping reaches my ears and I crane my neck to see that we are in an arched stone hallway.

The stones are covered in some sort of glowing moss, but other than that, there is no other light source. Only part of the wall is made of stone; odd sections are missing, only to be replaced by some sort of grating, interwoven like flowering vines that were encased in metal. I can't see what is beyond. There is nothing but a misty darkness.

Iorwerth stops in front of a grate that reveals a dark room beyond. He opens the door, gesturing for us to step in. I tug on Ravven's shirt to keep him from walking through the door. "I want to see my brother," I rasp. I wonder how I must look, bedraggled, barely able to stand, and making demands when I don't even have anything to bargain with. Not that I would ever make a bargain with Iorwerth.

Iorwerth had pretended to be charming and to actually like me and I guess I'm just hoping that it wasn't all just an act.

He smiles slightly, but it looks almost triumphant. "I shall see what I can do about that. But I'm afraid that you have to enter the cell with Crowe for now."

I press my lips together and nod. Still a prisoner, still alive, and for some unknown reason my connection with Ravven is the reason for both.

Iorwerth smiles and flicks my cheek with the tips of his fingers in a strange caress. Ravven moves away dragging me with him as he steps into the cell.

Iorwerth waves his arm and the door shuts with a clang, but I can see his twisted but beautiful smile through the slats. "Until we meet again, little bird."

Ravven guides me over to a slab on the far side of the cell that looks like it is supposed to be some demented version of a bed and drops me onto it probably all too eager to be done with the physical contact. I know I am, even if Ravven takes his body heat with him, leaving me exposed to the chill air of the dank cell. Coldness wraps around me like the antithesis of a blanket.

I slump against the stone. So much has happened in such a short amount of time and I don't even know why half of it happened. I suppose all those stories and warnings were right, the faerie world is certainly a twisted, dangerous place. Not that I doubted them.

I can't seem to muster up any feelings other than exhaustion. Not pain or fear or loneliness or anything anymore. Whatever that queen did to me, it was so intense it burned away everything else. I shudder and pray that it never happens to me again.

But I don't have time to be exhausted. I'm a prisoner and honestly escape is the only viable option here. I start running through my resources, which are kind of pathetically few. A few lockpicks that probably won't work on an invisible door, a dagger that would be illegal to use here, and a faerie I can't trust.

I eye Ravven as he paces back and forth, his arms hanging awkwardly in front of him, his clothing rumpled and the blood now dried. By all rights we are both prisoners, have both been roughed up by our captors, we should be allies. With our combined efforts we might just get out of here alive. But he is a faerie so nothing is that simple.

"Why are you helping me?"

The queen tortured me and Ravven was the one who asked her to stop. Why? Were my screams giving him a headache? Why would he help me? Why does he ever help me?

He saved my life when he didn't even know me. And I'm beginning to believe his explanation about his game less and less.

There are not enough coincidences in the world to explain Ravven's presence in my life.

Ravven turns to me, his lips quirking as if he is enjoying some inside joke. "You assume I am helping you."

Ah, there it is, vague non answers. For being such volatile beings, faeries border the line of being dangerously predictable.

"You're assuming that I'm assuming," I mutter. I'm kind of proud of how faerie that answer sounds.

Ravven shrugs. "Perhaps I am helping you. More likely than not, I am helping myself."

"Now you are being cryptic on purpose." I scratch the bridge of my nose as I consider him. He's deliberately twisting his words to confuse me. But the more I get him to say the less he can hide. At least I hope so, but I am probably underestimating his ability to be a faerie. "What's going on here and what part do you play in it?"

Ravven steps forward but rather than replying he simply kneels next to me and lifts my arm to look at it more closely. He looks almost concerned but that isn't possible so the dark lighting must be playing tricks on me.

I've been avoiding looking at my arm because I feel absolutely sickened by the handprint on my arm. It is almost completely blue, save for at the edges where it is raw and red. Frost gathers in the middle and hasn't melted at all. Nor has the vibrancy of the mark faded even a little bit. I wonder if it will ever go away.

What did she do to me? Is it permanent? I feel like crying when I think about what happened. Quite honestly, I am very likely going to die down here and there probably is nothing I can do to stop it. Doesn't change the fact that I'm not ready to die. Not yet. Not now. Not like this.

"A word of advice, it is not best for a mortal such as you to go about extolling your virtues. Do your best to not be so vain," he says, his voice so condescending that it would put an elitist to shame. "Believe it or not, it is not actually wise for a mortal to draw those faerie's attention."

I scoff and pull back. "Are you seriously calling *me* vain?"

He blinks at me. "You act as if you are surprised."

"I am! Why would you say that I am vain?"

"Why would I not? You are the vainest mortal that I have ever met," he says simply.

My blood rushes to my face, heating my temper with it. Anger always follows embarrassment for me. "And how many humans have you actually met?" I demand.

He's silent for a long moment, suddenly finding his elegantly long fingers interesting.

I huff a laugh. "It's really funny, you calling me vain when you are the vainest faerie I have ever met."

His eyes fly up to mine, they are ocher. "And how many faeries have you actually met?"

I blink at him, a little shocked at having my words thrown back at me. Maybe I haven't met too many faeries, but that doesn't change the fact that Ravven thinks that the sun rises in the morning just so that it can show the rest of the world his beauty.

He continues to watch me, but I can't tell what he's thinking. His face is insufferably arrogant and reveals nothing else. "But I suppose I already know that mortals are capable of lying."

I choke on my own scoffing laugh. "Excuse me, are you saying that I am lying by calling you vain? You're so vain that on Earth we have a whole song about how vain you are!"

Ravven blinks in surprise. "There is? I did not know that you mortals were so utterly obsessed with me."

I stare at him blankly, too shocked to even comprehend what he is saying. Oh my gosh. He's serious. He actually thinks that someone in the human realm wrote a song about him.

He shrugs. "I suppose I shouldn't be surprised. It's just, it's been so long since I've been in the human realm. A hundred years is very long in human standards, as I understand it."

And here I am. Even more shocked. Please someone pick my jaw off the floor and hand it back to me. I know faeries are immortal, untouched by time, and unbothered by age. But it is still hard to wrap my mind around the thought that the faerie in front of me was around for World War I.

He looks at me for a long moment as if wondering what he said that made me go silent. Probably so he can figure out how to make it happen again.

It is with a great effort that I manage to close my mouth.

"In truth, I was not speaking of my surprise for you believing me vain. I am so utterly perfect that even I must admire myself."

You're so vain...

He continues, "No, I was simply expressing my surprise that you would even lie about me being the vainest faerie you have ever met."

"What?" I choke, finally being shocked out of my shock. "You are!"

He levels me with a hard look that seems to say, *I know you are lying you naughty mortal.* "You have met Iorwerth have you not?"

I blink at him in surprise. I have to admit Iorwerth is also vain. How he acted like his very presence was a gift to me. Maybe just all faeries are vain.

Ravven turns and gracefully rises despite his hands being bound. "On the subject of Iorwerth, I think it best that you avoid him."

"And I think it best if you don't tell me what to do," I say slowly, crossing my arms. I regret it immediately as my arm protests. I drop my arms at my side and settle for shooting Ravven a challenging glare. How dumb does he think I am? For that matter how exactly does he expect me to avoid Iorwerth when Iorwerth is my freaking captor?

He releases a breath and looks away. "I apologize for coming across as too commanding."

"Wait. You apologize?" I'm gaping again. I know it's not attractive at all, but somehow this fae keeps shocking me senseless.

He takes an infinitely long time to blink as if he is thinking over all of his options. "Is that not what you mortals say to each other when you anger one another, but wish to keep speaking?"

I'm too stunned to say no and Ravven must take it as a yes. "Anyway, the reason I said what I did is because Iorwerth is a Gancanagh. The very purpose of his existence is to seduce young maidens and destroy their lives when they let him in."

And here I am, pretending to be a dead fish again. Because why the heck is he telling me this like he's actually worried that I'll be messed up by this Gancanagh?

Though the fact that Iorwerth is a Gancanagh makes his attention for me make more sense. Because he is trying to seduce me. But that once again raises the question of why Ravven gives a darn about what happens to me.

"And hopefully you are not idiotic enough to actually ignore my warning."

I clear my throat. "Please, he's not even my type. I don't go for..." *Painfully handsome.* "Faeries." It's pretty much the same difference, but I'm not about to admit that I find Ravven painfully handsome. He doesn't need a bigger ego.

I look away so that he can't see the truth written across my face and my glaze falls on the door. I study it from my spot on the slab because I still don't feel up for getting up just yet. I try to locate some handle or lock or anything I can jimmy or pick for escape, but I find none.

I shiver and resist the urge to cry. I have experienced enough cold to last my entire short, measly mortal lifetime. But something tells me that if the Unseelie court doesn't kill me, their blasted winter palace might just.

"Oh," Ravven says, straightening. "Then I suppose we shouldn't have any problems and I needn't have to warn you of all of the other faeries that will prey on your attraction for them."

"Wait," I squeak. "What other faeries?"

Ravven looks at me like I am the naivest being to ever step foot into the faerie realm. Maybe I am. "There are quite a few, most of whom reside in the Winter Court, but I suppose you needn't have to worry yourself too much about it. Most of them prefer young men as their victims."

My eyebrows draw further together as I settle back onto the slab, trying to curl into myself to remain warm. "Do you think my brother is all right?"

Ravven leans back on his heels, looking slightly shocked. "How should I know that? You forget I am a prisoner just as much as you are. And more so Iorwerth doesn't even like me."

I sigh. "I just don't know what is going on. I guess I was kind of hoping you had some clue seeing as this is your world."

"Did you not ask Iorwerth after him?" he asks, tilting his head, his eyes a bright cyan that they look like they shouldn't belong in his face or in this dark cell.

"I did ask."

"And what did he say?"

"That Thomas is fine," I mumble, staring down at the handprint on my arm.

Ravven pushes to his feet. "Well then, I suppose you have nothing to worry about. Faeries, after all, cannot lie."

There's something ominous in the way he says it and it sends shivers racing down my spine.

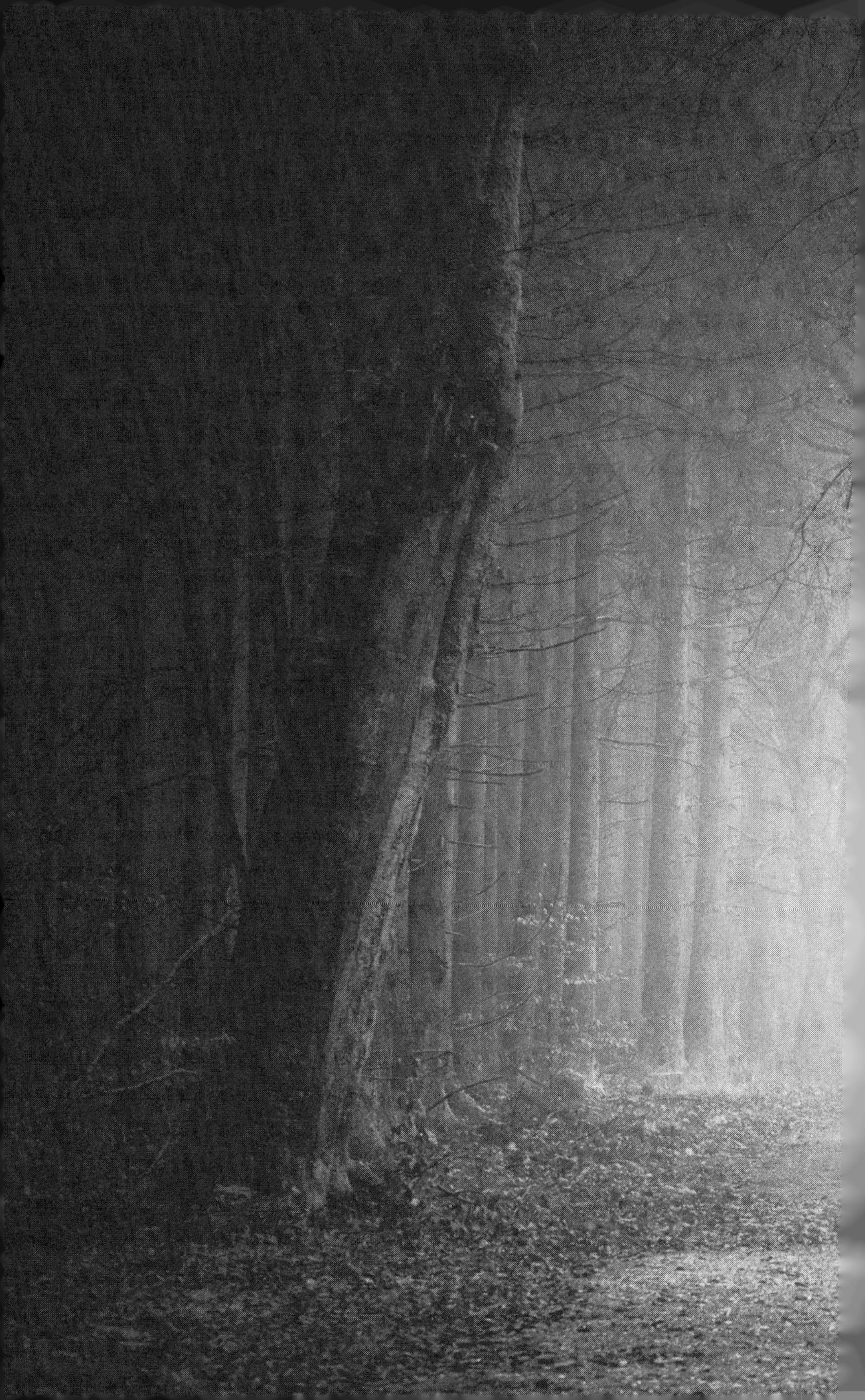

CHAPTER ELEVEN

I'm pretty sure I'm going to drown in the darkness. Or the silence. Or from inhaling too much water from the dank air. I don't know which one is going to claim me first, but my death will most certainly be caused by drowning and it will happen in this cell. Probably in a few minutes.

I turn to see Ravven, who is standing by the door to our cell, completely still as he has been for the past... I don't know how long. I don't have a watch on me and I haven't grown desperate enough to start counting the seconds, but it certainly feels like forever.

After so much happening so quickly; it's almost as surprising as it is torturous to wait. I don't even have a stupid clue about what I am waiting for. I hope it isn't my imminent death. My fingers inch to fiddle with my charm only to remember that it isn't there.

Or perhaps I will be forgotten down here. My mortal needs forgotten by my timeless captors and they will come down in a hundred years to discover that Ravven's cellmate is nothing more than a corpse. Will I decay if I die here?

I quickly shake that thought from my mind and decide that it's time for a distraction. I sit up, resting my back on the wall even though the ice slices through the fabric of my shirt. At this rate I'm going to just freeze into a block of ice.

"Hey, Ravven, I have a question for you." Not that he has bothered answering any of my questions. But it is better than wondering about the decay rate of the faerie world.

"And the silence was so sweet," he murmurs wistfully.

One of these days I'm going to punch him in his perfect nose.

"So, many of the faeries including the Gancanagh are known on occasion to take on human lovers." I say Gancanagh because that had been the faerie we had been talking about earlier, but honestly most of the faerie types other than the Solitary ones are known to do this. The Sidhe faeries are well known for carrying off mortal maidens and even young men to their world where they are never seen again. I wonder whatever happens to these humans. Mom and Dad rescued a good deal of them back when they were younger, but the Sidhe's only kidnapped more and fortified their palace under the hill so that Mom and Dad could not get in.

Ravven snorts. "Love is a temperamental word, even in the human world. Here it is nonexistent. Plaything is a better term for it."

I squirm in my seat remembering the Winter Queen. She had called me Ravven's plaything. But why the heck would she assume Ravven has one? Ravven is a Solitary faerie, they rarely seek companionship outside of themselves and even when they do it is usually only ever with fellow faeries.

The only thing humans have to fear from Solitary faeries is what they will trick them into doing.

Was that the only explanation she could think of for why Ravven would be traveling with a human? Or is Ravven Crowe known for kidnapping my kind? Was that why he had said that he would see me later? Was he planning on kidnapping me?

The thought fills me with disgust and horror, until I remember that I kidnapped him first. Who is worse? The kidnapper or the kidnapper that kidnaps the kidnapper.

I scratch my head, desperate for a distraction from my distraction. For once I would rather my thoughts not take the dark twisted route but instead try out the light and happy path. I try to keep my expression neutral to hide what I had been thinking. I lace my fingers over my knee. "So, what happens if a child is born from such a union?"

Ravven looks at me startled. "What do you mean?"

"I mean, if faeries and humans are able to... uh, breed an offspring. What would that half faerie half human be like? Would they be mortal or immortal?" My face heats up and I wonder why I even decided to ask this. I mean, yes, it's a question that I have wondered about before, but perhaps Ravven was not the best person to ask that. Scratch that, there is no perhaps about it. It would probably have been preferable if I'd asked Cliodnha.

Ravven arches a brow as he leans back against the wall. There's something about his expression that is decidedly smug. "Most faeries would not know, seeing as when a child is born of such a union, it is not uncommon for the faerie parent to kill the child. They do not know what such a creature would be, and they fear the unknown, so they destroy it before they learn."

"Oh," I say, my stomach churning as I turn my attention back to the crags on the wall. I fiddle with the soft fabric of my sleeve. I decide that it's best to change the subject. I should not have even brought it up in the first place. Not when we have much more pressing issues. I glance back at him. "If I were to free you from your handcuffs would you be able to use your magic to help us escape?" I don't have my key, but I do have lockpicks and they should do the trick. Providing I don't break all of them in the attempt.

Ravven glares down at his hands as if they offend him. "I wish that I could say yes. But do you truly think that Cliodnha or Iorwerth would just lock me in a cage that I can easily escape?" He nods to the glowing moss, covering almost every surface both in the cell and along the wall outside. It's our only light source. "That substance dampens my powers. Even if the iron were removed, I would still be weakened. In this court, I am not as powerful as I would be on my own. If it came to a fight, I'm afraid it might be a little more slippery. I can assure you, Cliodnha will not relinquish me that easily."

"What does she even want from you?" I ask, glancing back at him.

Ravven clenches his jaw and looks back away. "I do not wish to talk about it."

"Yeah, well I do. And I've been kidnapped, held hostage, and tortured so I think I deserve an explanation."

He looks back at me and scowls. "Everything is about you now?"

"Not everything is about you either!" I cry, throwing my hand up. "Besides, it's best if I know what is going on, considering that she seems to want to use me to get whatever she wants from you. If I know what that is, I will be better prepared to deal with it. *Please*."

Ravven releases a heavy sigh and shakes his head as he moves to the middle of the cell and sits cross legged only a few feet from the bed. "I don't see what the faerie queen thinks she can get from me through you seeing as I detest you." He grimaces and I wonder if his mind went immediately to where mine did. The handprint on my arm. Or maybe he was just thinking about my screams which probably grated on his ears.

"But since you are liable to torment me to tell you and will probably continue to do so for all eternity, I will acquiesce. It started many years ago. Over a century."

Perfect, just my luck. How did I somehow end up wrapped up in a conspiracy a hundred years old? So not cool. I haven't even lived for two decades. How the heck am I supposed to deal with this?

Ravven tilts his head, a lock of dark hair falling across his forehead. I wonder how much time on his hair it took for him to create the perfect combination of careless and neat. His eyes are distant and a deep blue like the sea at night. "Cliodnha was seeking allies in the neutral courts to help her destroy the Summer

Court once and for all. She came to my court and began trying to make an arrangement with me."

His mouth twists wryly. "I wanted nothing to do with war. I had seen what it had done to the Seelie and Unseelie courts—there is a reason that they are the two smallest faerie courts. I did not want my people to suffer in such a way, but Cliodnha... she would not take no for an answer. Clearly that is made evident by the fact that she is holding me in her court now a hundred years later. Something to keep in mind, pest. Faeries never forget a grievance."

Even though I tell myself not to, I'm starting to feel a little bit more respect for Ravven. He's spent a hundred years being hounded by a creepy winter queen because he didn't want his people to suffer? Still doesn't answer my question. "But that doesn't explain why *I* am here. How do I fit into any of this?"

"She thinks that you are important to me." Ravven waves his hand, quickly correcting himself. "Obviously not in a personal way, but faeries are very territorial of their mortal pets and it is considered a great blow to their pride if they cannot protect them. Which was why she did well... *that*."

Both of our eyes travel down to the handprint in my arm and I try not to shudder as I recall the pain.

"She was testing the strength of our connection."

"But we don't have a connection!" I cry, slapping the cold slab underneath me with my open hand.

Ravven presses his lips together. "I'm afraid that the way I reacted led Cliodnha to believe otherwise. She now thinks that as long as she has you, she can make me do anything that she wishes."

I shake my head. So Ravven didn't actually save me when he spoke up, he just embroiled me deeper into the sticky webs of faerie politics. "If that's what she was doing then why did you even speak up?"

My heart thuds loudly in my ears. And is that reason strong enough for him to help me next time?

"I—" his eyes flash crimson before turning to black as he finally looks down. "I thought it would be helpful to have a human ally in a court such as this."

I arch my brow. "You mean in a court that kills humans?"

He shrugs. "As frail and ugly as you are, even I must admit that you have some skills that are to be... desired. Your capability to lie is a trait that could be crucial in maneuvering through the courts. You could get away with anything. And you can wield iron—even if you cannot do so openly without being tried for breaking the Fair Law, it still is a skill that could incapacitate a faerie. Which leads into the fact that I still need you to free me. I would rather not spend all eternity trapped in these handcuffs."

I tilt my head. "So, you think that we could be allies?" The very idea is foreign. Becoming allies with a faerie? Use them, yes, but never trust them. Rule number one. Never put your life in their hands. Because they will destroy it. But perhaps the only way that I will survive is to be destroyed a little bit.

Ravven sneers slightly. "As much as I dislike it, we are imprisoned together. It would seem that no matter our mutual dislike for the other, we have a common enemy."

I bite down hard on my lip as I consider this. He is right. And even if his presence is what has gotten me into this mess, I also can't help but feel like it is the only reason that I'm not either dead or Iorwerth's pet.

"What do you have in mind?" I ask breathlessly before I can rethink all of my life's choices.

Ravven smiles and spreads his hands out. "I believe that we must come to an... *agreement* in order to get out of this alive. One where we both have equally to gain or lose if we succeed or fail. Respectively, of course."

I swallow hard. To make a bargain with a faerie... I would break rule number two. We have a reason for this rule. No matter what I say, the faeries have a peculiar knack of taking it and making it deadly.

I silently consider him for several long minutes. Ravven waits patiently but I suppose he has the time to do so. I consider my options. My chances of survival. I am trapped in the Otherworld. No, worse than that, I'm trapped in the Winter Court. Thomas is who knows where, with who knows who. I'm a pawn being used to try to start another faerie war. My rune is gone so I'm already breaking rule number three, and liable to be used against my will. And I'm imprisoned with a vain, arrogant Solitary faerie who seems to be the key to all of this. He possibly hates me, but has also gone through a lot of trouble to keep me alive.

At the moment, my only assets are my ability to wield iron, my capability to lie, some lock picks, and Ravven. And even if I hate the idea, even if it goes against everything that has been drilled into me, I fear that the only way to keep that Ravven from turning against me is to make a bargain with him.

Truly turn him into an ally. And hope and pray that he doesn't find some way to back out of it.

I can do this. I am smart enough to figure out a bargain that leaves no wiggle room for Ravven to stab me in the back.

With a deep inhale, I nod even while my mind screams at me for being foolhardy. My heart pounds and adrenaline pumps through my system like I'm about to go cliff jumping, instead of just speaking to a faerie. Actually, the latter is certainly the more deadly option. "Okay, I'm listening."

"I already have a plan," he states simply. Of course, he does. He's a faerie. He will probably only ever stop scheming when he is dead. Maybe not even then.

While I was lying here drowning in the silence, his mind was probably thinking of a thousand and one ways to save his pretty little hide.

"And what part do I play in that plan?" I ask, nervously fiddling with one of the pockets of my boots. The one where I keep the lockpicks.

"That remains to be seen." He looks me over for a long moment, contemplating. "But getting out of these handcuffs would be a fine start."

"I don't know, I think the handcuffs work to our advantage. The Winter Court might let their guard down if they think you are still trapped in them. I say we wait to remove them at the opportune moment."

Ravven presses his lips together. "Why, pest, for as ugly and mortal as you are, you certainly think like a faerie."

I don't know why, but I am oddly complimented by that even though essentially he is saying that I am evil, conniving, and twisted.

He holds up a finger. "Now I think we can come to an agreement. Naturally we shall help each other escape. But in return for showing you a way back to Earth I will require that you render me one service that only you can accomplish."

My heart stutters. There are so many loose ends to that one statement. He could make me do *anything*. He could ask me to drop dead and I would have to do it. And yet... with my rune gone, he could make me do it anyway. The second I free him of those handcuffs I open up the possibility of becoming his puppet.

Somehow, making this bargain is the only way that I can actually have power in this situation.

I swallow hard. "You will help both Thomas and me escape the Winter Court in *any* way you can and then you will do everything in your power to bring us back home. *Whole and in one piece.*"

"Awfully specific, are we not?" Ravven says, tapping his long fingers together.

I glare up at him. "Agree or we will not have a bargain."

He holds up his hands in a pacifying gesture. "Very well, I agree."

I inhale a shuddering breath. And now comes the moment of truth. "And I agree that in return for your aid, I will give you *one* service that is within my power to accomplish. So long as it isn't anything terrible."

Ravven's eyes glint. "And how do I know that you are not lying? I am bound by my word, if I break it, I die. But you are a mortal and have no such restrictions. What would stop you from double crossing me?"

I release a deep breath. "I'm not going to double cross you."

"You could still be lying," he insists.

"I already gave you my word. What more do you want me to do? Swear on my life?" I am only half jesting, but Ravven's eyes spark.

"Swear on something else. Swear on your humanity."

I suddenly find it very hard to swallow. My humanity? With a jolt I realize that there are far greater things at risk here than just my life. I'm in the faerie world, anything could happen. Even immortality.

But I've already gone too far. There's no use turning back now. Maybe my fate was sealed the second I stepped through that portal onto the faerie world.

I have to force the words from my lips. "I swear it. I swear it on my humanity."

Ravven nods once and his eyes land on my face. "Very well, mortal Jaye, I shall hold you to your word with a blood bargain."

I clench my hands to keep them from trembling. A blood bargain? The most sacred and ancient of promises, one that extends from worlds to humans as well as faeries.

Ravven eyes me keenly. "You are not planning on going back on your word already are you? Before the bargain has even been completed."

I shake my head numbly and clench my fist. My fingernails dig into my flesh. It's one thing to make a bargain that is only bound together by the Fair Law, one that has no hold over me. Ravven was clever to make me go through with a blood bargain. Any other way and I could have broken my word, hang the consequences, curse my conscience.

But with a blood bargain, we will be equally held to keep our sides. Or there will be real and lasting consequences. Even for me.

Especially for me.

My humanity...

I squeeze my eyes shut and remind myself that I'm doing this for Thomas too. That I don't have any choice. Ravven can't ensorcell me into completing any bargain; such a thing is forbidden in the Fair Law. But he can still always force me to do whatever this one task is *without* a bargain.

I pull one of the lockpicks out of my pocket and pray for luck. There's a faint stabbing pain in my index finger and then I pull the lock pick out and pass it to Ravven without a word.

Don't make a bargain with faeries...

He smiles wickedly in a way that causes my heart to stop beating as he pierces his own finger and holds it up. Crimson watered down by silver with golden highlights bubbles against his bronze skin.

Gritting my teeth, I hold up my finger and touch it to the tip of Ravven's. No solemn handshakes. That is far too human. No, simply a touch of our fingers so that our blood mingles on our pads. A zing like electricity shoots up my arm and I frown. Is that normal for a blood bargain?

Ravven is the first to pull away. He shakes his finger out and nods. "So now by blood we are bound."

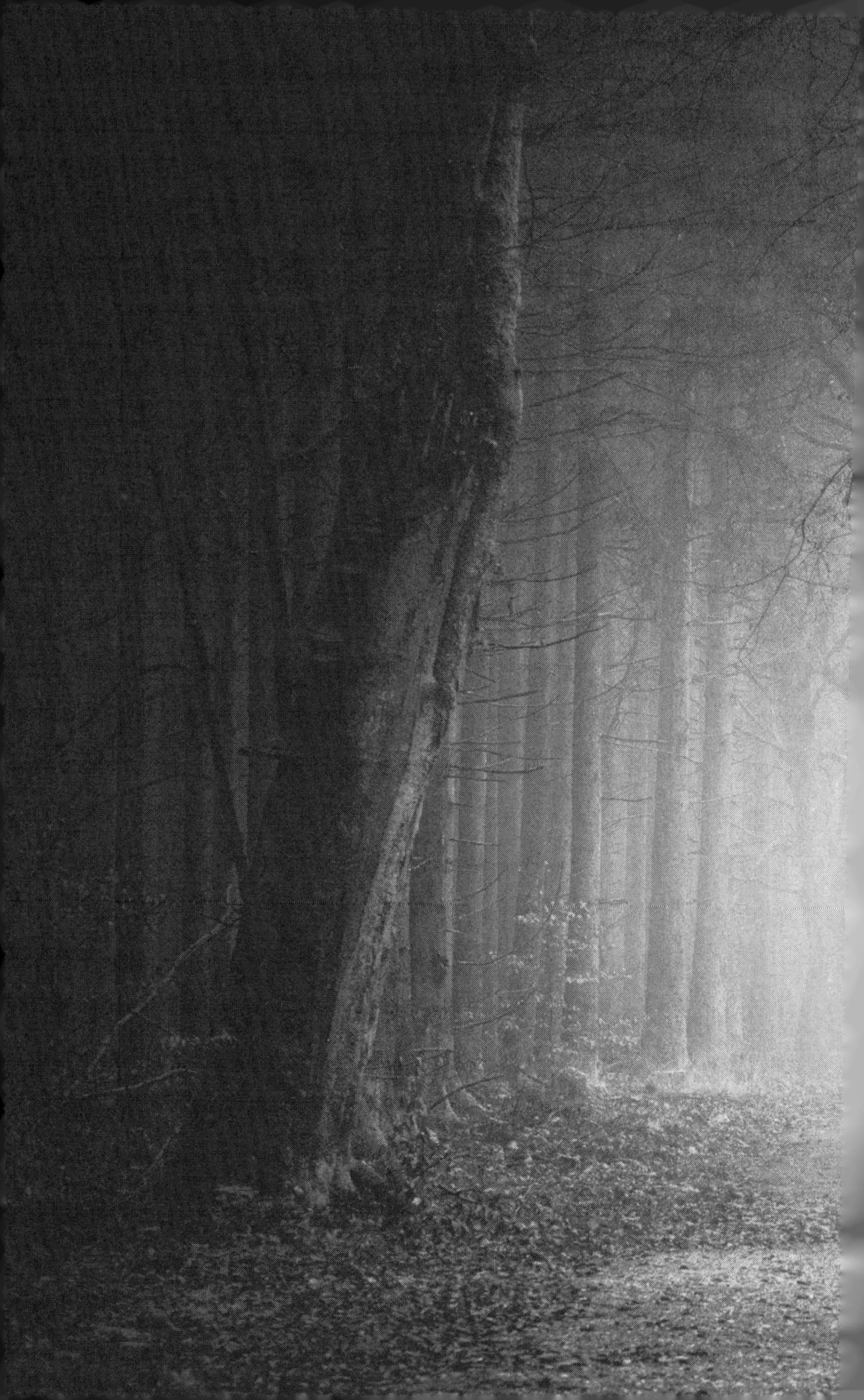

CHAPTER TWELVE

Your fates are entwined now. The death of one will be the death of another...

I had thought that the Banshee was out of her mind. And now, we are bound by blood. Crap, I'm like a living breathing self-fulfilling prophecy.

I consider the faerie standing in front of me and try to ignore the triumphant gleam in his dark eyes. A faerie. Demented, twisted, untrustworthy. And yet my ally now, even if the mere thought of it gives me chills.

There are three ways to kill a faerie. Only three. Time cannot touch them. Magic cannot kill them. They are invulnerable to everything but these three things. Iron, the only true weapon that humans have against faeries and so of course banned from being used as a weapon upon pain of death. And a very painful death at that.

The other two are the only ways that faeries can kill each other. The first of these is to learn a faerie's true name and force them to destroy themselves. To learn a faerie's true name is to have complete power over them. Because of this, no faerie dares to utter their true name out loud. Some even forget their true name.

The final way is to destroy a faerie's item of immortality. I'm not one hundred percent sure what that even is; the faeries do not exactly share that kind of information with the Guardians. It's bad enough that humans have at least one way to kill them. All I know is that supposedly these items of immortality are as closely guarded as the faeries' true names. Though since they happen to be an item, they cannot just vanish into nonexistence by forgetfulness. No, these are an actual tangible thing that must be guarded.

All I know is that for the remainder of the time that my fate is supposedly tied with Ravven's, it would be in my best interest to keep him alive. Shouldn't be too hard. He is an immortal, after all.

Now staying alive myself... that will be the tricky part.

The sound of footsteps echoes in the room, blocking out the sound of the dripping. I look briefly at Ravven, but his face is completely impassive. Arrogant as always though his eyes are now slightly red. I have to admit, his red eyes are unsettling, like he's a vampire.

Let me tell you, a person doesn't want to be trapped in a dungeon with only a vampire for company.

There is a creaking sound of the door swinging open and I look to the hallway outside our cell. I'm surprised to see Iorwerth outside after such a short time has passed since he dropped us off here.

His hands are clasped behind his back. I wonder what sort of magical enthrallment the door is under. And if there is some way to hack it, since obviously it isn't locked in the usual way that lock picks can solve.

He smiles. "My, my, cozy are we?"

Ravven turns to him and flashes a smile. "We could actually do with a few extra comforts. Perhaps an extra bed, or a door that opens readily."

Iorwerth blinks once slowly. "Well, I'm afraid that I cannot provide that. I have come for the mortal. As promised, I have gotten permission for her to see her brother. Are you coming, little birdie?"

The way he calls me birdie makes my insides shudder. It's so different from the way Dad uses my nickname.

I push to wobbly legs and ignore Ravven as I step past him, even though I can feel his gaze boring through my skin.

His words of caution from earlier still echo in my mind. I will not be a Gancanagh's prey, but perhaps a Gancanagh will be mine. I step out of the hallway and inhale the musky air. Iorwerth smiles wickedly and waves his arm. "After you."

I nod and with one last look at Ravven still sitting in the cell which is suddenly looking a lot more inviting, I follow the Unseelie faerie, hoping that he's actually taking me to see my brother and not somewhere far more sinister.

I feel completely defenseless knowing that Iorwerth can do anything to me, make me do anything, and I am powerless to stop him. I never knew how much courage my rune bracelet gave me until I was forced to live without it.

I don't think I breathe fully until Iorwerth leads me out of the dungeons. I ball my hands into fists as I follow him through the trees again and try not to think of what I'll do if I end up in the Winter Queen's throne room again. I don't think I can handle another torture session today. Actually, I don't know how I handled the first.

But instead of continuing forward, Iorwerth turns sharply to the left and steps between two trees. With only a moment's hesitation I follow him. After squeezing past the trees, he leads down a hall made of frozen vines all interlacing over our head, like the latticework in the prisons, only instead of that metal, this is all ice.

However, a second later a voice calls behind us telling us to stop, reminding me that I never should have breathed easily in the Winter Court. It takes everything in me to be able to turn around. I want to become an ice statue but at the same time I'm scared that is precisely what the Winter Queen is going to turn me into. Which doesn't make sense, but I'm currently too scared to rationalize my fear.

"How did you find the dungeon?" the Winter Queen says with a smile like she asked me what the weather was.

I arch my brow. "Cold. Bleak. Dungeony."

The Winter Queen smiles, speaking of cold and bleak. "I believe that we can cut past any pleasantries."

We cut past the pleasantries when you tortured me, but okay.

"I am not so proud that I am incapable of seeing humans for the valuable tools that you are. I know that you... think for yourselves."

The way she says it, it's like having to admit that physically pains her. "I'm thinking a few choice things about you right now," I mutter. I don't know fully why I said that seeing as she can go from zero to torture really fast. But I guess I have a death wish or something.

She flashes me a look that looks more like a death threat than amusement. "If you wish to leave my dungeon, to keep you and your brother alive, then you really must accept your roles as pawns."

I cough. I can't help it. It's the chilly dry air or something.

"Only I am giving you the power to choose. Will you be my pawn or Crowe's?"

I tilt my head and suppress the urge to shiver. Could a little warmth be too much to ask? Even in the Winter Court? I can't feel any of my extremities. "Just say what you want from me."

"You have a power over Crowe. One that your kind does not usually have over our kind. I want you to utilize it. Make Crowe see reason. *My* reason. And you have my word. I shall have no other need of you or your brother."

Gosh, when she says it like that it sounds like she fully intends to kill us. Which she probably does.

"Consider my words, mortal. He must side with me in the war. You will not like it if he does not."

I'm pretty sure I won't like it if he does. How did I even get involved with a brewing faerie civil war? I'm not even a faerie!

The Winter Queen turns around and glides off. She mildly reminds me of a ghost. Pale and ghastly.

I turn back to Iorwerth who is smiling at me. "You do hold sway over Crowe. You fascinate me, little bird."

The only sway I hold over Ravven I got by kidnapping him. Which is probably what got me into this mess in the first place. Probably not the best decision I ever made. I hug myself and glance at Iorwerth, trying really hard to keep my lip from trembling. "You were taking me to see Thomas."

"Right this way." Iorwerth starts down the hall again. At the very end of the hall is a large door made entirely of ice. It's partially open and through it I can hear laughter and talking.

I frown and quicken my pace until I'm almost walking in front of Iorwerth when we reach the door. It opens further upon our approach and I squint as I take in the room.

Bright warm sunlight streams through the windows high up on the wall, sparkling across the ice walls, but not in the blinding manner of the throne room. Large, ornate rugs cover the floor and silk tapestries hang from the wall. For the first time since waking up in the Winter Court, I actually felt like I could be warm.

I mean, I'm still freezing my tailbone off. But in this room, I could ignore that fact.

My eyes land on the giant bed sitting against the wall right across from me. There's a person lying in it. I recognize a familiar head of tousled auburn hair.

Thomas. I breathe his name, afraid to even say it out loud in case he disappears. Since waking up imprisoned, I didn't even let myself worry about him because I was too terrified of what was happening to him. And yet there he sits against the pillows looking just fine. More than that, perfect. A large easy grin rests on his face, showing his dimples and his face is flushed with color.

"Jaye!" he says, slumping into the mattress, if possible, his grin grows even more. I don't know how his face doesn't split in half. Although he is shirtless and a large bandage winds around the bottom of his torso, he doesn't appear to be any worse for wear. "Thank goodness you're here, I was starting to grow worried about you."

Only just now starting? But then, I suppose he may have only just woken up.

I step forward, when suddenly the second most beautiful woman I have ever seen steps in my path. The most beautiful being the Winter Queen.

This faerie is lovelier in a warmer way. She has brown hair, and while her skin is pale and looks to be carved out of porcelain, her cheeks have a rosy hue. Her lips are a lush color, just darker than the pink of her cheeks. She has wide blue eyes, rimmed with lashes and a petite curvy figure. She is wearing a flowing dress of the same color as her icy eyes.

"Iorwerth," the faerie girl says with an easy smile, revealing dimples that put Thomas's to shame. "How pleased I am to see you. My guest has been growing quite anxious for the care of his sister." She reached out and trailed her hand down my arm. She doesn't actually touch me though, rather her skin hovers an inch above mine. "And now you can put his fears to rest."

Iorwerth smiles in return and for a second, I want to cover my eyes because it's all too much. They are too beautiful. "I wish that I could remain longer, but alas, my queen requires my services." He tips his head as he backs away. "I will return to retrieve the mortal girl."

I barely listen to the faerie girl protest as I rush past her to the bed where Thomas is sitting. I wrap my arms around him. "You're all right!"

"Careful there, sis!" he cries as he wraps his arms around me. "Aoiby may be an excellent healer, but that doesn't mean I'm a good patient."

I pull back, frowning slightly. "Abby?"

"Aoiby," Thomas corrects. "That's my nickname for... well, how rude of me, I didn't even introduce you."

He gestures to the faerie girl who had wandered over and was watching our little display of affection like it was the most interesting thing she had ever seen, her hands clasped in front of her chest.

"Jaye, this is Aoibheann," Thomas says, a goofy smile covering his face when he says her ridiculous name. But instead of snickering, he pronounces each syllable like it is sacred. "But I call her Aoiby for short and she allows it. Aoibheann, this is my sister Jaye."

A dazzling smile pulls at the dark-haired faerie's lips. "I know you have not been here long, but he has told me so much about you. Mostly while fretting for your safety. I told him you were well, in the care of Iorwerth, but now he can finally believe me. Please take a seat and I will get you some refreshments. I've heard that humans have a tendency to grow weakened when they have not sustained themselves."

I most certainly was not well in the care of Iorwerth, but perhaps the faeries don't count a little bit of torture as anything to concern themselves over. After all, I can walk, can't I? Well, I couldn't earlier but technicalities.

I sink hesitantly on the bed and look over at Thomas. Is it safe to eat food here or will it just be a way to curse us? I can't remember if all faerie food is unsafe, or just the faerie fruits. Fine time for my knowledge of faeries to fail me. I know that the Sidhe race is known for enchanting their food, but do the other courts do this as well?

I'd always thought that I knew a lot about the faerie world, until being forced to live off of that information, only to find it all too lacking.

I raise my eyebrows in silent question, but Thomas isn't looking at me. I follow his gaze as Aoibheann disappears into another room in the back. Thomas leans closer to me, dropping his voice. "I think I'm in love."

I stiffen and turn to him. "She's a faerie," I hiss back.

"I know, isn't she just perfection?"

I grip his shoulder. What is wrong with him? His eyes do not have the tell-tale glazed effect of enthrallment. Perhaps he is being ensorcelled into saying this. There's no knowing if his charm is missing as well as mine. "Need I warn you of how dangerous it would be to fall in love with a faerie?"

His eyes dart to me, they are uncharacteristically dark. "I thought perhaps I would have to warn *you* about that."

"What?" I hiss. "Thomas, don't be an idiot. There is nothing going on between Ravven and me!" Other than our business arrangement, of course.

"Ravven? Odd that you would say him first, I meant that other faerie? What was his name? Iorwerth? Has he been looking after you as diligently as Aoibheann has me?"

Considering that he stood by while I was tortured and then locked me in a freezing cell, I would say the answer is *no*.

Not to mention that he is a Gancanagh and probably just wants to seduce me so he can destroy me later. "Gross. Don't even suggest such a thing. I'm pretty sure that he's evil."

Thomas shakes his head. "He isn't."

"What?" I demand. Thomas wasn't there in the throne room with the Winter Queen when the only faerie who actually stood up for me was Ravven. Thomas doesn't even know him other than the three sentences he said to that Aoiby chick.

"He can't be evil," Thomas says, shaking his head again. "Aoibheann seems to like him and I trust her judgment in character."

"You barely know her," I say as if Thomas has simply forgotten this fact. "She's a faerie—an Unseelie faerie at that. Do you even realize where we are? This is the Winter Court!"

"I realize that," Thomas says, graying just slightly. Good, at least he hasn't completely lost both his mind and his good sense. "But..."

"But? There are no buts."

"With Aoibheann there are. She's not like the rest of her kind. She's good and kind and gentle. She took me from the other faeries to care for me and protect me. I think she genuinely cares about me. Did you ever stop to consider that maybe our family is prejudiced against faeries? That maybe they aren't as bad as we have been told. I mean, they haven't really done anything to us. These Unseelie faeries that are supposedly evil have taken a lot of effort in tending my wounds. Reunited us."

Okay, this is getting really delusional. But I understand him in a way. When I first met Iorwerth, he was charming and even though I knew I shouldn't trust him, I wanted to. But that was his magical glamour working against me, blinding my senses to what he really was. A Gancanagh. An Unseelie faerie. A servant of the queen who wouldn't bat an eye at torturing me, for no reason whatsoever than to get a reaction from Ravven.

"You're being glamoured, Thomas. Snap out of it."

"I'm not glamoured," he replies harshly. "I'm just asking questions you don't want to know the answer to. Because what are you without your holy rage against faeries?"

"First of all, that's harsh and uncharacteristic of you. The real Thomas would never say that."

"I am the real Thomas!"

I roll my eyes. "Fine, the unglamoured Thomas. Secondly, have you forgotten that Ravven has stated that faeries aren't capable of love. Least of all Unseelie faeries."

"And Ravven is an expert in such matters," Thomas says, shooting me an accusing glare.

"Uh, yeah, he's a faerie. He's lived in this world his entire life. I'm pretty sure that he knows what they are capable of. Or not capable of. He isn't just a prejudiced Guardian who should be disregarded." My voice has a little more venom than is really necessary. Especially if he is glamoured. But I can't help it. I'm mad. How could Thomas disrespect our family so? Say that my only purpose is derived from hating faeries?

"Why is everything about Ravven anyway? How come he can suddenly be trusted and Aoiby can't? What have you been up to while I've been recovering?"

I shift in my seat. Well, let's see, there was torture earlier today, then a short imprisonment with Ravven where he explains just how dire my position as a pawn is, I made a bargain that I probably shouldn't have, had to deal with the Winter Queen again, and then I was brought here.

I reach up and rub at my forehead, somewhat violently. This conversation is not going at all how I thought it would. I didn't think that I would have to convince Thomas to even try to escape. "These faeries want to use us to start a civil war. I'm just siding with the one that doesn't want war."

Thomas snorts. "Oh my gosh, Jaye, you had me going there for a second."

"What?" I ask, frowning. "You think this is a joke?"

Thomas peers into my eyes, the smile dies from his face as he seems to realize that I'm not actually joking. "Why are you so concerned about a war amongst the faeries?"

"Oh, I don't know because maybe if the wrong side wins, they might decide that Earth is fair game. The Tuatha De Danan barely survived the last war, and they are basically the only faeries who would even *consider* helping a human."

"Again, you are assuming that the Winter Court is evil."

I don't know what to say. I'm half tempted to scream *that's because they are evil!* in his face, but just then Aoibheann comes back in, swaying her hips and with a skip in her step. A walk that should not have been able to be mastered by anyone let alone by someone carrying a tray of cups shaped like closed flowers, but somehow managing to look both innocent and seductive at the same time. And I'm not even sure how, but I *want* to like her.

She's a faerie, I remind myself. An *Unseelie* faerie, which is even worse than just being a faerie. She is obviously not as innocent and kind and gentle and whatever else it was Thomas said about her, as she appears. That's not how the faeries work. Whether Thomas accepts that fact or not.

They are vain and selfish and worst of all treacherous.

And I made a very, very dangerous bargain with one.

I swallow as I watch her make her way over to us. Now would be a good time to have a faerie guide, someone who could tell me if it is even safe to eat the food she offers. Of course, I wouldn't even know if my faerie guide had any intention of betraying me or not, so maybe not.

I squeeze my eyes shut to try to relieve my headache. Oh, why did the faeries have to be so untrustworthy? Why do I have to be trapped in their world?

I feel like I'm drowning and I have no idea which way is up and which is down. Which leaves me fearful that any direction I swim will only end up with me swimming farther from the surface that could be my salvation. I'm going to end up drowning myself.

Just like the Banshee said.

I look over at Thomas, trying to find something to stabilize me and drive the panic attack away. But he's sitting there, munching on whatever cookies

Aoiby brought and drinking the drink as if it might not be possibly poisoned or enchanted.

She smiles sweetly at me and holds out the tray. "Would you like some?"

I wave my left hand, my right one I keep in my lap, suddenly afraid to let anyone see the hand imprinted on it in case Aoiby insists on caring for it or Thomas insists on not caring about it. "No thank you, I'm not hungry."

In truth, I'm starving, but this is one of those circumstances where I am glad that humans can lie.

Aoiby's eyebrows shoot up. "Surely, you cannot mean that. You must be famished, you look wan."

Or maybe I just look wan because of the torture.

I shake my head. "No thanks. I ate a really big supper just before coming here. It was huge. I couldn't eat another bite."

I'm just grateful that my stomach doesn't rumble loudly, giving me away.

Aoiby sets the tray down with a frown. But at least she drops the subject. I just wish that she would have set the tray a little farther away so I don't have to smell the ridiculously strong scent of the cookies and the clear crisp scent of whatever beverages were in the flower shaped glasses.

Of course, even if she had tossed the food out the window, I'm pretty sure that the smell is imprinted in my nostrils, intoxicating my senses. A sure sense that they are most probably enchanted in some way. My eyes dart to Thomas and I try to figure out some way to knock aside his food without getting Aoibheann mad at me.

Aoiby sits down at the foot of the bed and then curls up in an extremely familiar way at Thomas's side. "Won't you continue with your stories, mine?"

I gape at her. Did she just use *mine* to address Thomas?

She turns to me and must interpret the look of confusion on my face. "Your darling brother has been telling me all about his childhood. They are such amusing stories."

I look over at Thomas then back to Aoiby. Does he actually think it wise to tell her all about our Guardian training, which was a large portion of our childhood? Then she would know just what we're capable of. Underestimation is literally the only thing we have going for us. The idiot. I could strangle him. "Um, why don't you tell us about you instead?" I force a smile to make it seem less like a demand and more like a request. "I am ever so curious."

Aoiby runs her hand across the bed, a little too near Thomas's barefoot for my liking. If she sneezed, she might accidentally hit it. "What do you wish to know?"

I shrug, my mind desperately trying to come up with something. Honestly, the only thing I want to know about her is how to defeat her. The tiny iron dagger in my boot feels like a heavy weight. "Iorwerth said that you were the queen's sister," I say at last.

I resist the urge to move my hand over the stinging handprint on my forearm, but Aoiby must interpret my words because her gaze flicks down to my arm anyway. She looks back up at me and smiles yet again. I want to smack the smile off of her face because what is there to smile about anyway? Does she find what her sister did to me *funny*? Actually, scratch that, she is a faerie, *of course* she does.

"Yes, I am Cliodnha's younger sister. She rules and I..." she inhales a deep breath as she looks around the room. Her eyes land on Thomas again and she bats her eyes, smiling again, this time it is shy. "I just try to find ways to amuse myself."

Hmm... because that didn't sound ominous at all.

But instead of getting freaked out Thomas smiles back. "I can imagine that living for an eternity can be quite grueling."

"Not always," she says and this time she really does touch his foot.

Oh, gross. My empty stomach churns as Thomas doesn't pull away.

This is dire. This is very, very dire.

Aoiby waves her arm. "But enough of me. Tell me more about you. I find the mortal world ever so fascinating."

Thomas doesn't even pause before plunging into the story of how he got his first dagger. Explaining how it wasn't iron because he was cursed to not be able to touch iron. I grimace. He's revealing his weakness too?

Has he told her about my lack of both a curse and a gift?

I sit there, trying not to murder either Aoiby or Thomas as they prattle on. I don't know how long we all sit like this, but my body must be keeping track of the time because I can't stifle the yawn. Aoiby's eyes, that I have decided are oddly like those of a cat, slide quickly to me. She pushes off the bed. "And here I have kept you for too long. I shall go retrieve Iorwerth so that he can take you back to your... accommodations."

Translated; my cell which I share with a faerie who may be vain but I am beginning to think might actually have a conscience. At least compared to these other faeries.

She glides out of the room and I turn quickly to Thomas who is staring after her dreamily.

"Please tell me this is all just an act," I bite out.

He startles and turns to me. "An act?" He scowls, beginning to look like my brother, the dazed expression leaving his face. Maybe he's broken out of the enthrallment, but then he says, "What exactly would I be acting about?"

"Thomas, you cannot honestly believe that you have feelings for a faerie? Even you can't be that stupid."

He shrugs. "I don't know what I'm feeling."

Which is far from the resounding *no* that I want to hear.

"She's a faerie!" I cry.

Thomas slides his gaze to me. "We seriously need to have this conversation again?"

"Thomas, I swear if you throw Ravven into this conversation again I may very well strangle you."

He arches his brow as if I somehow just proved his point. What has become of my overprotective older brother? He should be threatening to beat up any dude he thinks that I may like. *Especially* if said dude is a faerie.

"Where is he anyway?"

He's rotting in a cell downstairs, thank you for asking.

I want to argue further, but I don't have long. Aoiby could return with Iorwerth at any given second. "Thomas, we have to escape," I say, clutching his hand. I glance back toward the door to make sure that they haven't already returned.

Thomas stiffens. "Why do we have to? We're not prisoners, Jaye. Nothing bad is happening to us here."

Easy for him to say. He wasn't tortured. And yet I still can't bring myself to tell Thomas about what happened to me. I tell myself it's because I don't have time, but if I'm truly honest with myself it's because I'm afraid that it won't make any difference to him.

"Thomas, we did not come here of our own free wills." I shudder remembering the icicles slithering across the ground after me. "Whatever happened to getting home?"

His eyes soften. "We will get home. I can ask Aoiby to help us."

I shake my head. Asking the captor to aid in our escape doesn't seem like a good idea at all. "Ravven and I are planning to escape—"

"Ravven? Again with him?" he demands. "I can't believe your gall, Jaye. You're free to trust him as much as you like, but the second I trust a faerie that has spent the past day caring for my every need, I'm naïve?"

I release a frustrated breath and pull away. "I don't trust Ravven! But we do have an... arrangement." I don't dare mention the bargain. At this point he would probably use it as further ammunition against me. "Whether you choose to believe it or not, these faeries are not nice. Don't you realize that they are only using us as pawns? We are humans, Thomas, basically insects to them. We need to be careful, so, so careful, especially now that we are no longer protected from any curses."

Thomas's eyebrows draw together. "Did Ravven tell you this?"

That doesn't change the situation. "Faeries can't lie, Thomas."

"But somehow Aoibheann is doing so?" he demands, arching his brow.

"They can still mislead us!" I cry, my temper fraying.

"But it's only Aoibheann that is capable of misleading, not your precious Ravven?"

"He's not *my* anything."

Except for perhaps "partner in crime."

Thomas shakes his head and shrugs. "Fine, you believe your faerie and I will believe my own. Aoibheann will help us, just you wait and see."

I bury my face into the blankets and let out a screech. When I lift my head, I glance toward the door and stiffen when I see Aoiby and Iorwerth coming toward us. I'm out of time. I turn back to Thomas and clutch his hand. "Just, be careful who you put your trust in, brother. Guard yourself. And be ready when I tell you."

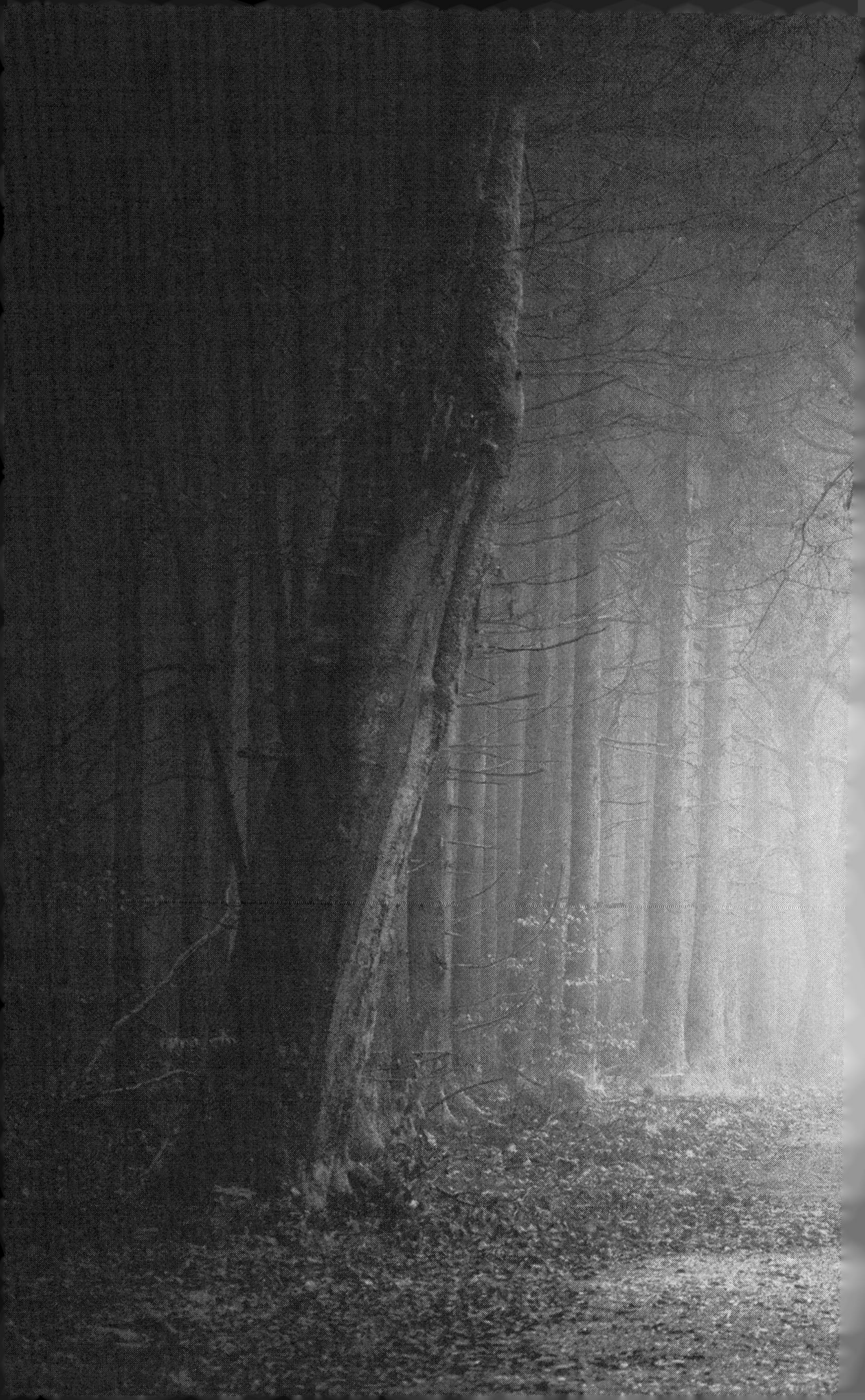

CHAPTER THIRTEEN

Ravven is in the exact same place I left him, sitting cross legged in the middle of the cell. As if he hasn't moved an inch the entire time that I was gone. He turns his head as we approach. I can feel his eyes tracking my every movement.

Iorwerth pulls open the gate and I step through, but before I'm all the way past him, he leans so close that I almost think he's going to kiss me. I force myself to not shrink away, but he simply smiles in a sultry way and murmurs, "I will see you again soon, my little bird."

"Promises, promises," I say back, and I manage to make it sound only a little sarcastic.

Then he leans back and I dart into the cell, afraid that if I wait much longer, he actually *will* kiss me.

Iorwerth shuts the door with a chuckle and once again I am imprisoned. Yet I can't help but feel relieved that there is a grated door standing between me and Iorwerth now. My pulse is racing and I think that there was a part of me that actually half thought that he would bring me back to the queen for another round of torture.

I shove my hair behind my ears and rub the goosebumps forming under my sleeves as Iorwerth walks away. I look down at Ravven, trying to figure out when he suddenly became the person I had to rely on. "I'm worried about Thomas."

Ravven's eyebrows rise still higher. "Well, I'm rather worried about us myself."

I jump to my feet and pace away. "I think he's under an enthrallment." That's not completely true. He doesn't look or act like he's under an enthrallment. But he's certainly not acting like himself either.

I don't know what is going on anymore. To Thomas. To me.

The longer I'm in this world it's becoming harder to determine what is enthrallment and what is truly a temptation.

"I highly doubt that," he says quietly.

I whirl on him. "Oh, and you're the expert on faerie enthrallments?"

"I am a faerie," he says with a cocky grin. "Or did you forget that in the short time you were upstairs."

I blow out a breath and sit back down on the bed. "You didn't see him. He's fawning over Aoibheann like... like... like a lovesick puppy."

Ravven's attention turns to the ceiling of uneven rock. "May just be Aoibheann's charms. There is no enthrallment required to fall under her spell. Believe me, I am well acquainted with her work."

My stomach sloshes and I look at him with disgust. "I don't like it. It isn't good for Thomas to form this sort of attachment with her when she most probably has a darker ulterior motive."

"Oh, she most certainly has a darker ulterior motive." Ravven chuckles as if the idea amuses him. I glare at him and he arches his brows. "I'm not entirely sure what you expect me to be able to do about anything. I am locked in a cell. Not to mention..." he holds up his bound wrists.

My head is pounding but still I try to sort through the swirling thoughts barraging my mind. "Let me get this straight. So, the faerie queen is holding you hostage until you agree to a treaty with her?"

Ravven dips his chin once. "It is as you say, small annoying mortal."

I choose to ignore the last part as I continue pacing. "And obviously we can't have a true treaty because with your court's aid they could win the war, right?"

"They would indeed be triumphant," he replies, seemingly more interested in straightening his sleeves than our current conversation.

"And if the Winter Court finally triumphs over the Summer Court then what?"

"Then winter will reign supreme. Oh, and they will probably turn to wage war against humans next. Your precious line of Guardians would not be enough to stop them and their pure unadulterated hate for you mortals."

I ignore the shivers snaking up my arms and down my spine. "And I'm important in all of this because they think I can be used against you."

Ravven finally moves, shifting uncomfortably.

I release a frustrated groan as I look at him. I shake my head and look down at my arm. Proof of how much I meant to the faeries. They didn't bat an eye over torturing me. They simply used me for their own political gain.

"Why is this even so important?" I say softly.

He looks up at me. "I do not understand. I just said that winter would reign supreme if the war was won. That you humans would be terrorized by the Unseelie faeries. How could you say that is not important?"

I shake my head, holding up my hands. "Not that. Why are *you* important?"

Ravven pulls back, looking insulted. "Why am *I* important? Why am *I* important? I am the most important piece on the board and you ask *why*?"

I pray for the patience to deal with this arrogant shallow faerie. "Yes. Why does the faerie queen need you? Why doesn't she try to make this treaty with some other random Solitary faerie?" I gasp as a sudden thought comes to me. I stare down at Ravven, more beautiful than the ordinary faerie that I have seen and especially more than the Solitary faeries which are practically by definition ugly. "Are you the king of the Autumn Court?"

His eyes widen with surprise then a sharp peel of laughter bursts from his lips. It's so unnatural to hear him create any laughter louder than his usual mocking chuckle that I jump. "How amusing of you to suggest the sort!"

His laughter grates on my nerves. I cross my arms and scowl at the wall over his head. "No need to mock me. Besides, you haven't actually answered my question."

Ravven presses his lips together with amusement. "No, I am not the *Autumn King*. The Autumn Court has no rulers. Who could tame the free spirits of the folk there, after all?"

"I knew that they didn't have a king, I just didn't know if that had changed. If maybe you had somehow taken over," I say defensively.

"We are not in the human world," he says unhelpfully. I already kind of know that. "Your world changes in the blink of an eye. Kingdoms rise and fall, peoples are wiped out, civilizations crumble. All in the blink of an eye. Since the war between the Seelies and Unseelies ended, there has been no change in our world. Your world, however, is unrecognizable in that same passage of time."

I look down at my grimy fingernails, wondering what it would be like to live in a world that never changed. A world where there was no need for newspapers, or even news in general. Where people didn't die every day and everyone lived on for eternity in the same painful existence. At first it seems almost tempting, but then I decide that it isn't. The faerie world is an illusion. Change is supposed to happen and anything existing without it is unnatural. The faeries are unnatural.

I clear my throat, realizing that I have been silent for too long, disappeared too deeply into introspection. Ravven is staring at me with a curious expression on his face. "So, you still have not explained why the queen wishes to make a treaty with *you*."

Ravven studies me for a long moment before looking away. "I am stronger than most of my kind. She believes that if I join her then the others will follow."

"And Thomas and I are just pawns in all of this," I say as I step toward the slab of rock and sit down on it feeling wane.

"Aren't all of you humans?"

I shoot him a glare. Just my luck, the only halfway decent faerie and he also has a terrible view of humans. I hate faeries. I hate this world. I just want to go home.

That's the moment when I decide that this might be too big of a job for even luck and I send up a silent prayer for deliverance. Or a death that isn't painful. But preferably deliverance.

I cup my chin in my hand as I stare at the door. I should probably get to sleep, but the thought of sleeping down here with only a slightly less malicious faerie as my only companion is almost enough to give me nightmares without even drifting off.

Still, I'll need all of my strength tomorrow and considering I haven't even had any food, I need to rest.

I lie down on the bed and squeeze my eyes shut, trying to ignore Ravven. I tell myself that he isn't staring at me, that he's probably staring at the wall over my bed or something else, but it does no good. I can feel his eyes boring into me.

I peel my eyes open and glare at him. I was right, he was looking at me although I have no idea why. "Can't you look at something else?"

"Yes," he says, but he doesn't move and I realize that he has absolutely zero intention to.

"I thought that you found me ugly."

"I do." Still he doesn't move.

I sigh and close my eyes again. *Just ignore him.* However, even while doing my best to ignore him, I find that I have another pressing problem keeping me from my sleep.

The cold.

I don't know how long I lie there shivering, trying to sleep, the cold of the slab seeping up through my bones, but soon enough I can't feel my toes and my nose, and my hands are quickly going that way as well.

"What is that thing your body is doing?" Ravven asks at last, his voice piercing through the odd haze that has come over me. It isn't sleep, it isn't half as restful. But it's still a form of losing consciousness.

"W-what is what thing-g?" I demand. I reach a numb finger up to move my hair over my ear to try to keep as much warmth as possible from leaking from my quickly freezing body.

"Your limbs appear to be convulsing, only slightly but in a way that affects your whole body."

"I-it's called sh-shivering, dummy."

He's silent for a long moment. "Why is your body doing this shivering thing? It does not look overly comfortable."

"Be-because that's what people do when they're cold."

"... You're cold?"

I open my eyes wide enough to glare at him. "Oh, wow, h-how long did it take you to figure that out? Of-of course, I'm cold! We're in the flipping Winter Court! It's like ten degrees below zero down here and I don't even have a c-coat!"

I wrap my numb hands around myself and try to rub along my arms, careful not to let anything touch the handprint, which seems to only be making me colder.

Ravven pushes to his feet and brings his hand to his chin. He considers me for a long moment before waving his hand toward me like I'm a fly he's trying to shoo away. "Well, can you stop this *shivering*? You are making this horrible clacking sound and I can't concentrate while you are doing it."

I fully glare at him now. "Well, I apologize for being human."

His eyes widen as if he's surprised that I actually said that. "Apology accepted."

Ugh, whatever did I do to *deserve* this?

He lets out a frustrated growl. "You're not stopping. If anything, I would say that the clacking is getting worse."

"It's called chattering," I snap. "And how can you not be cold?"

Ravven adjusts the sleeves of his dark blue tunic and looks me over. "I suppose we do not feel things the same as humans. Just another way your race is inferior to mine if you would let something so small as cold cause you discomfort."

And his race allows something as small as iron to destroy them.

I shudder. "You don't happen to have a blanket hidden somewhere in that ridiculous outfit of yours..." I trail off as he stiffens, looking miffed. "I didn't think so."

I sit up and pat the slab next to me. "All right, I guess this calls for a dire solution. You're going to have to climb up here with me."

"What?" he gasps.

"I need your body warmth or I'll probably freeze to death."

"You want me to come... *close* to you?"

I nod.

"But you're a mortal!" he gasps, looking more offended than he would probably look if I had asked him to kill himself.

I roll my eyes. "Which kinda makes this so necessary, or did you not hear me when I said that I would freeze to death? Oh, don't look so horrified. It's hardly ideal for me either."

He still doesn't look convinced and I blow out a frustrated breath which fans around my face. "We have a bargain, remember? It will be kind of hard for me to keep my end of it if I die."

"You are rather needy," Ravven grouses, but at least he takes a reluctant step toward me.

"Yeah, yeah, I know, just like my entire rotting race," I say, reaching for his hands and yanking him onto the slab of stone next to me. Warmth radiates from his skin like the warm rays of sunlight. I feel my muscles begin to relax. I would wonder why I didn't do this early but this was kind of a last resort.

"You said it, not I," Ravven replies, straightening his collar and shooting me an angry look like he's offended that I even touched him.

"Lie down," I instruct, ignoring his remark, or how much more beautiful he is up close.

Ravven lies down stiffly and glances at me out of the corner of his eye. "Like this?"

"Good enough," I say, I lift his arms as much as he can with the handcuffs still firmly held into place. Then I crawl into the space between them. It's embracingly intimate, but warmth radiates from all sides now and I focus on that. I try to ignore the way his breath hitches and the strange pattern my own heart has taken to beating.

He shifts behind me and clears his throat, his breath ruffling the hair on the back of my head. "Is all of this really necessary?"

I yawn which sends a jolt of panic through me. "Oh no."

"What?"

"Hypothermia starts with drowsiness."

He stills. "What is hypothermia?"

"It's the way humans die when they are too cold."

He is silent for a long moment. "You humans certainly die far too easily."

"You're telling me," I mutter. But I'm not shivering so hard and I don't feel close to death. So maybe I am just tired. Given the day I have had, that's probably it.

Ravven doesn't move at all, not even the twitch of a muscle. I half wonder if he has fallen asleep when he whispers. "This is most unseemly."

"I still hate you," I mumble, sleep making my voice groggy. I press my fingers between his hands resting in front of me. "Just in case you are starting to get any ideas."

He shifts uncomfortably under me. "Ideas about what?"

"Exactly my point."

"Do you actually make an effort to not make sense?"
"You said it yourself," I say past a yawn. "I act like a faerie."

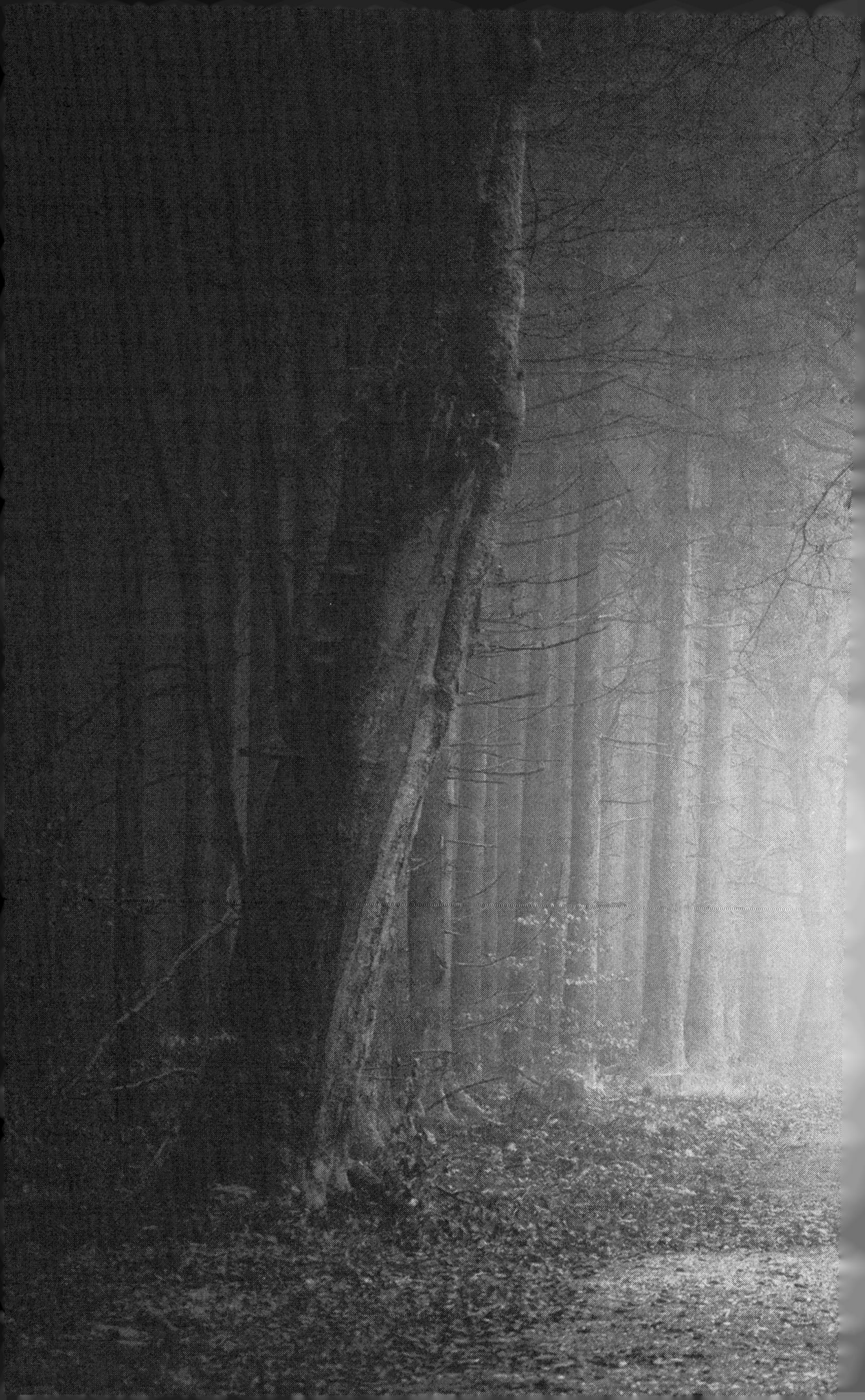

CHAPTER FOURTEEN

Something touches my nose. The sensation penetrating the hazy mire of my dream filled brain. I blink my eyes open, barely able to see the world past my blurred vision. But I do see Ravven's hand right in front of my face. His finger pokes my nose again.

"What. The. Actual. Heck. Are you doing?" I grumble, my voice is raspy and harsh sounding.

"I thought I would inform you that someone is coming."

I struggle to duck out from between his two arms, which is a little difficult because somehow he ended up lying on top of my hair. Finally, I am free, I sit up on the stone slab and run my fingers through my now very tangled hair. "There are other, more effective ways to wake a person."

"You sleep rather soundly for someone surrounded by enemies."

"I had a traumatic day okay. We can't all be immortal and perpetually refreshed."

Ravven runs his hand through his hair, although it looks somewhat awkward since he has to move both of his hands together, and his hair all just falls back into his face at the end.

Just then Iorwerth finally decides to join us. He smiles as he leans against the bars. "Did we have an enjoyable night?"

"*We* certainly had no such thing," I reply, stretching stiffly and decidedly ignoring Ravven.

"A pity," Iorwerth says, but the look he gives me isn't exactly pitying. "And here I come with good news."

"No news coming from your lips could ever be considered *good*, Iorwerth," Ravven says, somewhat sullenly. His eyes are now a dark yellow. Not the warm yellow like the sun. This yellow is cold and harsh, exactly something I would expect to see in the Winter Court, though perhaps not from someone like Ravven who was my source of warmth last night. Ugh, no. I am not going to think of him like that.

Iorwerth's gaze slides to Ravven and his smile grows. "Oh, but that is where you are wrong. You see, the Winter Queen is throwing a ball. And she has invited the two of you to be her guests. Is that not delightful?"

"Dreadfully," I mutter.

Iorwerth's smile grows. "As such I am to escort you back to your precious room, little bird. So that you can freshen up. Can't have the queen's guests appearing in such a state."

Too late for that. Seeing as I am already in this state.

I eye Iorwerth then glance back at Ravven. "Do I have a choice in this?"

Dress up isn't exactly my favorite thing. Dressed up like some sort of life size doll by psychotic faeries is even farther down that list.

"Afraid not. I shall bring you food as well. Wouldn't want you to starve, now would we?"

I certainly don't want to starve, but I doubt these faeries would care too much beyond the inconvenience of losing a part on their board.

I sigh and push to my feet then I glance at Ravven. "Quick, what here is safe to eat?" I ask as Iorwerth clears his throat impatiently.

Ravven arches a brow. "Safe to... *eat?*"

I nod. "Yes, I'm starving and I don't know what might be enchanted or not."

"*Starving?*" Ravven spits the word like he's learning a new spell and how to recite it.

"Yes, it's what happens to people when they do not eat enough."

Ravven surprises me by rolling his eyes. "And let me guess, it is fatal."

"Well, yes," I snap, waving my arms at the look of long suffering on his face rather than concern. "Sometimes, but in all honesty I'm more likely to die of dehydration first."

He heaves a heavy sigh. "I'm not even going to ask what that is. Very well then, I suppose that there is no knowing truly what food placed before you would be enchanted or not, but if you were to happen to have any iron to touch to the food, it would certainly drive the enchantment away. There, you have my answer. Now you no longer need to die."

As if it is that simple.

"I'm not going to die," I say like it really is that simple and then I turn and step out of the cell after Iorwerth.

Iorwerth looks me over almost possessively as the cell door slams shut behind us with a bang. "Don't you trust me?"

I force a smile even though I would rather tear my lips off. "Let me think about that for a second... no!"

Iorwerth smiles benevolently at me and chucks my chin with his finger. "Of course, pet."

Somehow with the way he says it, like I belong to him, it almost makes me prefer Ravven's derogatory 'pest'.

Iorwerth pauses and looks me over. "Do you happen to have iron on you?"

I shrug innocently. "Wouldn't you like to know."

My iron dagger burns into the side of my leg through my boot's hidden compartment. I don't know what I would do if they were to take it away from me. My last little bit of my peace of mind. The dagger's handle is also made of iron which makes it difficult for any faerie to touch it, but they could always find another way to rid themselves from it. As long as they are not directly touching it...

My heart thumps in my chest as I realize that he could simply command *me* to disarm myself and I would be helpless.

"That is why I asked," he says airily as he turns his attention forward and we move down the passage. For some reason he doesn't force me to rid myself of the dagger.

Suddenly, Iowerth comes to a stop. I don't know if we're far enough away for Ravven to not be able to hear, though I wager not. Whatever he has to say next, Iorwerth probably wants Ravven to hear him. I know exactly the type of game he is playing and it is a twisted one with a lot of pawns and only one king.

"You should forget Crowe," he whispers, running his fingertips down my arm. His touch feels like a thousand spiders marching across my skin, but I force myself to keep from brushing him off. As long as Iorwerth is pretending to be nice to me, he isn't being mean to me. "He is a prisoner here just as you. What can he do for you? But I can protect you. I can make you *mine*." He leans so close that his nose moves my hair aside. Then abruptly he pulls back with a feral smile.

I swallow hard and stare ahead. "And what if I don't intend on becoming entangled in such a way with *any* faeries? No offense, but that tends to not end well for humans who do it."

"Don't you realize, little bird? You are already caught in the web. You will fall just as your kind always does against our beauty and raw power. You mortals crave us as you crave air."

Not this mortal. I shove all thoughts of Ravven and last night from my mind. Never this mortal. I turn and begin walking again in the direction we had been heading, Iorwerth follows me a few seconds later.

"At the ball tonight, you will see the whole of the Winter Court. And then you will see that I am the most beautiful."

Oh lovely, more Unseelie faeries. Just what I needed.

"I'm not saying that you aren't beautiful," I say although I can't reasonably figure out why I am even having this conversation. "But you are evil."

Iorwerth laughs. Which is good, I guess. Means I didn't offend him. "We are all evil in some way or another."

He waves his arm toward the now open door of what is going to be my room for the rest of my captivity. "And here we are. Make yourself comfortable, my lady bird. I shall return shortly with something to sustain you until the ball."

I sit down on the bed and try my best to make myself comfortable as Iorwerth leaves. It's hard to be comfortable in a freezer though. Ugh. Couldn't we have been kidnapped by the Summer Court? I know that the answer is no of course because I highly doubt that the Summer Court would even bother to kidnap me. No, I had to somehow end up mixed up with the Unseelie faeries who have a personal grudge against humans.

I sigh and stare at the jagged wall, as I try not to think about Thomas, somewhere in their walls, alone with that faerie who he thinks he loves. Or Ravven sitting alone in his cell probably scheming.

I feel a little like the top three faeries that I met divided us up. The queen got Ravven, Iorwerth got me, and Aoibheann—or whatever her stupid name is—got Thomas.

But I think the true question is what they really want from us. I mean, other than war.

I shake my head and focus on getting ready and doing the things that I couldn't do in the cell with Ravven.

My new room has a chamber pot thrown clumsily in the corner, which is disgusting, I know, but a desperate girl can't complain too much.

When Iorwerth arrives with a tray of food, I'm back to sitting on the cold slab, too tired to try to escape before I get any food in me. He sets the tray on the slab next to me and steps to the wardrobe which he opens.

"I believe you will find that they fit you wonderfully," he says. "They are sewn from magic so as to fit anyone who tries to wear them."

Iorwerth glances back at me. I have no idea what he could be thinking behind that creepily charming smile and those cold, cold eyes.

"How convenient."

"Not convenient, little bird. Simply how things are here. You will become used to it."

The heck I won't. I'm leaving as soon as I can.

Iorwerth leans closer to me and I shrink back thinking that he might kiss me. I almost fall off the slab of stone, when Iorwerth pulls his lips up, revealing that the teeth in the back, right where his molars should be starting are actually jagged and long, like fangs. He steps back and bows to me. "I shall leave you to your meal. And then I suggest you prepare for the ball. It begins at sundown." He smiles again. It's back to his charming smile, without those horrible sharp teeth. "And you should know that the sun never lasts long at the Winter Court."

Then he whirls and is gone out the door.

I've never felt so relieved to be left alone.

I swallow my queasiness and force myself to turn to the meal, which looks more like a freezer burned pile of mush than anything else. I'm so hungry, though, that I'm actually desperate enough to eat it.

First, I pull the slim iron dagger out of its hiding spot in my boot and touch it to the plate, then into the contents of the cup, which is like a water slushie. It's close to being frozen, but not quite. When I'm done, I say a quick prayer that this meal won't kill me, or be my last meal, and then I eat.

The food and drink are cold and tasteless, unless cold is a taste. After eating this meal, I'm beginning to think that it is. I experience more brain freezes than I have ever lived through in my life. When it's finally all done and I'm about to gag, I quickly turn away, pressing my hand over my mouth. I can't afford to lose the nutrients no matter how tasteless they are.

The sunlight trickling through the small window is much darker than last time so I make quick work of seeking out a dress. I try to find something that will be comfortable and practical, but the entire wardrobe consists of ball gowns. And not a lot of them have sufficient material.

I finally give up on finding something practical and grab the nearest dress, spurred by my terror of Iorwerth returning and finding me in any state of undress.

The top of the dress is the palest blue I have ever seen that it's almost a white. The very bottom foot of the dress is stained a dark wintry blue. It has no sleeves, which I think is dumb considering I'm in the stupid Winter Court and already freezing my butt off. Still at least it covers more than some of the other dresses.

I frown, but pull off my shirt. Then I pull the dress on over the leggings. Once it is over my head, I pull up the skirts and stuff the shirt into the waistband of my leggings. It isn't ideal, but at least I can change into it later. It will have to do for my practical outfit, because I'm pretty sure my chances of escaping are a lot less likely when all I have are ball gowns at my disposal. The skirts are wide enough that they hide any bulge from the shirt.

Once my shirt is safely stored away, I set to work adjusting the dress. It represents everything I hate in clothing. The skirt is long and cumbersome, hanging around my legs in layers and layers of unnecessary petticoats. And it is sleeveless, which leaves my torso feeling far too exposed. I adjust the top half of the dress again, trying to allow myself the most privacy I can get in this blasted dress.

I glance toward the wardrobe. Do any of these dresses have sleeves?

"You look beautiful. But then, I'm sure you always do."

I startle and turn to see Iorwerth leaning against the wall by the door. My heart stops for a full three seconds as I wonder how long he's been standing there. If he saw me dressing myself. If he saw that I'm still wearing my other clothes underneath...

He strides toward me, his hands raised and places them on either side of my face. For a terrifying half a second, I think he's going to snap my neck, but then he gathers up my hair in his hands and begins twisting.

He looks at my face and chuckles. "Try not to look so terrified, my little bird. It would hardly do for you to go to the ball with your hair in such a disorderly state. It would be an insult to our fair queen."

I try to wipe the terrified expression off of my face.

Our queen? She isn't my anything except perhaps my enemy. And captor. I suppose there is no getting around her being that as well.

My head grows almost painfully cold and then Iorwerth steps back. "There," he says, smiling down at me. "Perfection. Or at least the highest that a mortal can achieve."

My hair stays perfectly in place, despite the fact that Iorwerth had let go of it. My head feels oddly heavy and when I reach my hands up to investigate, my fingers touch cold ice. I pull back with a shock. Iorwerth froze my strands of hair together to keep them in place.

Iorwerth holds out his hand. "Come now, little bird. It is time for the ball."

I cross my arms, trying not to be sick all over my lovely impractical ball gown. "Do I get any choice in the matter?"

He smiles at me benevolently. "Of course not."

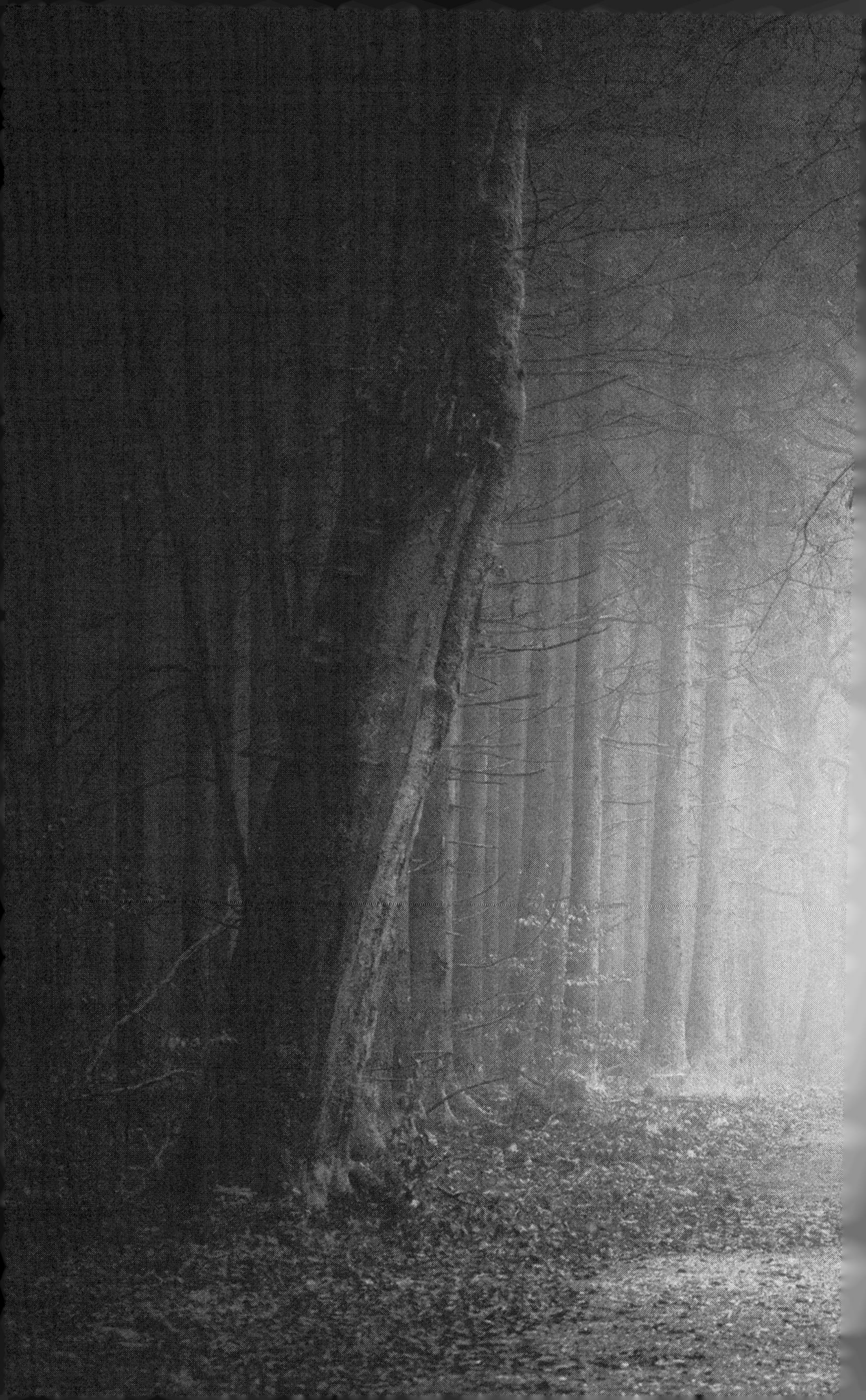

CHAPTER FIFTEEN

I force myself to breathe deeply through my nose so I don't pass out, and I follow Iorwerth into the largest room I have ever seen. If it can even be called a room, considering the fact that most of the ceiling is missing in a large oval over our heads. Already the sky is dark, even though only a few minutes ago, the sun was only just starting to set. The floor consists of a fine layer of powdered snow that immediately seeps through the seams of my boots and numbs my feet. The walls are made of transparent ice, though I can't make out anything beyond because the world has become too dark.

It is so cold that immediately my arms are covered in goosebumps.

I try not to shiver as I take in the inhabitants of the room.

I will admit that there are fewer faeries here than I had expected. I can make out no more than a couple hundred of them. Are these all of the members of the Winter Court? Ravven had stated that their numbers were severely depleted after a war with the Seelie faeries, but even then, I never would have imagined a whole faction of faeries being so utterly depleted that they could all fit in a single, if not huge, room. What is the Summer Court like?

The faeries all look very different from the ones that I have met, and not half as beautiful. I notice that the majority of the inhabitants in the room have obsidian black skin and snow-white hair.

I suppose they could all be considered attractive in an otherworldly sort of way, but none of them are the blow-your-socks-off, make-you-forget-your-name sort of attractive Iorwerth, the queen and her sister, and Ravven are.

I spot Ravven standing near a throne in the middle of the huge expanse, at the queen's right. I regard him suspiciously, wondering how an ordinary Far Darrig could be more beautiful than the members of the Winter Court.

But then my eyes move to the second person standing near the queen's throne. It's the other faerie from the throne room. The dark haired one that I don't know the name of. The one who actually seemed to have felt sympathy for me. Lying on the ground behind him is a giant fearsome black beast that is at least the size of a bear.

Iorwerth leads me toward the throne. Another couple steps up beside us just as we reach the throne. My heart jolts when I realize that it is Thomas and Aoibheann.

I anxiously look my brother over. Thomas appears to be well, and not at all like he might have been tortured since the last time I saw him. He is wearing a dark blue tunic that has a collar that extends all the way to his neck and silver leggings. Even dressed as a faerie, it is almost painfully apparent that he is human with his shock of auburn hair and the healthy glow of his complexion. Unlike the bloodless winter faeries with their gaunt cheekbones and hollow eyes.

I turn my attention back to Ravven. For the first time since the Autumn Court we are all together again. Maybe now would be a good time to at least attempt an escape. If I have to spend one more second here, I think I might just go mad.

Ravven also has a very healthy glow to his skin. He's not an Unseelie faerie so it shouldn't bother me. As a member of the Autumn Court, I wouldn't expect him to look like a faerie of the Winter Court. No, what surprises me is that of the Autumn faeries I have seen, indeed even his fellow Far Darrig, they all seem to have more of a faded, almost gray complexion. But Ravven's skin is brilliant and rosy. It glows like sunlight itself radiates from it.

I squeeze my eyes shut and shake my head. And why does this even matter? If Ravven can help get me out of this Winter Court then I shouldn't care at all what his complexion is like.

Iorwerth stops before the queen and bows. I pause, wondering if I should curtsy or something. Beside me Thomas and Aoibheann also bow.

I bite down hard on my tongue and bend stiffly at my waist. I'm pretty sure I did it wrong in some sort of feminine handbook because my skirts almost throw me off balance, but I don't want to risk angering the queen. She tortured me when I'd never even done anything to her. The last thing I would want to do is actually give her a reason to hurt me.

Not when I need my strength in order to escape.

She smiles at me, pale as ever. I decide that her complexion resembles that of a corpse. No life whatsoever. "And now all of my esteemed guests have arrived and the ball can begin." She waves her hand and smiles down at me. "Do have fun, little mortals, as you are wont to do. Dancing your sorrows away, never knowing if the day would be your last so you live life while you can."

I glance over my shoulder as the Winter Court, which up to this point had been standing still or milling aimlessly through the room, suddenly spring into action as if someone had injected them all with caffeine. Most of them begin dancing though several head toward the icy tables lining the walls.

I turn toward Thomas. "Care to dance with me?" It will give me the perfect opportunity to talk with him again. Especially, to discuss our escape.

"I'm dancing this one with Aoiby," Thomas replies with a dreamy smile as he looks over at the faerie at his side. "Sorry, Jaye. Why don't you dance with one of your faerie boyfriends? You certainly have plenty."

I swallow down the urge to scream and stare after my brother as he walks away. I know for certain that something is wrong with him. Thomas is the most overprotective brother to ever walk the earth. He would give his own best friend a bloody nose if he thought he looked at me for too long.

So, who or what is this person who looks like my brother that is walking away from me?

"But Thomas...don't...dance with...faeries!" I grind out, but it's too late because he has already disappeared into the crowd.

To dance with faeries is a dangerous thing. For a brief second, I'm glad that at least we're not at the Spring Court, where a certain sort of faerie that legend has it is so beautiful that if a mortal man dances with her, he will completely lose the will to live.

But still, I don't trust Aoiby and dancing with faeries more than opens up the opportunity for them to enchant you. Faeries have a sort of magic in dance. It is why they enjoy it so much.

A cold hand lands on my upper arm and I start, turning to see Iorwerth standing there, leering down at me. "Since your brother is so obviously busy this dance. Perhaps I could dance with you."

But don't dance with faeries!

Ravven is at my side faster than I can say "ensorcellment", and wrapping his significantly warmer fingers around my other arm. He smiles coldly at Iorwerth. "Find your own human pet."

I am no one's human pet, but since that is a statement that I doubt either faeries would listen to, I keep my mouth shut.

Iorwerth snarls. "Perhaps I already have."

Ravven peers around the room before looking back to Iorwerth. "Then perhaps you should go fetch them, because I do not see your human in this room." He yanks me toward himself, and Iorwerth finally relents.

"This isn't over, Crowe. You forget where you are," Iorwerth snarls in a deadly tone.

"You forget what I am," Ravven says back, his tone just as deadly. And I start to feel terrified that I am going to end up ripped to pieces, the prize in some sort of macabre game of tug of war.

Iorwerth grins coldly, his fangs out in the open for all to see. "I know just what you are, a prisoner."

Ravven tilts his head. "Say that again to me tomorrow."

Iorwerth snarls but then stalks off. Ravven grins smugly and holds out his hand to me. I don't accept it. "No offence but I make it a habit to not dance with any faeries."

"Walk with me at least," Ravven says, glancing back toward the queen who is watching us with a keen expression.

We walk alongside the dancing faeries. I try to spot Thomas in their midst but they make me too dizzy to watch for long. I glance around to make sure that no one is paying explicit attention to us and lean closer to Ravven. "What was that statement about?"

"Perhaps, the correct question is what is going to happen tonight."

"Fine then, what is happening tonight?"

"How should I know? It has not happened yet."

I swear, I'm going to strangle him.

I glance back toward the queen and stiffen when I see that Iorwerth appears to be telling her something. They are both looking toward us. Oh great. "If this is about our plan to escape then why did you have to go and make a show like that?"

Ravven lifts his chin. "I cannot help if I make a show. It is only in my nature."

Even more than that, curse Ravven's pride. What if his words ruin our chances of escaping?

I shake my head.

"Breathe, pest. Oh, and by the way, that is a fine dress. Too bad it is on you."

I shoot him a glare. What a sight we two make, a faerie and a human. One dressed up for a party, the other handsome enough to make his wrinkled clothes look glamorous, just standing on the outskirts of a ball swaying slightly. Oh, and he's handcuffed.

He chuckles. "You have a faerie's pride trapped in a human's body. You cannot accept that you are lesser than anything."

His words hurt. They stab through every layer of protection I have, piercing my heart and turning it into a bloody mess. It is perhaps the cruelest thing to ever say because if that is right then I am forever doomed to strive and fail. To want to be perfect like a faerie, but forever a human. I quickly look away to hide my pain as

I blink back tears. I want to argue with him. I want to snap at him and tell him how wrong he is, but I can't.

Curse him. He may actually be right. I can't stand to be less than anyone in any way. But especially not him. And nothing I do will change the fact that I will *always* be less than him.

It's ridiculous to even compare us. I'm a human. He's a faerie. Of course, there are going to be differences between us. He's flawless and will live forever. I am breakable and could quite possibly die tomorrow. But I also have emotions of anger, fear, and love. While he, like the rest of his kind, is as unfeeling as a lump of coal.

A very attractive lump of coal.

But right now, I'm wishing that I am also a lump of coal, and that these horrid emotions that are supposed to make me so much better than the faeries would go away. Because now I'm dangerously close to crying in front of a faerie and having him think even more poorly of me.

I blink rapidly, afraid to even say a single word because my voice will surely break. However, despite my best efforts the tears continue to build until they finally spill over.

Ravven chokes. "Are you *crying*?"

Of course, he doesn't know what starvation or hypothermia is but he knows what tears are. Just my luck.

"I had a long day, okay. I'm *tired*. I can cry if I want, okay I'm not doing anything bad."

"I didn't say that you were."

"Oh, don't pretend that you feel bad," I state, swiping angrily at my eyes and glaring at him hard.

Ravven opens his mouth to reply then closes it. For once I have Ravven Crowe at a loss for words. I just wish that I could feel triumphant about it, but I just still feel like crying harder.

"Very well, I will not," he says at last, glancing away as the music begins to slow. His eyes quickly dart back to me and he swallows hard, looking more uncomfortable than I have ever seen him, even more uncomfortable than last night. "But could you possibly please stop?"

I elbow him, my eyelids batting so quickly that I'm surprised they don't create a breeze, but unfortunately, they don't keep the tears from falling onto my cheeks.

Ravven's eyes widen as he stumbles back, probably more from surprise than any real force behind my blow. "Jaye—"

"Just leave me alone," I snap. "It's not like you can do anything to make it better." I turn and storm away. I just need a few moments to myself, to remember that hope exists and not everything is fickle and doomed.

I spot a little alcove cut into the ice wall and duck behind it to inhale a shuddering breath. I swipe at my eyes with frustrated, clumsy fingers.

Obviously, I have a lot of reasons to cry. I'm lost and imprisoned in a strange world by fearsome creatures who can lie to your face without saying a single untruth. I was tortured. I'm being used as a pawn in a game I don't even know how to play. I have no idea what is wrong with Thomas and I'm forced to break and bend every rule that I've ever been taught just to try to get out of here. Oh, and my hair is frozen in place.

I press my hand against my forehead. Listing these reasons does little to make me feel better. I still feel weak and useless for crying. My tears will get me nowhere. They're only using up the liquid that I need to keep in my system.

A dark shadow moves in my peripheral vision and I open my mouth to yell at Ravven again for trying to talk to me when I don't have myself fully under control.

However, the words freeze in my heart when I realize that the person standing there isn't Ravven, or even the familiar threat of Iorwerth. It's the dark-haired faerie from the throne room, the one that had shown sympathy. The one I'd seen standing next to the throne at the beginning of the ball.

I'm so surprised that I forget for a moment that I'm crying.

"Hello there," he says with a charming smile. "I was hoping to find the opportunity to get you alone."

My immediate thought is, *Oh great, another Gancanagh.*

What do I do to attract these guys? Simply exist?

A large dark shadow slinks past his legs, and I stiffen when I see that his creature has followed him over. It's even bigger when not lying down, with its long, tangled, midnight black fur that sways and twists around itself without any wind. It has a long snout and yellow eyes and a distinctly canine shape.

What is this? A faerie dog? I've heard of such things existing, but this creature doesn't fit the description I've always heard for such a creature. This one is transparent, not solid. And it is even bigger than I've heard they are supposed to be.

The giant dog steps toward me, making snuffling noises in its throat. I step away until my back is against the bitterly cold ice. Should I scream? It presses its clammy nose against my neck. I gasp for breath as panic crashes in my chest. Its cool musty breaths move my hair.

The dark-haired faerie chuckles. "Och, don't be afraid of Blackie. This pooka is nothing more than a melting heart. It's just been so long since he's last seen a mortal. He misses the scent."

In what universe are those words supposed to make me feel better?

He regards my face for a long moment and then whistles. "Down boy, it isn't her." The pooka immediately withdraws, moving to sit at his side. Sitting down, the creature almost reaches his shoulders.

I slump against the glass as I look the dark-haired faerie over. Truth be told, he doesn't *look* like a Gancanagh. It's not that he's ugly, it's just that he's not *perfection*. His black hair is too long and tousled, his features too angular, he's too tall and thin even by faerie standards, and his eyelids droop too far, making him look lazy. All of it is alluring in a way, but not in the way that Iorwerth, Aoiby, the queen and even Ravven are beautiful. By faerie standards, he's really quite standard. But he obviously can't be standard. Whoever he is, he is very powerful to be able to move in the closest circles of the Winter Court.

"Who are you?" I demand.

"Master Riagan, spymaster of the Winter Court at yer service," he says with a flourishing bow.

I frown as he rises from his bow. And what does the spymaster of the Winter Court want from me? I don't have any secrets. At least not any from the other courts. I doubt he would care much for my human secrets. Not that I really have any of those either. "Is there a specific reason that you wanted to talk to me?"

"There's a specific reason why ye would want me to talk to ye," he says with an amused smile, his eyes glinting like he believes he is the most hilarious comedian on the planet. "A word of advice for ye, lass. Don't dance with the faeries if ye value yer free will. And yer life. They have a nasty habit of never stopping until yer dancing off into infinity."

I raise my eyebrows. I already know that, but I think the more important question is what is Riagan doing telling me it. Why did he even feel the need?

"I'm sure Crowe is a safe enough bet though. Detests dancing, he does. Probably would not choose to dance for eternity. Also, since we are on the subject of things that could end badly for a mortal lass such as yerself, I would avoid the red liquid if I were ye."

My eyes stray to the tables to where several faeries are already slumped to the floor while others are dancing wildly around it. "What is it?"

"It is the combined juices of several faerie fruits. It's potent enough to intoxicate a faerie. Ye do not want to know what it would do to a mortal."

"Why-why are you helping me?" I ask, wrapping my arms around myself and looking him over. What reason could he have to help me, unless he isn't actually helping me. Though I don't know how him telling me what to avoid could possibly be *bad*.

He smiles and shrugs. "I'm not quite sure why. I suppose ye could say that I have a bit of a soft spot for humans. Troublesome thing, it be. Always getting me into all sorts of situations I'd rather not be in."

"That still doesn't explain why you are helping *me*."

"I told you, I have a soft spot for humans, it always clouds my better judgment even in these matters. Well, it was lovely to finally make yer acquaintance, young one. Do try not to do anything foolhardy in these next few hours. They are crucial, ye see. And since ye are also crucial, I would say that this is all very, very crucial. Do try not to ruin everything." With those last confusing words, Riagan presses his fingers to his forehead in a jaunty salute, before turning and striding off, his giant fearsome dog following silently behind him like a second canine-shaped shadow.

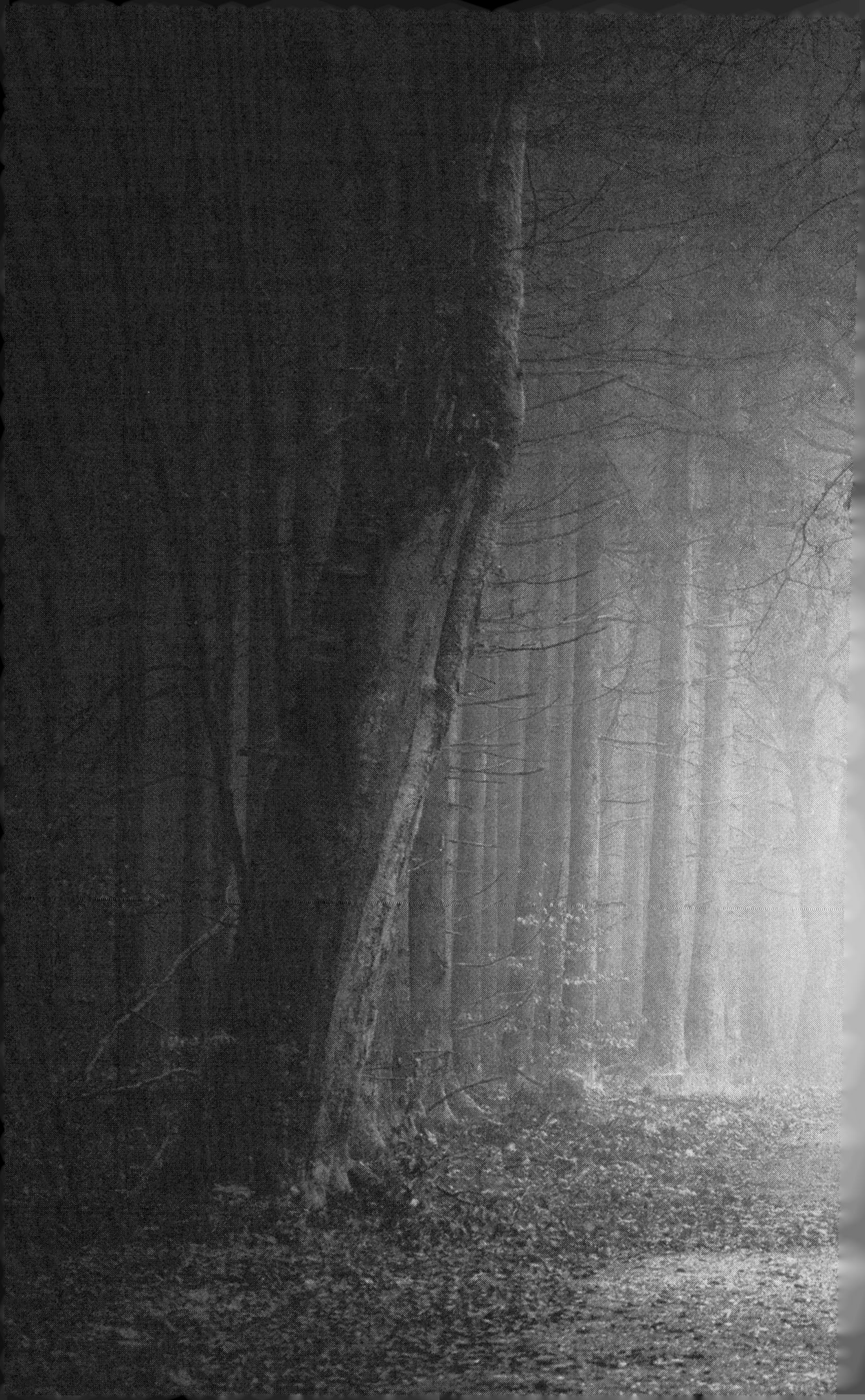

CHAPTER SIXTEEN

"There you are, my little bird, I was beginning to worry that you had flown off," Iorwerth says, materializing in the space at the opening of the alcove that Riagan had just vacated. My heart nearly leaps out of my rib cage as I'm jolted from my tumultuous thoughts over what Riagan could have even possibly have *meant*.

I need to stop trying to analyze the things that these faeries say. I will drive myself into madness... if I am not there already. How long can a human survive in the Otherworld without losing all distinctiveness of their humanity?

Because I'm afraid I'm already past that allotted time.

Iorwerth smiles as he steps into the alcove next to me, he runs his hand down my bare arms, leaving goosebumps in its wake and causing pain to flare up in the handprint on my arm when he touches it, before balancing my fingertips on his.

"Care to dance with me now?" Iorwerth asks, his voice musical and soft and so, so false.

I press my lips together. Just as much as I would care to fling myself from the peak of the highest mountain in this world. "Actually, I was hoping to speak with my brother."

"Later," Iorwerth breathes, the overwhelming scent of exotic fruits on his breath and his red stained lips gives me an idea. My eyes flit to the table. The red liquid. The faeries sprawled out on the floor. Iorwerth has me trapped with my back to the wall, quite literally, and I fear that the only way he will let me go is if he thinks he'll be gaining something else.

I lick my suddenly dry lips. "I'm rather thirsty."

Iorwerth's eyes brighten and his lips curl upward slowly. "Then the lady shall get what she so desires."

He steps back and it's all I can do to not release a relieved breath as he turns and saunters toward the table. Perhaps, if I am lucky, he will stop to get another drink and end up sprawled on the floor with the other faeries.

I pick up my skirts and hurry out of the alcove before I am cornered again. I scan the crowds for Ravven. I check first at the table which Iorwerth has almost reached by now. I find Riagan nursing a glass, watching the antics of the other drunk faeries with an amused look on his face, but Ravven isn't there.

I finally spot him at the other end of the room. He is standing next to the queen, though what they could possibly be discussing I have no idea. I know he can see me, because he stiffens visibly. I gesture for him to come join me. Or at least, I hope that's how he takes that gesture and not as some threat that means I'm going to kill him for making me cry earlier.

We have much bigger things to concern ourselves with than that.

Or at least that's what I tell myself, to make myself feel better about having cried.

Iorwerth has a glass in his hand and is now scanning the room probably for me. I quickly turn away, though I doubt I'll be able to hide for very long. My strawberry blonde hair stands out in this crowd of white-haired and black-haired faeries.

Which is what helps me find Thomas so easily. He's dancing only a short distance away. I'm horrified to see that it is still with Aoiby. I hike up my skirts and stomp across the trampled snow to where they are.

I roughly snatch his arm from Aoiby's perfect clutches and pull him away. While if a faerie so chooses, they can make it impossible for a human to break away while dancing, that does not mean that some outside force can't break them away. Both look up, opening their mouths as if to argue, but I don't give them a chance. "Sorry, sister cutting in." I tighten my hold on Thomas's forearm, until I think that I might actually leave bruises, not completely unlike the handprint still on my own forearm, barred for the world to see.

I don't wait for anyone to recover and pull Thomas deeper into the swaying masses. He keeps his gaze on Aoiby over my shoulders before finally releasing a breath and looking down at me with a frown. "That was rude."

"I don't really care," I reply with a flippant shrug. I glance over my shoulder trying to spot Iorwerth. I don't see him and my heart rate picks up. He isn't by the table anymore. I quicken my pace as I drag Thomas through the crowd.

When I finally burst through, I find myself right in front of one of the ice pillars, behind it appears to be a small side passage that looks to be relatively deserted.

I begin pushing toward it. This portion of the floor is not covered in the blanket of snow and so I have to walk carefully as my feet keep sliding on the slippery ice.

"Where are we going?" Thomas finally demands as I shove him toward the door.

"Away from the ball," I hiss, "So we can talk."

"What are we talking about?" Thomas asks, pulling his hand out of my hold. He arches his eyebrows.

I turn to him, placing my hands on my hips. "Oh, I don't know, let me think about it. How about our escape plan?" I snap, but I'm careful to keep my voice down. Even out here in the relative solitude of the hallway, we aren't safe to speak freely. I don't see any faeries, but that doesn't mean that they can't hear me. My eyes rove over the hallway, wondering why it isn't guarded. Are the faeries really so brazenly self-assured that they wouldn't guard us?

I don't know if we can just walk out here. I doubt that we can, but honestly, I'm desperate enough to try. Maybe when Ravven finally gets over here, we should just make a run for it.

"Escape..." Thomas begins, his eyes moving back to the door of the ballroom. "But—"

I swear, if he mentions Aoibheann...

"Get over her, Thomas. We are prisoners here; can't you see that?" I demand, shoving him.

Thomas shakes his head angrily. "We aren't prisoners. We are guests, Jaye. There's nothing to escape from. The only prisoner I noticed was Crowe who still is wearing his handcuffs."

I bark a laugh. "Seriously? So tell me, how often have you been away from your faerie escort in the past few days?"

"Aoiby only wants me to be comfortable. It would hardly be right for her to abandon me here when I have no idea what is going on."

"Real accommodating of her. But you know what, you're right about one thing. You have no idea what is going on."

Thomas stiffens. "I know that these faeries mean us no harm. If we need to worry about any of them, then it's really your boyfriend Ravven whose motive should concern you. We still don't know the part he played in the destruction of the faerie circle."

"His motive? His motive?" I cry. "He is being held hostage, I'm pretty sure that escape is his motive! Just as it should be ours."

Thomas still doesn't look convinced so I half lunge, half slide across the space between us and grip his shoulders. I shake him. "We are pawns, Thomas. Pawns in an elaborate game to start another faerie war. That's *all* we are."

He shakes his head. "But we're not. We're not prisoners here, Jaye."

"Did you not take the time to wonder where I have been this whole time that you have been sitting in the lap of luxury?"

Thomas opens his mouth, but nothing comes out. He stares at me like a dead fish. Mouth gaping, eyes bugging.

"For your information, I was locked in a flipping dungeon. I nearly froze to death, thank you very much for your concern." The only reason I wasn't was because Ravven and I... Well, we had to put forth major survival skills that may have looked suspiciously like snuggling but definitely wasn't.

He blinks. "But... why would they... why would they treat you like this?"

"I think the real question you should be asking yourself is why you weren't treated like this. Did you know that I was tortured, Thomas? *Tortured*."

He stumbles back, like I slapped him. His eyes rove over me as if he's trying to discern the damage. They land on my arm and horrid ghostly handprint. "You-you—"

"Your precious Aoiby's sister did this to me. While Iorwerth watched." Riagan too. Oddly enough Ravven was the one who spoke up for me.

Thomas inhales sharply and lifts my arm to inspect it. He turns my arm in his hand before looking up at me. He shakes his head. "This can't—Aoiby is different. She probably didn't know—I'll ask her. She can help us."

I grab the front of his tunic, keeping him from leaving. "You'd better not even think about it. We aren't going back to the ball. We're leaving, now."

"But why? Does the ball tire you so?"

I blink slowly and stare at Thomas, but I know that he didn't say that. The silky smooth and slick as oil voice had come from behind me. I turn slowly to see Iorwerth standing in the middle of the hallway behind me, looking a little too beautiful for comfort.

He strides toward me, his attention on the crystalline chalice clutched in his hand. He tilts it, allowing its blood red contents to slosh around before looking up at me. "I brought you your drink," he says, holding out the glass with a smile on his face.

I feel the blood drain from my face. I don't want to know what just one sip of that drink would do to me. The wicked gleam in Iorwerth's eyes are all the answer I need. Nothing good.

I back up a step into Thomas who steadies me with his hand. "I'm-I'm not actually that thirsty anymore."

"Nonsense," Iorwerth says in a completely reasonable tone. He holds the glass up higher. "Take a drink."

"No."

Iorwerth's eyes flash, but not with anger. With excitement. My heart begins pounding double time in my chest. "You interest me, little bird. You have a strange draw on our kind. On Crowe. On me. You may be mortal, but you are ravishing."

He glides toward me another step and I back up. My feet almost slide right from underneath me, Thomas catches me. He puts his arm in front of me as he moves around me to block Iorwerth from me. "Stay away from her."

I nearly cry from relief to see my protective older brother and the angry glint in his eyes. I had half thought that he had disappeared completely in the depths of his infatuation for Aoibheann.

Iorwerth's eyes flick to him impatiently and he rolls his eyes, looking almost tired. "Step aside," he growls and with his words Thomas's body stiffens. Then like a puppet on strings, he lifts one leg then the other moving away from me, leaving nothing but a precious few feet standing between me and Iorwerth the creepy.

I watch him with speechless horror. Thomas's eyes stare at me, just as horrified. I've never seen anyone be ensorcelled before. It's a horrible thing to behold. Just like that and Thomas has no control over himself anymore. Iowerth could make me drink without even trying.

Iorwerth keeps striding toward me as if nothing at all is amiss. And I guess for him it isn't. I back up until my bare back hits the cold wall. I inhale sharply and Iorwerth smiles as he holds the glass up.

I clench my fist, ready to fight whatever spell he puts on me, but my body remains under my control. I remain where I am, completely still, my entire body tensed.

Iorwerth regards me, a small furrow forming between his wickedly perfect brows before he shrugs off his confusion. "Very well, if you will not drink it for yourself, then I could always *make* you drink it."

He raises the glass so that it is on level with my lips. "If the ball has tired you, then I'm certain that we can find other ways to entertain ourselves. But first you simply must try the drink. I am certain that you will find it absolutely... *freeing.*"

"The only freeing I want, is to be free of your presence," I spit at him.

Iorwerth laughs as if what I just said is the funniest thing in the world. He presses the chalice to my lips and I shrink back in disgust at the feeling of the cold. I press my lips together and shake my head. Iorwerth leans closer and raises a finger to my lips as if he was going to personally pry them apart. I don't give him the opportunity. I open my lips just enough to bite him.

Iorwerth hisses and yanks it away. "You beast!" he cries.

I could say the same of him except that I'm back to clamping my lips shut.

I shove at him with one hand while my other reaches for my knife. Wielding a knife against Iorwerth may garner me a death sentence, but I'm not sure if I will survive whatever Iorwerth has planned for me anyway. I raise my leg so that I can have easier access to my boot where I have my knife stowed. But it doesn't seem to matter what I do, because all my hand meets are layers and layers of fabric. Where is my blasted foot?

"You will drink this," he snarls. He presses his whole hand against my chin and pushes it so hard that I can't help but open my mouth. He raises the glass and I grope desperately at my heavy skirts, trying to find my boot underneath.

The cup touches my lips, a horrible vile cold thing and then suddenly it's gone as Iorwerth is yanked away from me.

I gasp in relief as droplets splatter my shoulder, burning slightly on impact and staining my skin red. I fall to my knees with his body no longer holding me up and look up to see that Ravven has pressed Iorwerth to the wall. Ravven snarls, his eyes flashing a violent yellow and my heart stutters. He looks absolutely terrifying, so terrifying that I'm tempted to flee from *him*. In fact, I might if it wouldn't mean abandoning Thomas.

"You shouldn't have done that, Crowe," Iorwerth gasps. "You always play your hand too soon." Then he shoves against Ravven, who stumbles back.

"You know nothing about my hand," Ravven spits back.

They stalk a few feet away, both looking like they will strike at any moment. But Ravven is handcuffed still. And even if he wasn't, he already said he couldn't beat Iorwerth while in his court.

"The queen will be interested to know just how far your connection to the mortal girl runs."

Ravven arches his brow. "Then why don't you run off and tell her."

Iorwerth's eyes glance down to Ravven's cuffed hands. Then he smiles at us. "It amuses me that you think you can escape. Very well, you all stay here and I shall play the role of the messenger. I also need to inform Aoiby about how problematic her... pet is."

Thomas makes a strained noise then Iorwerth waves his hand. Thomas collapses.

"Thomas!" I gasp.

"I'm fine," he grunts.

Ravven watches Iorwerth leave somewhat uneasily and then turns to me. "Pest, I think now is that moment we were waiting for to free me."

I don't argue. I can barely think straight. Something is wrong, everything is oddly fuzzy. My limbs are heavy. Is it just the panic?

I pull out my lockpicks and insert them into the hole. I bite my lip as I focus on undoing it. Something isn't right though; I see at least three pairs of handcuffs and Ravven has six hands respectively. Finally, the musical click reaches my ears. Not a minute too soon, I seem to have lost all motor functions and slump to the side.

Ravven uses his newly freed hands to catch me.

"Jaye!" Thomas cries in horror. I want to inform him that I am fine, but I can't move anymore. I can't see either. I can still hear though.

"Mvtalach," Ravven spits. "This is why Iorwerth left so easily. He knew she had faerie fruits in her system."

"What can we do!" Thomas demands, his voice rising in panic.

"Quickly, do you still have the Fear Gorta's boon? Summon him here. With our combined magic we should be able to transport us out of here. There is a root in the Autumn Court that should clean her system of the faerie fruit."

There is a snapping sound and then a raspy voice. "I am here to fulfill my debt."

"Get my sister and Ravven out of here."

"What about you?" Ravven demands, which I'm thankful for since I still can't speak.

"I can't—I can't do anything against Aoiby. I wish I could but I just... I can't."

"Mvtalach," Ravven spits again. "You fool, you are bound to her now. By my wings, that was fast—you didn't fight it at all?"

"You need to get Jaye out of here. She looks awful."

"Very well," Ravven says. "You mortals... you are always more trouble than you are worth."

"Don't I know it," Thomas says with a humorless laugh. And then I lose all grasp I have on the material world.

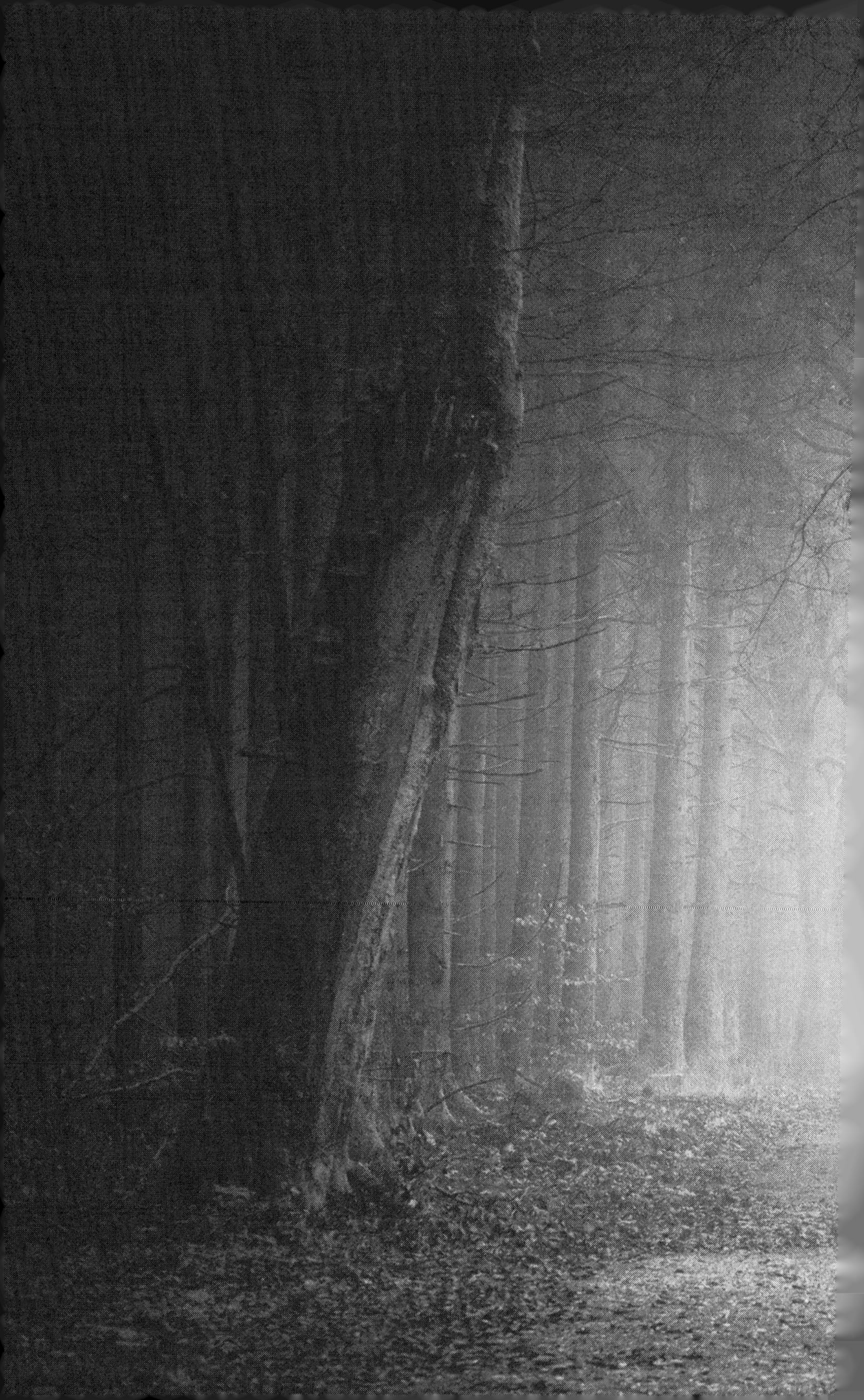

CHAPTER SEVENTEEN

I'm no expert on the outdoors or wildlife or flora or fauna or whatever it is that experts are experts on, but I'm pretty sure that I'm lying on a patch of moss.

I blink twice trying to make the world stop swaying, until I realize that the world isn't swaying. The trees above me are. An orange leaf breaks away from the bough and floats down toward me landing on my cheek.

I frown and try to lift my hand to knock it off, but my arm only does this weird diving flop thing where it rises only an inch above the ground before plopping back down on the moss in defeat.

"I'd probably give it a few minutes more. You appear to still be slightly paralyzed."

Oh yeah, cause that's something a person wants to hear.

I frown, my eyes darting around, trying to find the person responsible for speaking. I don't recognize the voice. There is no one in my line of vision, just swaying multicolored trees. My heart pounds in my chest as I stare up at them, forced to look there and nowhere else.

Where am I? Last I remember I was in the Winter Court.

The *Winter Court*.

Oh goodness, *Thomas*.

"Quit your human reactions. I can hear your hummingbird of a heart pattering like the rain. It's giving me a headache. I'm certain that it will be out of your system in only a few more minutes. You wouldn't have woken up if you weren't almost over it."

I still have no idea who is speaking, but the distaste in his voice does nothing to comfort me.

I try to steady my breathing and tell myself that if this mysterious stranger had meant me any harm, he would have done so while I was still unconscious. Unfortunately, I cannot fully comfort myself because this is most likely a faerie that I am dealing with. And one can never apply reasonable thoughts to a faerie.

"Who-who are you?" I manage to push past my stiff lips. My words are only slightly slurred.

"Someone who would rather not have to deal with you."

My finger on my left-hand taps and I hold my breath as I move another finger. In a few more minutes, I'm able to lift my head. I push to a sitting position, more relieved than I could even imagine to have my ability to move back, though my shoulder of my right arm still feels a little numb.

I turn to the person who was talking to me to find a Far Darrig standing only a few feet away, glaring down at me as if my very presence offends him. Which considering that he's a Solitary faerie, that's probably exactly the case. Though, it's not like he can very well blame me for being here. *I* certainly did not bring myself here.

How did I get here?

I look around sharply, seeking out either my brother or Ravven, but neither of them are there. Fortunately, neither is Iorwerth. Given the array of gold, bronze, and red leaves drifting slowly down from the majestic trees around us and the chilly but not frosty breeze, I would say that I'm not in the Winter Court anymore, but rather the Autumn Court. Though how I made it to the Autumn Court is beyond me.

I could almost think that perhaps that was all just a dream if not for the fact that I am sitting here wearing a frosty blue ball gown and the red handprint on my forearm.

The Far Darrig steps toward me and I scoot back, the heavy skirts impeding my movement. "Who-who are you?" I demand, desperately searching for an escape. I grope at my boot, but my dagger is gone. I don't know where the stupid heck it went. Who took it? Did it slip out sometime? But I feel a whole lot more helpless with it gone.

The Far Darrig draws to a halt and heaves a heavy sigh like what is about to happen next physically pains him. Finally, he opens his mouth, his dull dark eyes searching my face. "I am Keane. I am Ravven's father, though I believe that only one of those things actually matters to you."

I shake my head as if that will somehow help me process what he just said.

This guy-this guy is Ravven's *dad*? I frown and peer more closely at him, trying to find a resemblance between the two. They are both tall and skinny, though Keane's joints seem far knobbier than Ravven's elegant form. Keane's face is covered in wrinkles and frown lines, his heavy eyebrows are drawn down into a scowl. Keane does have the same patch on his cheekbones that is more golden than the rest of his skin. The only truly remarkable resemblance between the two is their shockingly black hair, though even there Keane's hair is wild and untamed and Ravven's hair seems to be placed in perfect order to allow for the most symmetry with his face.

"But you're his *dad*?" I don't know why the idea is so strange to me. Everyone has a father, even faeries. But I guess I never thought about any family Ravven would have. I didn't consider anything about him when I kidnapped him. Crap, I'm a monster.

He harrumphs. "Just like my son to bring perfect strangers to my doorstep. I always told him that he was too social to be a Solitary faerie but he never listened to me. Nay, he claimed that he was solitary enough, but let me tell you," the Far Darrig grouches, pointing a finger at me, "Solitary faeries do not willingly make friends."

He says that like he is making some important point, though I have no idea what it is.

Especially since Ravven and I are not friends.

I swallow hard and stare down at my hand. Honestly my head is reeling. I never really considered much about the dynamics of faerie families. New faeries are born, but not overly often. From what we Guardians have managed to get from studying the faeries over the years, they have a population growth of about three faeries every century. Faeries rarely ever die and so no one seems to care about posterity. Plus, they are such selfish beings that love does not come easily to them, if they ever experience it at all. A faerie family, a new faerie born, these are rare things.

Especially in a court such as the Autumn Court, where the Solitary faeries avoid attachments at all costs.

I rub at my temple and tamp down the urge to ask Keane how old he is and how old Ravven is. What does it even matter to an immortal faerie living in a world where time does not change?

Ravven and any family he might have are not important right now. What is important is Thomas and finally getting home. My stomach twists. And fulfilling my bargain. I shake that thought from my head. No, Thomas first. I need to make sure that he's all right. That he escaped Aoibheann. "Where-where are everyone?"

"*Everyone?*" Keane cries, jumping back. "What do you think this is? A bloomin' ball? Bad enough that I have to deal with the one of you."

I clench my fist around the voluminous skirts of my ball gown. "No, I actually know what a ball looks like, thank you very much. What I would like to know is, where is my brother and where is your—ah... er... son?" I bite down on my lip hard and wince over how quickly my fiery response became something pathetically awkward.

Keane regards me warily like I might start talking again or somehow pull a whole ball out of my skirts. Finally, he clears his throat. "I can't say much for this brother of yours, but I can tell you where that accursed laggard of a son of mine is."

I arch my brow as I take in his wizened face. I could almost like him just for that comment if not for the fact that he is a faerie. And a Far Darrig at that. And Ravven's dad. "And where is that?"

"Not here," Keane grumbles, looking up at the multicolored trees above him. "Lad said that he wouldn't be long, said he would try to be back before ye woke." He scrubs a hand over his lined chin. "Should have known better than to even bring him into the world."

I arch my brow higher. "Do you not like your son?"

Keane looked at me like I'm an impertinent toad who decided to ask him the exact funds of his bank account. "I don't see how it is any business of yours," he grouses, "but if you must know, I like Ravven just fine. Or at least I did back when we had a proper relationship and never saw each other. But I can surely curse the day that he was born when he drops in out of the blue dragging a guest along with him yelling about roots—*my* roots that I don't have to share..."

"Just one?" I ask, my heart dropping. No, no, no. Thomas is fine. He's here with us. He has to be. I don't know what I would do if he isn't.

"Thank everything in the skies, yes, just one. You're trouble enough."

My heart drops completely. Thomas isn't here.

There's a loud flapping somewhere beyond the trees. Then a twig snaps and I, like the frightened rabbit I must be, about jump out of my skin.

Keane raises his head. "Oh, that must be the ungrateful boy now."

As if summoned by his father's words, Ravven steps through the trees looking every bit the Autumn prince I had mistaken him to be. Instead of the dark blue tunic he had been wearing in the Winter Court, he is now wearing an ankle length coat the color of burnt red, a black shirt that is embroidered with gold and trousers the same color as the dirt. He stops short, his deep blue eyes scanning over the clearing before landing on the man who couldn't possibly be this gorgeous creature's father. "In order to be ungrateful, I must first have something that I should be grateful about, don't you think?"

Crap, he looks *good*. I should slap myself. I'm gaping.

Keane blows out a breath and shakes his head. "Always far more trouble than you are worth. But then, so is everyone so why should my own son be any different?"

"You tell me," Ravven says dryly.

"Where's Thomas?" I demand, lurching to my feet. I need to stay focused here. There are way too many things vying for my attention in this all too beautiful all too confusing world but only one of them actually matters.

Ravven looks at me and raises his brow. "You know full well where he is."

"If you say that he is in the Winter Court I will murder you slowly."

Ravven presses his lips together. "Then I will say nothing."

"You left him!" I cry, surging across the short space between us and shoving him hard. Wiping the arrogant expression off of his face. Ravven stumbles back.

"Ugh, people," Keane mutters behind me.

Ravven backs away from me, straightening his shirt sleeve. "As you will recall, you left him also."

"I was *unconscious*, it's not like I had much of a choice."

"And you think I had more of a choice than you? If anything, it is your fault for getting yourself paralyzed and forcing me to move up the timetable."

He can't pin this on me, I can't handle that responsibility. I didn't *ask* Iorwerth to try to drug me. "You promised. You swore to help both me and Thomas."

Ravven grimaces. "Do not remind me of what I am already well aware of. But I also made an arrangement to do everything in my power to get you out of the Winter Court. And at the moment you were the only one that I had power to save. As it was, without the magical aid your brother bought with his boon, none of us would have escaped."

"We can't just give up on Thomas!" I cry.

Ravven rubs at his chin like he is considering doing just that.

"Ravven," I growled. "You made an agreement. We had a deal."

He frowns. "Yes, quite unfortunate."

I'm about to yell at him more, but just then my stomach rumbles loudly.

"What was that sound?" both Keane and Ravven demand, glancing at the sky as if looking for storm clouds.

I roll my eyes. "It was just my stomach. I'm hungry. And cut that out it wasn't that loud."

Ravven looks at me and then back at his father. "You didn't feed her," he accuses.

Keane raises his chin. "Don't know why I have to be your errand boy."

Ravven runs a hand across his face. "You know how delicate humans are. They die if you don't feed them."

I roll my eyes. Yeah, sure and he's such an expert on what kills humans. He didn't even know what hypothermia was. He only knows about starvation because I told him.

Ravven snaps his fingers and then someone appears only a few inches away. I jump and let out a little squeal before I recognize the emaciated, ghoulish figure. It's just the Fear Gorta. He must have been the magical aid Thomas brought with his boon.

Why is he still here if he already paid his debt?

"Could you retrieve our... eh... human some food?" Ravven asks.

"*Your* human?" I demand and Ravven grimaces.

"I'm not yer housemaid, Crowe," the Fear Gorta growls.

"Of course," Ravven says with a charming smile. "I do not have a house and you are no maid."

The Fear Gorta huffs and disappears, a minute later he reappears holding a steaming bowl of something that smells divine.

Keane throws up his hands and stalks toward the edge of the trees. "There are far too many living beings in my rath. I will return when I am no longer pressured to have to speak to you."

As he disappears, the Fear Gorta steps toward me and offers up the bowl. I want nothing more than to snatch it up and gobble up every last bite, but I force myself to still my hand.

Instead I look up at the Fear Gorta suspiciously. "Tell me that this isn't enchanted or cursed in any way that will harm me."

The Fear Gorta rolls his eyes. "And why would I do that?"

Because I don't have my iron knife and I'm not about to end up cursed and bound to a faerie for all eternity just because of some hunger pangs.

"Because she's a suspicious creature," Ravven says at last. "Go on, Daithi, tell her."

The Fear Gorta rolls his eyes. "This is ridiculous, Crowe."

"Is it now?" Ravven asks mildly, his hand over his mouth. His eyes dart to me and then back to the Fear Gorta. "How so?"

The Fear Gorta grumbles and stomps his foot. "You know as well as I do that I can't stand humans, let alone would I want one as a slave."

"Just humor her," Ravven says, rolling his eyes.

"Fine, I swear on me bloomin' immortality that this here bowl of food be not poisoned or otherwise tampered with," Daithi grumbled. He shot Ravven a glare. "Happy?"

"I am, but it has nothing to do with how I feel and this mortal here is temperamental."

I hesitantly accept the bowl and turn a glare at Ravven. "We aren't done with this conversation."

He rolls his eyes. "Just eat so you don't collapse and then we will discuss it."

"I'm not going to collapse," I say. And then because I'm worried that I just might, I quickly spoon the food into my mouth.

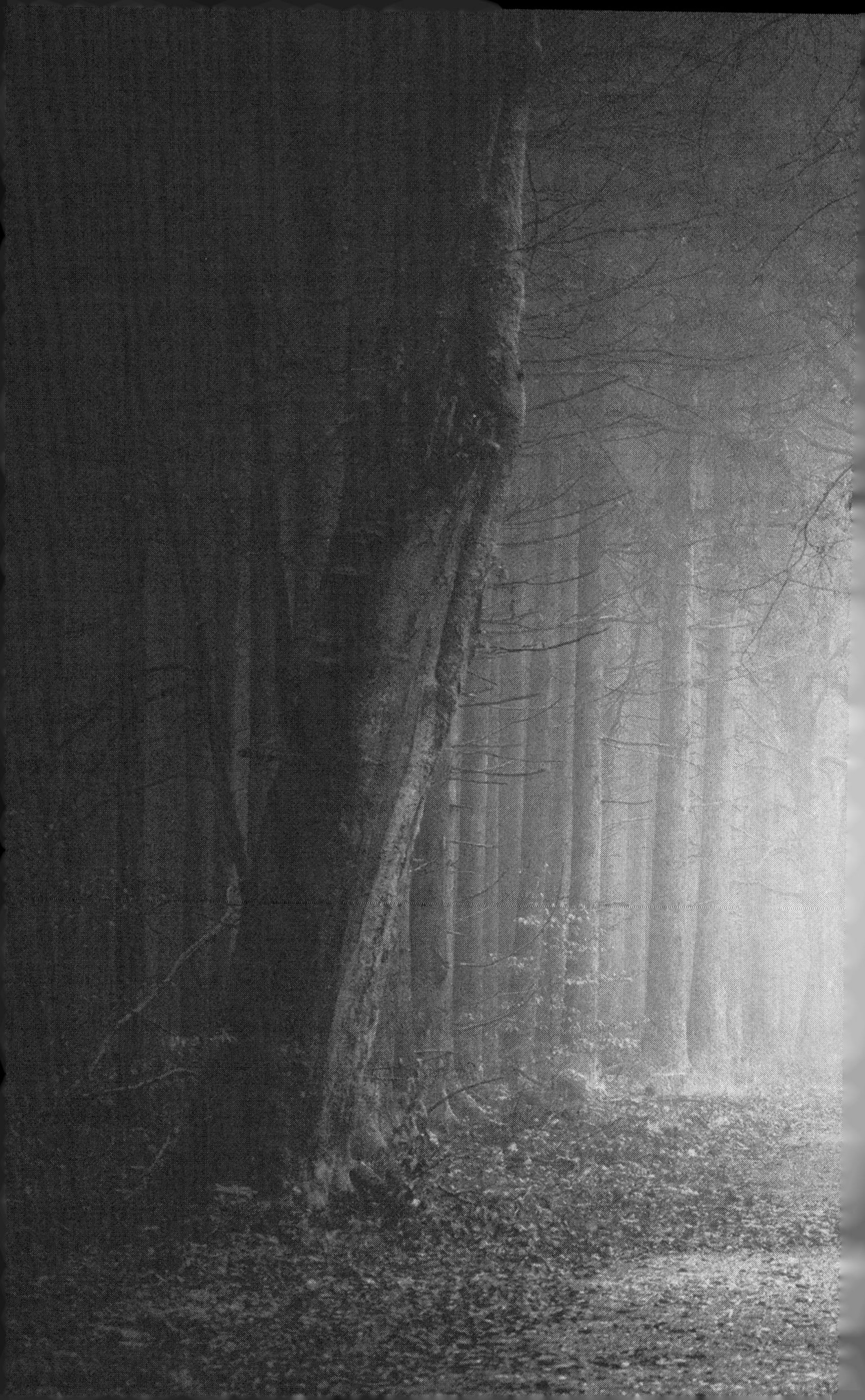

CHAPTER EIGHTEEN

The soup is some sort of savory meat with a distinct leafy flavoring. I finish it quickly, maybe a bit too quickly that I'll probably have a stomach ache later. I arch my brow at Ravven. "Okay, I'm done eating. Talk."

Ravven taps his finger against his arm. "I do not think that you will like what I have to say. Nor do I think that I will like your reaction to it."

I stiffen. "What?"

"Now before you go do anything violent, recall this is not my fault. This is on that foolish boy who fell in love with that witch Aoibheann."

"What-what does that mean? That he fell in love with her?" I whisper, my lips almost so numb that I can't push the words out.

Ravven presses his eyes shut and shakes his head. "Aoibheann is a Leanhaun Shee; they are beautiful and known as the muse for humans because of the artists and bards that they have managed to ensnare in their hold. But woe to the mortal that falls in love with them. Because if they do then that mortal becomes the Leanhaun Shee's slave for all eternity. She draws the life force from her slave until there is nothing left but their whimpering spirit."

I'm too stunned to even cry. I *want* to cry. I want to scream and rail. I want to fight and kick. But I can't do any of that. I'm trapped, frozen in place, gaping at Ravven in horror.

He looks away, resting his hands on his hips. "Obviously I will keep my side of the bargain and return you to your home. But as for the boy... he is out of my reach."

I shake my head, trying to dislodge the ringing. Trying to knock away his words. "No—we have to get him."

Ravven paces away, a lock of his dark hair falling across his forehead. Suddenly he stops and turns to me, his maroon coat billowing behind him and ruffling the leaves.

"Absolve me of my word," Ravven spits. "Please, I will still help you. But to help him, it is im—" he pauses and bites at the word like he wishes he could say it, but can't. "It is unwise to go after him."

"Were you going to say impossible?" I demand.

Ravven stares forlornly at me, his eyes sparking with frustration. If he could lie, he would now, but the Fair Law holds him silent.

"But it isn't impossible is it?" I say, arching my brow. "Otherwise you would just say so."

"What I have in mind—it is ill advised."

"I've never let that stop me before," I state, pacing away.

Ravven frowns. "That is hardly comforting."

I stare at him and then shake my head as I shrug. "Whether you are comforted or not is really the last thing on my mind when my brother is enslaved by an Unseelie faerie. You gave me your word. More than that, we have a blood bargain and you know full well that cannot be absolved by either of us. So, hate to break it to you, but you are going to help me."

Ravven opens his mouth as if to argue, but he has no arguments to say. Frustration oozes off of him, I can practically see it in the set of his shoulders and the way he clenches his hand. "What makes you think that I can even help you?"

"You said you already had a plan in mind."

"I also said that it is ill advised! We will very likely both die trying to accomplish it."

"I like risky plans, they're my favorites."

Ravven releases a deep breath and turns around. "You are going to be the death of me, I know it."

I tap my finger impatiently against my elbow. "Stop being melodramatic and spit it out already."

He releases a heavy sigh. "Very well, there is a way that you can help your brother, but it is dangerous. And it is idiotic. And did I mention that it was dangerous? Because frankly I am too beautiful to die so please take that into your consideration."

I tilt my head to the side. He is pretty, that's for sure. But beauty is only skin deep. "It's considered, now get on with it."

He rubs at his jaw. "If you must know. The only way I can figure that you can save your brother from Aoibheann's clutches is to kill her."

My eyes widen and I gasp. As much as I hate the witch, I don't actually want to kill her.

Ravven must read my hesitation because he sighs. "There is no other escape for the Leanhaun Shee's slaves save for death. Either hers or Thomas's."

I swallow and nod, scratching my cheek. "Yeah, sure. I guess that makes sense." In a cold-hearted brutal way. "But if we have to kill Aoibheann then why did we leave the Winter Court? That's where she is." Also, there is the matter of how we will manage to kill her. Especially now that my iron dagger is missing.

Good gosh I think I'm gonna upchuck my soup.

Ravven scoffs. "As if you could kill her anyway. The faeries would not take kindly to a mere mortal murdering one of their own. It is against the Fair Law for a mortal to harm a faerie with iron. I doubt they would even give you a trial and if they did it would only be to proclaim you guilty. They would kill you which you would probably choose to save your brother, you mortals are such a sacrificial lot. But if you die, it still breaks our blood bargain, so that would hardly help me. And if I were to try to protect you, they would just kill me as well for trying to defend someone who has broken the Fair Law. Oh, and it would probably start a war or two."

I arch my brow. "So, we kill her stealthily. The faeries can't try and execute you if they don't know who you are?" I try to sound flippant but it is hard to talk around the lump in my throat. My grandma wielded iron against a faerie once in self-defense. And that was how they killed her, exactly how Ravven described it. No trial or anything, they ensorcelled her and forced her to tear herself apart with her bare hands.

Ravven shakes his head. "No, the risk of getting caught is still too great. You probably didn't hear the part about both of our deaths and war, but I'm actually trying not to allow that to happen."

"What if *you* kill her then? Faeries do not have laws against murdering each other, right?" Just if mortals are to murder them...

Ravven presses his lips together, his eyes a swirl of black and yellow. "I don't think you understand. It is no small task to kill a faerie. Let alone one who is related to royalty. Besides, I do not have her item of immortality, nor do I even know what it could be."

I blink. "So, we find out what her item of immortality is."

Ravven regards me for a long moment. "You don't even know what an item of immortality is, do you?"

"Of course I do," I snap, crossing my arms.

He arches his brows. "Oh really, then what is an item of immortality?"

I feel heat begin to crawl up my cheeks. "Well... it's an item that a faerie has... and it has something to do with their immortality."

Ravven releases a breath as he rolls his eyes. "Mortals lie so easily," he says, twisting absently at the golden ring on his finger. "When a faerie is born, the essence of their magic is embedded into an object. This object is their item of immortality and as long as this item exists so does the faeries because as long as their essence exists so will they."

I bite down on my lip as I try to wrap my mind around the faerie logic. "Like the way that a mascot for a restaurant is immortal as long as the restaurant is popular and thriving?"

Ravven stares at me as if I am an uncomprehending child. "No, nothing like that. It's like when a faerie has an item that is as immortal as they are. Some of the old faeries made their item their castles and as their castles crumbled and became decrepit, so did they. When their castles finally fell, so did they. A faerie's very life force is linked to this item."

I scratch behind my ear and nod. "Okay, so that still doesn't really make sense without my mascot and restaurant analogy but okay. Moving on. So, we find her immortality."

"Even if I were to somehow magically find her item of immortality which I can assure you would be well guarded, I cannot kill her. I may not be held accountable by the Fair Law, but Cliodnha would need no other reason to declare war against my—against me. Do you care so little for our politics here?"

"Well, excuse me, but my brother is having the life drained out of him. Would you rather we sit down and discuss how to properly murder faerie royalty? I certainly would not want to get it wrong."

Ravven blinks. "Are you being serious?"

"No!"

"Oh that's..." He pauses and runs his hand across his face. "Sometimes I cannot keep up with you humans, you seem to lie for the sheer enjoyment of it. But anyway, it will be very difficult to kill Aoibheann without starting a war. We'll probably both be dead before it gets out of hand, but still, I would rather not destroy both worlds as I leave."

"What are you suggesting? We get the Winter Queen's permission to kill her sister? Or do we get another court's backing?"

Ravven shakes his head emphatically. "No, any interference from any other courts will lead to war."

"This war is seeming pretty inevitable."

"It doesn't have to be."

I reach up to rub at my temple. "Could you please stop talking in riddles and just spit it out."

Ravven's lips curl up slightly, but his now completely black eyes are grave. He holds my gaze as if pondering the wisdom of actually telling me. "*You* kill her."

"I thought you already said that I can't kill her. That they would kill me. And you would die trying to protect me, bound by our blood oath. And there would be war. You stated it all quite clearly."

He holds up a finger, a mad glint in his eyes as a wicked smile pulls at his lips. It chills my heart. This faerie is far more cunning than I give him credit for. No, more than that. I see that he *thrives* from figuring out an impossible puzzle piece and utilizing it. He is not an unwitting pawn at all, but actually a master player. And somehow, I'm starting to feel like I've been played. Even though our blood bargain is probably the only reason that he's even still here speaking to me and not off enjoying the solitude of his own company, I'm suddenly regretting making it. Because, I'm not sure that wasn't what he wanted. "Only if you kill her by breaking the Fair Law. But if you did not break the Fair Law and did not have the support of any one court then Cliodnha would have no right to kill you and no reason to start a war."

If iron is off the table... there are only three ways to kill a faerie, and learning her name wasn't even suggested. This must be why Ravven finally explained to me what an immortal item is. "Wait, so I'm supposed to find her item of immortality and destroy it?"

My palms suddenly feel extremely clammy and I have trouble swallowing.

How am I supposed to do that? If humans destroying a faerie's item of immortality is a thing, then why do the Guardians know nothing about it? In all the generations that my ancestors fought against the faeries, *especially* the early years where they killed as many faeries as the faeries killed them, why is there never a recorded use of a human destroying a faerie's immortal item?

Ravven does nothing to help my rising anxiety by throwing back his head laughing toward the bright swaying boughs overhead. "By the moon, girl, but you are quite full of yourself."

I cross my arms tightly over my chest, trying to fight off the blush rising up my cheeks. "What?"

"That you actually think that you can destroy a faerie's item of immortality?" he shakes his head, resting his hands on his hips. "You, a mere mortal? Defeat an immortal such as Aoibheann, without cheating with iron? She would have the backing of the entire Winter Court, and you are a mortal."

"Okay, I get it!" I cry, throwing up my hands. "I'm a mortal. Do you think I am not already well aware of that fact?"

He regards me for a long moment. "I suppose that every beat of your frail heart, bringing you closer to your inevitable demise, would be hard to ignore."

I step away from him, rolling my eyes. "Okay, what did you have in mind then if not destroying her immortal object?"

Ravven immediately sobers up, the strange glint returning to his eye. He stretches his fingers slightly toward me as if he is reaching out to touch me. The mortal with the frail heart. But he pulls back. "You have to become the Fair Assassin and earn the right to wield the Blade of Gold and Iron."

He delivers these words like they must hold some sort of significance, but they simply leave me feeling confused. "Fair Assassin? What the heck is a Fair Assassin? And for that matter what is the Blade of Gold and Iron?"

Ravven smirks. "The Fair Assassin is a mortal held in the highest esteem by the faeries; they live among us as our personal killer. If a faerie has a feud, instead of being forced to find some impossible way to destroy them, they can hire the Fair Assassin to do it. The Blade of Gold and Iron is an ancient blade that was forged for the first Fair Assassin's use. With this title, you will have the right to kill any faerie you so please. Even with iron. *Especially* with iron."

I rub at my temples. This is too much. He wants me to become an assassin? I don't want to kill anyone! My stomach twists, except for apparently Aoibheann—but only because it is the only way to save my brother.

Ravven's smile turns mocking. "And now you see the madness of it all. Naturally allowing a human to carry the title and the mantel to be able to kill any faerie she or he so pleases, is not something that is granted easily. In order for you to be given the title of Fair Assassin, you must first pass a test held by each of the courts. It's in the law of fairness, if you can overcome the greatest obstacles that they can devise for you, then you will become the Fair Assassin. Over the centuries, there have not been very many Fair Assassins and for one reason or the other... they did not remain alive for long. The faeries have their own assassins, you know, and a mortal is so much easier to kill than an immortal."

"Okay, that sounds..." *daunting. Suicidal. Ill advised. Maybe I should have listened to Ravven when he said that this was a bad idea?* "Difficult."

Ravven chuckles. "Difficult does not even begin to describe it. You will have to complete four tests that will challenge you in ways you could not even imagine. If it is the Autumn Court that petitions for you to become the Fair Assassin then you will be forced to complete the challenges put forth to you by the Summer, Undersea, Spring, and yes, even Winter Courts. You will have to complete each task within the cycle of the moon. If you fail or if you are too late, they will kill you. They will kill me too." Ravven grimaces. "A death sentence for a faerie is not a pretty thing. They torture them, and the faeries unable to die are healed by their magic only to endure the pain all over again. Until finally, to end the eternity of suffering—and believe me, it can last hundreds of years—they finally reveal either their name or their item of immortality."

I swallow hard and nod. Okay, so maybe difficult doesn't cover this. My stomach churns at the thought of what could happen to not just me, but also Ravven if I fail. Am I really so selfish to drag him into this? "Why are you helping me then?"

Ravven smiles a cruel, biting smile. "I don't have much of a choice. Death by betraying a blood bargain is just as painful a fate. So, while you were... eh, unconsciously succumbed to human weaknesses, I called a gathering of the faeries and we must leave for the Court of Dreams and Nightmares soon."

I stare at him, my mouth gaping. He knew all along that I would agree to this? Then again... it's not like either of us have any choice. I have to save Thomas and his blood bargain probably compelled him to do it.

I nod and run my hand through my hair. The strands hang limply around my shoulders, the ice having all melted away while I was unconscious. I find several leaves nestled in the tousles. "Okay, so we have to go to this Court of Dreams and Nightmares, then. What the heck even is the Court of Dreams and Nightmares?" I've never heard of another court. And why does it have to be named the Court of Dreams and *Nightmares?* Is the name Court of Dreams not catchy enough? If so, then why couldn't it have been called the Court of Dreams and Unicorns? No. I suppress a shudder. Not unicorns. Puppies maybe?

Ravven takes one look at me and sighs, throwing his eyes to the sky. "Stars above have mercy on me because you certainly will not."

"You said there are only five courts. I only know of five courts. I don't really see how this Court of Dreams and Nightmares fits into this. I mean, I'm bad at math, but I'm not that bad."

Ravven heaves a heavy breath and picks an invisible thread from his shoulder which he flicks away. "There are only five living courts. The Court of Dreams and Nightmares is nothing more than a shadow of a court."

I swallow hard and try not to shiver. "A shadow—how does something become a shadow of a court?"

"When it is no longer used," Ravven says, looking at me. "The Court of Dreams and Nightmares was the first court of the faeries. Back when there was only one court and only one queen and all the faeries were united."

I blink, staring at him, trying to make sense of the words that came out of his mouth. "The Otherworld wasn't always divided into five courts?"

"It hasn't been so for centuries. It started with the Tuatha De Danan breaking away, deciding that they would rather rule than be ruled. Then one by one all of the other courts followed suit. They dethroned the queen and the world was broken into five pieces. Shortly after that was the war because apparently without someone there to make certain that they got along... faeries do not get along.

"Since then the Court of Dreams and Nightmares has sat abandoned in the Forest of the Night, what was once the heart of the Otherworld. As a neutral court it was used as a meeting place for the faeries of the different courts to speak to each other when needed. Naturally there were not many reasons for individuals that hated each other to wish to speak to each other so it's not used very often. But any such rites such as the challenges given to a contender for the Blade of Gold and Iron would take place there."

I take a deep breath and release it slowly. I didn't get half of that but quite frankly I'm scared to ask again. Ravven already thinks I'm an idiot. Best not to give him any more reasons to. "So that is where we must go," I say quietly, wishing that he will shake his head and say no, that we will be heading to the Court of Daydreams and Butterflies which is situated in the Forest of Light.

But Ravven simply smiles in his disconcerting manner that makes it seem like he is enjoying all of this despite how many times he stated that this was a horrible idea and it would probably end with us both dead and says, "Precisely."

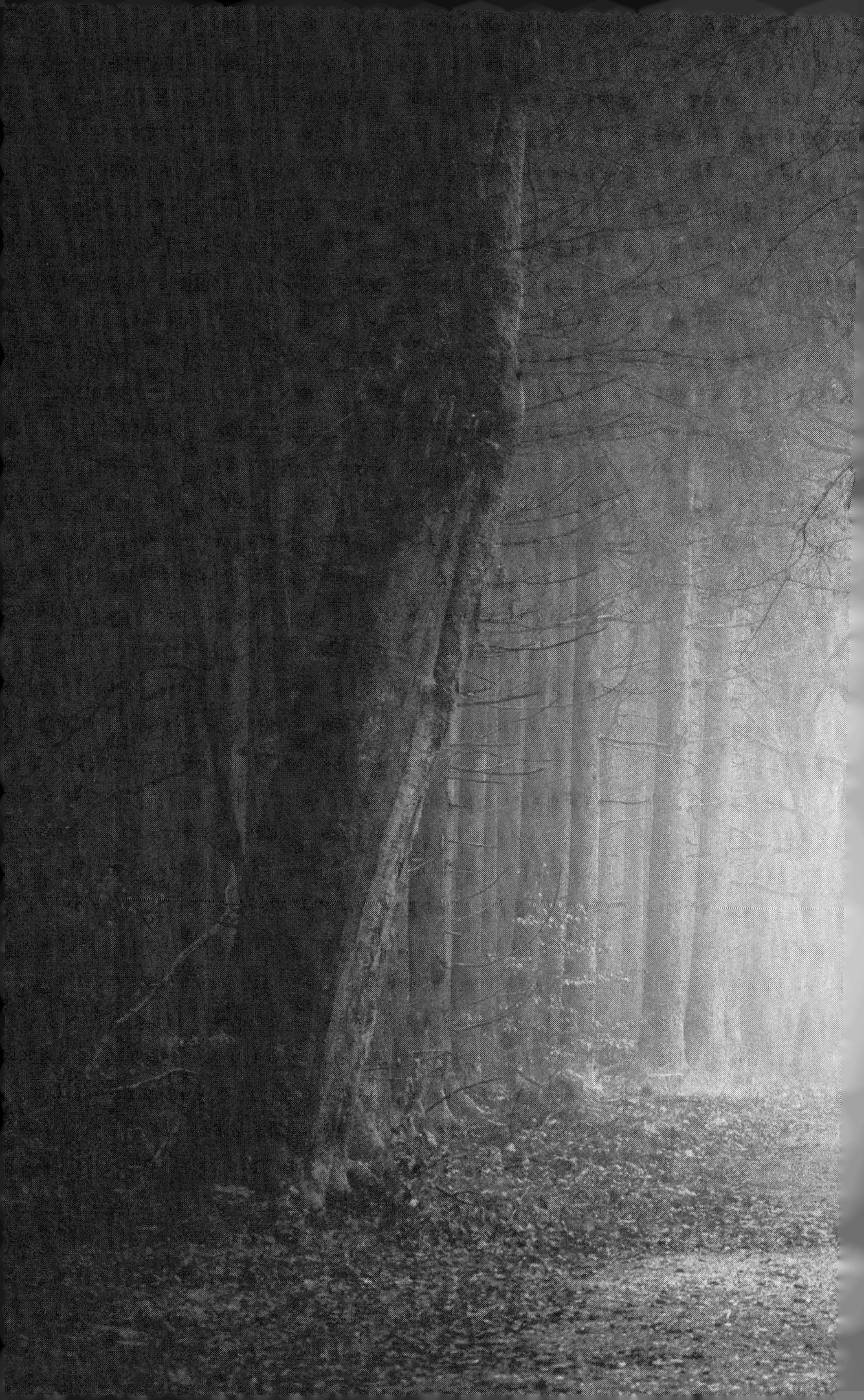

CHAPTER NINETEEN

I try to fight back my panic. So, I made a dangerous bargain with a faerie? No biggie. Sure, I'm actually planning on trying to become the faerie's special assassin. And yeah, they'll probably put me through a series of dangerous tasks in order to become that assassin. And I'll probably end up assassinated if I succeed. But right now, I'm not even sure if I will make it past all the faerie tests. Historically speaking, I have not had the best of luck since entering the faerie world. No matter how hard I try it's just one bad thing happening after another. Boom, boom, boom.

I'm going to have to figure out how exactly to come out on top, even over Ravven, who undoubtedly has his own reasons for helping me become the Fair Assassin. Faeries are exactly like their glamours, you never know just what you're looking at until it's too late and you're tumbling off a cliff that had looked like a meadow.

But as long as Ravven proves useful, I will use him.

And then I will kill Aoibheann and save my brother.

As soon as I stop feeling like I'm going to throw up.

Ravven clears his throat behind me and I turn with an arch of my brow. It takes everything in me to keep my expression schooled. Calm and in control. That's what I need Ravven to think I am.

Who am I kidding? Ravven thinks I'm a decaying corpse. No other front necessary.

"We should begin our journey to the Court of Dreams and Nightmares if we wish to make it to the Forest of Night and be already prepared when the other courts arrive. It's considered ill form to call all of the faeries and then arrive late."

"Right, yeah, I suppose it would be. So where is it?" I turn in a circle as if half expecting some sort of yellow brick road to appear to lead me to this shadow of a court.

Ravven rubs his jaw. "It sits in the center of the Otherworld, but in order to get to it..." he pauses and shakes his head. "Dragging a mortal along would take too long. Not to mention you would probably die at least six times in the journey."

I cross my arms. "I can only die once."

Ravven arches his brow. "Can you? Well, that is inconvenient."

Oh yes, terribly. Another point against me being a mortal. "And what? Faeries can die multiple times?"

"A faerie does not die," Ravven says stiffly, "not like you mortals do, dropping to the ground like snowflakes. I had hoped that since you are so expendable that you were allowed a second or third chance to try to escape death after it claims you."

"No such luck."

"Hmm." I don't like the way Ravven is looking at me again. Like I'm about to drop dead.

I clear my throat and resist the urge to tell him that I am feeling perfectly healthy. Actually, I am a tad light headed but I'm sure that's nothing. "You were trying to make a point earlier. How are we going to get to this Court of Dreams and Nightmares then?"

"I do not think that you will like my suggestion."

I stiffen. I'm really not liking how he keeps saying that I'm not going to like things. "What is it?"

Ravven's mouth twists into a wry line. "I *could* teleport you there with my magic, but for a frail mortal such as you it would probably be an overwhelming experience."

My stomach drops at the thought of traveling across space in the blink of an eye again. I rub at my temple, trying to drive back the headache that is threatening to rear its ugly head. "Is there no other way to get there? How did we get from the Winter Court to here?"

"Teleportation, but you were rather paralyzed."

I release a heavy sigh. "If I survived it once I suppose I can survive it again."

"We can only hope. You dying at this moment would be terribly inconvenient." There's something in his voice. Something foreign. Concern? Probably for himself.

I snort. If I survive any of this it would be a miracle but I don't bother saying that. Why would Ravven care anyway, I am just a decaying corpse.

But then I wonder, would traveling this way a certain number of times kill me and if so, how many times can I safely travel without dropping dead?

Oh gosh, Ravven is right, we humans are fragile creatures, always having to wonder if the next second will be our last. What would it be like to be a faerie, almost invulnerable, immortal, never having to worry where their next breath will come from? But then I shake my head. I know what it would be like. It would be twisted, unfeeling, lonely. Living forever as such a flawed creature is unnatural. The faeries are unnatural. And even as fragile as I am as a human, I am one hundred times better off mortal than immortal.

I swallow hard and look up to see that Ravven is staring at me. It's unsettling the way that he looks at me now. Like he can't pull his eyes away, even though I still see the distaste in his eyes as he looks at me. I shrug and glance away wishing that he would stop. "Are we going or not?"

Ravven swallows and holds up his hand. I stare at it as if it is some sort of viper about to pounce. He flexes his fingers. "It may be easier for both of us if we are holding hands."

I hesitantly slide my hand against his warm palm and try to ignore the fact that our skin is touching. He's only a faerie, nothing special. Nothing to warrant the way my pulse is picking up. I tell myself it's panic. It's definitely panic. "Really?"

"I don't actually know," he says with a smirk. "But in the name of you not dying, it's worth a try."

I glare at him and open my mouth to snap at him, but then he tightens his fingers around mine which totally distracts me. Then my feet have been yanked out from underneath me and I'm falling, even though I'm still standing upright. My head pounds as the blurring of the bronze and orange of the Autumn Court fades from view into dark stone.

Ravven releases my hand as the world clears around me. I stumble to the side across the smooth flagstones, tottering like I'm intoxicated even though I'm certain that the faerie fruits are out of my system by now. My tongue feels like a ball of wool and the contents of my stomach are doing a dance I'm going to dub the *slosh and turn*.

I nearly careen into the wall, but then warm hands land on my shoulders and steady me.

"Did I kill you?" Ravven demands, his voice high and slightly laced with panic. I would laugh if my head didn't still feel like it was going to implode. I shake it slightly, as much as I can manage.

"No," I croak as the ground bucks underneath me. "I just need to sit down." I slump down as Ravven holds me steady enough that I don't collapse completely.

The cool stone soaks through my shoulder blades as I lean back against the wall and draw in several deep breaths. I squeeze my eyes shut until the dizziness and vertigo finally pass.

When I crack them open, Ravven is sitting on his heels across from me, watching me with an anxious expression. It's somewhat amusing now that I'm no longer feeling like I'm going to throw up all over him. Perhaps next time he will think twice before he makes a blood bargain with a "frail" human.

I groan as I push to my feet. I don't have time to sit here recovering, not when Thomas needs me.

Ravven lunges across the short distance between us, holding out his hands as if to catch me, but I'm not going to fall. "I'm fine," I say, brushing his hands away.

His eyes travel up and down me before returning to my face. He arches his brows. I wonder how terrible I look. "Are you certain that you're not going to die?" Ravven asks, his voice a deep rumble.

I breathe deeply through my nose, trying to calm my stomach which is still sloshing slightly, but only manage to inhale his scent. He smells like sunlight and fresh air. How can a person even smell like sunlight and fresh air? I guess I already know the answer to that. Ravven is a faerie; he is not a person. "Someday I might. But I think we are safe for now." I pat his shoulder and try not to look into his eyes as they soften from a faint red into a darker purple.

Unfortunately, no matter where I rest my eyes, I feel a shuddering ache in my heart. His lips are definitely the least safe place I could ever look because the second I catch sight of them, my mind fills with dangerous notions. But his high perfectly sculpted cheekbones or dangerously quirked dark eyebrows are no respite. Not even his forehead is safe, with a soft dark curl sweeping over it in a carefree manner. I clench my fingers to resist the urge to touch the curl and find out what his hair feels like. Does faerie hair feel the same as human hair? This is a question that I never had the need to ask before.

What is wrong with me?

I decide that his right earlobe is the only moderately safe place to look.

He really is gloriously handsome, isn't he?

He's also a faerie and I will not be swayed by glamours and illusions and lies thinly veiled in the truth.

As if reading my thoughts, Ravven quickly pulls away with a grimace. "You really are quite ugly are you not?" he says and my heart drops. Yes, of course, I can't believe I forgot his views of physical appearance.

He reaches a hand up, and I startle when his fingertips touch my cheek. They trail down to my chin as his eyes move across my face, as if he is trying to assure himself that my face is truly shaped the way it is. He could have saved himself the trouble and my heart the pain and just asked. Because it is. "Truly abominable," he mutters under his breath.

I step away, smacking my back into the wall and swat his hand away. "Then stop looking," I hiss. Seriously, what is his problem? Is he a sadist? Does he truly gain pleasure from causing me pain? I know that's a ridiculous question, he's a faerie. Odds are very, very high that he's a sadist just like the rest of his entire stupid race.

The true question should be, since when did I give Ravven the power to hurt me? His insults didn't use to hurt like this.

He is a faerie. *Of course,* he's going to hurt me if I give him the ability to do so. He won't even care when he does. He'll probably just find it amusing.

I cross my arms and scowl at him. "I apologize that I don't have the time nor the wish to wear a paper bag over my head, but maybe you might save yourself some unnecessary pain by not following my every movement with your eyes!"

And save me the unnecessary pain too.

Ravven stiffens with a scoff. "I most certainly do not follow your every movement with my eyes. How vain of you to assume such a thing."

I breathe deeply, regretting not having my dagger because it sure would be great to carve him up right now.

Ravven presses his lips together in displeasure, as if he knows what I'm thinking. Why is it that he keeps seeming to know exactly what I'm thinking, even so far as saying things eerily similar to what I thought? I frown as this thought comes over me. Am I actually saying these things out loud, is Ravven able to read minds, or am I just paranoid? Since two out of those three things would be very bad and might threaten to kill me with embarrassment, I sincerely hope that I'm just paranoid.

He quickly pulls his gaze away and begins walking further into the dark hall. "It cannot be too long before the other faeries arrive. Come, let me take you to your chambers. You should probably situate your appearances or whatever it is you humans do to hide the fact that you are decaying corpses."

I hurry to catch up with his long strides, as my eyes attempt to burn holes into the back of his head. "You know very well that the second I entered this world, I ceased aging." I ceased *changing*. It's weird to think that I could be in here for a hundred years and not grow a single gray hair. There are still a lot of ways I could die, but at least here, old age is not one of them.

Ravven's steps falter slightly. "I am well aware of that fact," he says tersely. Then he begins walking even faster than before, the coat tails of his ankle length coat flapping behind him.

I have to practically jog to keep up with him which leaves no room for conversation. Which is just as well because I don't see why I would want to converse with this pompous, cruel fae that I have allied myself with. He'd only have more ways to insult my race, my intelligence, and the way I look.

I wish that I had more ways of insulting him, but unfortunately other than being rude and arrogant he doesn't seem like the rest of his race, actually taking the time to help a human—even if I'm still not entirely sure that it isn't for his own gain. It would be a blatant lie to say anything bad against his looks. And even if I am capable of lying, I'm not sure if even I could lie that well. Not that he would believe me if I did. He seems to be quite the admirer of himself.

I shove my hurt away and bury it six feet underground. There, now I shouldn't care about what Ravven says. Unless my feelings become a zombie, but there's nothing much I can do about it then.

"So, this is the Court of Dreams and Nightmares?" I ask as Ravven leads me up a circular staircase. The walls and floors of the castle are a smooth gray and all perfectly uniform. They almost glow with translucence. They have dark veins interlaced within them that seem to steal the very light from the room.

The effect of these both fills me with calmness and joy and then immediately afterward, robs me of it, filling me with a deep dread instead.

"Yes," he replies simply. He climbs the stairs far faster than I can easily keep up and I find myself having to skip every other step as I practically fling myself up the stairs to catch up. I'm embarrassed to say that I am breathing hard before we're even halfway up. I stay near the wall because there is no side or railing on the other side, instead there is a black pit that leads back down the stairs. You know, for those who wish to get down the stairs the quick way and will have no concern for their physical safety.

The whole staircase is somewhat eerily lit, with certain portions thrown into dark shadows, though I'm not entirely sure where any of the light is coming from since there aren't any candles or lanterns or chandeliers in sight. Surely the faint glow from the stone wall isn't illuminating the whole room.

Finally, Ravven reaches the top of the staircase. We must be in some sort of tower because I can't fathom how any other portion of the castle could be up so high. I slump against the wall, breathing hard, and risk a glance down the stairs. The view gives me vertigo and I quickly turn back to Ravven and the room at the top of the staircase.

It's like a complete transformation has come over the castle. Gone are the smooth stone walls and floor, or perhaps they aren't gone, but instead are covered. A thick brown rug that resembles dead grass in many ways lies at our feet, and red and gold tapestries showing designs of leaves blowing in the wind cover the walls. Flickering gold and red fires light the room from candles, hanging from the ceiling and supported by golden leaf-shaped holders.

My mouth drops open and Ravven looks back at me, an amused smile on his face. "Welcome to the Autumn Court's wing. Each court has a portion of the castle dedicated to them when the faeries come to stay here."

"Wow," is what I say in reply.

Ravven shakes his head and turns and strides farther into the room to where a series of large ebony doors are situated and opens one.

Perhaps we are not at the top of a tower after all because the rooms sprawl out and there is far more space than if we were in the small confines of a tower.

Ravven steps aside to reveal a room that's decor seems to be a combination of the hallway and stairwell and of the Autumn Court. No tapestries line the wall, in their place are large pillars protruding from it made of a rich brown wood and embellished with gold. At the top, they had gold leaves pouring down and on the leaves stood tiny burning candles, giving the room a soft glow. The only perceivable carpet are spots of leaf shaped fabric covering the floor as if I were outside and they had drifted down there from the wood and gold trees however when I nudged at them with my foot, they did not move, despite the fact that they appeared to have been simply scattered there. The wall and floors visible appear to be the same as that glowing marble outside the Autumn wing.

The wooden pillars and their flaring golden leaves give the room the appearance of being filled, despite the very small amount of furniture actually in the room. Sitting along one wall is what appears to be a bed, draped under a scarlet canopy. Near it is a large wooden wardrobe made from the same wood of the pillars, engraved across its majestic doors is a pattern of leaves. That's it.

The wall across the door consists of a giant balcony made of pale marble. My eyes stray outside, but it is dark out—the only light coming from the giant moon in the sky. It had been day when we were still in the Autumn Court. I don't know how it could have come to be night so suddenly. When Ravven had transported me before, it had seemed instantaneous without any time having passed.

Ravven walks past me as I stand there contemplating this. He opens the doors to the wardrobe to reveal dresses, dozens of them in all sorts of colors. I frown and pull out a dress, only to find it exactly my length despite being in a world of overly tall faeries.

I look back up to all of the dresses and suddenly have to wonder why Ravven has so many dresses that are easily accessible. And appear to be my size.

I pull up the sleeve. "Where did these come from?"

Ravven tilts his head, looking taken aback. "How silly of you to ask such a thing."

I swallow and nod. Of course, I should cease to be awed and surprised by this faerie world, despite the fact that it runs on a substance that is almost completely nonexistent in my world. "Magic," I whisper. Iorwerth had said as much about the dresses in the Winter Court.

I am answered by only Ravven's chuckle.

I look back over my shoulder to see him striding toward the door. He pauses and looks back at me. "Be certain to ready yourself. The other faeries will arrive soon. Tonight, you will be presented to the courts."

And with those words and a swish of his coat, I am left alone with only my enchanted dresses and whirling thoughts for company.

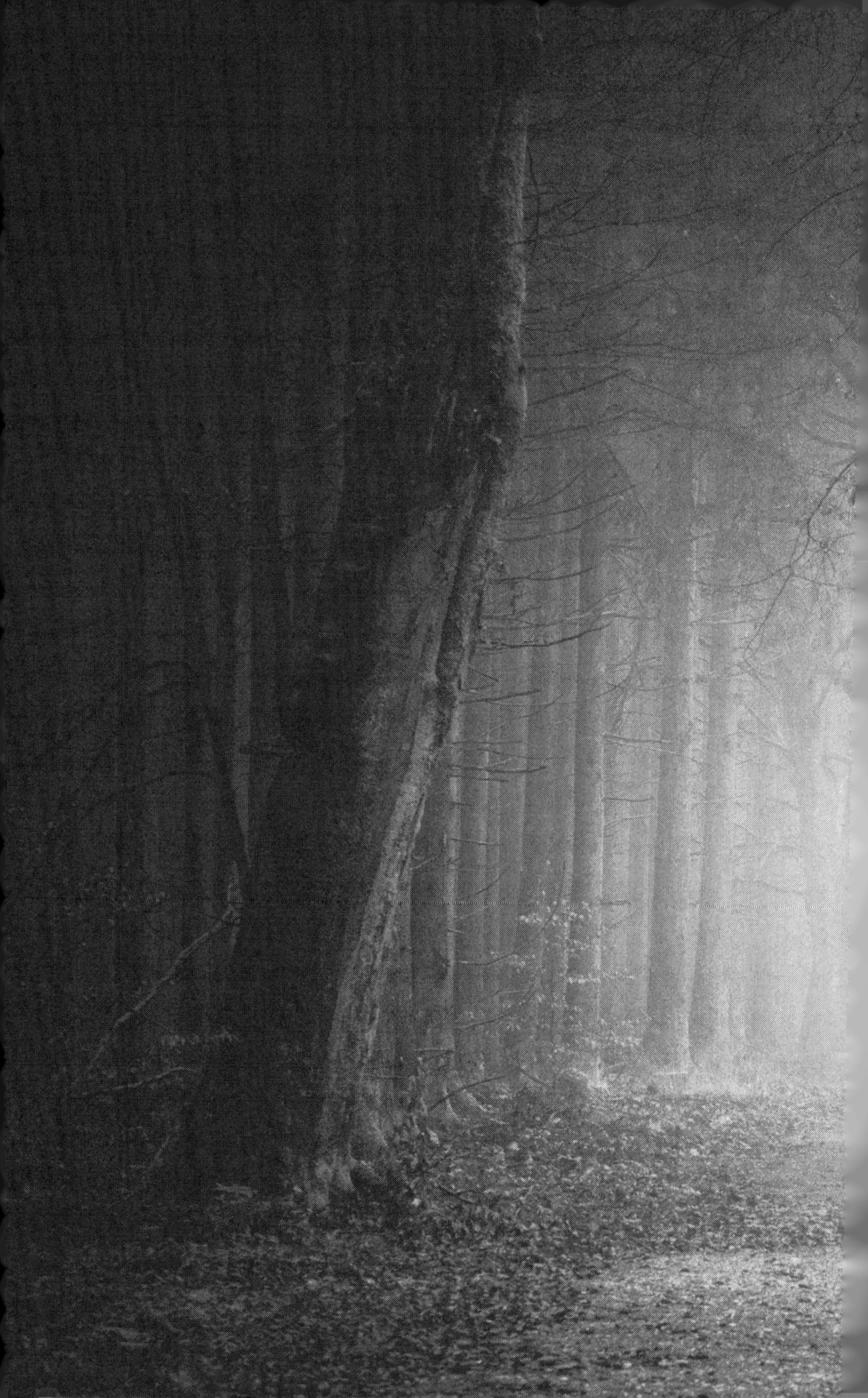

CHAPTER TWENTY

I find that staring at the gently glowing moon above my head calms me. Considering that I'm freaking out over half a dozen things, the least of my worries is wondering if the pale pink dress with sleeves made of precious gems interlocked together is appropriate for when one is presented to five courts of faeries.

I stare at the moon until my eyes blur and try my best not to panic.

"What exactly are you doing?"

I startle as I turn to find Ravven leaning against the pillar right outside the large open balcony doors.

He no longer looks like an Autumn prince. Instead he's wearing a black tunic as if he is trying to match the night itself. As he steps toward me, the moonlight reflects off of it turning it to a shade of deep purple. Then it's black again and I'm blinking. Can faerie clothes ever be just fabric and thread? As if faeries aren't beautiful enough without wearing enchanting, dazzling clothing.

Ravven looks me over, a small smile hinting at the corner of his mouth. "Congratulations. You look almost passable."

"Uh..." was that a compliment or a backhanded insult? Knowing faeries, I would say that it was probably a complimentary backhanded insult, but still. Coming from Ravven though this must be high praise considering his first words to me were to lament how utterly hideous I am. "Thank you?"

He chuckles and strides forward. "There is no need to sound so uncertain."

I look back up at the moon. Isn't there? Even if he's a faerie and incapable of lying, I still have to question everything he says to make certain that he is not deceiving me with carefully concealed truths. And even if he is a faerie, I still have to feel an irritating and very, very dangerous tug of attraction toward him. I need to cut that tie, but I don't know how. I think only distance from his almost intoxicating looks and unfortunately endearing childlike innocence can cure me now. When I am back home, I will laugh over the fool that I was.

But for now, I'm just happy to have him standing here with me. And why shouldn't I be? At least I have an ally in all of this. And I think... well, I know how dangerous this sounds. But I think Ravven is a good ally. Perhaps even a good person who just tries really hard to hide it. I haven't forgotten that he is a faerie, but thinking back to everything that has happened and even I can't deny how much he has aided me. I doubt I would be alive at this point if it weren't for him. It may be stretching it to say that he cares about me, but he certainly had more than one opportunity to step back and just let me die but he did not.

If I had to have my life in someone's hands, I suppose I could do far worse.

He closes the distance between us, that half smile still on his lips, and looks me over. "I suppose I could have done worse when it came to choosing a human ally," he says, causing my heart to race as I reconsider my thoughts from earlier of how he might be a mind reader.

His dark gaze flickers to the silent trees beyond me, finally releasing me from their clutches. I breathe in relief and then immediately chastise myself. I *need* to get myself under control. Things will end very badly for me if I do not. My heart will be broken, and I'm not entirely sure that Ravven won't succeed in breaking the rest of me if I give him the power to do so. He is still a faerie no matter what happens.

"You never told me what it was you were doing," he murmurs, his voice soft and silky.

"I was looking at the moon," I answer and then frown because it's a bit of a weird thing to say. But Ravven doesn't mock me, instead he leans over the railing of the balcony, his arm lightly brushing mine. I jerk away like his touch is fire and I am very, very dry wood. His smile widens in some sort of sick enjoyment from my discomfort, but then he turns his gaze up at the moon.

"Highmoon is almost past," he says softly to himself.

I turn to him. "Highmoon?"

Ravven stares another long moment at the moon before turning to me. "Yes, Highmoon. In the Forest of Night, the sun never rises. Instead day and night are determined by the moon's position in the sky." He raises his hand. "Highmoon." He drops his hand. "And Nethermoon."

"Oh," I say because I don't know what else *to* say. "Okay."

Ravven straightens and adjusts his dark tunic. "The other courts are gathering now." His lips pressed together in a hard line and for once he doesn't look like he knows everything and that the world is his plaything. For once he looks just as lost as I always feel. "Are you certain that you are ready for this?"

I laugh nervously, unsettled by his grim expression. "What if I am not?"

He shrugs. "Then we will probably die."

I swallow hard. "Oh, well, when you put it that way, I guess I am ready after all."

Ravven's face is still unsure as he holds out his hand to me. I stare at it for a long moment before I realize that he wants me to take it. I slide my palm against his, marveling at the smooth flesh. There's not a callus on his hand. It isn't rough at all, but instead is as smooth as a flower's petal. A faerie's hand.

Ravven wraps his fingers around mine and gives them such a small, almost imperceptible squeeze that I almost think I imagined it.

"You already know not to trust the Winter Court," he says as he holds our hands up between us at my shoulder level and leads me off of the balcony and into my room. I frown at the odd positioning of our hands, but then decide that it must be the faerie version of placing a hand in the crook of an arm. "But avoid the Spring Court as well, as if your life depends upon it, because it most likely will. The Summer and Undersea Courts should hold you no ill intent, but they are not your friends."

"Okay, got it. Trust nobody. And here I was going to dance with every faerie I met and eat any food offered by them and make blood bargains with them all."

Ravven turns to me, a startled, horrified expression on his face.

I can't help but laugh. "I'm kidding!"

Ravven shakes his head, not looking amused in the least. "Don't do that."

"Don't do what?" I ask, frowning.

"Don't joke about such matters."

Well sheesh, some of us need humor to help get through the stress.

He leads me out of the room and back into the main chamber of the rooms for the Autumn Court.

I am surprised when I see two other faeries are there, both wearing scarlet coats. The first is Keane, Ravven's father, and the second is that Fear Gorta, Daithi. They both look almost comedic, Keane with his shock of black unruly hair and his lined face and Daithi as emancipated as ever, every bone protruding from his skin as if there is nothing between them.

Neither of them speaks as we enter, though Keane harrumphs.

Keane perhaps I would expect to see here since Ravven is his son, despite how much he grouses about it. But I am utterly stunned to see Daithi. Why is he still here? He already paid his debt with Thomas, didn't he?

"What are they doing here?" I demand.

Ravven glances at the other faeries for a second before turning away like it isn't strange at all that they are there. "The same as any of the faeries, I imagine. They are here to see whether you succeed and become the next Fair Assassin or whether you are going to die a horrible death. Of course, they are the only ones who know that is the true reason for why they are here. The rest of the faeries just know that I have called them, though they will learn soon enough."

I swallow hard as he leads me to a door, past the stairs that we climbed up. The door leads out into a hallway, made entirely of the glowing black and white marble and gold. It's so magnificent that it makes my eyes hurt, and I almost forget about the churning in my gut until we step into a large ornate room. The most spectacular thing about this room is the people—or should I say faeries? So many of them, some beautiful, some terrible, fill the room. I can't even begin to guess what all of their types or courts are.

A part of me wants to take a long moment to geek out over this. I have always been somewhat fascinated by the faeries. But I am the type of person who likes to learn about deadly races from a distance. And this is far too close for comfort.

The center of the room is empty save for five thrones, sitting around a circular marking in the ground. Three of the thrones have an inhabitant sitting on them.

The thrones all appear to be made of different material. As Ravven strides toward the center of the room, with the other faeries parting like water before us, I recognize the Winter Queen sitting on a throne made entirely of ice. It can't be the most comfortable seat, but Cliodnha doesn't show it. I don't spot Riagan, Iorwerth, or Aoibheann standing around her throne where they usually do. Though many of the other thrones do have people standing next to them.

A woman sits on the throne to the far left. She has stunning blue hair, looking at it is like gazing into the Caribbean Ocean. Her skin is a paler, murkier blue, and both her lips and her odd, non-human eyes are brilliant green, matching the shimmering dress she is wearing. Scales trail up her neck and her forearms. Her fingers are webbed.

Her throne appears to be made of seashells and coral.

If I had to wager a guess, I would say that she was the queen of the Undersea Court. A grim faced, dark-haired faerie stands behind her. He is also wearing shimmering green clothes, but doesn't look half so otherworldly or like he just dragged himself out of some lagoon.

The next throne is empty. It is made of petals and intertwining brambles. A faerie stands behind it. He has glowing blonde hair that descends to his shoulders, framing his angular face, and is wearing an outfit of deep purple. His blonde hair and perfect features can mean only one thing. He must be a Sidhe faerie and thus a member of the Spring Court. He clenches his jaws when he sees us, a look of utter hate crossing his face.

It causes my insides to fill with chills. He doesn't even know me and already he hates me. I decide that I don't like him. And not just because I dislike Sidhe faeries on principle.

The next throne, and possibly the largest is made of a blanket of lush grass and moss with flowers rising up from it. The man sitting on it has a haughty expression and a sharp hooked nose. His hair is the cross between white and blonde and hangs in straight sheets all the way to his waist. There is something commanding about his expression that I did not see on the other ruler's faces except for the Winter Queen. He must be the Summer King.

Just to its right is the Winter Queen's throne. It's slightly smaller than the Summer King's and she does not look happy about it.

The smallest throne is completely empty with no one standing around it at all. It is made of antler horns with a scarlet seat and toadstools growing out of the bottom. It must be for the Autumn Court—except the Autumn Court has no leader.

I wonder what the other courts think of the faeries of the Autumn Court and their complete lack of ambition, choosing instead to live a solitary life, but I catch the Undersea Queen looking at it and smirking with contempt.

As we reach the edge of the empty circle, Ravven releases my hand and whispers, "Do be a good little pest and stay here and don't get into any trouble." He strides forward toward the five thrones and their varied occupants, ignoring the holes I am glaring into the back of his shimmering tunic. I force myself to remain still even though I feel open and exposed surrounded by all of these faeries without Ravven to protect me.

I remind myself that Ravven is just as dangerous as all of the other faeries, though now that I've seen so many others of his kind, that thought falls flat. Because the fact of the matter is that I actually feel *safe* around Ravven. I know that I can't trust him, but I can't seem to change the fact that I can relax around him.

Ravven steps onto the circle in the center of the floor and it rises up into the air with a rumbling groan. Antlers dotted with flowers extend from the empty pit in the ground where the circle had been before, pushing the platform up higher until I'm sure that everyone in the room can see it.

"Ravven Crowe," the Summer King says and as he speaks, it is as if his words lend warmth to the room. "Tell me, what is the reason that you have summoned all of the courts together in this way. Do you have an announcement to make?" The Summer King looks pointedly to the blonde faerie standing behind the Spring Throne.

The Sidhe smiles mockingly. "Yes, Ravven, do you have an announcement to make?"

The Winter Queen stiffens and though she doesn't look at me, I can feel her attention trained on me all the same. I wonder if Iorwerth and Aoibheann and even Thomas are here and what they are thinking. I can't even hazard a guess except that Thomas is probably calling me every word for idiot right now.

Ravven smiles a brief, mocking smile. "Indeed, I do have an announcement to make. But I fear that your Majesties will not like it."

"I dislike the very breath you breathe," the Sidhe says with a yawn.

Ravven shoots him a withering look. "I was not addressing you, Cinaed, since you are no ruler."

The Sidhe, who must be Cinaed, withdraws, a snarl almost marring his perfect features. Almost.

"Get on with it, Crowe," the Undersea Queen says, sounding bored. "I wish to return to my lands. This palace is too dry for my tastes. How you can all stand to remain up here at the mercy of the bitter wind, I cannot fathom."

Ravven looks at her and smiles indulgently. "Very well, my lady. Then I shall say what I came here to say. I, Ravven Crowe, in the name of the Autumn Court, bring forth a human champion, ready for the trials of the Fair Law in order to attain the right to be called the Fair Assassin and wield the Blade of Gold and Iron."

The Winter Queen looks at me, her face as expressionless as her empty eyes, the only sign that she sees me and recognizes me is the slight pursing of her pale blue lips.

I swallow hard as a shiver races up my arms—it feels like I'm being pierced by a thousand tiny icicles. The handprint on my arm throbs.

"I see," the Summer King says. "And does anyone from the Autumn Court wish to challenge this faerie's claim that their court will bring a human contender forward?"

The room fills with a rumble of voices and the shifting of fabric. I glance around, as it seems that many of the other faeries are doing the same, and notice that Keane and Daithi are standing right behind me.

"What would happen if someone were to challenge Ravven?" I whisper.

"Oh, then the two would have to duel over which claim should be heard. The faerie remaining standing is the one who wins. Unfortunately, the loser then has to give up their true name so that they can be commanded to destroy themselves. It is the way that duels to the death work here, as according to the Fair Law."

I gasp slightly and look at Ravven standing in the center of the room atop those antler stairs. "A duel to the death?"

Keane chuckles humorlessly. "I wouldn't concern myself over it. Only the Autumn Court can challenge him right now since it is in their name he is proceeding. And in order for any member of the Autumn Court to challenge him, they must first be in attendance."

I frown, wondering at his words until I scan the room. I see faeries dressed in pinks and greens and golds and blues of every color, but none in the customary red color of the Solitary faeries that make up the Autumn Court. It appears that the only faeries from the Autumn Court in attendance are Ravven and Keane and Daithi. It looks like not a single other Solitary faerie even bothered to attend.

As the silence continues to grow, Ravven turns to us and raises his eyebrows, I don't know how a being could ever look more arrogant than he does now as the Summer King releases a breath that is like a warm breeze. "Then according to the Fair Law, the other courts accept the challenger."

At those words, every eye in the chamber turns to me. I try not to think about what Ravven and I just did, but that proves useless as Keane leans closer to me. "Well, now you have what you want. You will either become the next Fair Assassin or you will die trying. Congratulations. Try not to kill my son in the process, will you?"

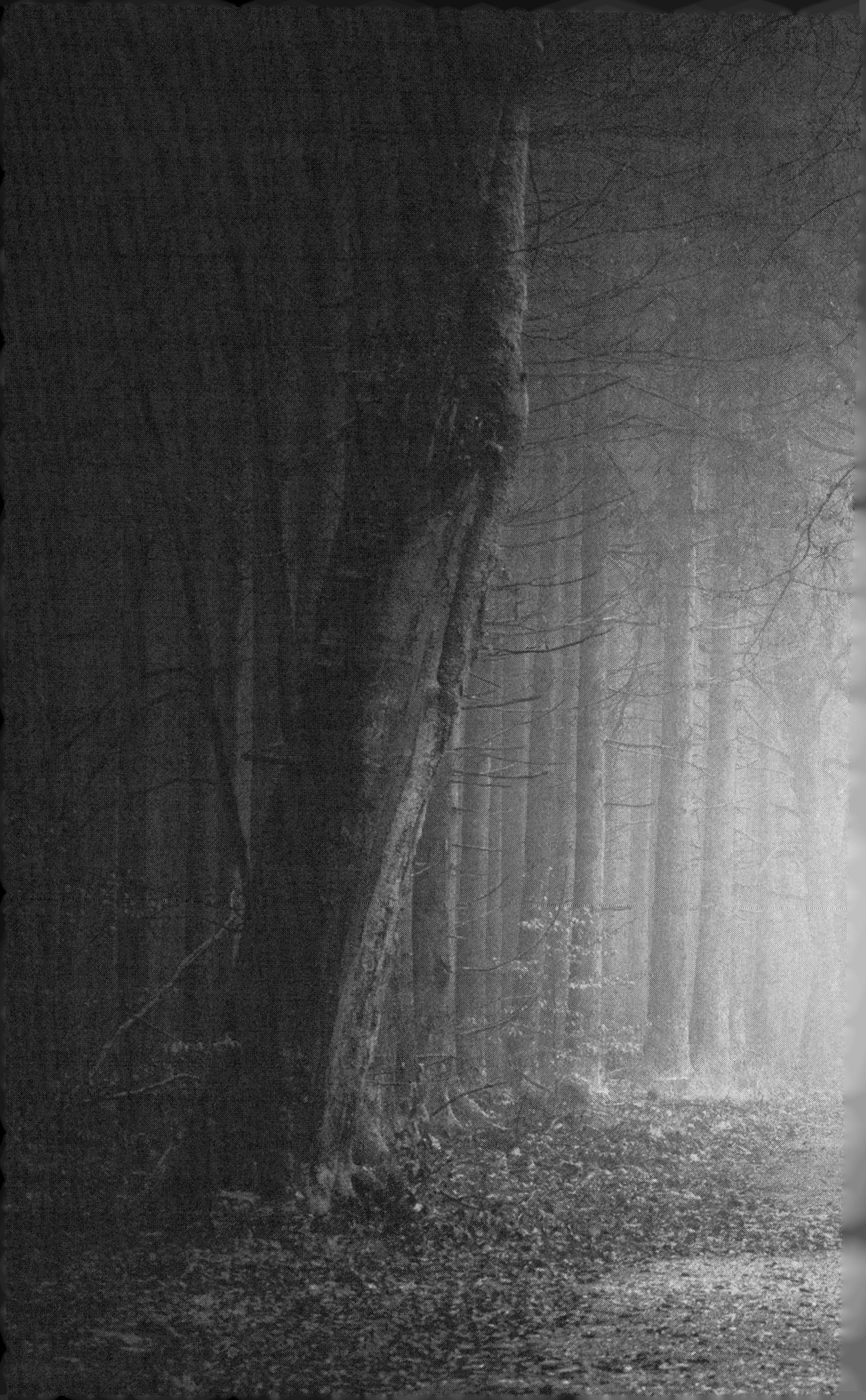

CHAPTER TWENTY-ONE

I want nothing more than to sneak off to my room to have a proper panic attack, but it appears that the faeries have other plans for me. As soon as the announcement is made, music echoes down from the chambers and goblets begin floating through the room. Like just floating there like ghosts are toasting us. Some faeries begin dancing, but most crowd around me. Wanting to touch my hair or my skin or wanting to know my name and everything there is to know about this newest trinket of their world.

When I look around, I see no kindness or gentleness or hope in their expressions. Not even fear. No, only curiosity. Only excitement. Only a ravenous hunger.

I get the feeling that they want to know me now while I'm still alive, so a thousand years from now they can still boast of having known the contender for the role of Fair Assassin who died in the most gruesome way possible. Which is probably the reason that many ask for a strand of my hair as a trinket, something that I refuse. One even asked for a fingernail.

"It's a pity she won't last long," one says to their companion as they leave. "I would dearly love the excuse to remain in the court longer. This place is so much bigger than my measly rath under the hill."

The other faerie sighs. "Yes, such grand balls are thrown every night when the courts are in attendance of the Court of Dreams and Nightmares. My queen rarely holds such grand events at the Winter Court."

I just came from a grand event at the Winter Court and I have not the slightest wish to ever go through that again.

Then they are gone and another wave of curious faces and pinching fingers fills my world.

I think I'm going to go mad and I'm wondering where Ravven and Keane and Daithi disappeared to—probably somewhere secluded, curse the Solitary fae for leaving me—when suddenly a hand is grasping mine and pulling me away. I look up surprised to see the faeries stepping back with disappointed looks on their faces but stepping back all the same. Stunned, I whip my gaze around to the girl who is pulling me away. She's about my height, which is something odd to see in this world of tall majestic faeries and she has long curly red hair that puts my hair to shame for even considering being strawberry blonde because of the vibrancy of the colors.

She pulls me into a small alcove at the end and turns to me with an easy smile. "Ach, I thought maybe they were going to crush ye if I didn't get ye out of there."

I smile in turn, though it feels uncertain, and run my hand over my skirt. Why on earth should she care? Not that we are on Earth anymore. "Thank you."

I study her more closely; she has bright green eyes and a somewhat pale complexion. Freckles cover her face. She's wearing a dark blue top and skirt that splits down the middle to reveal pants and sturdy boots underneath. A sword hangs at her belt, clanging into the wall as she leans against it, crossing her arms nonchalantly though her eyes scan the room alertly.

She's young. I don't know what about that surprises me considering all of the faeries, with the exception of the Solitary ones who don't seem to care how they look, are all young looking. I suppose it's one of the perks of immortality. But there's something about her that seems younger than them. The faerie's youth is ageless, I couldn't even begin to try to place their age only that they are young. This girl, though, only appears to be fourteen or fifteen.

Just like the other faeries, there's something about her youth that seems fake. But unlike the other faeries, I place what it is almost immediately. There is a deep and ancient sorrow in her eyes. The sorrow of one who has lived generations and seen terrible things.

And yet, despite all of this. There's still something different about her.

She arches her eyebrow and smirks at me. "Have ye satiated yer curiosity yet?" she asks. Her accent is a heavy brogue.

I feel the heat spread to my cheeks, but I can't pull my eyes away because my curiosity isn't satiated.

She tilts her head. "But excuse me manners, yer probably just wonderin' who I am. Ye must forgive me, it's been so long since I've been in human company... I'm afraid that these faeries are rubbin' off on me."

My brows draw together as I study her harder. Her complexion isn't blindingly perfect but instead marred with freckles and too pale. She's too short and holds herself with a sloppy easiness rather than her every movement being like a graceful dance.

She juts her chin out. "My name is Eilis. I be a guard of the Undersea Court."

"You're a human," I whisper.

She laughs merrily, not seeming to be angered by my abrupt accusation. "Yes, I be that as well. The Fair Folk call me the Iron Maiden for me talents. Even if they do make an exception to allow me to wield iron due to the fact that I've been here since before the Fair Law was even created, I'm not allowed ta kill 'em. Unlike what ye wish for." She suddenly stills and regards me with a hard expression. "And ye be a human as well. It be nice to meet ye, how is the human world? What has become of it in all of these years?"

"Uh…" I say. I swallow hard as I scratch behind my ear. Well, that would be a far easier question if I knew what era she lived in originally.

She looks at me and smiles compassionately. "Or you do not have to say. I can imagine that much has happened in all of these years. I doubt I could even recognize my home if I tried. That is one thing that the humans do that the faeries do not in their timeless courts—change. And when the faeries do change, it shakes the world and nothing can ever be the same again." Her tone takes on a bitter edge.

"What was the world like when you left?" I ask, tilting my head, trying to figure out who exactly she is or how long she has been here.

"I'd much rather hear how it is now."

I shrug. "I mean, it's fine. There haven't been any world wars recently. America is still standing. I'd say it's all good."

"America?" Eilis says, scrunching her nose as if it is a foreign term.

I nod mutely. "Yes, it's where I'm from."

"Oh, is it now? Must say, I've never heard of it, course I never traveled much before comin' here."

I frown. Never heard of America? "Where *are* you from?"

"I'm from Ériu's land. Though I t'wasn't even there for two decades so I can't say it be me home." She waved her arm at the chaotic room around us. "This world is me true home."

Ériu's land? What the heck is that? I've never heard of it before? Given her accent, I have the sneaking suspicion that she means *Ireland*. And that terrifies me. "How long have you been here?" Then something else that she said strikes me across the cheek. She was here before the Fair Law.

Holy crabapples.

How old is the human girl standing in front of me?

"Time doesn't pass here like it does in yer world," she says with a merry laugh. "I don't know what time has passed in the mortal world, it could be hundreds, perhaps even a thousand years. I don't think I would even recognize our old land if I were to return or whatever this *A-mer-E-ca* that you are from. Or what these world wars are. Give it time and ye will be the same as me. Soon everyone and everything you know in that world will die and ye will have nothing left but the faeries and their world."

"Speak for yourself," I mutter, crossing my arms. "I still fully intend on returning to Earth." I plan on dying with everyone and everything I know.

"Are ye now?" Eilis asks, arching her brow. "Good for ye. Not many can resist the tempting charms of this world. I know that I certainly did not. So, tell me, what is yer homeland like?"

I shift uncomfortably. "It's a whole other continent. I don't think you've heard of it, at least not from when you were born. Most countries didn't even know of its existence for a while."

"Hidden continents," Eilis says with a laugh. "How amusing, what will these humans come up with next?"

"And you don't know about electricity?" I ask. I'm grasping at straws. If she doesn't know what America is, of course she won't know what electricity is.

Eilis looks at me and raises her eyebrow. "Is this another hidden land, perhaps it is under the sea?"

I shake my head. "No, humans discovered ways to uh... make stuff happen more easily." Oh sheesh, I'm messing up this explanation thing. "Like making lights turn on with the flick of a switch."

"So, humans finally discovered magic?" she said with a small nod.

"Well, I'm pretty sure that there is more science involved... but I will admit, I don't really understand the finer tendencies to electricity myself."

"Sounds like magic to me," Eilis says. "And I should know."

Suddenly a new thought comes over me. "How are we even able to speak to each other? I can't think that you speak English."

Eilis turns to me and raises her eyebrows. "English? No, no, I don't even know what that is."

"It's what I'm speaking."

"What you are speaking is the language of the faeries. Upon meeting a faerie, humans learn it. Almost instantly. Like I said, magic," Eilis smiles slightly. "*English*," she mutters in an amused tone under her breath.

I want to ask so many questions, my lips are brimming with them threatening to spill them out of my mouth before my tongue can even form the words, but then another voice fills my ears. A voice that is far too smooth and nonchalant and far too familiar. "Hello, Eilis. Have you missed me?"

Eilis stiffens, a dark expression crossing her face. "I reckon I missed you, Riagan, as one would miss a werebear."

The spymaster of the Winter Court strides into view, a smirk on his arrogant face. "I should imagine. I miss dear Darragh dreadfully." He sighs. "I wonder what he's been up to all these years."

I look between Eilis and Riagan and raise my eyebrows. "Do you two know each other?"

Eilis frowns as she looks from me to Riagan. "Wait. Do you two know each other?"

Riagan's smile grows. "Why of course me bonnie bell, I met our lovely wanna-be assassin here when she was being held by the Winter Court." He turns to me, ignoring the looks of murder that Eilis shoots at him. "We had some very stimulating conversations."

I really just found them confusing.

Just like I'm finding this conversation to be far too much trouble. Faeries should all have tape placed over their lips so that they can all stop confusing me. It isn't fair.

Eilis snorts. "The only person you would care to have a conversation with is yer own mirror."

Riagan stares off into space. "I do know myself quite well from many long-sided monologues."

I rub my temples; this is not the conversation of indifferent acquaintances. This is the heated banter between two people who feel very strongly about the other. I swallow the slimy feeling in my throat. But if Eilis is a human from the Undersea Court and Riagan is the spymaster of the Winter Court then I imagine their paths probably don't cross that often. "But you know each other, how?"

"No need to sound so jealous," Riagan says, reaching up and adjusting a jewel on the shoulder of my dress. He backs away holding his hands out, a satisfied smile on his face. "There, much better. And truly, there is nothing to worry about. Eilis and I worked together... once upon a long time ago."

"But obviously it means nothing," Eilis says, her tone forced as she glares at Riagan. "Well, nothing other than the many headaches I suffered. He was annoying even then."

"And she was short tempered," Riagan says back, his tone perfectly nonchalant and cool like he'd never cared about anything in his whole life.

Eilis snorts and rolls her eyes. "And did you have a reason for coming here or was it only to torment me?"

Riagan flashes her a wicked smile. "As much as I enjoy tormenting you, me bloom, I actually came here because I have a message." Riagan shifts his position and turns to me. "Your brother gives his regards. He also says and I quote, 'Jaye—' I hope that you don't mind the informality, I am simply quoting, anyway he said, 'Jaye, don't do it. Leave now while you have the chance. You aren't doing me a service if you get yourself killed. Or Mom and Dad either.'"

I cross my arms, a scowl taking over my features and Riagan steps back. "Oh dear, I told him that you wouldn't take this message well." He throws up his arms. "Do not stab the messenger."

I purse my lips and look down at the ground and the gown around my feet. Finally, I take a deep breath and look up. "Thank you, Riagan, now can you deliver a message for me?"

Riagan leans against the wall near where Eilis is leaning. She straightens and steps away. "Certainly. As a spymaster it turns out I'm not much more than a glorified messenger anyway."

I inhale a deep breath through my nose. "You tell Thomas that I'm saving his sorry butt whether he likes it or not."

Riagan's mouth twitches. "Well, if you didn't stab me, I'm certain that Thomas will."

I shoot him an apologetic smile. "Thank you, Riagan."

He releases a heavy breath and straightens his sleeves carelessly. "At least it's nice to know that not all humans are as without manners as our Eilis here."

"I'm not *yer* anything," Eilis says, crossing her arms tightly.

Riagan raises his eyes and stares at her for a long moment and in that moment Eilis's angry expression begins to slide off her face. Her arms drop to her side. I look between them, wondering what is going on when Riagan straightens. "No, I suppose that you are not. But that doesn't change the fact that you were once."

Eilis's face turns a deep crimson and she backs up a step, seeming to have forgotten that the wall was right behind her. "Oof," she mumbles, rubbing at the back of her head. She glares at Riagan and then me.

I hold up my hands, unsure what she has against *me*. If anything, I'm probably the only one here who understands her pain of being too close to a faerie she definitely should not be close to.

Riagan backs away. "It appears that I've overstayed my welcome. I'd better go…"

He turns to leave, but I lunge forward and grasp his sleeve. "Can you—would you please keep an eye on Thomas. Just until I am able to save him." I don't know what I'm thinking trusting a member of the Winter Court. Their head spymaster at that. But there's something about Riagan, a light in him that did not exist in any other member of the Winter Court. Besides, he had told me that he cared about humans, and faeries cannot lie.

Riagan stares at me a long moment before nodding once. "I cannot promise that I will be able to do much, though. Not while he is Aoibheann's. But I shall do what I can."

As he turns to leave again, the giant black beast that always seems to be following him barks and rushes past him to us. I nearly have a heart attack until I realize that it is lunging at Eilis and not me.

"No, no, boy," Riagan says with a snap of his fingers. "Come along."

The pooka ignores him, choosing to sniff instead the front of Eilis's dress. It lets out an excited bark and suddenly seems to brighten. Its translucent fur is no longer so dark. The giant beast seems to be practically emanating happiness.

"Come along, Blackie," Riagan says, his voice suddenly sharp. I startle. I hadn't thought him capable of anything more than a drawl.

The giant black dog whines low through its nose and nudges Eilis's hand once more with its nose before it turns and lumbers off after its master.

Eilis inhales a shaky breath and tucks her hair behind her ear. She looks at me out of the corner of her eye and then quickly turns her attention to straightening the sleeves of her outfit. Finally she turns back to me. "Anyway, sorry about that. Riagan can be..." she trails off as if searching for the word. "Riagan," she says at last. Her gaze is so solely focused on me it's like she's trying very hard not to look anywhere else.

I nod. Just like Ravven can be... *Ravven*. And every other faerie here can be like... *faeries*. There is no other way to describe them. They simply *are*.

"Don't forget to not dance with any of the faeries," Eilis says, tapping her finger against the hilt of her sword as she looks over the crowd.

As if I need the reminder. "Why are you so freely helping me?" I ask, glancing back at her. I remind myself that this girl has associated with faeries for far longer than she has associated with humans.

And she can actually lie.

Eilis turns to me languidly and arches a brow. A small smile pulls at the corner of her lips. "You're the first human that I have seen in... oh, so many years." She huffs a tiny laugh. "It's been so long; I can't even tell you how many years it's been." She shoots me a sideways glance. "I would rather not see any harm come to you."

I hadn't realized how comfortable I had become in a world where no one else around me could lie, until I'd met someone who actually could. Every word out of her mouth could be a blatant lie and I wouldn't know.

"How did you even end up in the faerie world?" I ask, fiddling with the jewel that Riagan had already adjusted.

"Oh, me parents died when I was a young girl, before they could arrange a marriage for me. I was thrown out on the streets. I almost starved so many times. I almost died in so many ways. But then my queen—" she abruptly cuts herself off. "But then I was carried off to the faerie court, and I've been here ever since."

"And you've been serving the Undersea Court this whole time?" I ask, shifting uncomfortably. What would make a human choose to serve the Undersea Court? Doesn't seem very practical to me.

"Not this whole time," Eilis says softly.

"If you don't mind my asking," I begin., "If you have been in this world for so long then why did you never... you know, become a faerie? That is possible isn't it, for a human to become a faerie?"

Our Guardian texts say that it is, though they don't detail how.

"It is possible," she says stiffly. "But unlikely. In order to become a faerie, they must choose a court to join and then prove themselves to that court. But yes, if they did pass these tests, they would be allowed to drink from the well and become faeries."

"And why did you never do this?" I ask, wrapping my arms around myself at the chill her words give me. *Swear it on your humanity...* So, there is a way to lose it.

Eilis's eyes flash. She straightens. "Because I didn't want to become like *them*," she states, looking out over the crowd.

I resist the urge to retort with, who would? Instead I say, "Why didn't you leave then?" If she doesn't care about the faeries so much, why would she stay in their world?

She looks at me, her eyes are hard as if they are actually emeralds. "Because I couldn't leave them."

A bit confusing. One moment she seems to detest the faeries, the next she loves them ardently. But then I am starting to feel the same way toward a specific faerie in particular.

She presses her lips together and inclines her head. "If you will excuse me, I must go attend to my queen."

I watch as she strides through the crowd. The faeries make way for her. They view her, not with the derisive contempt as a creature considered less than them, but instead with a sort of respect for something that they do not understand.

I suppose that there is actually a chance for a human to exist in the faerie court after all, even without becoming a faerie.

But then, who would actually want to be a faerie? I can't judge Eilis for her choice when death seems like a better option than immortality, even if I kept my humanity to remain here forever as a human it still seems like a nightmare. To spend the rest of existence trying to make my way through the treacherous world of the faeries and to so completely lose focus of my own world so that I am more faerie than human at the end of the day.

And yet I also understand her, and the pull she must feel toward this world. To these faeries. I hate them, I despise them and yet... and yet... I can't. I've only been here for a few days, and already the draw to their magic and their chaotic existences is like a magnet.

One that I must ignore, because to follow that pull would mean the end of everything that I hold dear.

I draw my eyes from the swirling mass and scan the room. I don't even know what I'm looking for until my eyes land on him. Ravven Crowe. He's standing alone, on a small raised platform jutting from the wall. I spot the spiral stairs next to it and begin to shove my way through the crowd. They no longer seem interested in me, but instead on the madness. Many of their mouths are stained red and the more I watch, the more the room seems like a zoo instead of a ball. One where all of the animals have broken from their confinements.

I pick up my pace and make it to the bottom of the stairs. Hiking up my skirts, I hurry up until I come to a stop next to Ravven. He is leaning against a silver railing that appears to depict several shooting stars curling to the ground, their tails holding up the banister.

"I hate balls," he mutters as soon as I reach the top. "So do Keane and Daithi, so do all self-respecting Solitary faeries. We were the only ones foolish enough to actually attend. And to think, the prospect of this every night." He waves his arm out, sneering with disgust.

I move over to stand next to him and lean my elbows on the banister. "Where are Keane and Daithi now?" I ask, scanning the crowd from my now higher vantage point. I spot Eilis easily enough with her flaming red hair. She is standing next to the Undersea Queen who has moved away from her throne and now is standing close to the handsome faerie who had been standing behind her when I first saw her.

Faeries dance around them, not the least bit concerned with the solitary figures in their midst. Watching them dance reminds me of Eilis's warning to not dance with any of them. Probably why she is not dancing now. But that was not a warning that I needed, though both she and Riagan seem very concerned about me.

"They retired to the Autumn Wing like self-respecting Solitary faeries," Ravven mumbles.

"Why haven't you left yet?" I ask, tracing the silver engravings with my fingers.

Ravven shoots me a pointed look. "It wasn't from my own desire to stay, if that was what you were wondering."

I study him as he holds my gaze and I get the feeling that he stayed for me. How is it that in such a short time that I have gone from hating him and wondering over a thing so simple as him saving my life, to finding his concern endearing.

I shove all of that aside.

He is a faerie. No matter what he does for me, he does it for himself first and foremost.

As if reading my thoughts, Ravven nods. "I had to make certain that you didn't do anything foolish and ruin everything. Risk your life. Possibly get yourself killed and consequently me. Now that you are my contender, our lives are linked further. If you die or lose, they will kill me as well."

"Oh, fun."

"I do not find it such. Though I suppose that *you* would find the idea of me dying amusing."

I shove his shoulder with a snort. "That was that sarcasm, idiot."

Ravven frowns, perturbed. "Could you please stop using it on me. It is always so... confusing."

"I don't rightly think that I could," I state, rubbing my finger over the rail. I crane my neck to look at him. "Sarcasm is in my blood. I don't even notice anymore when I use it."

"And you wonder why you are such an unlikable person."

I roll my eyes. "And you're a perfect saint."

"If you say so. I'm surprised though, by your admission."

"That was sarcasm!"

Ravven grimaces. "This really cannot continue going on, if we are supposed to be able to communicate which we should if we want to survive these trials, we have to come to an agreement. Since this *sarcasm* is apparently so important to your speech then you must, in the very least, give me some form of hint or clue to know that you are not actually meaning what you say."

"Since apparently the different inflection of my tones isn't enough."

"You could always blink twice," Ravven mutters, his tone growing wistful as a small smile pulls at his lips.

My heart clenches. He's beautiful. But not the beautiful that I've grown to expect, the haughty arrogant kind. No, there is a softness to him after all, and it only serves to cause more pain in my chest cavity.

"Sure," I say, my voice coming out in an oddly breathless tone. With that smile, I think he could get me to agree to anything.

I quickly yank my gaze away from Ravven, trying to get control over my quickly beating heart, especially since according to Keane, faeries can hear my heartbeat. I freeze when I spot a familiar shock of auburn hair and an endearing face.

Thomas. He's here. He's really here.

My frail human heart breaks in two.

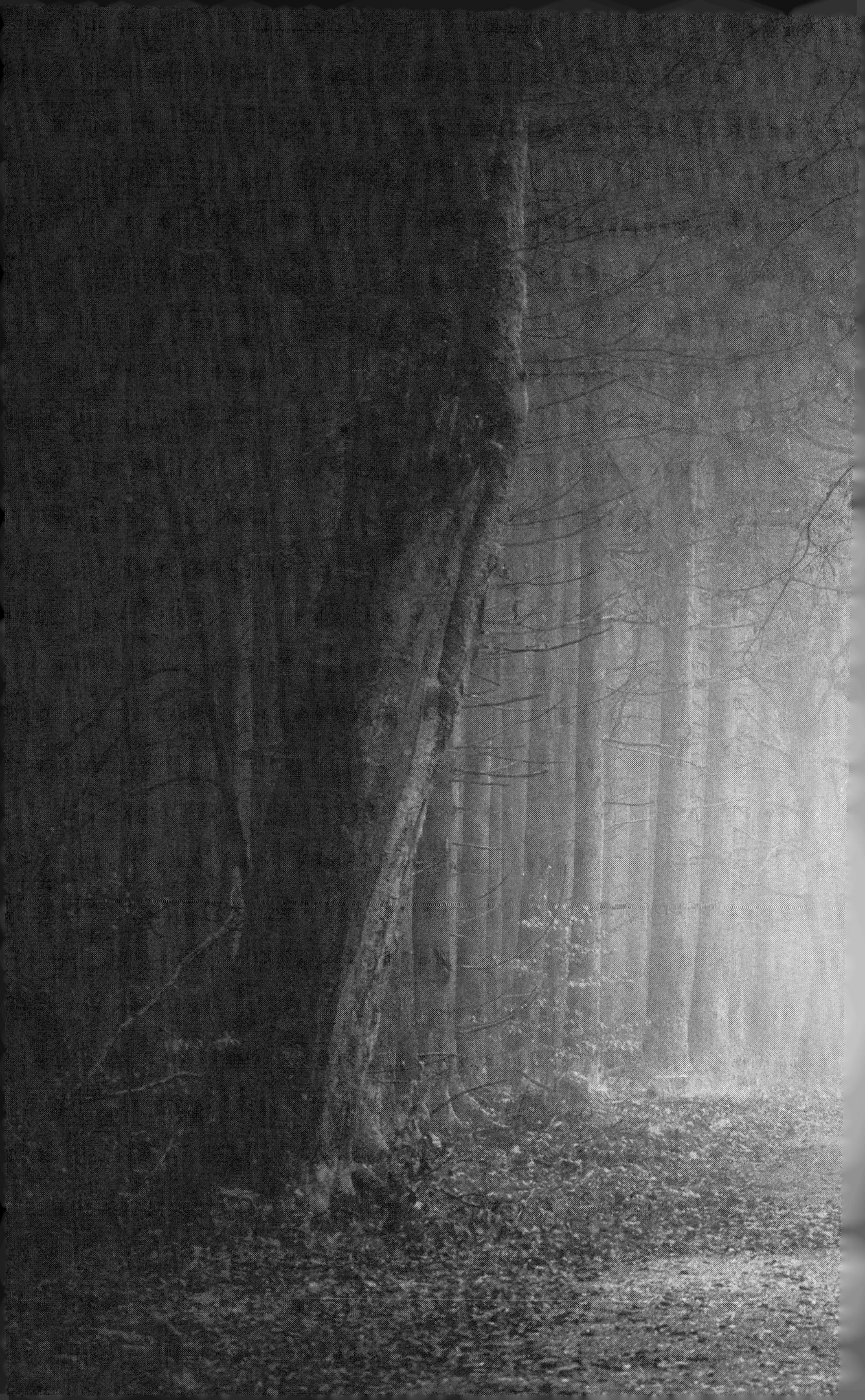

CHAPTER TWENTY-TWO

Before my thoughts have a chance to catch up with the rest of my body, I'm hurling myself down the stairs and flinging myself across the ballroom.

I wish I could forget what I saw. To forget the hollow gaunt face of my once robust older brother. But even then, I know that I must truly be a human, despite the world that I am in. Despite the immortality that seeps into my very pours. Because it's a lie, I can't forget, I don't want to forget. I can never forgive these faeries of what they've done to my brother.

I slow down as I near them, my chest heaving. My step falters as I try to convince myself not to rip them apart with my bare hands. Not that I conceivably could but I am mad enough to try. I step around the group of tittering faeries and into their view.

Thomas looks up, probably sensing me immediately. Even when he isn't a wolf, his sense of smell and hearing have always been superb. I've never been able to sneak up on him.

As his blue eyes, the exact same shade of my own, meet mine I freeze.

I stare at Thomas and he stares at me each with equally horrified looks on our faces. Thomas looks even worse up close than he had from afar. His complexion is so chalky, the stone floor has more color than it. His cheeks are hollow, and he has circles darker than the Forest of Night lining his eyes.

Finally, Thomas closes his eyes, breaking the eye contact between us, resignation replacing the horror on his face. "Jaye, what are you doing?"

"What does it look like I'm doing?" I whisper back.

I step toward him and Thomas stumbles back closer toward the small cluster of Unseelie faeries. "You shouldn't be here, Jaye. You should be back home by now, not trying this *idiotic* plan. I know you're doing this because of me."

"Of course, I'm doing it because of you!" I spit, my eyes flashing. "I'm going to save you."

The Unseelie faeries standing around Thomas regard me stonily as Thomas pales further. Aoibheann looks at me like I'm some sort of bug, Iorwerth with interest, and Riagan with concern before his face becomes completely neutral.

"Ah, my little Jaye-bird, I am so pleased to see that you have found your way back to me," Iorwerth says, stepping toward me. "What a fierce little assassin you would make. A pity you will die."

Faeries can't lie. Iorwerth must not think that I have very high chances of survival.

Thomas steps forward and grips my wrist. I gasp at how cold his hands are. "Jaye, please go. Go home," he finishes quietly.

"I'll go home when you do," I say determinedly, my hand sliding up his wrist to grip his fingers. I hold onto them tightly. Seeing him here reminds me of every reason I can neither give up or die. My brother is still alive, and I am going to make absolutely certain that he remains that way. He will not become Aoibheann's shade. Not while I still have breath in my lungs.

Thomas shakes his head. "Please, Jaye, you still have so much life left to live. Don't waste yourself on me. I'm a lost cause."

"Not to me you're not," I state, clenching my teeth. "And I never want to hear you talk like that again."

Thomas looks away. "Go home, Jaye," he says again. "Mom and Dad shouldn't be forced to wonder what became of both of us."

"They won't wonder what happened to either of us," I state firmly. "Because I'm going to win this contest and then I'm going to save you. Ravven is going to help me, we won't lose."

And if we do? Well then, I guess we die and Thomas becomes a shade, but at least it won't be because of my lack of trying.

I regret that Ravven has become messed up in this. Correction, that I dragged him into this. He doesn't deserve to die for my selfishness, even if he is a faerie. But I have no choice. And neither does he since he swore with blood. When this is all over, I will complete his task, whatever that might be.

"Please, Jaye, I'm begging you. Don't go through with this. Have your faerie boyfriend take you home. Please just go home."

"I'm not discussing this, Thomas," I snap.

"Listen to your brother," Aoibheann says with an airy tone. "He obviously does not want your help."

My gaze slides to her and I feel my fury bubble up further. "I'm going to kill you." I'd kill her now, Fair Assassin, faerie war, or no faerie war, except I don't have a means without my iron knife.

She laughs gaily. "I don't see how you can, little mortal."

I grit my teeth so hard that it causes pain to shoot up my temple.

Iorwerth's hand lands on my shoulder hard and I grimace. "You're making a fool of yourself, my little bird, making enemies where they are not."

I lift his hand from my shoulder. "You've enslaved my brother. Your queen wishes to do the same with my whole people. And I dislike you personally." I look Iorwerth over with disgust. "By my reckoning, we're enemies already."

He smiles again, but this time it is strained. "You act as if you know what is good for you."

"I do," I spit. "And it doesn't include you."

He leans so close that the sour scent of his cold breath fills my nostrils. "Are you so sure of yourself?"

"You really ought to control your pet, Iorwerth," Aoibheann says, her tone bored. Her gaze flickers to Riagan, who is watching all of this with an amused smile on his face. Though his posture is uncharacteristically rigid for his easy going manner. "Shouldn't he? I mean, I have complete control of my pet."

At her words, Thomas grimaces and grows paler even as he steps toward her without her even having to speak the command out loud. She rests her finger on his shoulder.

I see red.

I no longer care that Iorwerth is standing next to me, or Riagan is subtly shaking his head, half his face hidden behind his hand as he stifles a yawn. Or that all I have are my bare fists.

I don't care that I haven't even started the tests, let alone completed them or about anything Ravven said about us possibly dying if we go about this wrong.

All I care about is that faerie and her hand on my brother.

I throw myself at her.

Riagan's pooka barks loudly, but he shushes it as if he has nothing more to worry about other than his pet making a fool of itself. My fingers claw at Aoibheann's neck. I want nothing more than to rip the life out of her, but simply touching her flesh hurts. Though it's all worth it for the widening of her eyes and her sharp inhalation of breath.

"When I run you through," I hiss at her, "I will laugh as I watch the life drain from your eyes. Killed by a mere mortal, *how pathetic.*"

My hands touching her neck are growing cold, it's like trying to strangle a block of ice. What I wouldn't give to have my iron knife back. I would kill every blasted faerie who stands between me and my brother's safety.

"Unhand me now or you will never compete in the tests," she hisses, finally regaining her composure.

Two warm hands grasp each arm and suddenly I'm yanked away from her.

"I will kill you!" I scream at her. "I swear I will kill you."

"Hush, lass," Eilis says, yanking me harder. Ravven has my other arm and together they manage to pull me back another few steps. My chest is heaving with rage, but I'm beginning to see clearly again.

"Not now, pest," Ravven says quietly into my ear. He squeezes my arm, though not unkindly. As if he is sympathizing with me and my pain, though I know that cannot be what it is.

Faeries are not sympathetic.

Eilis tugs me harder. "Come along now, Jaye."

Iorwerth is shaking his head at me with a smirk. "And so, these are your allies? Are you just hoping that they will not betray you? Oh, how you will come crawling back to me, and maybe when I'm done with you, I will make it so that you are still able to crawl."

It happens so fast that I don't even have a chance to snap at Iorwerth. Ravven whirls on him and backhands him so hard that it's like a rumble of thunder. A flash of purple and blue light erupts from the impact and Iorwerth goes flying across the room.

Ravven stares after him for a long moment before straightening. He turns to me and grabs my arm. "It is late," he says in a strained tone. "We should probably return to our rooms before we start a war."

With that, he drags me away. I stumble after him, peering over my shoulder as Iorwerth pushes to his feet and shoots us a venomous glare. Every faerie in the room is watching us.

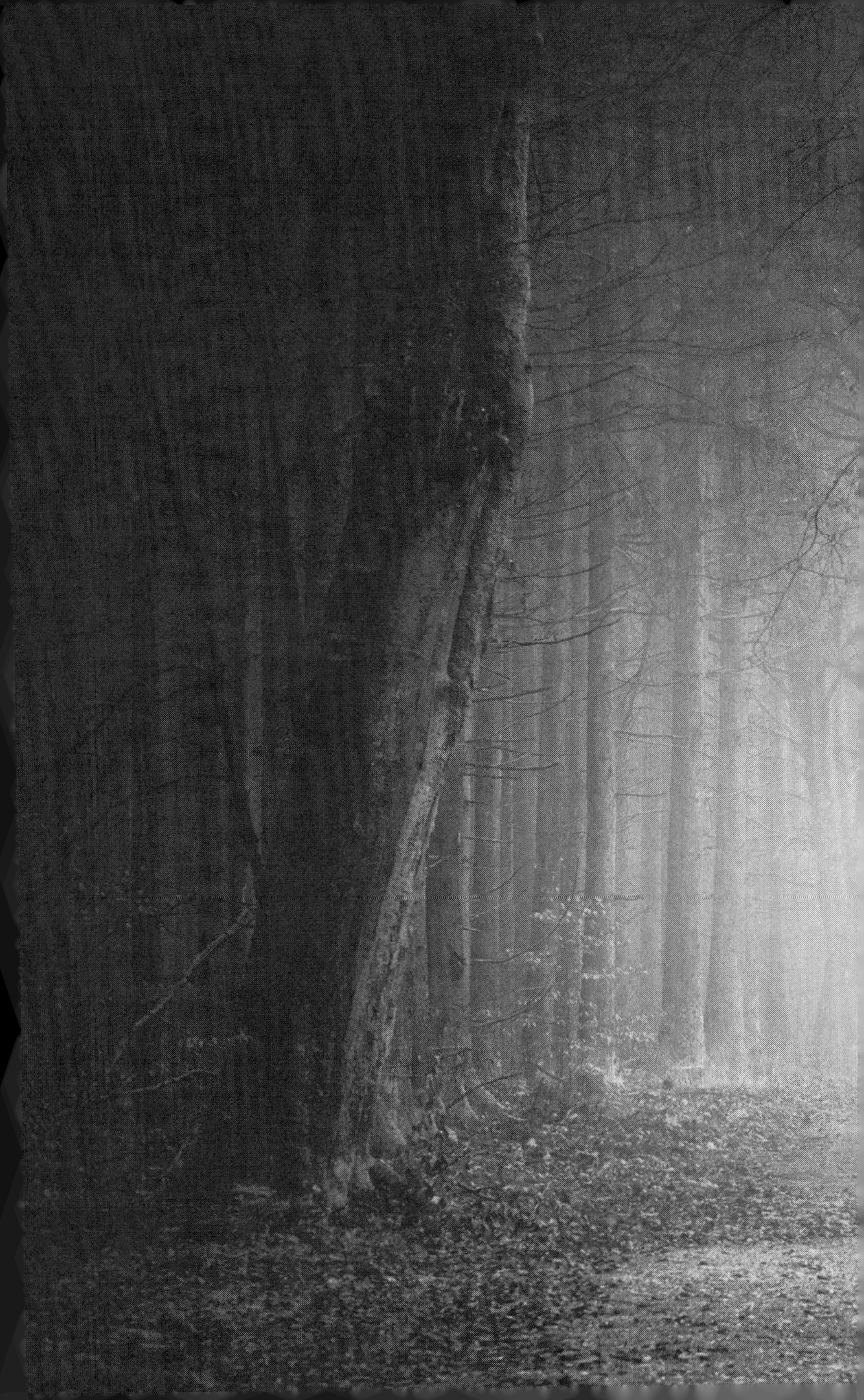

CHAPTER TWENTY-THREE

I inhale a shuddering breath as the door to the Autumn wing slams shut behind us. I sag against the red embroidered pillows sitting in the middle of the floor, almost feeling the impact of the door shutting in my bones. I'm grateful that Keane and Daithi are nowhere to be seen, because I don't want them to see this. It's bad enough that Ravven and Eilis have to be here to witness me as I dissolve into tears.

I draw in a shuddering inhale as the first tears begin to fall. My brother! *Thomas*. Did I make things worse for him? Will he be punished for my actions? Thomas is already so much less than he had been only yesterday; I don't know how much more he can take.

Eilis and Ravven appear to be having a hushed conversation nearby, but I can't hear a word they say over the sound of my own sobs.

"Could you stop being so pathetically human for just one moment and focus on the matter at hand?" Ravven asks, whirling to face me. "We have much ahead of us and you need to control all of... *this*." He gestures wildly before stopping and pinching the bridge of his nose like this has all gotten to be too much for him. "My magic, you certainly have a special talent of taking something bad and making it so much worse."

"I'm sorry," I say, wiping at my eyes, only to find more tears to replace it. Ravven is right, even if he could have said it in a nicer way. I need to get control of myself. My tears, my anger, my human emotions they need to stop. I'm in the faerie court now, cool and calculating indifference is the order of the day, not passionate feelings.

If only I can convince my heart of that.

"Ach, leave her be, Crowe. Ye honestly don't know how relieving it is for me to hear another person cry," Eilis says, plopping down next to me. She drapes an arm over my shoulder and shoots Ravven a hard look. "Ye have no idea what it is like here with these faeries, all so blasted stoic. Wouldn't cry if their family died."

She smiles wistfully, "Though most faeries don't really care about their families to begin with. Not in the long run anyway."

Don't know how *that* is anything to be wistful about. Though, it does make me wonder about Ravven and Keane. They appear to be at least on civil terms, and while Keane had spoken gruffly earlier, he was still here, in a show of support, even though that means having to *be near* other faeries.

I wipe at my eyes. "Don't try to make me feel better. I made a mess of everything."

They're both silent.

"Didn't I?" I prompt.

"Yes," Ravven says, crossing his arms

At the same time Eilis says, "No, of course not."

I look between them and laugh bitterly. Out of the two of them, I know who is telling the truth. The only one who can't lie.

Eilis clears her throat. "Not a mess that cannot be cleaned, at least. Keep yer chin up, lass. The fight has only just begun."

I stare down at my lap. "Are you sure that it is even a fight that I can win."

"I think ye have a fair shot," Eilis says.

Since I can't gather much comfort from her words, I look to Ravven and arch my brow.

He smirks arrogantly. "I think ye have a fair shot," he says in a perfect imitation of Eilis's brogue. "You have me helping you, after all. How can you fail?"

I stretch my legs out. My skirt tangles underneath me and I grunt in frustration. Blasted contraptions.

"Ugh," I state, rubbing at my temples.

"Ye need rest," Eilis says, resting her hand on my shoulder. "Everything will look better in the mornin'."

"It is impossible for me to look better than I already do," Ravven mutters. "Besides, we don't have time for *rest*. There is too much to do before tomorrow."

Eilis frowns at him. "Some people really do need to sleep, Ravven."

I look up at them, frowning as my eyes land on Ravven. "You don't sleep?"

Ravven arches his eyebrow. "Why do you find that fact surprising?"

Well, for one, humans tend to die without sleep. Two, he doesn't look like a person who has gone without sleep. There are no dark circles around his eyes, there is no exhaustion creasing the features of his face. He looks perfectly whole.

"Do faeries not sleep then?" I ask, trying to sound nonchalant and not like a total idiot. My books on faerie mythology had never told me anything about that.

"Faeries don't need to sleep," Eilis explains, taking pity on me as Ravven snorts. "Though most of them do sleep when it suits them since the rest offers up a respite from at least a few hours of immortality." Eilis's tone grows hard as she frowns down at her lap.

"Only the weak faeries with nothing better to do." Ravven shakes his head, a smile curving at his lips. "I have not slept for more than a hundred and twenty years. Don't look so surprised, pest, I thought you would have noticed this when we spent our night together in the Winter Court."

He could say that in a less suggestive matter. Sheesh, he makes it sound downright obscene.

Eilis's eyebrows rise and I fight the urge to blush. "We were imprisoned in the same cell. We had to... um, snuggle for warmth so I didn't freeze to death."

"*Snuggle*," Ravven repeats with disdain flavoring his voice.

Eilis's eyebrows lower. "That doesn't sound like you, Crowe."

"The mortal hardly gave me a choice. It was that or let her die, and we had already made a blood bargain so obviously I could not let that happen."

"Ye made a blood bargain. Now that *really* doesn't sound like you, Crowe."

Now it's time for my eyebrows to rise as I study Eilis. What *is* she doing here? She serves the Undersea Court, so why is she here in the room with a Solitary faerie from the Autumn Court and his human contender?

"How well do you two know each other?"

Eilis looks at Ravven, but he doesn't return her gaze. His focus is on the tapestry. She shrugs. "Well enough. Though I will admit not perfectly well. But enough of that. We are wasting valuable time especially if you are supposed to have some time to *rest*. We have much to prepare."

"For?" I prompt.

"Tomorrow," Eilis says with a heavy sigh. "The Undersea Court has asked for the privilege of holding the first test."

My stomach somersaults. I doubt I'll be able to sleep after that kind of information. Whether I need it or not. "What is the test going to be about?" I ask.

Eilis shrugs. "That I cannot say for certain, but fear not. The Undersea Court is neutral in their opinion of ye, the test will probably include a test of yer metal and yer integrity. Servin' in the Undersea Court, I have proved to them that not all humans are lying thieves. They should have no problem allowin' ye to pass the test so long as ye prove yerself worthy, so I can say that whatever instructions they give ye, follow them to the letter and do not die and ye should pass well enough."

Follow the instructions and don't die. Sure, that sounds simple.

I look into Eilis's sparking green eyes. Knowing that she is human causes me to reconsider her age. She looks possibly younger than me, but her aged eyes cause me to wonder how old she truly is. How much she has truly seen?

"Why are you helping me?" I ask, frowning. Just because she is a human doesn't mean that I can trust her. She's lived in the faerie world for so long that she's probably more like a faerie than her own kind.

Eilis tilts her head as she looks at me. "You don't have to fear me. I mean you no harm."

"I can't believe what you say. Every word out of your mouth could be a lie."

Now I understand Ravven's problem with trusting me to make a bargain.

"Do not fear, Jaye," Ravven says, speaking at last.

I turn to him abruptly.

He smiles in what he probably thinks is a reassuring manner, but it only succeeds in causing my heart to flip three times over because of how utterly breathtaking it is. "For the time being, Eilis wishes to help us."

"And how long will that last?" I mutter, unable to help myself.

Ravven looks at Eilis as if he isn't so sure of the answer himself.

Eilis tilts her head in amusement as she looks us over. "I suppose we shall see."

How comforting.

I purse my lips and Eilis laughs, patting my hand. "Never fear, Jaye. I am fond of you. Besides, my court is neutral. What reason would I have to harm you?"

Lots of reasons. I just don't know any of them.

"Neutral?" I ask instead. This is the second time she's called it that.

Ravven dips his head. "The Undersea Court and the Summer Court should have no problem with you as long as you prove your loyalty to them. It is the Winter Court and the Spring Court that you must worry about. Their tests shall be particularly painful, as in, they will try to make certain that you do not survive."

I grimace. "Painful. Of course, my favorite thing."

Ravven looks at me sharply, but then his expression relaxes. "You were lying again, weren't you?"

"It's called sarcasm," I state defensively. "It's not a lie because it is never intended to be believed." Then because I remembered our code, I blink twice.

Ravven shakes his head, but a ghost of a smile crosses his face. "Unbelievable. Humans lie so much that they try to find ways to tell the truth while still lying."

I don't bother trying to argue, I just inhale a deep breath. "If these courts are so set against me living then how am I supposed to be expected to complete their tests?"

Eilis stands. "That is not something you need to worry about now. Tomorrow is the Undersea Court, focus on that." She smiles, looking completely ordinary, like a normal girl from Earth and not a part of the faerie world, older than time itself. "Get some sleep, Jaye."

We both watch silently as Eilis sashays out of the room. I'm surprised when Ravven is the first to break the silence. "Her help will be invaluable." The way he says it, it's like he's trying to convince himself.

I peel my gaze from the empty doorway and look at him.

He turns his face to me, his face passive, his tone flat as if he's resigned himself to some fact. It makes my pulse pick up a notch. "It is against the Fair law for any faerie to aid you now that you have become a candidate. Other than your faerie patron, that is." He raises his eyebrows, making it clear just who my faerie patron is. "Just as no faerie can harm you other than the court you are currently vying for the favor of. Which is why Aoibheann did not attack you earlier. Even if you were severely tempting her." The corner of his lips turns up. "All the same, Fair Law or no, you must stop being so tempting."

I cross my arms. "You know, I don't actually make it my goal to make people want to kill me."

"Don't you?"

I narrow my eyes at him, but I don't exactly have any arguments to make because I had just been forcibly escorted from a ball for attacking a dangerous queen's sister. "So, what does this have to do with Eilis?"

Ravven taps his long finger against his chin. "While the Fair Law prohibits any faerie from helping us, Eilis, as a human, is not actually bound by the Fair Law. She can do anything she wants. Including help us."

"But why *is* she helping us? Why would she choose to do that?" Did Ravven make a deal with her as well?

Ravven scratches the nape of his neck and shakes his head. "I'm not sure exactly. I trust her about as much as I trust anyone."

Meaning, not at all. What must it be like to live in a world where you can have no friends? Because if you do. It is very likely that they will kill you someday. It must be a lonely existence indeed. While I might not be the most social person, I know I can rely on Thomas and my parents. That they love me. That they would die for me. And I would die for them, as evidenced by this crazy scheme. Would Ravven give his life for anyone? Even his father?

Or me?

I quickly shake that thought out of my head and scratch at my jaw as I push to my feet. "I hope for both of our sakes she doesn't turn against us."

Ravven releases a breath as he steps toward me. "You may not believe me, but I do understand your plight, learning to exist in a world such as mine. A world where one can only ever survive. There is no one you can trust and that is a frightening thing. I know that you cannot nor will you trust me." He takes a final step, closing the distance between us and lifts his hand, tracing the back of his knuckles lightly against my cheek. His eyes are a magnificent royal purple as the fruity scent of his breath washes over me and he continues. "But trust me when I say this. You will make it through these tests, pest. I will see that you do. My love for myself is too strong to allow myself to die now."

I inhale a shaky breath and try to force myself to remain calm. I cannot, I absolutely cannot show Ravven the effect he has on me. It's bad enough that I have to *feel* it myself.

If only it didn't have to feel like my entire body was on fire. What is wrong with me? We were this close at the Winter Court, closer even. And yet my heart is beating pathetically in my chest despite his own admission that I can't trust him.

"Do you—?" I begin, cursing myself for my shortness of breath and my inability to hold back a blush for even a second.

"Do I what?" Ravven asks, blinking down at me. Is it just me or is his voice breathy as well? He doesn't step away even though I wish he would. And I pray that he never will.

"Are you putting me under an ensorcellment?" I demand. Oh goodness, can my heart calm itself down? I am certain that Ravven can hear it thumping wildly.

Ravven throws back his head and laughs, breaking the spell between us. He shuffles back a step. "*Me* put *you* under an ensorcellment? What a ridiculous notion."

I cross my arms. "No need to mock me. It could happen."

"It never could. I value my existence far too much to even attempt such a thing." His eyes fade from the purple to black.

I swallow hard and nod. "Good, just making certain that you would know that there would be consequences if you ever tried such a thing."

"Honestly, I think I'm too beautiful to be harmed, but obviously, you don't seem to care for such things as beauty."

Oh no, I care about beauty. I care about beauty far too much, otherwise I would be able to pull my eyes away from Ravven's face, no matter how perfect it is. How his hair is the blackest shade of black I've ever seen and his face glows with that beautiful golden hue.

I really need to learn how to ignore such things.

I also need to learn how to breathe.

But until then, I wait breathless for what I know will come. For Ravven to say something to insult my looks. I know the second he does, I can reestablish the correct perspective of him and perhaps banish this lightheaded feeling.

But Ravven doesn't say it. He doesn't say anything at all. He just stares at me the same way that I'm staring at him. As if waiting for something that isn't going to come.

I'm the first one to finally break the silent bond between us by looking away. I clear my throat and try to get control over my racing childish thoughts. "Even if you weren't ensorcelling me it still shows how dangerous it is for me without my rune protecting me. I am powerless against any other faeries who would try to control me."

"Are you now?" Ravven says, looking me over. "Odd. But I have a hard time envisioning you being powerless."

"Obviously, you see the danger that this poses though."

"I do not," Ravven says. I whip my gaze to him and glare. Of course he doesn't, he's a faerie. He's the one who does the cursing, he never has to worry about *being* cursed. "But since you obviously are expecting me to do something, I can offer you a boon. A blessing of sorts. I can use my magic to protect you from any curses of other faeries. No one would be able to ensorcell you or curse you in any way save for me."

I swallow past my suddenly dry throat. Just like a faerie boon. Maybe I'll be protected from others, but Ravven will still have complete power over me. Of course, without this boon, Ravven would still have complete power over me, and at least it would protect me from other faeries like Iorwerth or Cliodnha.

I don't trust Ravven; I'm not ready to break rule number one just yet. But I do trust him more than the other faeries. Better to be in his hands alone than in the hand of every doggone faerie in the whole world.

"Okay," I say at last. I wipe my sweaty palms down the front of my pants. "Let's do this then."

Ravven's mouth twists as he steps toward me. He raises his hand, a swirling glowing purple mist circling around his fingertips. "This will only hurt a little," he murmurs.

"Wait," I say. No one said anything about hurting. But before any more protests can escape my lips, Ravven touches my forehead and suddenly I'm knocked from my feet as I'm hit with the force of a speeding car.

I blink open my eyes to find myself lying sprawled out on the other side of the room. My head is pounding from where it smacked into the floor and I feel like I've been punched right in the center of my chest.

I sit up with a groan and look around the room, trying to recollect what it was that happened. My eyes land on a crumpled form wearing dark clothes lying across the room from me.

A startled cry breaks loose from my throat. "Ravven!"

He doesn't move.

"Ravven?" I cry, I struggle to push myself to my feet, but just as I get them underneath me, my traitorous knees give out on me and I collapse back to the ground.

Before I have the chance to get back up, he stirs and sits up, his beautiful face twisted in pain.

"Are—are you okay?"

Ravven pushes unsteadily to his feet, clutching his side. He grimaces in my direction. "I do hope you're happy."

Then he turns and limps off, leaving me wondering what just happened, and whether his boon worked or not.

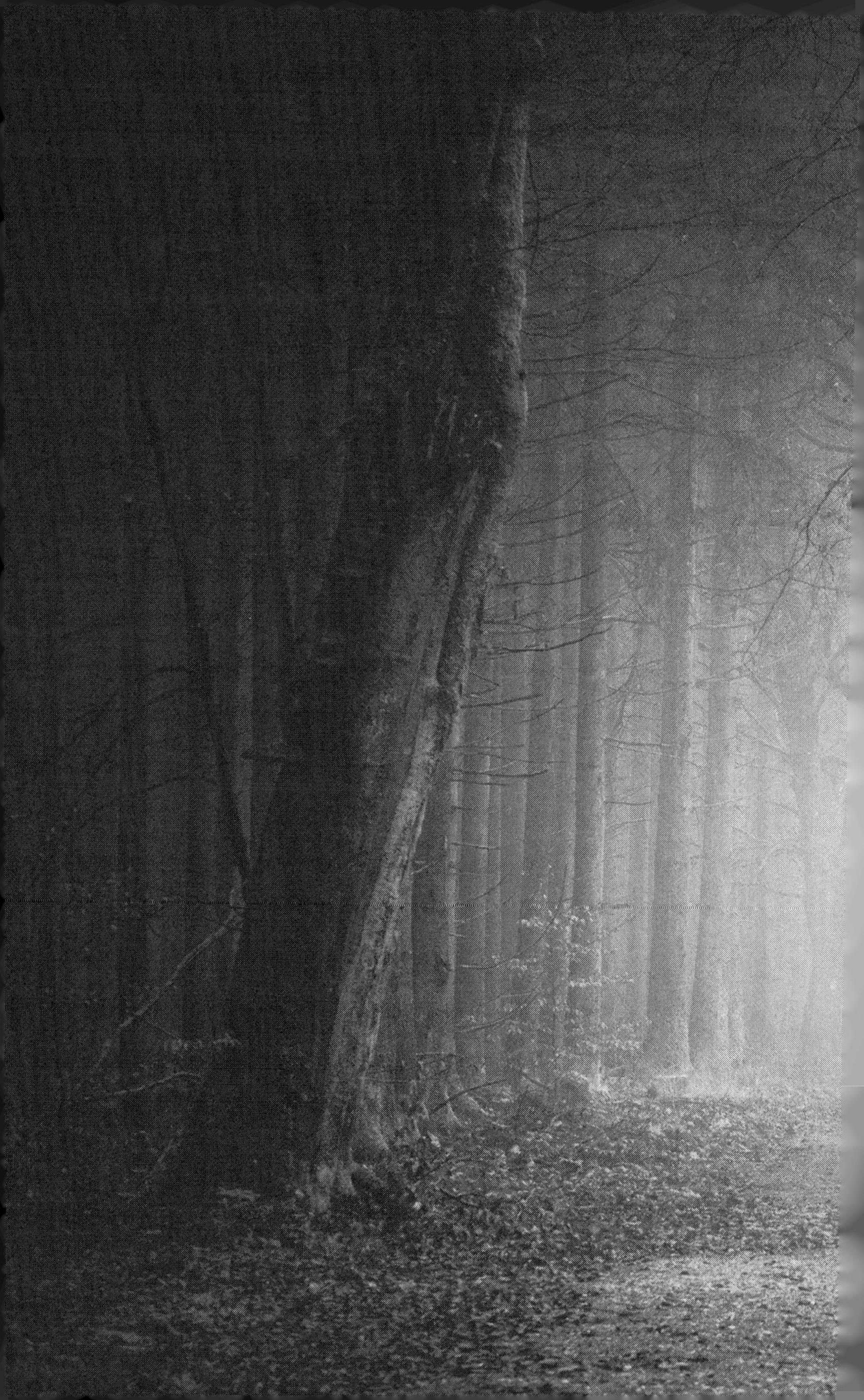

CHAPTER TWENTY-FOUR

The ground underneath me is invisible, and it is freaking me out. Below it, crystalline waters gently swirl. I'm not quite sure what I'm walking on. Given its transparency, I would say glass, and yet as my booted heels land on the floor, it echoes like stone instead. The reflection of the water shimmers on the walls and the arched ceiling over my head.

So, this is the wing for the Undersea Court. I inhale a shaky breath. Well, it certainly lives up to its name. I feel like I'm about to drown and I'm just in the entry hall.

I'm grateful to be finally wearing pants again; they are made of black leather and stiff but at least they aren't a ball gown. I'm wearing a black long-sleeved shirt with a collar which comes up to my throat. Little gleaming white designs line the sleeves and torso of the shirt. It comes down to my mid-thigh. I feel like with my somber black apparel I will fit right in at my funeral should the need arise for me to have one.

Ravven is striding beside me, silent as my shadow. He hasn't said much since last night, which is fine with me because I don't know what to say to him. At least he seems to have recovered completely from... *whatever that was* that happened. He is also wearing all black. His apparel was assembled of a long shirt tucked into a black belt and cloth pants, tucked into gleaming black boots. His black hair only adds to the dark appearance, to be contradicted by his sunny complexion.

The hallway we are walking down is empty save for us. The only sound being the lapping of water below and our clipping footfalls.

Ahead of us are large doors that appear to be made out of water, trapped inside of the slim confines of a glass prison.

As we near the doors, Ravven's gait slows. I pause and glance over my shoulder at him. His look is twisted with something akin to worry as he looks at the door.

I frown at him. "You should stop looking like that. Or you might just convince me that this is a bad idea."

Ravven shakes his head. "This *is* a bad idea. As you will recall, I told you of the folly of this plan when we started out. Unfortunately, it is too late for us to turn back now."

I nod. Well then... I step toward the doors, but then suddenly his warm fingers are wrapping around my arm and drawing me to a halt.

I stiffen. I hadn't heard him close the distance between us. I turn back, opening my mouth to tell him to unhand me, but his worried expression forces me to stop in my tracks.

"Be careful," Ravven whispers harshly. "These tests are not games."

And here I thought that they were. Silly me.

I swallow hard as my palms start sweating. "Wait. Won't you be joining me?"

Ravven smiles. "I most certainly shall be joining you, but I might not have the opportunity to say it later," he says, stepping back and putting some much-needed distance between us. "And the stars know you need to hear it said more often."

I cross my arms. "I'm not that reckless."

Ravven laughs bitterly. "And humans can lie."

I roll my eyes. Yeah, okay so maybe I am a little reckless. I wonder how much of my current circumstances have been brought about because of my reckless actions, but then I quickly shove that thought aside afraid of the answer. I don't want to know. I don't think I could handle the guilt of knowing. "Okay, fine, but you be careful too all right?"

No need to have Ravven on my conscience as well as Thomas.

Ravven arches a brow. "I hardly think there is any concern from me. I am far less breakable than you."

I huff a breath. "I'm not that breakable."

Ravven's eyes move down to my right forearm. The handprint is hidden underneath the layers of my shirt, but I know what he's thinking about. It seems that the Winter Court was so long ago. And yet, I also wonder if the haunting chill that has followed me since then will ever abate.

His gaze returns to mine and he smirks, the kind of smirk that would send the devil running for cover. "I suppose that we shall see."

Then without another word, he turns to the watery doors and shoves them open, striding through without another look back at me. I stand there for a moment debating whether I really want to follow, but then, do I really have a choice?

I force my heavy feet to move.

The room beyond is enormous, the huge domed ceiling is made of the same material as the floor had been, with the waters bending around it and yet looking like there is nothing there at all to hold the tides back. The walls are still made of the dark gray stone.

A throne is on a slightly raised dais, the blue haired queen sitting upon it. I suppose that the Autumn Court didn't need a throne room. Perhaps their room with the cushions was the equivalent to theirs.

Today the Undersea Queen's dress is a blue so dark that it could only be found in the deepest part of the ocean. The dark-haired male faerie is sitting on a slightly smaller throne to her left and that's when I realize that he must be her husband. A woman hovers just behind the Undersea King's throne. She has flowing dark hair that resembles his and I garner they must be related. My thoughts are further justified as I take in the rest of the Undersea Court. The king and the woman behind him are the only Undersea faeries here that look like they don't belong at the bottom of the ocean.

Positioned on the last step of the dais, looking refreshingly human, is Eilis.

Ravven strides up beside her before coming to a stop. I step up beside him. Eilis winks at me.

I stare at her back wishing that she would be a little more helpful, perhaps by telling me how I am supposed to act around her queen. Should I bow? Or heaven forbid, make some lame attempt at a curtsy?

Ravven, however, only inclines his head slightly, so I quickly follow suit.

"Queen Ursulle, King Tadhgan, members of the Undersea Court," he drawls. The other faeries in the room appear to vary between looking similar to their queen with scales and different colored skins. Then there is a cluster of surprisingly human, surprisingly beautiful women with gills who are wearing caps. They titter when Ravven starts talking. *Merrows.*

I decide that I don't like Merrows. Incorrigible flirts. According to my studies of them, they are always looking for other faeries, or even humans to marry because they do not consider the males of their own kind handsome enough.

"I thank you for your hospitality," he continues, the charm practically dripping from his tone.

The Undersea Queen waves her hand. "Cease with the pleasantries, Crowe. We all know that hospitality or no, I would have to host you in your test. It is as the Fair Law decrees."

I don't know why, but for some reason King Tadhgan appears to wince at his wife's words.

Ravven smiles charmingly. "But of course. We are wasting time. All that remains now is for you to give us your test."

The Undersea Queen purses her green lips as she taps her fingernail against the arm of her coral throne. *Tap, tap.* "Yes indeed. All that remains..."

Tap.

"Is for me..."

Tap, tap, tap.

"To decide what I shall do with you."

Tap.

Tap.

Tap.

Utter silence.

She smiles. I suppose she thinks it's supposed to be comforting, but all I can think about is how very sharp her teeth are.

My, my, what sharp teeth you have...

I swear if she says, "The better to eat you with," I will be out that door faster than anyone can blink.

I shift uncomfortably from foot to foot and try to swallow down my terror. It's nerves. It's all just nerves.

"My test for you, mortal," she says at last. "Is that you shall descend into the catacombs beneath this palace."

I frown. The catacombs beneath the palace? We already descended more levels than I ever want to walk again to make it to the Undersea Court's portion of the castle and she's telling me that we have to go down even deeper? If we go down any deeper, we will probably reach the center of the Earth. Or rather the center of the Otherworld.

"And you shall find for me the Chalice of Eagna which is hidden somewhere down there."

I arch my brow. "And what exactly is this chalice of... er, this chalice?" My voice squeaks and I wish that I hadn't spoken, but I also can't accomplish this test if I have no idea what I'm even looking for. I've never heard of it in my reading.

She looks at me amused and I realize that even if she had said mortal earlier, she had really been telling Ravven what the test was, not me. I grimace and try to hide my embarrassment. Though what does it matter if they all think I'm an idiot? Odds are they thought I was an idiot the second I agreed to this. I'm beginning to agree with them.

"The Chalice of Eagna is an enchanted cup that has been in the possession of the royal Undersea Court for centuries. One sip of the contents of the liquid within and the drinker is granted the answer to all of their questions."

My eyebrows rise. I can see why it would be a valuable trinket.

"I want you to retrieve it for me," she says, folding her webbed hands. "Be certain not to spill a drop. Not to take for yourself a sip. The chalice must be full when it reaches my grasp." She looks me over with a sinister eye and I determine to walk as carefully as possible when I pick up the chalice.

The queen raises her hands and gestures for us to leave. "We shall see if you pass this test, but if you do, you shall have the support of the Undersea Court."

Eilis catches my eye and winks again. Ravven's hand brushes my arm and I turn with him as the large doors swing open, held by two guards, one with grayish blue skin and one with a sea green skin. They have finlike ears and patches of scales on the lower half of their faces. Probably male Merrows.

They both smile as we walk past them, their teeth just as sharp and pointy as the queen's had been. I glance once over my shoulder at the court of blue, green, and gray with Eilis's hair a shining beacon, and then the heavy dark doors block my view.

"That could have gone better," Ravven says as the echoing sound of the door closing breaks the silence of the otherwise still passage.

"What?" I thought that it hadn't gone too bad. The Undersea Queen hadn't seemed too dangerous, she hadn't insulted or threatened any of us personally. And all we have to do is get some chalice, we won't have to fight any monster or do anything horrible after all.

"It's just... she could have chosen a simpler task for us, but I suppose she wishes to test me."

Of course, he's the one being tested, obviously not me, the contender here. I decide not to press the matter and instead ask, "What do you mean by simpler task? It's just a chalice."

Ravven arches his brow at me. "Have you not learned yet, pest? Nothing in the faerie courts is ever going to be just what it seems."

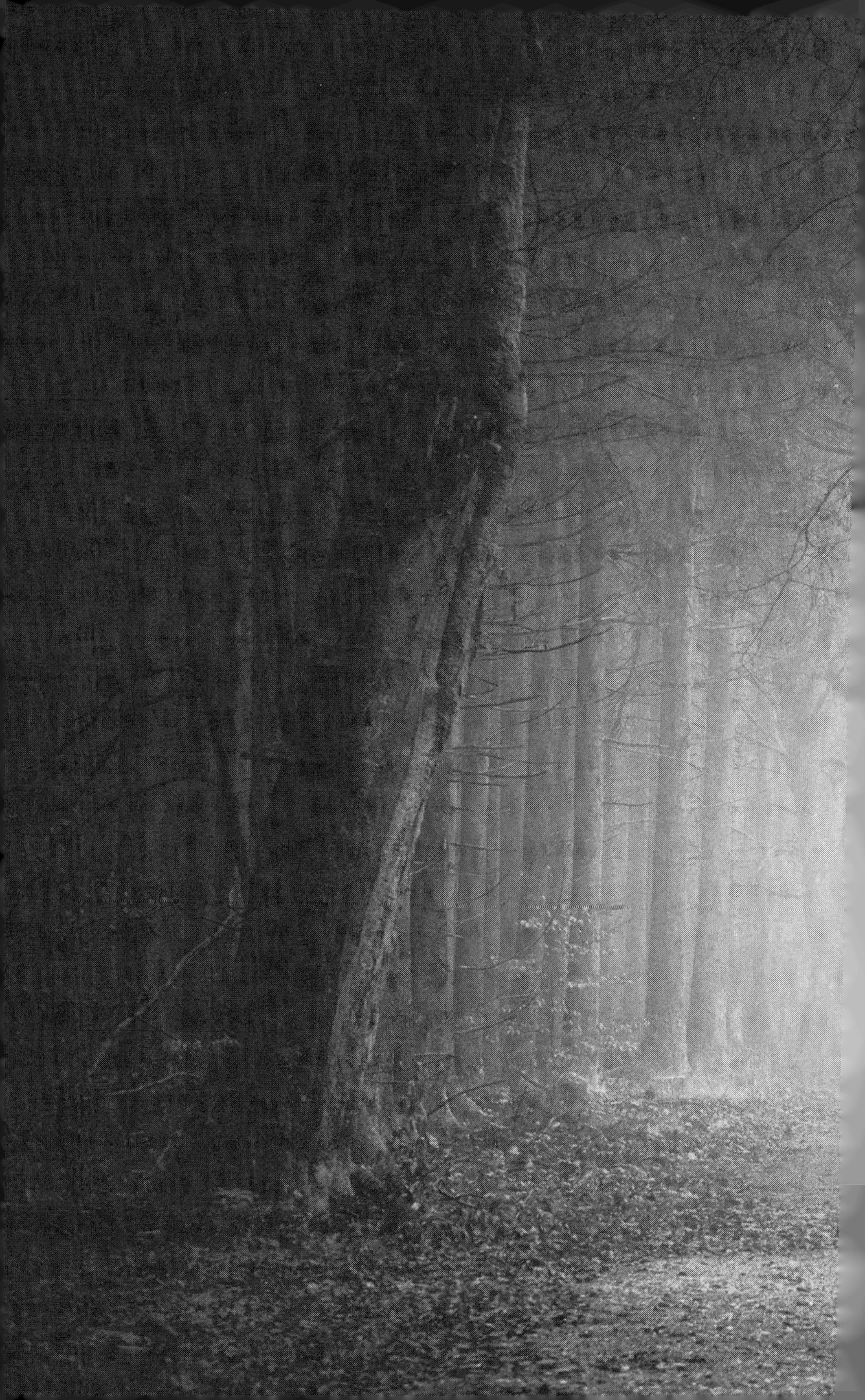

CHAPTER TWENTY-FIVE

The walls are practically made out of liquid. Or at least that's the way it feels when I have to brush my fingers against them to regain my balance after I slip on a damp patch of... well, actually I don't want to know what it was. The steps leading down to what I'm assuming are the catacombs of the palace are dark and slimy and treacherous, but fortunately Ravven is walking in front of me. Not so that he can catch me if I fall, but just the thought of him having to catch me keeps me from being too careless as we walk down, down, down in a never-ending spiral of slick stones and silence.

The silence is probably the worst. I can't figure out what is going on with Ravven. One second we are on at least civil terms the next it's the silent treatment. I decide that I have enough of this cold shoulder or whatever it is.

"I couldn't help but gather from your words from earlier, that you think that this will be dangerous?" I hop down a few steps, trying to keep up with Ravven's gait. Not only are his legs longer than mine and his movements far more graceful, but his eyes can probably see better in this gloomy darkness too. "Tell me truthfully what are the odds of me dying?"

Ravven doesn't respond as we slip further down into the bowels of who-knows-where. I let out a whistle. "That bad huh?"

"I don't know what waits for us below," Ravven says at last, his tone hard. He pauses and turns to me; I can't read his expression or see the color of his eyes because the top half of his face is concealed in shadows. He reaches out for me, but drops his arm to his side as soon as it brushes my shoulder. "Of course what is ahead will be perilous, but can you at least promise me that you will *try* not to die?"

"Rich of you to tell me not to die when this whole stupid plan was your idea," I say, crossing my arms. "Now you have me terrified of what lies beneath this castle."

He frowns deeply. "I don't see what you have to fear. Once you are dead, you no longer need to live with the consequences. I, on the other hand—"

"Now wait right there, mister," I interrupt, thrusting my finger into his chest. He recoils as if it is some dangerous weapon. His foot slips slightly and he has to steady himself on the wall to keep from falling down the last few stairs. "Don't you try to make my death about you, you selfish arrogant... *faerie*."

Ravven huffs. "Then who should it be about?"

I cross my arms. *Seriously?* "Um, how about me?"

He looks up at the ceiling, a smile curving his lips as if he is enjoying some private joke. "Please, you would suffer the least from your own death."

"You act as if I want to die!" I cry, throwing my arms out.

"Do you?"

"Of course not! Quite the reverse actually."

"Then why won't you promise me that you won't die?"

His words draw me up short. Why is he so obsessed over whether I die or not? This conversation is getting increasingly macabre.

"I don't have to promise you anything," I say with a roll of my eyes. "I hardly see how whether I die or not is your problem."

He tilts his head. "And how will your death not be my problem?" he asks, his tone lowering dangerously. "Considering I am very likely to be killed if you die."

"Well, then you will be dead and will no longer have to live with the consequences," I mimic. "And we will both be dead and worry free. Sounds lovely to me."

He stares at me for a long moment before finally saying. "You didn't blink twice."

I pull back. "Excuse me?"

"You said that if you were being sarcastic, you would blink twice. You were clearly being sarcastic there. I may be a faerie, but I can see that much."

I snort. "No need to sound so put out. Okay, so yes I was being sarcastic."

"You gave your word that you would blink twice and then you did not. How can I trust you?"

"How can you trust me?" I ask, guffawing. And this coming from the faerie? The faerie that just last night said that he didn't trust anybody?

He nods, averting his gaze to the dripping stone wall. "How can I when everything from your mouth is nothing more than a veiled lie. Sometimes, it isn't even veiled."

Veiled lie? It's only *sarcasm!*

I huff a breath and resist the urge to roll my eyes. "All right fine, I'm sorry."

Ravven begins to nod, but freezes when I blink twice.

"Did you—are you—" he stammers.

I smirk. I'm not sure if I've ever heard him stammer before.

"Confound it all, woman, you baffle me."

"Thank you," I say. I nod my chin toward the dark passage where the water is coming from. "Now, shouldn't we get going? We have a chalice to retrieve after all."

I glance at Ravven as I say this and my words die on my lips. Because the way that Ravven is looking at me, the chalice seems to be the furthest thing from his mind. His expression has softened and he is gazing at me with something akin to ardor, but I can't be right because this is the same faerie who called me hideous.

I am clearly imagining a lot of things. Like my heart's fluttering response to that look.

Ravven quickly pulls back. "Of course." He turns around stiffly, and steps down the last two steps, landing with a splash at the bottom.

He peers down at the two inches of stagnant water covering the floor with disgust.

I hop down beside him and pat his arm. "Cheer up. Just think, if it were a little brighter down here, the water could be reflective and you could have traveled with ease in being able to see your reflection everywhere you look."

He heaves a pained sigh. "That would have been nice, yes. May have even made all this worth it."

I smile teasingly at his back. "Well, I can see you all I want without a reflective surface, and I can tell you that it does not make it worth it to me."

Ravven grunts. "Obviously you have no fine taste for beauty. How could you when you are so—"

"So what? Hideous? Deformed? Mortal?" I silently thank Ravven for reminding me just why I must have been imagining that look on the stairs.

Ravven's shoulders tighten. "Yes, to all of those, but I was going to say desensitized."

I trip over a protruding section of floor that had been hidden by the murky waters and nearly crash into his back before I steady myself. "Desensitized?"

Ravven shoots me a crooked smile over his shoulder. "Of course. You are used to gazing on my beauty, it does not seem worth it if you have to pay a price for such an honor."

Well, he is ridiculous. I am about to tell him as much, but a low rumble from deeper in the dark passage kills any response before it has a chance to live.

I stumble forward a few steps and grasp Ravven's arm. His muscles are tense. "What was that?" I whisper.

He shoots me an annoyed look. "How am I supposed to know?"

I return a glare. "Considering I didn't even know that the Court of Dreams and Nightmares existed until yesterday, I would think that out of the two of us, you are the one who would know what lives underneath it."

Ravven shakes his head. "Why must I be the one to do everything? Perhaps I should have chosen a more self-reliant human to be my champion."

I scoff at him. "You hardly chose me. It was more... a really bad play of circumstances."

Ravven arches his brow, pressing his lips together. He turns his attention back ahead as another rumble fills the air. It sounds like a moan, a call. A roar. Like something that is alive, and probably quite hungry.

"Well, if you don't know what it is, and I don't know what it is." I swallow. "Then there is only one way to find out."

"Why do I get the feeling that you are about to say something foolhardy?"

"We need to go see what it is."

"And there it is. You never fail to disappoint, do you, pest?"

I ignore him and step forward, passing him. Ravven heaves a heavy sigh, but then I hear him sloshing after me.

Finally, the passage widens and brightens just a bit. We're now in a large circular chamber. It's filled with a large pool of dark water with only a small path extending in front of us. At the end of the path, in the very center of the room is a small circular platform with a pedestal on it. Sitting right on top of the pedestal is a silver chalice.

My heart leaps and I step toward it. Can this truly be so easy?

Ravven hand grasps my arm and yanks me back several steps just as another roar shakes the room. I glance around wildly until my eyes land on it.

I'm not entirely sure what *it* is. A giant creature surfacing from the water, with a snout and scales. It looks almost like a crocodile, only it's giant and it is blue. And it is definitely a dragon, not a crocodile.

"What. The. Heck," I breathe.

"It's a Lake Dragon," Ravven replies softly.

"How did it get in here?" I ask. It seems so huge even for this large chamber. No way could it have come through the passage we just entered through, and I don't see any other ways in or out.

"There must be some passage connecting this room to the Lake of Darkness under the waters."

Lake of Darkness? Sounds *lovely*.

I swallow. "Maybe—maybe it won't notice us." I take a hesitant step forward. I watch the hump of the back, followed by the tail as the creature disappears below the surface. I scan the water breathlessly.

I turn to Ravven when there is no sign of it. "Maybe it grew bored of waiting for us and swam to this Lake of Darkness of yours."

Ravven shoots me a dark look, one that quickly morphs into horror. "Behind you!"

I whirl, just in time to see a long slender scaly snake whip toward me. It collides with my stomach and as I go flying backwards, it occurs to me that this snake is actually the Lake Dragon's tail. It came at us from underwater. Sneaky.

I could almost feel a small measure of respect except I'm currently incapable of breathing and I just really wish that the Lake Dragon hadn't done that.

As the wind whistles past my ears, I wonder if I'm ever going to land. My stomach muscles cramp and I note how hard that creature hit me. Then I crash into something hard and unyielding. Pain shoots through the back of my head, and my vision fills with stars. I tumble down into the dark liquid below and begin to sink, too stunned to think about swimming up even as my lungs demand for air.

Faintly I hear a splash and see bubbles, but I'm too busy watching the Lake Dragon swimming toward me with an alarming speed, it's body swaying and its tail working as a sort of fin. It is sort of graceful, I could even appreciate the display, if I wasn't one hundred percent certain that the Lake Dragon was on its way to eat me.

Then Ravven's face is there, blocking my view of the Lake Dragon. Not that I care. If I was capable of speaking, I would tell him how beautiful he looks. Though when I open my mouth only bubbles come out.

I glimpse the Lake Dragon over his shoulder. Or more, it's mouth and rows and rows of its razor-sharp teeth. It's close enough that that is all I can see.

Ravven wraps his hands around me and I squeeze my eyes shut as a dizzying rush vibrates through my skull. I let out a cry and pry my eyes open as my stomach sloshes. We're sitting on dry land again. I gasp for air, which quickly turns into a gag as I spew out water and more water and still more water.

Ravven braces his hands on either side of me. "Are you all right?" His hair drips into his face. For the first time since I met him, he doesn't look immaculate. Except non-immaculate Ravven is gorgeous as well. And his wet clothes cling to his form in a way that I wish they wouldn't.

I nod, not trusting my lungs to work as I cough up more water.

Ravven glances down at the water and then stands. He moves to the edge. "Get the chalice." He whirls on me and holds up a finger. "But be certain not to drink a drop, no matter how tempted you might be. That is the test in it all."

"Yeah and the Lake Dragon is an inconvenience," I mumble, swiping my hair out of my face.

Ravven smiles. "Precisely. Behave while I am gone."

I still, every muscle and bone and blood cell turning to stone. "And where are you going?"

"To distract the inconvenience while you retrieve the chalice." He backs toward the edge of the platform.

"Ravven don't," I cry, scrambling toward him but slipping in the water still dripping off of me.

He smirks. "Careful, pest, or you might actually sound like you care."

My hand flies out from underneath me and I grunt as my elbow hits the stone.

"Don't wait for me," Ravven says. "I shall return on my own time."

"Don't!" I cry again, but it's too late. He's already stepped back and disappeared into the water with a splash and a sea of bubbles. "Ravven!" I scream, partly in worry but mostly in rage.

I slap my hand against the cold stone with a wet splash.

I don't know what to do. Ravven told me to go, but surely, I cannot just leave him here. A roar echoes through the chamber even louder than any of the other roars of the Lake Dragon. I grimace. He's trying to distract it until I can retrieve the chalice, and here I am sitting here, wasting all of the time that he is buying.

I lift my head and glare at the chalice, sitting there taunting me. With the rest of my strength left, I push to my feet and take off running toward it. My soaked boots don't want to gain any traction, so I almost slide past the chalice, but I grab the pedestal at the last second. I pull myself up and wrap my shaking fingers around the stem of the chalice.

The cavern is devoid of sound as I lift the chalice, so I can hear the clink distinctly. I try not to think of what that means as I turn and walk as quickly as I dare back down the narrow aisle.

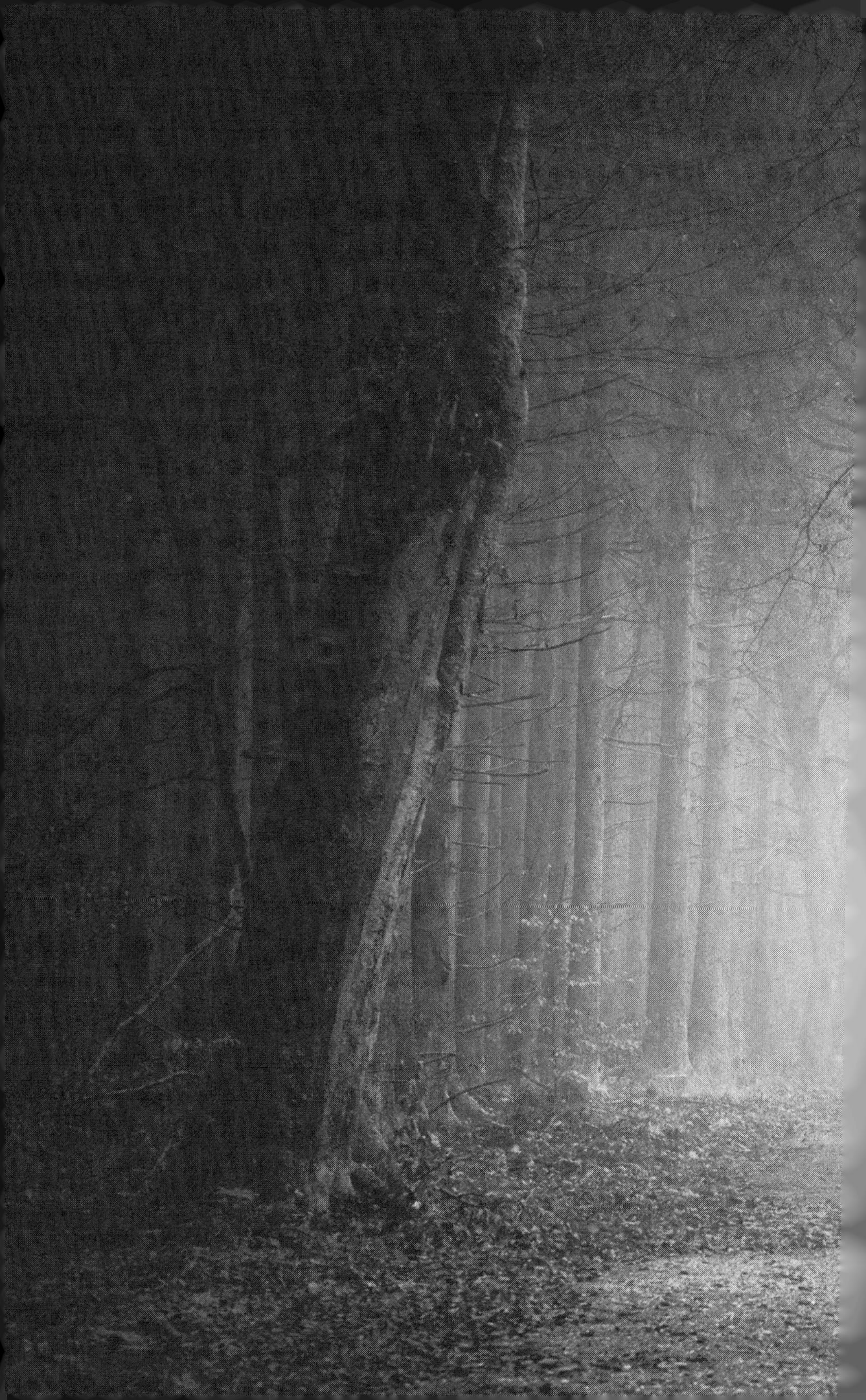

CHAPTER TWENTY-SIX

My hand trembles as I pull away from the throne, not a minute too soon. I had managed to hold off the tremors and kept my hands still as I carefully made my way through the passage, back up the stairs and all the way to the Undersea Court, all the while making absolutely certain that I didn't spill a drop.

But now with the chalice gone, safely in the queen's hold, my whole body is wracked with shaking. Probably from my wet clothes clinging to me. And somehow water got clogged into my tear ducts and that is definitely the reason why I feel like crying.

The Undersea Queen looks briefly into the chalice, not half as long as she should have given the care I took to obey her command not to spill a single drop. Or the temptation I faced when I started thinking about all those questions I would like answered. But I had to think of Thomas's safety. That's all that matters. Not my curiosity. Not even Ravven.

The Undersea Queen arches one perfectly blue eyebrow. "Well done, young mortal. You have completed the test. But tell me, where is your faerie escort?"

"He—" the word lodges in my throat despite my previous assessment that Thomas is all that matters. Where is Ravven? Surely not dead. He wouldn't take me this far only to abandon me on the first test, left to wander blindly on my own?

"I am right here, your excellence. And I am quite honored by your concern."

My heart jolts so far that I legitimately fear that I'm going to have a heart attack. I whirl just as Ravven strides into the room, dripping water all over the transparent floor. I wonder if the Undersea faeries even care, given how much they must like water.

He smiles charming as usual, and magnificently, gloriously soaked. "Did you miss me?"

I'm not entirely sure who he's talking to. Me, or the Undersea Queen, or just everyone in general.

He strides to my side and looks at the Undersea Queen without even sparing me a glance. I try to cover up any pain, it's ridiculous that I feel it anyway. I should just be relieved that he isn't dead and I'm not on my own. I shouldn't feel slighted by a faerie who barely even tolerates me.

She smiles. "Very well then, since the cup has been delivered, I have nothing more to say. You have completed the trial that I gave you. According to the Fair Law, you now have the Undersea Court's support, contender."

I raise my eyebrows, noting that she hadn't said that we had her support because we impressed her. Or proved ourselves. No, we have their support because of the Fair Law. Without it I doubt she would give it. Something tells me that she isn't an easy person to please, and she is supposed to be the neutral one.

Ravven bows and I even drop into a sloppy curtsy. "Thank you, my lady," I say, lifting my chin.

She holds my gaze for a minute before finally turning to her husband, summarily dismissing us like we did nothing. Like we didn't just go up against a freaking Lake Dragon.

A warning glance from Eilis stops me from speaking up. Instead, since we've obviously been dismissed, I turn and leave. No one in the Undersea court tries to speak to me or congratulate me. I may have completed my first test, but I'm pretty sure that they all still think that I'm going to die.

Once I'm past the large doors, I turn around to see Ravven slip out behind me just as the doors bang shut.

"Where have you been?" I demand.

"I told you, I was distracting the Lake Dragon."

"But *how*?"

He looks at me and smirks. "Believe it or not, Lake Dragons are surprisingly easy to distract. Especially hungry Lake Dragons like the one we saw. All you have to do is swim in front of them and they lose their minds."

I swallow hard. "You think it was hungry?"

Ravven chuckles. "Do you think it got much food in that room? Even in the Lake of Darkness... well, there are some prey that even a Lake Dragon wouldn't eat. But enough of that. The Lake of Darkness was actually looking surprisingly well."

"The... Lake of Darkness?" Ravven had mentioned it once or twice, but I still had no idea what the heck it was.

Ravven smirks. "That indoor pool must have drained into the room from somewhere and I am pleased to say that I was right in assuming that it was the Lake of Darkness. I found the underwater passage connecting the two and swam down it. The Lake Dragon followed close behind. Obviously, it was a good distraction since you made it back here in one piece. A remarkable feat if you think about it."

I nod, but bite down on my lip as it feels like my brain rattles around in my skull. My head seems to hurt more and more in every passing second since I smacked it into the wall in the catacombs. "Well, mostly one piece."

Ravven looks down at me. "What? Are you hurt? Did you somehow manage to get yourself hurt in the time that I was gone?" His words are tinged with such a fierce anger, it's like he is angry at me for any injuries I might have sustained. I suppose he might take personal offense considering that he was nearly eaten by a Lake Dragon to try to protect me.

I shake my head as I reach up to massage the back of my scalp. "No, not after you left."

The jerking motion awakens a fresh wave of pounding in my head. I grimace, I hope that stupid Lake Dragon didn't give me a concussion.

Ravven frowns. "What is it?"

I massage the lump underneath my hair. "It's just my head. I bumped it when the Lake Dragon smacked me across the room. It'll probably hurt for a while."

Ravven frowns as he looks me over. His fingers rest gently on my shoulders as if he's trying to somehow hold me together.

"I'll survive," I snap. Probably. I mean, unless the damage was worse than I thought and my brain is swelling at this very moment and... I quickly banish that thought.

Ravven's eyebrows shoot up to his dark hair. "Really? Because often I wonder if you will. You should not be in this world. You do not belong here." His tone grows bitter.

A sharp pain pierces my heart. Here he is, once again reminding me that I don't belong. Not here. Not with the faeries. Not in their world.

I'm just a weak inconsequential human.

I clear my throat and start walking down the hall, ignoring my hurt feelings or the surprised look in Ravven's eyes. "I should probably go get dry." I glance over my shoulder as I reach the door that will lead up into the rest of the Court of Dreams and Nightmares. Ravven hasn't moved. I pause with my hand on the handle and force a smile, trying to hide any traces of my pain from his suspicious glance. "You should probably go get dry too."

I turn away again, wondering if that sounded as bad as I think it did.

"Jaye—"

That one word, my own name nearly startles me out of my skin. Ravven rarely ever calls me Jaye. Mortal? Yes. Pest? Heck yeah. Rotting corpse? Well, actually with my head injury, I can't remember if he called me or Thomas that, but it was definitely said.

He only ever calls me Jaye when there is something big and life threatening. Like when I was tortured.

I whirl so quickly that a wave of dizziness washes over me. I brace my hand on the wall and rub at my temple. When my vision clears, I see that he has stepped closer to me. So close that I only have to extend my fingers to touch him.

"What?" It's supposed to be a firm question, but instead it comes out hopelessly breathy.

Ravven doesn't answer me for a long time. He just stares down at my face, his eyes a deep purple.

"I'm sorry," he says at last.

I frown, perturbed. "What do you have to apologize for?" Last I checked, I was the one who dragged him into this mess, not the other way around. Actually, Ravven is being suspiciously helpful. I remind myself again that I can't fully trust him. Constantly having to remind myself to not trust anyone is getting exhausting and makes my head hurt worse. "Is there something you are keeping from me—" I don't even get a chance to finish my sentence before Ravven is leaning forward and pressing his lips against mine. Hard. Stifling any attempt of mine to speak.

I inhale sharply as his arms wrap around me and press me to his hard chest.

What is he doing?

I'm stone. I'm stillness. I'm shock itself. Ravven Crowe detests me. Even if our relationship has grown since we first met, I'm still nothing more than a disgusting little human. A pest.

Why is he kissing me like he might die if he doesn't?

And then something snaps inside of me, breaking through the layers of stone on my arms and my hands are reaching up, twining into his hair. His glorious silky damp hair. And now I know what faerie hair feels like. It feels like hair, the softest hair possible. My lips move against his, trying to memorize their shape and feel.

I rise up on my toes to get closer and he moans.

Fire explodes in my chest. Stars fill my vision. Electricity runs up and down my body and then back again. And then suddenly he's yanking away and I'm stumbling against the corner of the wall next to the door, gasping for breath and trying to remember who I am.

Ravven grimaces as he clutches the back of his head and I half wonder if I pulled his hair. Then his eyes land on me and they fill with terror as he slowly lowers his hand from his head. It falls limply at his side as the terror morphs into horror. He lurches back.

I wince. Was the kiss really that bad? I had thought it was pretty great. Magical even, and I know that it is ridiculous to say that. I'm sure any girl thinks that any kiss with a super-hot faerie is magical, but that doesn't change the fact that it felt magical.

Or maybe it was something much, much worse than a bad kiss. Because Ravven legitimately looks like he is about to either be sick or pass out. His normal golden hue has become a chalky gray and his eyes are such a bright red that they practically glow in the dark passage.

"Ravven...?" I ask, swallowing hard at how husky my voice is. I straighten and step toward him. "Are you all right?"

He shakes his head, jerking back another step. "Yes... only... I... farewell." And with those four stilted words, he sweeps past me and races out the door without even a backwards glance. Which is just fine with me because he doesn't need to see me slump back into my corner and bury my face into my hands to hide the tears streaming down my face.

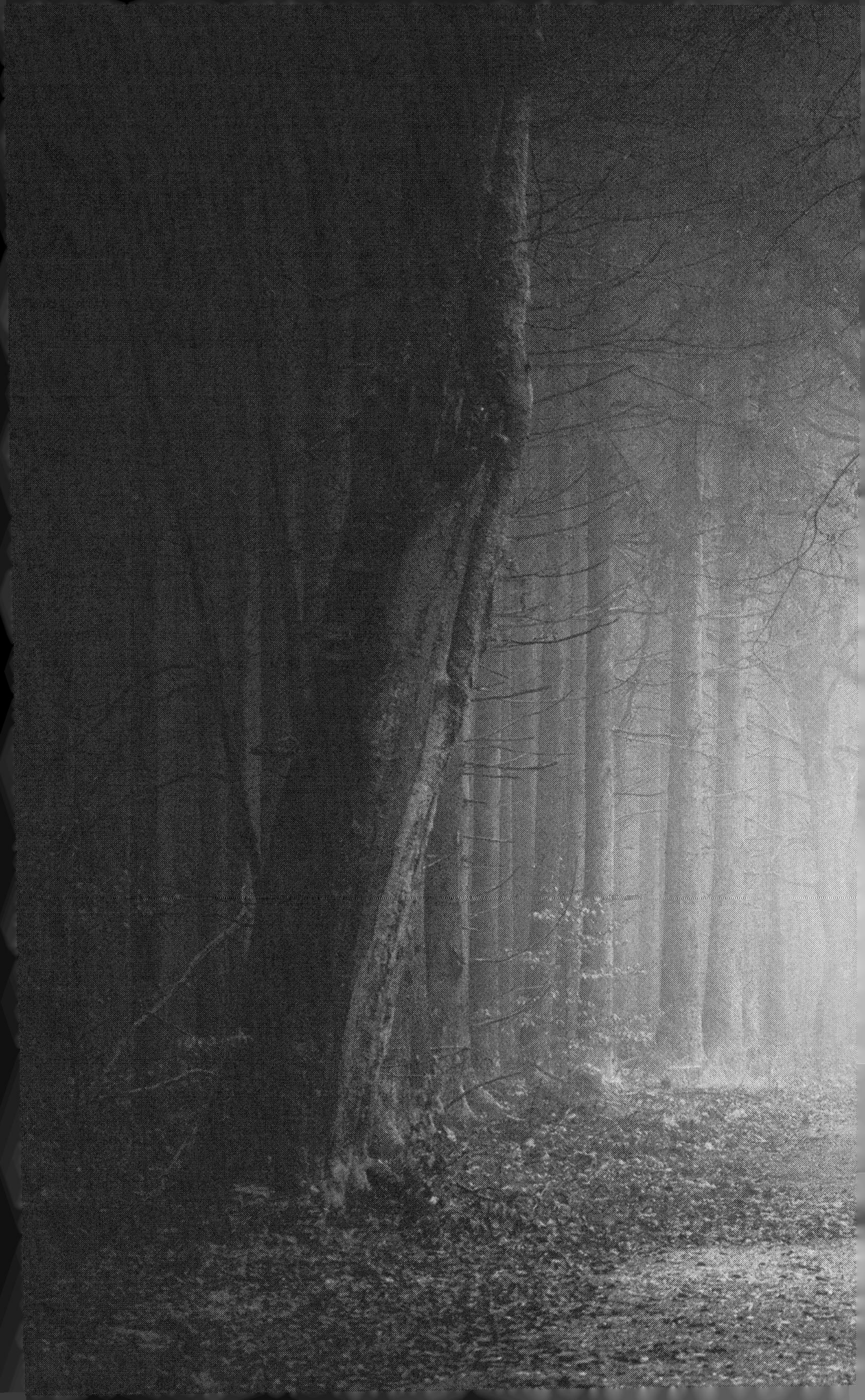

CHAPTER TWENTY-SEVEN

I guess I didn't hear the door from the throne room open, because I didn't know Eilis was there until a soft lilting voice is asking, "What troubles ye, my friend?"

I wipe at my eyes and look up to see Eilis staring at me with concern filling her bright green eyes. I shake my head. "It's nothing. It's stupid. I always seem to cry over the stupidest reasons."

I always seem to cry because of Ravven Crowe.

Eilis's mouth twitches. "Do not fault yourself for being human. Every time I believe that I have forgotten how to shed a tear, it arrives as if it has been summoned, and often it is for a ridiculous reason just as ye suffer."

"Yeah, you pretty much described my struggle precisely." I straighten, wiping my eyes again.

"You are going through an ordeal, and even though you may be surrounded by these ethereal beings, you are only human. That is not a fact that ye should forget. It is yer humanity that offers ye a distinctness from them."

"Good for me," I mutter with a huff. I've never wanted to be more than a human in my life. But now, a part of me wonders what it would be like to be a faerie. To fit in with this world. To be someone who actually had a future with Ravven.

I shove that thought away angrily. I don't *want* a future with him.

Ravven Crowe is not worth anything. Least of all my humanity, my life at home, or my family.

Eilis's eyes dart toward the door. "Where is Crowe?"

"How should I know?" I ask a little too bitterly. Eilis's eyes dart back to mine and she hums knowingly.

"I wish that I did not know yer pain," she says at last; she smirks, but there's an edge to it like she also harbors anger. "But I am certain that every mortal girl who is lost in a world of faeries does. Come." She holds out her hand. "The ball shall begin soon and ye certainly cannot arrive looking like this. Just because ye are mortal does not mean that ye have to give these faeries a reason to remember that fact."

I don't know why I do it, but I slip my hand into Eilis's. Warm, calloused skin meets mine. Her skin isn't smooth as silk like the faeries, but instead rough and weathered. She squeezes my fingers and pulls me forward.

"Where are you taking me?" I ask as she leads me back down to the throne room.

"To me chambers. I'm assuming that ye do not wish to risk running into Crowe again for a while?" she pauses and glances back at me as if waiting for an answer.

I debate this question for a long moment before nodding. "You're right."

She dips her chin. "I thought as much."

She pushes open the door and I straighten my spine, hoping that the tears didn't cause my eyes to swell up, or leave behind any residue on my cheeks to betray my pain and my human frailty, but no one is in the room.

"They be all preparing for the ball," Eilis says as I glance around the empty throne room. It seems dead without anyone inside.

Eilis steps toward a door along the wall and steps in. After a short walk down a hallway that looks like something out of a mermaid's castle with coral and starfish lining the wall, she opens a door to the right and pulls me in.

I'm shocked to not see a single sea urchin. It's a surprisingly... non undersea room, with a simple bed and wardrobe and a vanity. The walls are unadorned. One could almost forget they were in the portion of the Court of Dreams and Nightmares dedicated to the Undersea, if only they ignored the transparent floor. A large rug that looks homespun covers most of it anyway.

Eilis releases my hand and steps toward the vanity. "Through the door to your left ye'll find the washroom," I look over to see a small wooden door. "Ye should wash that scent of dead sea critters out of yer hair."

I smile faintly and go into the washroom. It is outfitted with a simple tub and a toilet. An elaborate bird bath like contraption appears to be the sink. Since coming here, I've wondered what the faeries do as far as plumbing goes, but as I pull the tap on the bath, I realize that it is probably magic that keeps this system running. Of course.

The soaps I find are all scented like sweet water. If they were sold at home they would probably be labeled, "Ocean Breeze" or something like that.

When I step out of the bathroom, wearing a soft pale blue towel, Eilis is waiting. She's transformed from the human guard to an otherworldly princess. Her hair is pulled back in an elaborate braid and she is wearing a floor length dress made entirely of shimmering green scales. She looks like a mermaid. She looks like *the Little Mermaid*.

She smiles when she sees me. "Excellent. There ye are." She holds up a dress made of a shimmering Caribbean blue material. The cut is simple, slightly off the shoulders with sleeves that extend to the elbows. The truly remarkable portion of the dress is that the bottom half of the skirt looks like it's a fish tank. Myriads of fish are sewn into the skirt and when Eilis moves, the ripples in the skirt makes it look like they are actually swimming.

"Well, I will look like a fishy queen."

Eilis smiles. "Don't let Ursulle hear ye say that. She be territorial at best."

I change quickly. It isn't too hard to pull the dress on. Eilis probably likes her clothes easy to get into.

"And now for the question of what to do with your hair."

"I—" I trail off, lifting a limp strand of my damp hair and a droplet of water rolls off my finger. I have no idea what to do with my hair. I don't have a hair dryer.

"Not to worry," she says as she bustles me to the stool next to the vanity. "I've had plenty of practice working with wet hair. Ye'll not look like a drowned pooka by the time I'm done with ye."

"How do you..." I pause and trail off over how ridiculous my question is.

"How do I what?" Elis asks as she pins another lock of my hair up.

"How do you survive? In the Undersea Court, that is. I'm assuming that it is—" I cut myself off, biting hard on my lip as a blush takes over my face.

Eilis smirks at me in the mirror. "Undersea? Well, you would be correct. It is. But the court itself... well, it's hard to explain to someone who has never been there, but there are magical barriers around the water. Part of the court is submerged completely in water, and the other half is dry as the land. The water never broaches into the dry side or in from outside, that's the handy thing about magic. And I just tend ta stay in the areas of the court where I can breathe."

I nod, but freeze when Eilis smacks my shoulder. "We'll have none of that now. You will ruin my work and I'm almost done."

Finally, she steps back and waves her hand. "And there we go."

My hair is in several coils around my head, leaving only a few softly curly damp strands hanging around my neck.

I raise my brows. Eilis transformed me from a drowned... uh, pooka into an enchanting mortal maiden. I've never been one to care much about how I look, but in this world, beauty means everything. Eilis just gave me everything. "Thank you."

215

Eilis smiles. "I'm just glad ta help. Ye must look yer best if ye want to earn these faerie's respect."

I half turn in my vanity and peer up at her. "Why are you helping me? What would you have to gain?"

Eilis tilts her head. Her smile turns devilish. "Would ye believe me if I said that I simply wanted to help out my fellow mortal?" Her voice drips heavily with disdain.

"Well, I might have believed it until you said it like that."

Eilis laughs and glances down at her feet. Finally, she looks up at me. "I have me own reasons for helping ye. Same as Crowe does. But never fear, I have yer best interest at heart. That is more than can be said for others."

My stomach churns and I adjust in my seat. By others does she mean Ravven? "Do you know what Crowe's—I mean, Ravven's reason for helping me is?"

Now that is something I would dearly like to know.

"Crowe is young. He is only concerned in the present. He does not see the big picture."

I gape at her. *Ravven is young?* If she can say that when he speaks of hundreds of years carelessly then how old is she truly?

Her eyes are ancient as she returns my gaze. Gone is the carefree mortal. This girl has lived longer than any human ever should, seen things that humans should never be permitted to see. And she has done things that are too terrible to even be remembered.

That is the story that her eyes tell.

She smiles coolly. "Now I on the other hand... I have been at this so much longer. I can see the greater picture of the future. It is a blank canvas, wide open and simply waiting to become what a soul needs it to be."

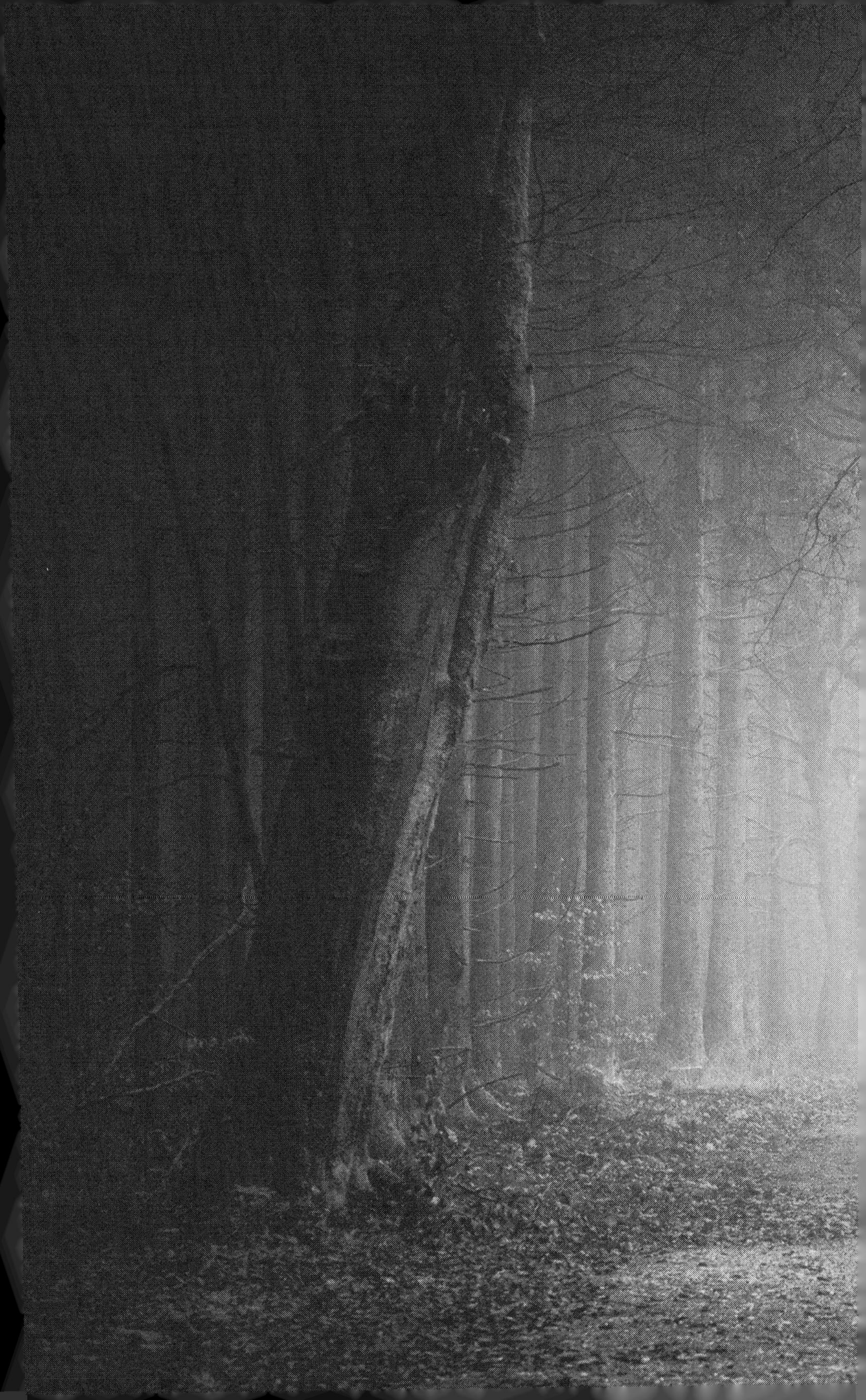

CHAPTER TWENTY-EIGHT

The ballroom is chaos when I arrive, and for the first time I wonder at the wisdom of this. The four courts all gathered in one place. That faerie war seems very inevitable and if one little mortal could cause it what would a roomful of faeries do? Faeries that dance and cavort and howl, and I even catch a few of them fighting with each other, all around me. They're back to ignoring the human in the room and even though Highmoon has only just set and the ball officially began, already most of the faerie's mouths are stained red.

Eilis sneers as she takes it in. Her eyes linger on a faerie in the midst and I realize that it is Riagan leaning languidly against a wall, a goblet of the red liquid in his hands. "I may love the faeries, but sometimes they disgust me."

With all of these faeries dancing around, the liquid in their glasses sloshing around, I'm overcome with anxiety. All it had taken was a drop of that liquid to touch my skin before I was paralyzed.

"I call it the Oblivion Potion," Eilis says, her eyes hard and flat. "It is the only evidence that not all faeries are happy with their existence. They would never admit it, but they would not drink if they were not trying to forget something."

She shakes her head.

"Have you ever tasted any of the faerie fruits?" I ask, rubbing at my shoulder. Eilis has lived in this world a long time.

Eilis snorts. "Stars no. I would not be standing here next to you if I had."

"I don't see Ravven," I say more to myself than anyone else.

"No, I bet that he would avoid the Oblivion Potion."

I glance at Eilis, surprised. I hadn't been even expecting a response. "Why is that?"

"Ye'll have to ask him that yerself." She begins striding through the convulsing crowd. "Ye must excuse me, but I've been away from me queen for too long."

I hurry to follow her. As much as I'm not sure about Eilis, I know for certain that I do not want to be left with these faeries. "Why do you serve the Undersea Queen?"

Eilis turns and raises her eyebrow. "What do ye mean?"

"I mean, out of all the courts, why do you serve hers? I can understand not wanting to serve the Winter Court, but why not the Summer Court? Aren't they the good guys?"

I bite down on my lip as Eilis's expression becomes livid. I hold up my hands, stepping away. "I'm sorry. I shouldn't have asked. It's none of my business."

"Not everything is as it seems in the faerie world," Eilis says, holding herself stiffly, her eyes still flashing. "The sooner ye get that in yer head, the longer ye'll live."

And then with those curt words, she inclines her head and walks away.

I shake my head and return to searching for Ravven, but I can't find him anywhere. If he left me to attend this ball on my own in favor of never arriving, I will probably kill him. Heck, I might just kill him anyway. Oh, *why* did he kiss me and complicate an already far too complicated relationship? I thought he couldn't stand the sight of me!

Suddenly a hand grasps my arm. I startle and whirl only to see Riagan's lazy half charming smile. It puts me at ease immediately, until I realize that is probably the exact purpose of that smile. To put people at ease.

I roll my shoulders back, trying to remove the tension. It's claustrophobic surrounded by all of these faeries, all of this stifling magic, and every single one of these craftily veiled lies.

"Would you care to dance with me, my lady?"

He holds out his long-gloved hands and I stare at it like it's a snake. Riagan himself told me not to dance with faeries and now he's asking me to dance with him.

I cross my arms tightly. "Why did you call me 'my lady'?"

"It is the proper form of respect, suiting yer title of Fair Assassin."

I snort. Riagan's pooka runs around us in a circle, barking and snapping at any faeries he deems are standing too close. They move away, some with titters, others with hisses. I inhale deeply, relieved to be able to breathe again. "I'm not the Fair Assassin yet."

"But I have no doubt that ye will be," Riagan replies easily. He raises an eyebrow. "And ye are well aware that I cannot lie."

I'm also well aware that he cannot be trusted. He serves the Winter Court. And yet... he's only ever been kind to me. *"I have a soft spot for humans,"* he said. And even though he stands passively by while his court does its darn best to ruin my life, I sense no malice from him.

"Ye've already finished yer first test," he continues gaily. "And yer next test is from the Summer Court which should be quite easy."

I arch my brow. "My next test is from the Summer Court?" I didn't even know that.

"Did I say that?" Riagan asks, not sounding the least perturbed. "Well, bumble me, the things I let slip."

"How do you know that?"

Riagan raises his eyebrow and his expression is suddenly a lot less lazy and far craftier than I would have given him credit for. "Well, I have my ways. The Winter Court was incensed that the Summer Court got to ye first, so they'll likely be the next ta test ye, leaving the Spring Court for last if I am not mistaken."

Then I realize what he is doing and I inhale sharply. He's telling me information about the tests. He's *helping* me.

"Why are you helping me?" I demand. "Don't you realize what I plan to do once I have the title? I will kill Aoibheann and you serve the Winter Court."

"Ye made that fact perfectly clear last night. About killing Aoibheann," Riagan replies cheerfully. "And it is true that I am the spymaster to Queen Cliodnha."

"Then why? Why are you helping me when it means betraying the queen you serve?"

Riagan stares at me a long moment. "Because Eilis chose yer side, so despite the folly in all of the scheme and the way that I can see a hundred possible ways we could end up dead, I appear to have chosen yer side as well. But actually, it's very important that you keep in mind that I'm not technically helping ye." He smiles. "Seeing as due to that accursed Fair Law, I cannot. I am simply telling you something that any faerie would know. I'm certain you would learn this and more from any faerie you would choose to speak with. And as for my queen... well, betrayal comes easily to me. I find that I am very good at it."

I frown up at him, disconcerted by his answer. He's helping me because of a loyalty to someone who appears to despise him. Someone who I don't even know the full reasons why *they are* helping me.

"Who is Eilis to you anyway?" I blurt.

Riagan's smile falters and I half expect him to go ballistic on me like Eilis did, but he simply blinks and nods. "Eilis and I worked together in the past, serving the last High Queen. However, when her reign... *ended.*" The way he says ended makes it seem like there is more of a story. "We went our separate ways. We may have been close once, but we did not part on good terms. I'm afraid that the hundreds of years between us has practically turned us into strangers."

He lifts his head and I follow his gaze to where Eilis is standing beside the dark-haired Undersea King at Queen Ursulle's throne. She's watching us with an unreadable expression on her face. He sighs, somewhat wistfully. "But despite that fact, I still have a particular fondness for me wee mortal."

The haunted tone to his voice and the longing look on his face, make it seem like he has more than a fondness, particular or no, for Eilis. Something akin to love... assuming faeries can even love, which I'm not sure. However, before I can ask any more questions, Riagan looks down at me as intent as a hawk. "And what of you and Crowe, eh? What is happenin' between the two of ye? Love between a mortal and an immortal does not happen often."

"Who said that there was anything between us?" I ask breathlessly. Had Eilis seen our kiss and then told Riagan for some reason?

Riagan smirks. "I believe that you did just then."

"I... we're... not like that," I stammer, my face burning.

Riagan shakes his head. "Chin up, lass. Ye did not betray a secret. Ravven was the first one to give himself away."

I raise my eyebrows, too surprised to speak. What is Riagan talking about? I hadn't even known that Ravven had feelings for me until he kissed me. He always said that I was ugly. He calls me pest.

I'm still pretty sure that he detests me.

And I have no idea whatsoever why he kissed me.

"One does not often see a Solitary faerie care for another living being. Least of all how much Ravven appears to care about you."

I shake my head. "That's ridiculous. You're being ridiculous."

"Perhaps I am," Riagan says, stepping away. "But I think you will find in our world, that many things are ridiculous and it doesn't make them any less true."

"You're giving me a headache," I mutter.

He dips into a low bow. "I hope ye enjoy the rest of yer evening. And best of luck to ye in yer test on the morrow. Though, ye will not need it."

When he straightens, his grin is back and he whistles. The pooka turns and follows him and the faeries begin to fill the space that was left.

I inhale shakily and hunch my shoulders. I jump as an overly intoxicated faerie drops his glass, the red faerie fruits splashing on the hem of my dress. I need to get out of here before something horrible happens to me.

How could Ravven abandon me here tonight? He knows exactly how lost I am. How endangered I am. He's said so many times that I'm fragile.

I begin shoving my way through the crowd, trying to avoid any glasses or red stained lips.

However, before I can escape, a new faerie steps in front of me, blocking my path. He smirks in much the manner a cat would at a mouse trapped in a corner. "Ah, here is the little mortal who thinks that she deserves the place as our esteemed assassin."

I'm surprised that he even noticed me. None of the other faeries even care who I am. Not anymore. Yesterday I was big news, today I am irrelevant.

"That sounded a little passive aggressive." I cross my arms as I look the new faerie over. He seems familiar, though I don't know where I've seen him before. He is tall with shoulder length blonde hair and is just all around breathtakingly beautiful. Most faeries are, but this man's beauty trumps theirs in a way I've only seen in a few individuals. Iorwerth, and the Leanhaun Shee sisters, and Ravven. He must be a Sidhe, the beautiful but wicked faeries of the Spring Court who consider mortals as nothing more than their play things. As soon as I realize that, I figure out where I've seen him before. He was the faerie who had stood behind the empty Spring Throne.

I think I remember Ravven saying that his name was Cinaed. They hadn't appeared to like each other.

"Careful, or your tongue could almost be considered as sharp as that iron blade you wish to someday wield," he says with a laugh that is so fake that it's almost painful. His eyes flash yellow in a somewhat familiar way before fading into coal black.

"Who said I didn't want that?"

Cinaed laughs. "I can see why Crowe would choose to play with you. Truly I can. You are amusing. But you are probably wondering who I am."

Cinaed. A Sidhe faerie who does not like Ravven. I think I know everything that I need to.

He smirks. "I am Cinaed, High Lord of the Spring Court."

"Jaye MacCullagh," I say tightly.

His smile grows wider. I half imagine poison dripping from his straight, perfect, blindingly white teeth and then his attention strays to a short blonde-haired girl standing at his side. There's something slightly off about her, but I hadn't paid much attention to it just as I hadn't paid much attention to her. At first, I had assumed that she was simply another faerie eavesdropping on our conversation, but apparently Cinaed knows her.

"This is Sarah," he says with a wave of his hand to the small girl. I narrow my eyes as I try to figure out what is different with her, but then my heart launches itself into my sternum as I realize what it is. Sarah is a human. My stomach churns with the sickening reality. The Sidhe may not hate humans like the Unseelie faeries do, but they do not view them as anything more than animals. They are known for kidnapping humans to be their slaves and even lovers.

"She so wanted to make the acquaintance of a fellow human," Cinaed continues in his haughty, smooth as honey voice.

Sarah dips her chin. "It is my pleasure to—to meet you."

I can't even say, the pleasure is mine, because all I can think is how she is a slave. She must be a slave. She is a slave of the creature standing before me.

Cinaed steps toward me. "Come now, I did not realize that you would be rude."

"You're a monster," I mutter.

Cinaed startles and then follows my gaze to Sarah. He laughs. "Sarah is here of her own volition is that not right, my pet?"

"Yes, my prince," Sarah says, bowing her head.

Cinaed turns back to me and takes another step forward, reaching out. "What I can't figure out is why you are here."

I jerk back as his fingertips brush my hair, but he has already jerked back just as quickly. His perfect straight nose wrinkles in disgust. "Disgusting, you positively reek of Crowe. What have you two been up to? Shame on him. And with a human nonetheless. How the mighty have fallen."

I press my lips together, trying to tamp down the urge to blush. How can I reek of Crowe? So, we kissed hours ago. I took a shower in that time. I smell like Ocean Breeze.

"I don't see how Ravven is any of your business," I say bitterly as I try to shove past him.

Cinaed arches his brow. "Really? I would think he would be, considering that he is my last living relation."

My feet halt just as my heart does. *What?* Just... *WHAT???*

My mind grapples with that fact as I realize what was so similar about Cinaed's eyes. They change colors, just like Ravven's does.

Cinaed begins to bow, but then pauses and straightens with a disgusted look on his face as if he can't even be bothered with such a thing. "Give my cousin my regards." And with those words he turns and disappears into the crowd, dragging the human girl with him.

And I'm left in the crowded ballroom. Alone save for the faeries that descend upon me as if Cinaed's attention reminded them that I was someone important, all seeking favors and to dance and my hair to make into necklaces.

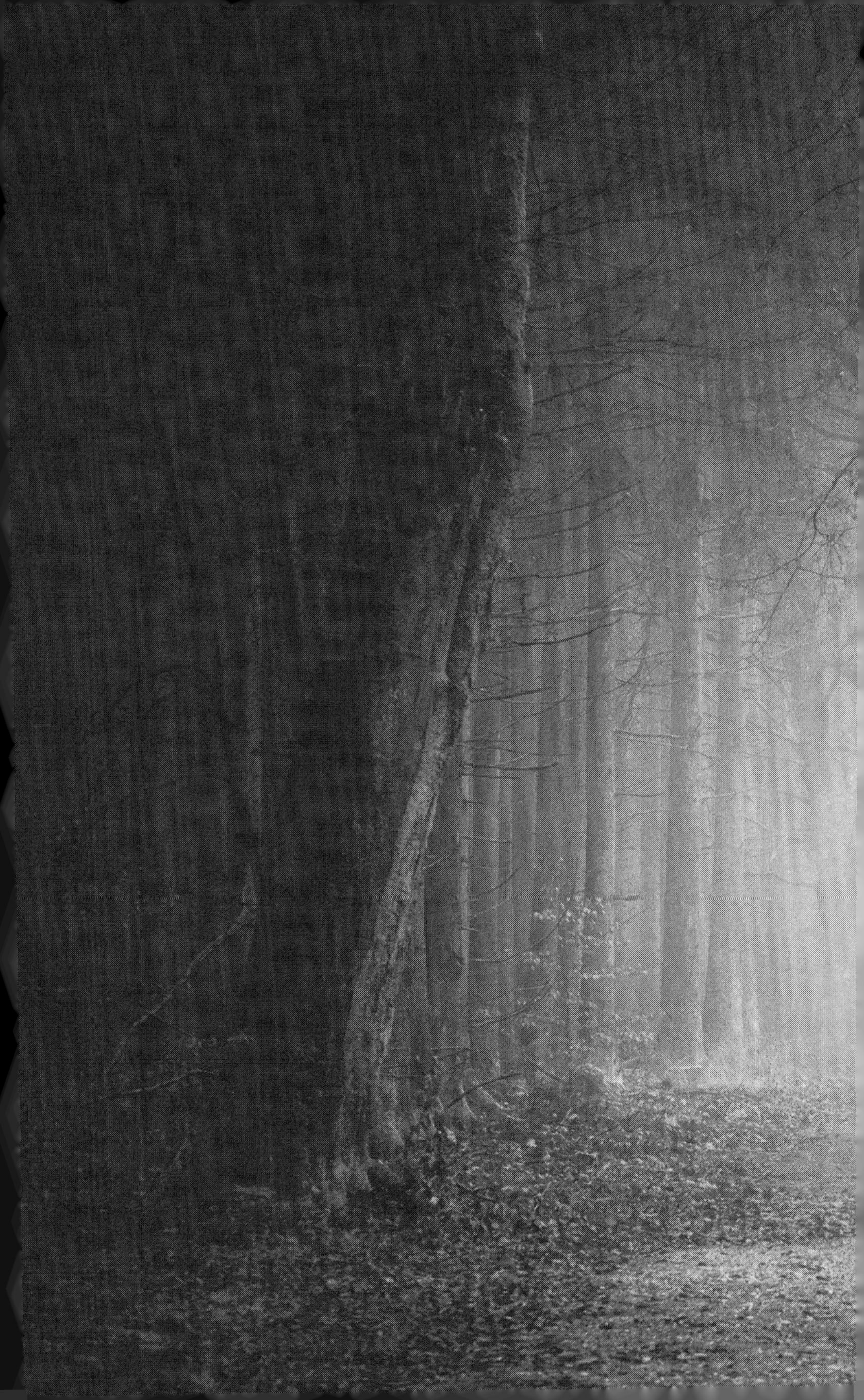

CHAPTER TWENTY-NINE

I don't know how I finally manage to escape the horde of faeries, but I'm grateful all the same as I race down the hall toward the wing of the Autumn Court.

I slow down before entering and try to compose myself. I'm trembling all over. Stupid emotions. Stupid stress. I raise my chin as I shove open the door. The only person in the main room is Daithi who is sitting cross legged on a pillow playing a reed pipe. He looks up at me, takes one look at me, and then slips away muttering about how his day was going well before he was forced to look at a human.

I grit my teeth as I stalk down the hallway of the doors, wondering where Ravven sleeps. I can't believe that I don't even know that. I pause outside one of the rooms, hearing the murmur of voices.

Twisting the handle, I swing the door open to find Ravven and his father standing across from each other, both in a deep conversation.

"How did you manage to accomplish *that*?" Keane asks wearily.

"I don't know," Ravven says, spreading his hands out. "Is there any way to reverse it?"

"I'm afraid there is nothing to do but either accept your fate or flee as far and as fast as you can because the damage has already been done, my son. Either way you look at it, your life is ruined, and you need to accept that fact."

"Hope I'm not interrupting anything," I ask, my voice so civil it half scares me.

They look up startled. Keane's face is alarmed, Ravven's is awash with emotions. First, he looks almost pleased to see me, then he looks frustrated.

Unfortunately for him, I'm just frustrated. "Where. Were. You?"

Ravven arches his eyebrow, his face becoming completely impassive. He sweeps his arm gesturing to the room and his father standing across from him. "Isn't it obvious? I was in here."

I stalk farther into the room. "You abandoned me!"

Keane clears his throat. "Perhaps I should..." he moves toward the door, but I step into his path. Keane freezes like a deer caught in the headlights.

Ravven rolls his eyes. "I hardly abandoned you. I'm your patron, not your nursemaid. Besides, I did not force you to go to the ball tonight." I'm about to ask him how he knows I even went to the ball since I haven't seen him all evening, but then I realize that I'm dressed in a ball gown. His eyes are on something on the hem of my dress and I realize that it is the residue of when the liquid splashed on my skirts.

Seeing it only makes me angrier. What if it had touched my skin again? What if I had blacked out in that ballroom with only those faeries? What would have happened to me then?

"You're my guide! And what about all of that talk about making certain that I passed my tests? Don't you think that could have been hard if someone killed me while I was wandering around abandoned?" I fling my arm out, nearly hitting Keane, who jumps back at the last minute.

"No one is going to kill you," Ravven says, rolling his eyes. I'm about to rip those eyes out. "I won't let them. So there, you have my word. You can go now."

"No," I spit, planting my hands on my hips.

He looks up surprised. "No?"

"That's what I said."

He releases a heavy breath and looks me over. "What is it now?"

I tilt my head. "You owe me answers."

"I owe you no such thing," Ravven says harshly, he pales slightly.

Keane once again makes an attempt to slip out the door. "I'm just going to..."

"So, you're not going to tell me why I just met your cousin downstairs."

Keane freezes and Ravven becomes like stone. I smirk in triumph and deliver the final blow. "Your cousin Cinaed who is a Sidhe faerie. The High Lord of the Spring Court, at that."

The blow lands just as I intend it to. Ravven grimaces. Behind me Keane curses every star that isn't in the sky above the Forest of Night. A creative curse, I should remember to use it sometime.

"So, it is true," I spit, crossing my arms. "And here I'd thought that Cinaed had magically found some way to lie, but you are his cousin, aren't you? I thought that you were a Solitary faerie!"

"I am," Ravven grits out. "That is what I chose to be anyway."

"But you aren't fully a Far Darrig are you?"

Ravven winces and then shakes his head. "No, my father, as you can well see—" he gestures to Keane, who looks like a trapped animal. Frightened and ready to fight if it comes to it. "Is a Far Darrig. My mother, however, was a Sidhe faerie."

"Bewitching woman," Keane spits like the most bitter of insults. "Had me in love with her before I even knew what was happening."

Ravven looks from his father to me. "I did not care for life in the Sidhe court so I left. I am more Solitary faerie than I am Sidhe." He smiles bitterly as if at some inside joke that isn't actually funny.

"Nothing to be ashamed of there," Keane says defensively.

"And when were you planning on telling me this?" I snap, swinging my arm out. Keane ducks.

"Never," Ravven replies coolly. "I don't really see how my lineage is any of your business."

"You're a Sidhe! A Sidhe, Ravven. They are horrid, wicked creatures and *you are one of them*. And you kept that fact from me for what reason? What could you have to gain from that? My trust?"

"I hardly think my mother's bloodline should affect your trust in me one way or another," he replies looking down at his fingernails.

He's right. I hate that he's right. That he's the one who has to remind me of the rule that I need to keep for my own survival.

Never trust a faerie. Sidhe or Solitary.

"You. Are. So. UGH!" I fling my hands up and storm out of his room, stomping down the hall to my own room. Once inside, I slam my door shut as hard as I can, hoping that they wince even if just a little bit whether because of their enhanced hearing or just because they dislike me smashing around their beautiful castle.

Still fuming, I change out of my dress and into a silvery shirt and matching billowy pants that come down to midway down my shin. However, by the time, I'm pulling the pins out of my hair, the anger has melted into weariness and despair. What am I to do?

When I was at the ball, I didn't even catch a glimpse of Thomas, and I'm absolutely terrified of what may have happened to him in the hours since I last saw him. What have they done to him? It's my fault—whatever they did in retribution against my outburst is my fault.

And what I'm doing to help him probably is only going to end in my death.

I can't trust the faerie that I need to trust.

I can't even trust myself.

Of course Ravven is a Sidhe. How else could he be so devastatingly beautiful if he *wasn't* one of them? I was so focused that I only believed what I wanted to believe and left everything else to be ignored. I had wanted Ravven to be a Far Darrig, because while they may be worse than most other Solitary faeries, at least they aren't the Sidhe race.

They only care about mischief. The Sidhe only ever care about themselves.

And on top of all of it, that kiss haunts me. I kissed a Sidhe. I allowed myself to become entrapped in his treacherous web. And yet, the spider doesn't even want the idiotic wayward fly. It's obvious that Ravven regrets it. And he's probably holding the kiss against me as well, even though it is hardly my fault. He was the one who kissed me. I had just been going along on my merry way oblivious as ever until he kissed me.

He kissed me and ruined everything.

Because now I want more. And more will destroy me. Ravven will destroy me. But not even knowing that can stop the longing.

My head throbs and I bury it in my hand. Outside the balcony, the night is pitch dark. It leaves the imagination to race as to what is lurking out there.

I shudder and pull the doors shut. I wish that they had locks, but I suppose that this is the best I can do. After that I climb into my bed.

I must have drifted into a weary sleep, because the next thing I know, my eyelids are fluttering open. I frown and squint into the darkness as the sound comes again. The soft click of the heel of someone's shoe hitting the marble floor. My eyes dart to the balcony doors.

They are wide open.

Someone is in my room with me.

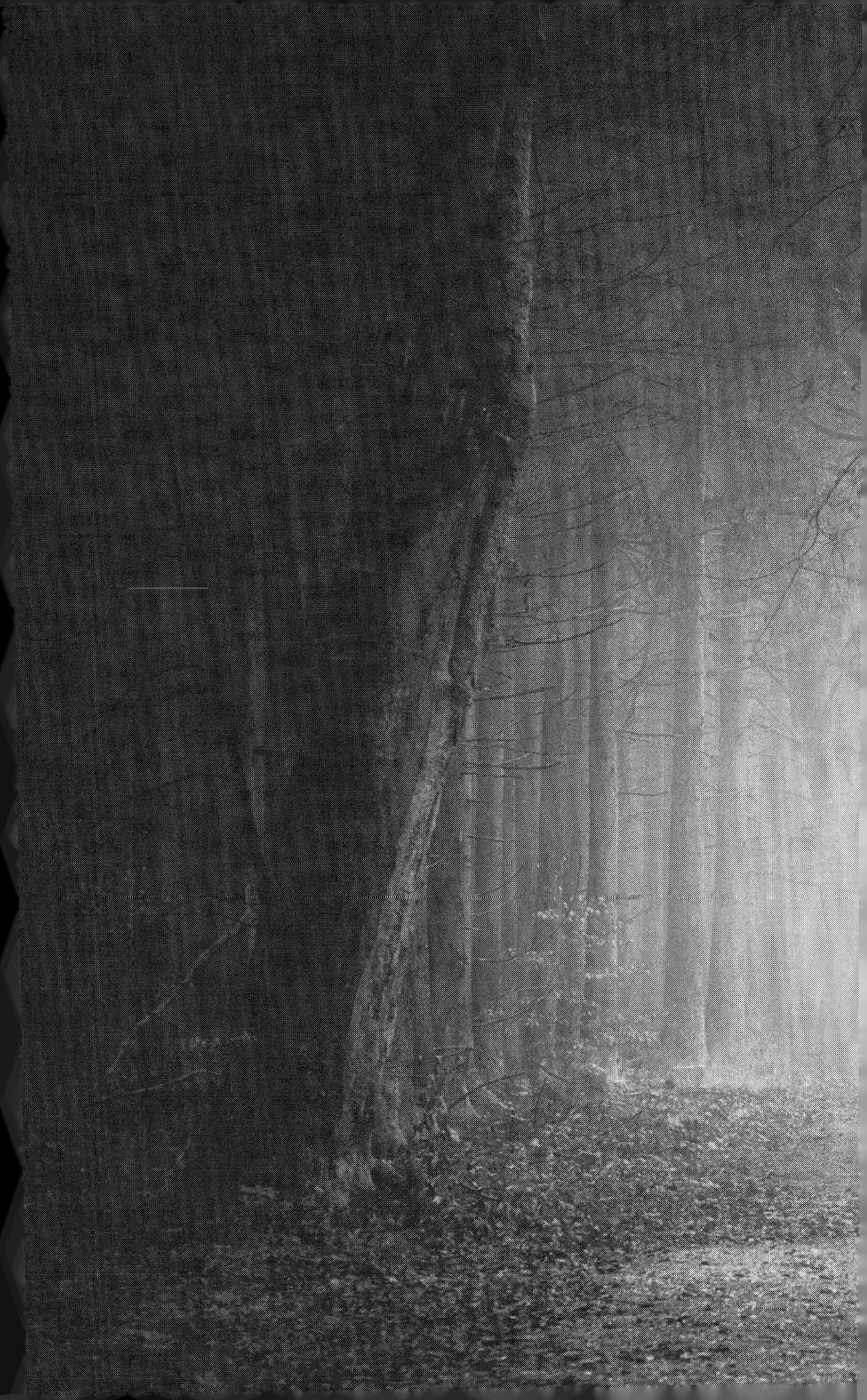

CHAPTER THIRTY

I lay still, wasting precious seconds wondering whether it is best to pretend to be asleep until they come closer and strike then, or to make a dart toward the door.

But then a thought slams into my consciousness with sickening clarity. This is no human attacker. How can it be? This is the faerie world. What am I supposed to do against a faerie attacker? I've just made up my mind to run for help even if that help is Ravven, Keane, or Daithi when the faerie speaks.

"Come, little human. Climb from your bed and walk to your balcony. Fling yourself from it without a single scream." The voice is smooth and rich like silk. And completely foreign. A misty fog of glowing pale red drifts toward me.

I whip my head toward the speaker with shock. "What?" I ask, my voice groggy with sleep.

"I said, fling yourself from your balcony. Come now, little mortal. You know that it is useless to resist."

"Um, how about no thanks?"

"No—I said to *jump*!" The red smoke reaches me and I brace myself for whatever it brings. There's a thump and the dark shadow of the faerie hits the wall. I'm knocked back onto my bed.

Before the faerie has an opportunity to recover, I spring from my bed. I don't know what just happened, but I'm not about to question it right now. I race toward the door. I reach toward the handle and my fingers just graze it before I am suddenly yanked back. The heel of my foot hits the tiled floor with a thump and I yelp.

"Silence," the faerie growls. I ignore him and let out a pterodactyl screech. It is quickly cut off when the faerie clamps his hand over my mouth. His other hand grips my hair, pulling it hard on the roots.

I clench my teeth to keep from groaning in pain. My elbow lashes out, but the faerie holds his body away.

"Stop that, cease your struggling."

Well, since he asked so nicely... I stomp on his foot. However, since he is wearing boots and I'm barefoot it doesn't make much of a difference.

"Why will you not do as you are told?" the faerie hisses, tightening his hold on my hair. Tears spring into my eyes.

Considering that he's asking me to kill myself, I don't see how that is so hard to figure out. Then I realize what it was he was trying to do. He was trying to ensorcell me. If it weren't for Ravven's boon, I could be dead right now. My heart thuds uncomfortably.

"Never mind, I suppose I shall have to find some other way to kill you. Shouldn't be too hard. You are still a mortal, after all."

So everyone keeps telling me.

He yanks me backward toward my bed. His hand releases my hair and I buck my head back, but freeze when I see the blanket on my bed beginning to rise and float toward me like tentacles.

It begins to twine around my neck and that is when my composure cracks. It was one thing when the faerie was trying to convince me to fling myself off of my own balcony, it's quite another when he decides to strangle me to death with a snakelike floating blanket. *I had been sleeping in that blanket!*

Already I can barely breathe. My heart pounds with anxiety, beating on my ribcage, trying to escape. Escape to where I'm not sure. What sort of difference will it make? I'm going to die. Ravven will find my corpse in the morning. Or someone else will. If the assassin even leaves anything to find.

What of Thomas? Will they kill Ravven if his contender is murdered in foul play?

So many lives hang on one key fact. My survival. But how am I expected to live when I can't even draw in a stupid breath?

I try to shriek but it comes out as a garbled gasp. I claw at the blanket, but it's no good. It continues to coil tighter and tighter, blocking off my air completely. I continue flailing, but already my limbs are becoming heavy. My lungs are beginning to panic and my heart just keeps beating harder and harder and harder...

Just breathe! My body screams at me, as if it is that simple.

The blanket is so tight that I'm worried it might crush my esophagus, black spots are filling my vision when suddenly the door bursts open and a dark figure rushes in. I know it is Ravven, even though my vision is blurring. I don't know how I know; I don't even know how it could be him, but it is Ravven.

Suddenly the faerie's hold on me is gone. I collapse to my knees as the blanket loosens slightly and I desperately rip it off, choking on the air that rushes down my throat. It burns, but the feeling of oxygen reaching my starved lungs is the most beautiful thing I have ever experienced.

I fling the blanket away, bracing myself against the bed with one hand and clutching my throat with the other as I turn my attention to the two dark shapes grappling across the room. The blankets rise and I lurch back, however they slither away from me toward the fighting faeries.

I try to shout, "Ravven, look out," but all that comes out of my throat is, "Ahheh hoo ouh."

I watch with horror as the rope, glowing an eerie purple color, snakes up the leg of the smaller of the two forms. The draperies around the bed lash out, snapping around the arms of the faerie and pinning him against the bedpost.

I try to stumble forward, but then the glow reaches the faerie's face and I realize that it isn't Ravven. His hair shines a pale gold in the dim light. I sag against the bed in relief.

However, my relief is short lived. I gasp as my hand explodes with a fiery pain. I clutch it to my chest just as Ravven swings his arm at the faerie. The faerie cries out, arching his back then his cry turns into a splutter as he sags down, held up only by the draperies.

My eyes widen as I take in his limp form then Ravven stumbles back, bracing himself against the wardrobe.

I turn my concerned gaze to him. Was he somehow hurt as well? "Ra—" I say again, in a softer tone, testing my throat. "Ravven?"

He turns to me and is at my side in three steps. He kneels in front of me, his hands running down my arms and patting my hair as if to make certain that there isn't any damage. "Are you all right?" he demands in a low tone. "Are you able to breathe?"

I nod. Sure, I can breathe *now*. But earlier... I shudder. That had been awful. It wasn't a peaceful fade from consciousness as I would have expected, instead it had felt like every blood vessel in my body would explode from want of oxygen.

"If I couldn't breathe, Ravven, I wouldn't be conscious anymore," I say, trying not to let on how shaken up I am. I need to stop letting my human weakness show. If I keep my voice at a low whisper, I find that I'm still capable of talking. Though it hurts like heck. Then again breathing hurts like heck. And I don't even want to try to consume anything at this moment.

"You are certain that you are all right?" he asks.

I nod and my eyes dart back to the dark figure still slumped motionless. "Who was he?"

Ravven follows my gaze and I feel anger roll off of him in waves. He rises and with a wave of his hand, the candles' light comes on, illuminating the room.

I gasp at the puddle of blood seeping across the floor toward us. I grimace and press my hand against my throat as the fire washes up my body.

Ravven grimaces as well. "He is dead."

"How—how did you kill him?" I ask, trembling. I thought that there were only three ways to kill a faerie, destroy their item of immortality, learn their name, or kill them with iron. Since Ravven didn't speak, it couldn't have been the faerie's name though how he figured out what the assassin's item of immortality was so quickly, I have no idea. I hadn't thought that destroying an item of immortality would be so bloody.

Ravven presses his lips together, staring at the body. I can't see much of my assassin because the bed is in the way. I brace my hand on the mattress and push to my feet. I gasp when I see the way that he died.

There, protruding from the faerie's chest is my iron dagger. The one that I had thought I'd lost in the Winter Court.

I look at Ravven accusingly. "My dag—" I gasp, but my voice rises too loud and the last part comes out as only and "Ah!"

Ravven smiles sheepishly. "I didn't exactly feel comfortable allowing you to continue to carry an iron weapon around. You are rather unpredictable."

I shake my head. "But how did you manage to carry it? Iron is harmful to faeries!"

"I kept it wrapped in cloth, which made the discomfort somewhat more bearable. It still has an oppressive heaviness to the air around it, but at least not excruciating pain." He grimaces and flexes his hand.

I step toward him and grasp his wrist. He tries to pull away but I tighten my hold. He flinches, but finally relents. Carefully, I turn his hand around and uncurl his clenched fingers to reveal the palm. It is horribly red, scalded, charred and oozing blood. I inhale sharply and look up at him.

He yanks his hand from my grasp, and hides it behind his back, his face impassive once again. "I didn't really have time to make sure that the dagger was properly wrapped before I used it."

I continue to stare at him stunned. Ravven used the dagger, was burnt by the iron handle, all to save me. What world am I even living in where a faerie would sacrifice something for a human? Let alone a faerie like Ravven for a human like me?

He waves his hand toward the dagger, obviously trying to draw my attention from him which is another first. Ravven Crowe not wanting attention... the world might be ending. "Do you want it back?"

I glance at him. That dagger had come in handy when he needed it. "Don't you?"

"I have carried it long enough, thank you," he says, pulling away from the dagger with a grimace of distaste.

I step toward the dagger. "Aren't you afraid I will be unpredictable in my use of it?"

"I think that you probably need it, my darling—"

"My *darling*?" I ask, but choke on my useless throat and it comes out as a rasp.

"Pest," Ravven says in a hard tone. "You did not allow me to finish it. I was going to call you my darling corpse."

I shake my head. Of course he was. I don't know why I would have thought that he was going to call me an actual term of endearment. I'm not important to him in any way that truly matters. Our fates are intertwined but that is it. He's faerie. I'm me. And those two can never meet. Even if they already did.

How many times do I have to keep reminding myself that nothing between us could ever work before I actually start believing it?

I stare at the dagger embedded in the other faerie's chest, his unseeing eyes staring forward. What a husk he has become. Once a beautiful unchanging creature, now just as dead as any human could become.

"Are you hesitating?" Ravven asks.

I shake my head. "No, of course not." And yet I still can't seem to make my fingers wrap around the dagger.

"I'm sorry, but I cannot touch it again. It really has to be you."

I shoot a glare at him over my shoulder. "I am well aware of that fact. And I am more than capable of pulling out the dagger." Then to prove myself right, I wrap my fingers around the iron handle before I have an opportunity to talk myself out of it. I pull it out, gagging at the wet *shlitck* sound that it makes and the strands of clotted silvery blood that cling to it. I drop the dagger as soon as it is free of the faerie's body. I gag again and press my other hand against my mouth as bile races up my already burning throat. I cannot throw up now. I squeeze my eyes shut and take a deep steadying breath.

When I open my eyes, I feel like throwing up again when I see the dagger sitting there in its bloodstained glory.

Ravven kicks it into a corner of the room. "I think that is good enough for tonight. We—well, you can clean it later."

He wraps his arm around my shoulder and turns me toward the door.

I hesitate against his pull and glance once more over my shoulder at the unfortunate creature who thought that it was a good idea to try to kill me. Now killed himself. I wonder if his last moments were filled with regret?

"Who do you think he was?" I whisper.

Ravven tightens his arm around my shoulders. "We'll discuss that later once you are somewhere more comfortable."

He opens the door to my room, revealing Keane and Daithi in the hallway.

"This is why I don't like company," Keane harrumphs. "Never appreciate the others' sleep schedules."

Daithi grunts. They both look up as we step out into the hall.

"Care to explain what is going on?" Keane asks in an acidic tone.

Ravven smiles. "Oh, the usual, an uninvited guest. Never fear, I took care of him."

"Good," Keane grumbles.

Ravven glances at the Fear Gorta. "Daithi, there is a body, one of the Spring Court in Jaye's room. If you would be so kind as to take care of it for me."

Daithi grins happily, the already drawn skin around his face wrinkling in a gruesome way. He looks so gleeful it's downright wicked. A thousand shudders race down my spine and I clutch Ravven's shirt as if I will use him as a human—or at least faerie—shield.

He tightens his hold and his thumb rubs up and down across my shoulder as if it is meant to be comforting instead of maddening. Daithi chuckles and skips off toward my room as Ravven ushers me forward. Keane gives us an accusing look as we pass.

"You can stay in my room for tonight," Ravven says, pushing open a door that leads into a room that looks similar to mine except the bed is larger with no draperies, and there is a small pool of dark water in the middle of the floor. I must have burst into Keane's room earlier, not Ravven's.

I stare down at the pool as we walk past. "What is that for?"

Ravven shrugs. "I have no idea. What is anything in this room for?" He leads me to the bed and sits me down on it.

"Thanks," I say, suppressing a wince as it feels like hard stones grate against my throat.

He looks at me and grimaces. "That must hurt terribly. Is there anything I can do to help?"

"Not unless you can heal it," I rasp.

Ravven pushes his lips together and I can tell from his face that he cannot. Faeries, for all of their magic, do not seem to know how to use it to help. Only to hinder and destroy.

Even their blessings can be curses in disguise.

"Then bring me some ice," I say with a roll of my eyes.

Ravven steps to the pool of water and waves a hand over it. Droplets of water rise from the pool and form in a sphere above it only to freeze together. He brings it to me and kneels at my side. "Will this do?"

I take it, wrapping the ice in Ravven's blanket to protect my hands from the cold before glaring at him. "Sure, you can do that, but you can't heal my stupid throat."

Their magic is in manipulation and even if it is a slightly trickier magic to manipulate something to be better than it is now, it's hardly impossible. If Ravven tried...

Ravven smiles sheepishly and shrugs.

I frown at him as I press my lips together. "And what about your hand?"

He glares down at his hand, now hanging limply at his side. "Faerie's magic cannot heal wounds made by iron."

I hold out my hand. "No, I mean let me see it."

He withdraws a step. "I am—" he pauses, seeming to realize that what he was about to say was a lie. "I do not need your help."

"Well, you're getting it from me anyway." I lurch off the bed and grab his hand, pulling him down to sit next to me. He perches stiffly on the edge like an uneasy animal unsure if he should flee or lash out instead.

I tug on his arm until he finally relents and gives me his hand.

However, the second I touch the ice to it, he hisses and yanks it back.

I look up at him. "Stop it. It might hurt at first, but the ice will numb it." He still looks at me, his hand staying stubbornly in his lap. I gesture for him to give it back. "Come on, Ravven, it must be hurting you terribly. Gosh, the pain is so written across your face that I can almost feel it hurting you."

Something about my words finally convinces him to hold his hand out.

I press the ice against his hand. He inhales sharply, his fingers curling, but he doesn't pull away. After a moment he relaxes. I look at him and smirk. "See? Now, where might I find bandages?"

Ravven huffs a breath. "Bandages?"

"Some cloth that I can wrap around the wound?" I ask impatiently.

Ravven arches his eyebrow and pushes off of the bed. Keeping his hand with the ice pack close against his chest, he strides across the room to his wardrobe and opens it. Then he comes back with a shirt. "Will this do?"

I accept the shirt and glance up at him. He really doesn't know anything about bandages, does he? But then I suppose that he doesn't need to when he is a faerie and supposed to be almost completely invulnerable. Against everything but iron. "I suppose it shall."

I grip the edges and yank with all my might until it begins to tear.

Ravven lurches back with a horrified gasp.

I look up at him and giggle even though it hurts my throat. "Oh, don't be such a baby. I'm sure you have plenty more where that came from. Now give me your hand."

He hesitates. "So, you can tear that into ribbons as well?"

I roll my eyes. "Don't be ridiculous." I pat the mattress next to me. "Now, sit down and give me your hand."

Ravven grudgingly complies, all the while watching me warily.

I huff a small laugh and try not to cause myself anymore undue pain as I set to work on wrapping it around his blistered skin.

As I finish tying the last bit of bandage together, hoping that I put it together right, I glance up at him. He is watching me intently, though I don't know what he is thinking. His eyes are purple and it's so beautiful that it makes me want to kiss him again. I quickly shove that thought aside and focus on the more important matters at hand. "Now, are you going to tell me who that faerie that tried to kill me was?"

Ravven presses his lips together and glances away.

"You told Daithi that he was from the Spring Court. And for that matter I thought that the other faeries couldn't interfere with me while I am a contender."

"He was from the Spring Court, or at least they sent him. And sometimes the rules can be broken if you are dedicated enough and find enough loopholes. The laws regarding the contender for the position of Fair Assassin only hold to those who reside in a court. My belief is he must have been an exile, promised with a pardon. Cinaed must have sent him." Ravven sighs and shakes his head. He buries his face in his hand. "I did not tell you the whole story between me and my cousin."

I lean back on my elbows. "You didn't actually tell me anything about your cousin."

His shoulders slope with defeat before finally he lifts his head. "I didn't always know of my heritage. That I had... that I was Far Darrig. I was raised in the Spring

Court, in the highest of all circles." He runs a hand through his dark hair, mussing it, and smirks to himself. "I did always wonder why I was the only person with black hair in a sea of golden light."

"A Far Darrig and a Sidhe?" I ask with a frown. I have never heard of such a thing before. It isn't impossible for a faerie to produce offspring with a faerie from another court, it's not common but it's not impossible. There isn't any sort of love between the Winter and Summer Courts, and the Solitary fae live a lonely life. The reason they are such a small court is that they do not have families. Just beings who are older than the stars, continuing their lonely existence, and never changing.

Ravven huffs a humorless laugh. "It does seem strange does it not? It should have been impossible, but one day my mother was traveling and she became lost deep in the forest of the Autumn Court. My father found her and after she convinced him to help her, he finally brought her home. Somehow... I suppose they were meant to be because before they knew it, they were bonded."

"Bonded?" I gasp quietly. I had heard of it of course. The faerie's equivalent of marriage, but I confess other than that I don't know much about it. No mortal does. It is something that stays primarily in the Otherworld. Just like the knowledge of the items of immortality.

"Bonding is... a strange phenomenon," Ravven says, slowly, carefully. He looks at me with a disconcerting expression. "It is when the magic of a faerie binds their soul to... another. They become one, feeling the pain of the other, hearing the thoughts of another. No one knows how it quite works, so few bonds form due to faeries being such inherently selfish creatures. It seems as if the bond will start to appear if they are around each other, finally snapping into place at some sort of monumental moment..." Ravven trails off and stares straight ahead.

"I wonder if it could happen between creatures that aren't faeries," I muse out loud. Does soul bonding happen to humans when they marry and they just don't realize it?

Ravven coughs. "Theoretically I suppose that it could happen, say between a faerie and a human." He quickly looks away. "With the faerie's magic being the one to bind them. But such a thing does not happen. There is no great love between faeries and humans. If there ever is, it is only one sided like the way Thomas feels toward Aoibheann."

"Felt," I correct. "So, you don't think such a thing has ever happened?"

Ravven rubs the back of his head. "I wouldn't know of course..."

I scratch my chin as my mind begins racing. I think of the odd connection between the human guard of the Undersea Court and the spymaster of the

Winter Court. They obviously have a past. And if any human has ever been bonded then surely it would be Eilis, who has existed in this world for so long. Perhaps a bonding was the reason that she never left... "Do you think that Riagan and Eilis are, you know, bonded?"

He looks up and then shrugs a little too nonchalantly. "I believe that there were rumors during the time of the High Queen, before the courts, that such a bond existed between them, but since then those rumors have proven obviously false."

"Why? Because they can't stand each other?"

Ravven lifts one shoulder. "And the distance between them. It has been centuries since the High Queen fell and they have hardly been together since then. Distance is possible with the bond, but it is uncommon. Though it did happen between my own parents. Keane wasn't ready for a family, he returned to his Autumn Court, leaving my mother with me and I was raised as a Sidhe, not even knowing of his existence for a hundred years."

I rub at my chin as I think of this underlying connection between Riagan and Eilis, something that they both try so hard to hide. If they truly are bonded then what side is Eilis really on? Riagan claims that he helps me because of her, but what if she chooses to betray me for his court?

"Anyway, when I found out about my heritage. I was hurt. I did not feel as if I belonged to the Spring Court. The night before I left, I dreamed of bloodshed and carnage." His lashes lower. "Sometimes faeries have prophetic dreams, I think that is the main reason most of them even bother with sleeping since obviously we don't need it. To get that glimpse of the future. But I ignored my dream and I left that morning. Within a fortnight my entire family was dead."

I gasp and pull back.

"Cinaed had murdered them," Ravven continues. "My own cousin. He had gotten a human slave to lace their drinks with molten iron. They were all too intoxicated to even notice until they were being torn apart from within."

His voice is laced with such betrayal and horror as if he is reliving the experience all over again. I've never seen a faerie display this much emotion. It scares me. It breaks my heart. I scoot closer and rest my hand on Ravven's clasped hands. He stares at it like it is some puzzle that needs to be solved, but he doesn't pull away.

"I never returned to the Spring Court, I had nothing left there. Keane was the only family I had left. I have not slept since that night." He looks up at me. "Because I know exactly what I will see when I do so again."

I try to swallow past the lump in my throat. Why am I going to cry? Why should I cry? This is Ravven's tragedy not mine. And yet his words strike my heart truer than any knife could. "Why?" I whisper. "Why would Cinaed do that? Why would he kill your family?"

You mustn't know.

I startle at the words. It's like my thoughts in my head had somehow adopted Ravven's voice.

Ravven's eyes dart down to the floor. "Because I had something that he wanted, and my family stood in the way. I still stand in the way."

I open my mouth to ask what it is, but Ravven continues talking before I can, as if sensing my intent. "That is what I want you to do, the favor I will ask of you once you are the Fair Assassin. To kill Cinaed."

I pull back, his words slapping me in the face. "You wanted me to kill your cousin?" I demand.

"I still want you to kill my cousin," Ravven replies in a stiff tone. "Nothing about that has changed."

"But-but," I splutter.

Ravven rolls his eyes. "I understand your confusion, you mortals do seem to be unduly attached to each other, but the fact of the matter is that I have been waiting one hundred and thirty years for my chance at revenge."

"But you want *me* to kill him?" I demand, jumping to my feet.

He looks at me as if I've grown an extra finger in front of him. "Yes."

"But I'm no killer!" How could he want to make me kill someone, even someone as evil as his cousin? I would forever have Cinaed's blood on my hands. Doesn't he see that?

"You're trying to become an assassin, pest, what do you think that means?"

I shake my head. "I only want to become an assassin to save Thomas. I don't want to actually assassinate anyone."

"Except for Aoibheann," Ravven mutters darkly.

I swallow the nausea at the thought of killing even her. Do I have that in me? "Only if she affords me no other choice."

"Cinaed has given *me* no other choice," Ravven spits bitterly. "He killed my entire family."

He looks up then, his eyes broken, his expression no longer stone, and all I can see is the face of a man who is hurting. Who wants vengeance. Who wants his family back. Who cannot live with the possibility that he might not get either.

And suddenly I find that I can't refuse him. I can't tell him that I won't do it. And it's not because of that blasted bargain I made with him. Even if it costs me my conscience. If I do this then I can make Ravven's life a little easier. Give him something in return for all of his help. Aid him one last time before I leave this world forever.

A final farewell to the faerie who is at this very moment trying to steal something he can never have.

He won't get my heart, but he will have his revenge.

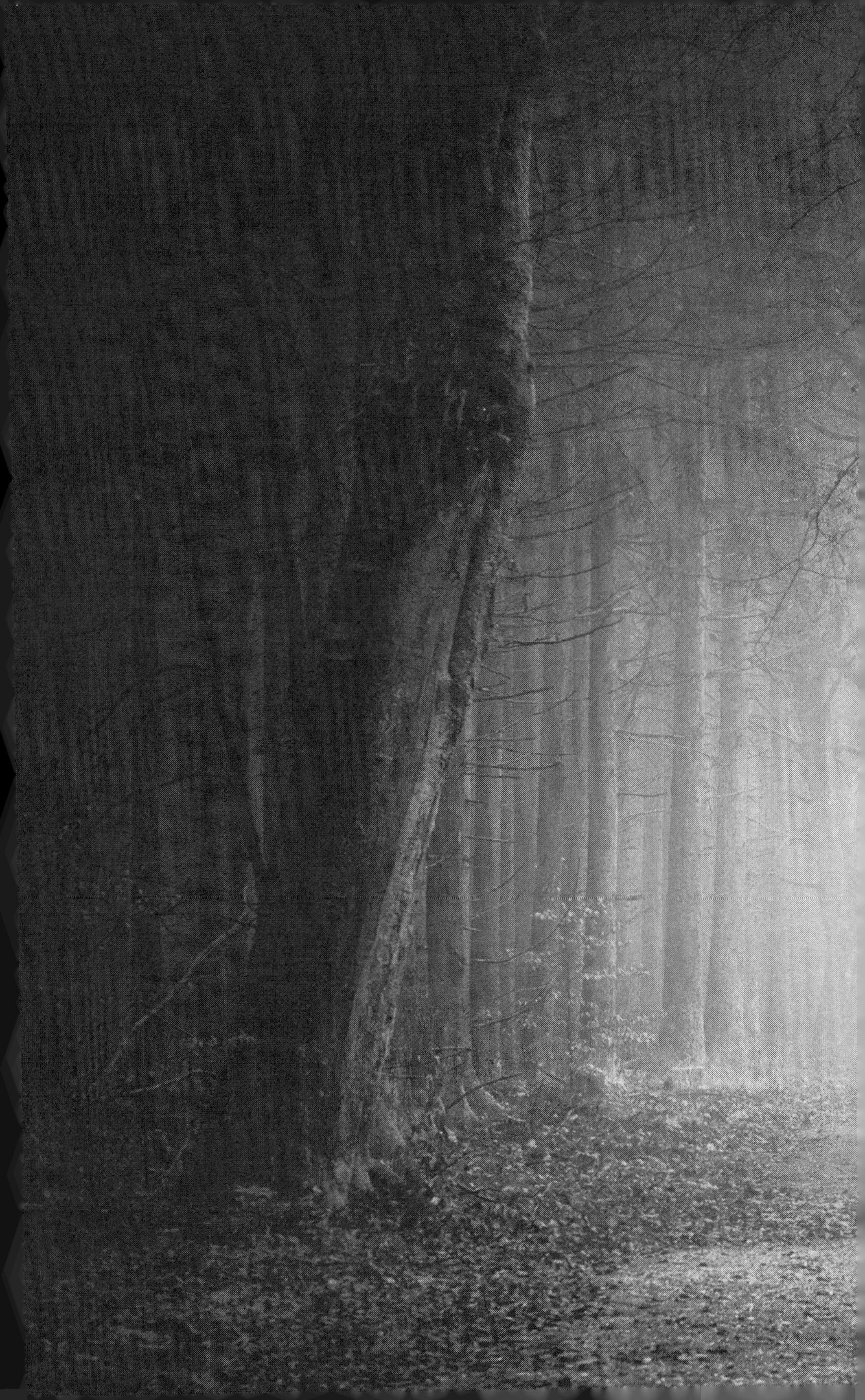

CHAPTER THIRTY-ONE

I would have thought that the Summer Court would be in a high tower, as close to light and warmth as they could possibly get. Instead it is situated right in the middle of the Court of Dreams and Nightmares far away from either.

"Actually, the real Summer Court is inside caverns in a mountain," Ravven says as if he knew what I was thinking. I bite down on my lip wondering if I said that aloud as well or if he really can read my thoughts. I don't remember anything about faerie's having that ability in my studies, but obviously the human lore on faeries did have its gaps. Was that one of them?

The corner of Ravven's mouth turns up, but it's a bitter smile.

He pauses outside of large double doors. I'm so startled by them that I pull up short. The Summer Court sort of just appears out of nowhere, you turn down a regular hall and then there it is. Not like the Undersea Court which had the long hall of water. Or the Autumn Court where you have to climb up so many winding stairs.

"Remember what I said about not insulting the Summer King?" Ravven says, straightening his jacket. "He is vainer than even Iorwerth and he will not take kindly to any of your human *sarcasm*."

I glare at him. "I'm capable of behaving civilly."

"Are you now?"

"Ha," I mutter, but I also shake out the golden skirts that I had chosen to wear today. It made me think of the sun, which made me think of summer, but now I'm worried that my ostentatious apparel will only make my less glamorous human features stand out all the more. The metal leaves that twine down my arms are cold and uncomfortable.

My hair feels heavy and unnatural on top of my head. When I had tried to leave earlier today with it down, Ravven would have none of that; instead he did my hair himself. When I'd asked how he even knew how to do hair, he had said he had used to do his mother's hair.

That ended the conversation pretty quickly. It seems that Ravven's mother is a sore subject.

I understand why he would want Cinaed dead. He killed Ravven's entire family. What I don't like is that Ravven expects *me* to be the one to kill Cinaed. And apparently, I'm not half as ruthless as I had always thought I was.

I jolt myself from my thoughts. I shouldn't even be thinking that. Right now, my main focus is to not somehow insult the Summer King with either my smart mouth or my poor fashion sense.

"Chin up, pest," Ravven says with a small smile. "You don't look half so hideous today."

I want to argue, but just then the door bursts open and I'm left speechless.

The Summer Court is not at all what I had been expecting. I'm not sure what I *had* expected, but it certainly wasn't this.

The first thing I notice is the blinding light. I squint and raise my hand to try to block some of it. When my eyes finally adjust to it, I realize that it is coming from a giant glowing ball floating in the air some feet above our heads. Like an artificial sun. The ground is made of soft grass.

All of that I could have expected from the Summer Court, even if I am surprised to see a sun and grass indoors.

No, what surprises me are the walls and the ceiling. We are in a cavern, which is almost as surprising to see inside the palace as the grass. Stalactites hang from the ceiling and the rough, uneven stone wall is covered in sparkling spots, which I quickly realize are gems. Precious gems lining the wall, not like ornamentation, but like they are embedded in it and need to be mined.

I try not to stare at the faeries lining the walls, but I can't help it. The Tuatha De Danan. The Seelie court. Supposedly they like humans, as much as a faerie can like humans, considering us their little pets and soldiers and warriors. Hundreds of years ago, they roamed the Earth freely amongst the humans, ruling the ancient Irish as gods, before finally departing back to the Otherworld. I believe that was about the time that the civil war between the faeries took place, if I have my dates right. Perhaps that was the reason that they returned to their own world, to fight for their claim against the Unseelie faeries.

Now there are so few of them. Same as the Winter Court they were nearly wiped out during the war between the two.

My eyes catch someone standing in the shadows in the back of the room. I freeze. It's Riagan. He smiles and winks at me before disappearing down a corridor. I blink and shake my head. What the heck is the spymaster of the Winter Court doing here?

Did no one else see him? Am I supposed to keep his presence a secret? Would it be considered betraying the Unseelies if I did not? A betrayal to the Seelies if I did?

My eyes dart to the Summer King and I swallow hard. My life depends on whether he wants me dead or not. He looks exactly like he did when I first saw him. His skin is suspiciously golden toned despite the fact that according to Ravven he lives in caverns within a mountain.

He smiles languidly. "Ah, welcome, my young friends. It has been so long, too long since a human has graced my court with their presence. All of these other courts appear to have their pets and yet I, who truly enjoy their company, am left abandoned."

I glance at Ravven. If this test is for me to become the Summer King's *companion* then he'd better just count us dead now. He smiles slightly as if he's amused, which if he knew my thoughts he wouldn't be. He is too beautiful to die after all. But perhaps, I'm just too stubborn to remain alive. He reaches down and of all things, grabs my hand.

He bows and yanks on my arm, forcing me to also bend at my waist. As I rise, my foot becomes entangled in my skirts and I wobble. I manage to catch myself before I take a spill in front of the entire Summer Court but still it was close.

"But you have not come to join my court, nay you come for your task, and indeed I have one for you. I wish for you to steal something for me from the Winter Court. I wish for you to bring the High Lord of Winter's most prized possession. An antler that he took from a white stage that he killed. Destroying a sacred creature before learning your destiny is a rare and powerful sort of magic. I very much want it for my own."

I inhale a shaky breath. Steal from Iorwerth, I think he is the High Lord of Winter anyway? It doesn't seem hard for me to guess what will happen if I am caught. I try to hold still as a shiver races down my spine.

"Prove to be a friend of the Seelies in this act and you shall have my support," Tibernus smiles warmly, but it doesn't meet his sky-blue eyes.

I dip my head. "Of course."

Ravven bows stiffly. "As you say it."

"Please do not disappoint me," he says with a heavy sigh as his eyes move over my body. "It would be such a waste of your gift."

Time crashes to a halt around me, just as still as it always has been in this world. "What gift?" I demand bitterly, forgetting for a second that the Summer King is not someone I can afford to have as an enemy, in my resentment over having been overlooked.

Ravven grimaces.

"The one bestowed upon you by my court on the first year of your birth," he says, his tone turning bored. I inhale and his eyes sharpen on my face. "Do not tell me that you didn't know of this gift."

"I didn't receive a gift," I state. My cheeks are hot and cold at the same time and I'm finding it increasingly difficult to breathe.

"Precisely," the Summer King says, a smile pulling at his lips. By now he looks mildly amused. "My people blessed you that you could never be cursed, but those wretched Unseelies cursed you that you could never be blessed. Since it was your birth blessing, the Fair Law made it so that they *had* to place at least one curse over you despite your gift. That was it."

Now I can't feel my face at all. My eyes fly to Ravven who is standing still as a statue next to me. He won't meet my gaze, but instead stares straight ahead at the gathered faeries of the Summer Court. "Did you know about this?"

That night before the Undersea test, I asked Ravven to put a boon on me, and he did. If he knew about my blessing and curse then why did he never say anything? Why did he pretend that I didn't have any protection against ensorcellments and enchantments?

Was my curse the reason that he was thrown across the wall for trying to give me a boon?

"Now isn't the time to discuss this, pest," Ravven says in a low voice.

I want to argue so badly, but then I follow his gaze to the rest of the Summer Court and I decide that I don't want to talk in front of an audience. So, biting my tongue I bow at the Summer King as he waves us away.

I follow Ravven out, keeping quiet until the loud door slams shut behind us with a deafening bang.

"You knew, didn't you?" I demand, whirling on him as soon as we are alone.

Ravven frowns as he dusts at the front of his jacket like I got too close and breathed my humanness on him. "Of course I knew. Both the Seelies and the Unseelies were quite proud of their original curse and blessing which broke from routine. Anyone who was paying any sort of attention on their little struggle for power would have known."

I stare at him in shock. All this time, I've been walking through the faerie world thinking myself susceptible to curses and below getting blessings and it seems as if everyone knew about it but me. "And why didn't you tell me? Why did you pretend to put a worthless boon on me instead?"

"To pacify you, pest. You were obviously fretting and I had wished to calm you some."

"You could have just told me the truth!" I cry, waving my arm.

"It seemed like too much to explain at the time. Too complicated."

"It didn't take that long for the Summer King to explain it," I snap, crossing my arms.

"I see that now," he replies, his eyes as black as midnight. "But what I do not see is how this conversation is going to get us into the Winter Court."

I glare at him for a long moment, but then I force myself to move on. Our twenty-four-hour countdown has begun. When we started this whole thing, Ravven had said that we would only have the cycle of the moon in the sky to complete each of our tests. And unfortunately, not a human moon either, the moon of the Forest of Night that rises and sets like the sun. I don't have time to yell at a faerie for doing something untrustworthy or I would waste all of my time.

So yeah, Ravven didn't tell me. And I don't know his full reasons for not telling me. I shouldn't take this personally, I really shouldn't. He's a faerie. We have no real bond and any affection that I imagine I am beginning to sense that he has for me is really just all in my head.

Isn't everything, love?

I shake my head and rub at my temples. I had always known that it was only a matter of time till I lost my mind here. It probably happened long ago when I actually started to *like* Ravven and if I'm honest with myself, trust him too. To an extent at least, because this news of my powers shakes my trust in him. And something cannot be shaken if it doesn't exist.

I can say that I don't trust him as much as I want, but the fact of the matter is that I no longer watch him like he will stab me in the back, my brain no longer screams at me every time he is near. My heart does pick up its rate, but for a whole different reason. For a whole other, utterly deadly reason.

I swallow hard and glance away. "If we are going to get into the Winter Court, we need to do it when they won't be there. We'll have to do it tonight—I mean this Nethermoon. During the ball."

"And the guards?"

I scratch at my jaw as I consider this. "Many of them will be at the ball guarding the queen." But how do I make certain that they all go to the ball? Then an idea strikes me. "What if we stage an assassination attempt?"

Ravven's eyebrows shoot up. "You do recall that you are not the Fair Assassin yet, do you not?"

I shake my head. "Not that we would actually kill her, and we would have to get someone else to do it. But we could make it look like her life was in danger to draw her guards out."

Ravven's mouth twists as he considers my words. "I think I might actually be able to find a Summer faerie fool and intoxicated enough that I could convince him of such a thing. And Cliodnha would remain to make certain that he was punished instead of allowing her guards to return to her rooms."

"You orchestrate that and I'll steal the antler," I state with more assurance that I feel. Break into the Winter Court? Find my way through it? Steal something from it?

"You wish to enter the Winter Court alone? It seems to me as if you court your own demise."

The only courting of my demise that I've done is falling for you, Ravven Crowe. I bite down hard on my lip to keep from saying that. The more I ignore my attraction for him the easier it will be to pretend that it never existed.

Ravven's eyes drop down to the handprint, bared for the world to see, wrapped in golden leaves. It doesn't hurt anymore, not like it once did. But I don't think it will ever go away, it hasn't faded at all.

I move my hand to cover it and shift awkwardly on my feet. "I won't be alone. Eilis will help me."

Ravven opens his mouth and I rush to add. "She *will* help me, Ravven, and she's the only one who can since she is a human. And we only have one cycle of the moon to do this or else our lives are forfeit anyway."

Finally he nods. "Very well then. You make your little human alliance; I'll send a messenger pixie to Eilis so you two can speak. But if you die, I shall be most put out." He taps a long finger against his chin. "I'll find some way to slip away after the assassination attempt to help you two. Obviously Iorwerth will have some charms protecting his room that you humans will be powerless against."

"You do that then," I say stiffly with a nod as I study my ally who I can't actually trust.

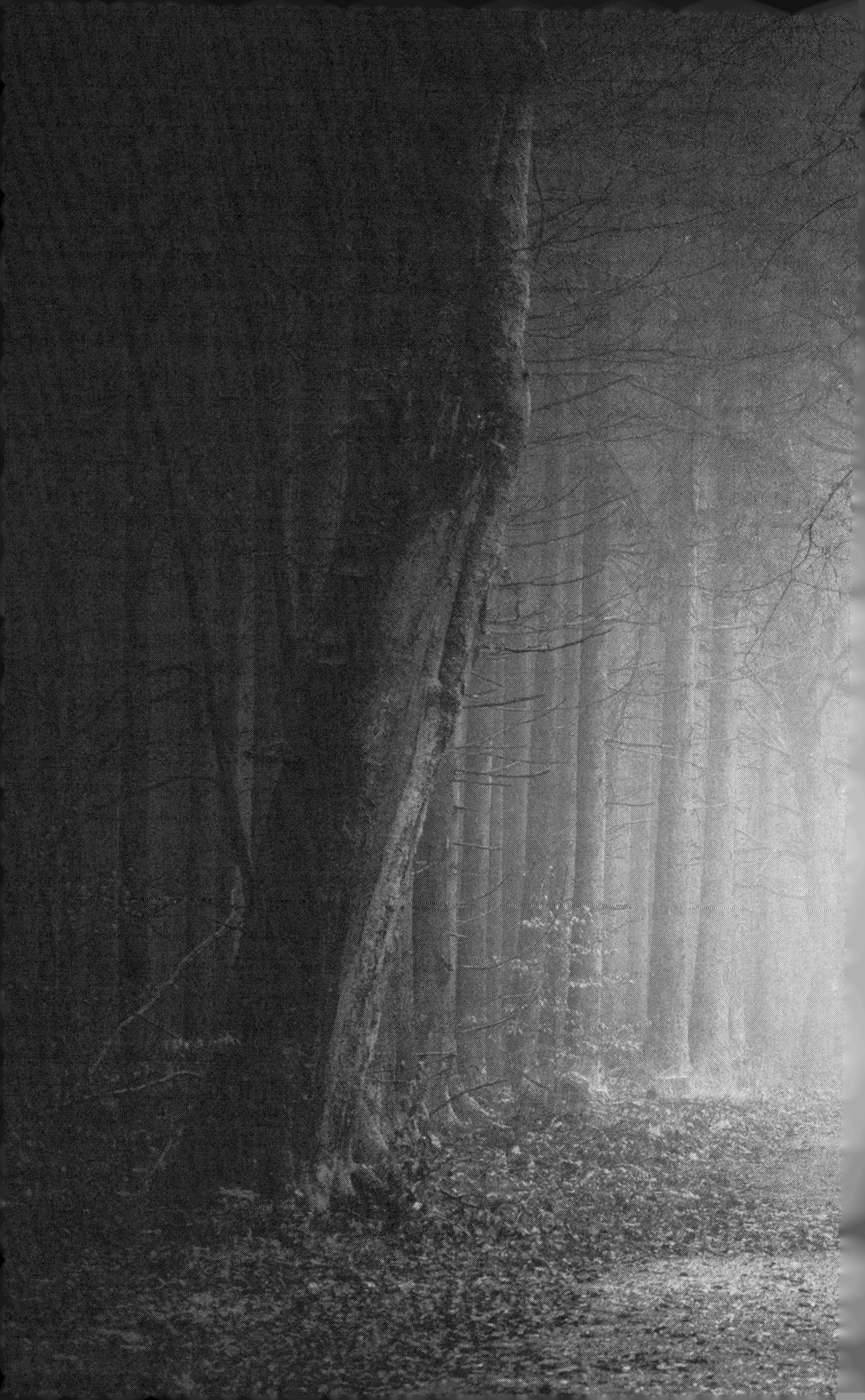

CHAPTER THIRTY-TWO

Ravven is waiting for me outside my room when I finish changing into something a little more practical. He reaches out and suddenly grasps my hands. I pull back in surprise, but he tightens his hold and slips something into the palm of my hand. Something that moves.

"Eilis says that she will meet you at The Sprite's Toadstool."

I stare at him. "Uh... okay? Where exactly is that?"

He rolls his eyes. "And you think that you can handle the Winter Court on your own. Follow the messenger pixie, it will bring you there." With those words, he turns and disappears into his room, leaving me alone.

I open my hand, allowing a small blue creature the size of one of my fingers to crawl out. It unfolds iridescent wings and takes off flying. I let out a little yelp and nearly let it escape in my surprise. I'm thankful that it is glowing or else I would have lost it immediately.

The pixie flutters down the stairs from the Autumn Wing and then stops in front of an ancient looking wooden door that is adjacent to the first room that Ravven and I appeared in when he teleported us here. I step toward the door and it opens on its own with a creak. I shudder, but the pixie is off again before my mind can linger too long on ghosts.

The cold wind of eternal night washes across my face as I step out into the Forest of Night. I race after the pixie through the dark woods wondering just what exactly is going on. A thought crashes into my mind that this is some way for Ravven to get me killed, but as soon as it surfaces, I shove it aside. Why would Ravven kill me now when he could have just let the faerie assassin do it last night?

He needs me just as much as I need him.

Then a derelict wooden shack, with a sagging roof and dark broken windows comes into view in the silver light of the moon. I draw to a halt, taking it in as the pixie flies through one of the broken windows.

My eyes land on a wooden sign lying on the ground, broken in half. On it are the words *The Sprite's Toadstool* with a picture of an ugly white creature with spiky hair and a wicked grin sitting on a toadstool.

I step hesitantly over the shattered sign and through the doorway, the door is hanging on its hinges, not doing anything to block my path.

My eyes land immediately on Eilis sitting on a rickety chair at a bar, her back to me. I blow out a relieved breath, telling myself that there is no way that Ravven and Eilis would have plotted to kill me, and take a seat beside her.

She doesn't look up, but keeps her eyes on some sort of drink held clasped in front of her.

"So, a little messenger pixie whispered in me ear and said that ye needed help," Eilis says lightly, taking a sip of the drink.

She passes a cup to me. "It is Starlight Water, gotten from the springs outside of the castle. It tastes differently than any water that exists elsewhere, but at least ye'll be able to think clearly later tonight when you need to because it steals slumber."

I stare down at the cup in my hand. The liquid is clear except where it twinkles every now and then like a star. I debate not drinking it, but then decide that Eilis is probably just trying to help me. And with my sleepless night last night, I will need all of the help I can get to stay up. I squeeze my eyes shut and take a sip. She's right, it doesn't taste like water—maybe almost like bubbling water, but bursting with so many flavors of fruits that I couldn't even name. The flavor takes me so by surprise that I cough and pull back. "This is really water?"

Eilis smirks. "Welcome to the faerie world."

I huff a small laugh, mostly more from nervousness and set my glass down. I turn to her and blow out a breath. "I need your help stealing an antler from Iorwerth."

Eilis laughs, her tinkling bell sound. "You certainly aren't one to beat around the bush are ye?"

"Reminds me of ye." I startle at the new voice and glance over my shoulder to see Riagan step into the room.

Eilis however stares angrily at her hands, not bothering to turn around. "What are ye doin' here, Riagan?"

"Oddly enough, I came here because I thought that it was the most likely place to find you," Riagan remarks, striding over to us.

I swallow hard, wondering how much he heard. How much he paid attention to. When did he come in? As charming as Riagan seems, as much as he seems to actually like me and Eilis, he is the spymaster of the Winter Court. Surely, he will tell them if he knew what I was planning. Then again, he was in the Summer Court; maybe he already knows.

"And it is a good thing I happened along, because it seemed as if ye were planning something foolhardy without me. Naughty you. How many times do I have to say that if ye are going to plan something stupid to make certain that I am included?"

I inhale sharply and stare down at the glass. Okay, I'm probably dead now. It was a nice life while it lasted. I toss back the remaining contents of the Starlight Water.

"No need to fear anything from me, lass," Riagan says with a charming smile, turning his attention to me. "I am well aware of what you are plannin' on doing, I was aware of it before you were. I may be the Winter Court's spymaster, but my truly loyalties lie with the Summer Court."

"Stop harpin' as if ye are so proud. Yer nothin' but a nasty spy," Eilis grumbles.

My eyebrows fly up. The spymaster of the Winter Court is spying on his own court for the enemy? What sort of political intrigue have I gotten myself wrapped up in?

"It takes some skill ta be a double agent, me bloom, when one cannot lie," Riagan says in a triumphant tone as his smirk grows. "So I would not say that is nothin'. Ye probably thought that me days as a spymaster were over when I destroyed me lying gloves long ago, when the Fair Law was made, didn't ye?"

Eilis bristles at this.

I adjust my position, trying to keep up with the conversation. "Wait, there was a time before the Fair Law."

I'd never heard of this.

There was a time the faeries could lie?

"Aye," Riagan says somewhat nostalgically. "There was. But at the end of the reign of the last High Queen of the faeries, she put a curse on all of us."

"Don't ye forget why she placed that curse," Eilis said, slapping her hand against the table.

"How could I when ye constantly are remindin' me of it?" Riagan replied blithely as he contemplates the ceiling of the shack.

Eilis growls. "Ye serve a traitor."

"And ye serve Prince Thadghan, which I think shows the sense that ye have."

"He's king now," Eilis says in a low and dangerous tone. "King of the Undersea Court."

Riagan ignores her and turns to me. "If ye ask me, I would say that it was the High Queen who betrayed her people when she placed them under that curse."

Eilis shoots to her feet. "Ye will not speak of my queen's sacrifice that way! She would not have done so if she had not been driven to it."

Riagan rolls his eyes. "It be easy for ye to remain loyal to her, me bloom, when ye were not affected by her curse."

Eilis cuts her eyes to him. "No, instead you choose to serve the man who betrayed our queen which led to her creating the Fair Law."

"The Summer King cares about humans," Riagan says stiffly. "Which should be enough for ye, but obviously not since ye refuse to serve him, all because of a feud that is centuries old. And ye hold it against me when I have yer best interest in mind."

Eilis snorts. "Best interest," she mutters contemptibly.

I'm rubbing at my temples. "Wait, I'm so confused. What is going on here? What are you guys talking about with the High Queen and the Fair Law?"

Riagan glances at me and raises an eyebrow. "Appears that the lass needs a lesson in faerie history."

Eilis rolls her eyes. "And I suppose ye plan on givin' it to her."

"I don't see anyone else volunteering," Riagan replies. He turns back to me. "Ye see, lass, there was once a time when there were no faerie courts and there was no Fair Law. This palace, the Court of Dreams and Nightmares, was the center of faerie life, the Forest of Night, the capital of the world."

Ravven had said something of the sort, but I hadn't thought too much about it. How could there have once not been the Summer and Winter Courts? My entire existence as a Guardian revolves around their meddling in human's lives.

"We were ruled by a High Queen," Riagan continues. Eilis stiffens at his words. "I was her spymaster and Eilis was the captain of her guard. She'd taken Eilis to our world when she was a young lass."

Eilis growls. "She saved me from the poverty and starvation that awaited me in me own home when me parents died of the plague."

Riagan sweeps his hand toward her. "As ye can clearly see, Eilis became fiercely loyal to that queen."

"Loyalty is a virtue that ye do not understand," Eilis says, turning away.

Riagan stares at her for a long moment, a look that I would never have expected to see a faerie give. Least of all one as seemingly carefree as Riagan. It is filled with longing and sorrow. "Perhaps," he says softly. "But then that would not explain how I somehow always end up aiding ye."

Eilis rolls her eyes. "I'm going to go get another drink," she says, stalking around the bar and to the back of the *Toadstool*.

Riagan shakes his head as he watches her go. "I'm sure ye can gather from the present events, the High Queen's rule did not last."

"You don't say," I mutter dryly as Eilis disappears into the back.

Riagan nods. "Oh, but I do. It was her own family who brought about the end of her rule. Her husband, King Tibern, decided that he was tired of ruling at her side. He gathered his loyal supporters, the Tuatha De Danan and created his own court. The Summer Court. The queen banished them from the Otherworld, but when they entered the human world, they found the people their easy recipients of their power."

How old are Riagan and Eilis? He's talking about ancient Ireland, before it was christianized. Back before the faerie's war and the Tuatha De Danan returned to the Otherworld when no one worshiped them anymore.

"It wasn't long however 'afor other faerie lords and ladies got it in their heads to create their own courts. The High Queen's rule was crumbling and she knew it. She resented Tibern and her people for all betraying her. And so, she decided to curse all of us. Even the ones who remained loyally at her side."

My breath catches in my throat as Riagan's easy voice grows harsh. "Aye, she cursed us. As ye know, faeries cannot actually curse each other. It is because our magic protects us to an extent from the magic of other individuals. But Aine was the High Queen. She had more power than most. She created the Fair Law, to make certain that faeries were always under boundaries, no longer limitless and free as we had once been. The cost of such a curse, killed Queen Aine."

"Oh," I say, unsure of what else to say.

"Eilis never understood. She is still blinded by loyalty..." He shakes his head. "She doesn't know what it is like to have yer free will stolen from ye."

I swallow. Because I can think of how it would be. How my chances and opportunities would shrivel up if I were to ever lose my humanity and become a faerie. Lying would be the least of it. I've seen the faeries how they are hindered from doing so many things by the Fair Law.

"I see."

"Aye," Riagan mumbles sadly.

"What *are* you doing here, Riagan?" Eilis demands as she strides back, an empty glass in hand. She sits back down and glares at him.

Riagan slides into the seat next to her and shoots her a wicked smile. "It appears that I am interested in the outcome of this young mortal."

Eilis rolls her eyes. "Don't pretend that you really care about her. Besides, I don't see how you can actually help since the Fair Law prevents your kind from either aiding or hindering her during her trials."

Riagan's face twists into a horrid frown at the mention of the Fair Law, but his smile quickly returns.

"I am not allowed ta help her, that is where ye are right, me bloom," Riagan says with a lazy grin as he leans against the table. "But that doesn't mean that I cannot in a drunken stupor boast to me old partner."

Eilis snorts as Riagan pulls a flask out of his jacket and tips it back. When he pulls it away his lips are stained red.

"Riagan!" Eilis gasps.

Riagan grins again, his smile lazier than before. "Because of me special position in the Winter Court I can certainly tell you that Iorwerth's room is three doors down from the queen's own. My room is across the hall from his. I will probably carelessly leave my door open. Should make it obnoxiously easy to distinguish what is his room if that were the case. Ye'll need Ravven for this part, Iorwerth is so smart to have charmed his room is he not?"

Riagan holds out his hand, but it hovers helplessly in midair, a key dangling from his fingers. He arches a brow. "It appears that this is as far as the Fair Law will allow me to go. Apparently, I cannot accidentally maliciously drop this key for ye to find. I would be powerless to resist however, if ye were to remove it from me with force."

The key dangles temptingly from his fingers and for a second, I think that it is a trap. Riagan stated his fight with Eilis how they don't see eye to eye. What if he wants her to die? But then I remember the look on his face when she hadn't been watching. How it had been frustration and sadness in his voice when he spoke of Eilis not understanding the Fair Law, not hate or anger.

Then Eilis's hand shoots out and grabs the key.

Riagan smiles and rises to his feet. "Bother me, it seems that I have misplaced me key. If it doesn't appear in me room by Highmoon on the morrow, I shall have to report its disappearance."

He totters across the room to the door, swaying on his feet.

"Riagan—" Eilis begins, half turning as if to go after him.

Riagan pauses, leaning heavily against the doorframe and glancing back at her.

"Thank you," she says softly.

He chuckles. "There be nothin' ta thank me over. All I did was get drunk." And with that, he lurches out the door into the dim light of the moon, whistling a jaunty tune.

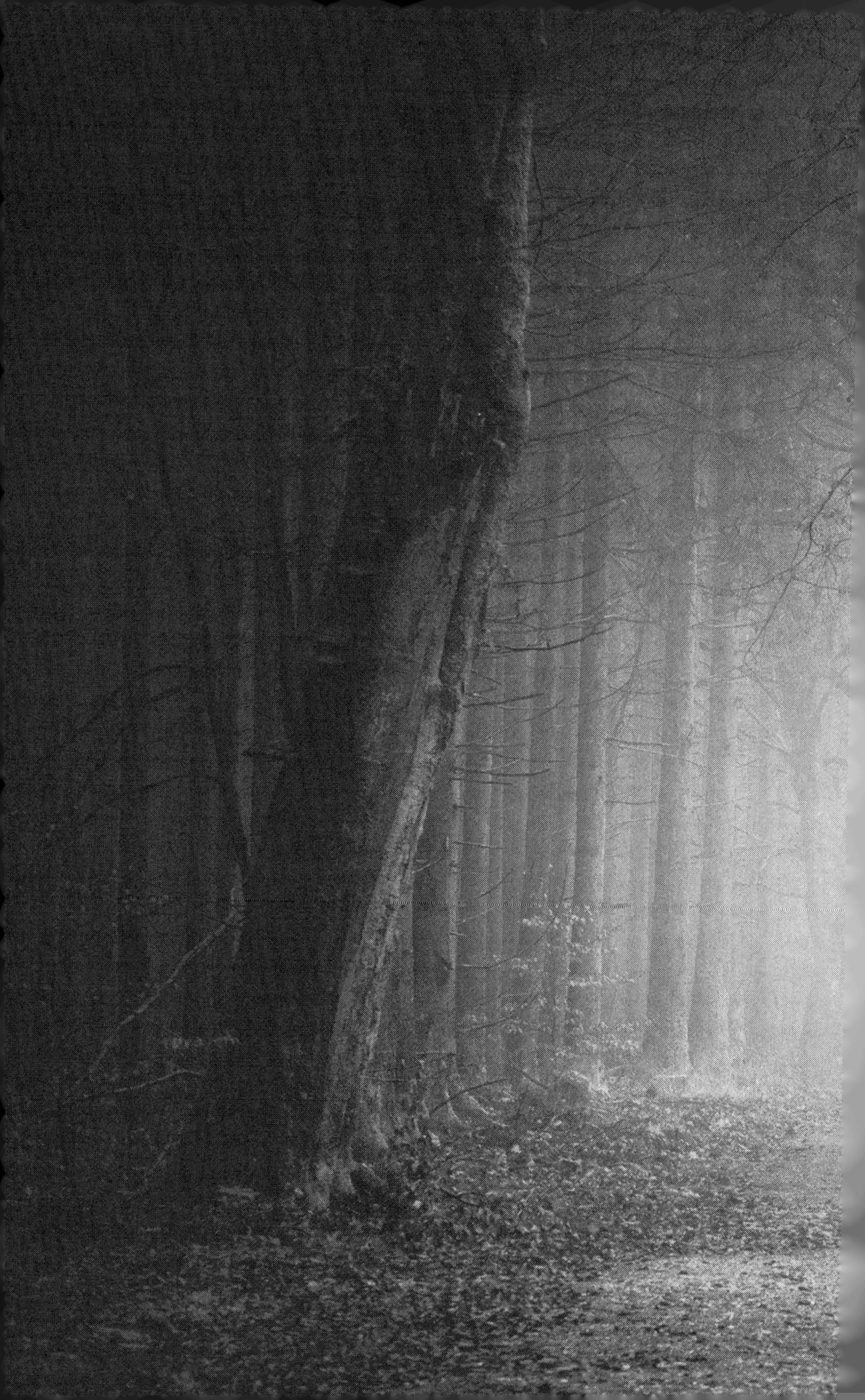

CHAPTER THIRTY-THREE

"So that worked," I say as I blow out a breath. It fogs around my face and I grimace at the cold as Eilis gently closes the door behind her. The walls of the Winter Court are crusted in ice.

"Did ye think that it would not?" Eilis asks, turning back to me and arching a brow. Her curly hair is pulled up around her head like some sort of fiery halo.

I shrug as my eyes dart around the dark, empty throne room. Eilis had stated that there might be some sentinels guarding the inner chambers, but it appears they all ran to their queen's aid when her screech shook the entire palace. What a sight that had been, the drunk Tuatha De Danan had started ripping off parts of her clothes and accessories, destroying them, raving about her item of immortality. It had caused a better distraction than I had thought. It distracted *me*. I had been curious to see how it played out.

Ravven had assured me that such a feat wouldn't cause a faerie war so long as the Summer King renounced the faerie and allowed Cliodhna to do as she pleased with him.

"I don't know, I just thought that maybe Riagan would have betrayed us."

"Don't hold yer breath," Eilis says, slipping the key around her neck. It hadn't worked like a regular key and lock would have. All she had to do was touch it to the door and it opened. A small smile pulls at the corners of her lips. "Riagan has a misguided loyalty. It is perhaps the only good quality that he has."

I press my lips together. What is going on between Riagan and Eilis is really none of my business, and I don't want to risk Eilis becoming angry at me by pressing further. It seems to be a touchy subject to her. Even though I would really like to understand her better.

Eilis brushes past me. "Keep close."

I do my best to follow, trying to walk as gracefully as she, but I keep slipping and sliding on the icy floor. We slip through a door along the wall that supposedly leads to their inner chambers.

Hopefully Ravven arrives soon.

In order for either of us to get into Iorwerth's room, we need Ravven to use his magic against the ward that Riagan claims is guarding it. But I don't know how he plans on getting in. He said for me not to worry about it, but I don't know how he plans on getting through the door without the key that Eilis and I have.

Who needs a door?

I startle at his voice, but there is no one other than Eilis in the hall. I swallow hard and shake my head as I follow Eilis. I have to brace my hand against the wall to keep my balance as my booted heels keep sliding across the floor. The last thing I need is a bruised tailbone for my efforts. It's so dark in here too on top of everything else. Everything is enveloped in shadows, even the darkness is hidden by still more shadows. As we pass a small window, I peek out, but I cannot see anything out there either. The night is pitch black without the light of the moon.

I hear a fluttering noise and glance over my shoulder to find a dark form standing directly behind me. My sharp gasp is cut off by a warm palm clasping over my mouth.

"Calm yourself, pest. It is only me."

I sag against the ice wall. Ravven. It's just Ravven. I try to tell my heart to calm down.

"What is goin' on here?" Eilis demands in a low hiss.

"Nothing, Jaye is simply overreacting. As per usual."

I knock his hand aside, which was still resting over my mouth and glare at him. "You nearly scared me to death."

Ravven's dark form straightens. "Do you mean to tell me that humans can be killed by fear as well?"

"It's— it's happened," I mumble, tucking a loose strand of hair that had escaped from my braid behind my ear.

"Is there something that *doesn't* kill humans?"

I huff loudly, perhaps a little too loudly. My eyes dart around the dark corridor. "If there is, I have yet to come across it."

"I wonder how you are still alive."

"Come on," Eilis growls back. "We do not have time for this."

"How did you even get in?" I demand, my voice barely audible to my own ears, but I know that Ravven can hear it.

"I flew in," he replies. "Through the window."

The same window I was just looking out? That thing was too small for him to crawl through. Besides he doesn't have wings. "No, you didn't."

Ravven chuckles. "Of course, I did, faeries cannot lie, or have you forgotten? You truly are a distrustful soul. You already know that I have Sidhe blood in me. That includes being able to shapeshift."

I open my mouth to reply, but then decide not to. Quite honestly, I have reached the point where I don't know what to say to Ravven anymore.

"How did you think I lured the Lake Dragon away?" Ravven asks with a derisive snort. "You thought that I actually outswam it in this form. Lake Dragons were made to prowl the seas."

I don't have a reply to that because that's exactly what I had thought.

Ravven must sense my reply in my silence because he chuckles softly. "And here I had been thinking that I had let my secret out then!"

"How *did* you escape the Lake Dragon?" I ask, glaring at his dark shadow. It's not like he can think me any more idiotic anyway.

Ravven glances at me and I wonder what he can see with his heightened senses. "I turned into a Lake Dragon myself and then led it on a merry chase."

Fortunately, he moves ahead to say something to Eilis so he doesn't see the shock on my face. No need for him to have any more reason to mock me. Ravven turned into *a Lake Dragon*???

I remember that last roar I had heard, the one that was louder than the other Lake Dragon's. That must have been Ravven.

I reach up and massage my forehead as I watch Ravven's dark form saunter ahead, walking seamlessly on the icy ground. There is so much about him that I don't know, and the fact that this surprises me is terrifying. I've barely even known of his existence for a few days. But somehow, I thought that I had come to know Ravven Crowe. And I don't know why I would.

Ravven and Eilis both draw to a halt outside an arched doorway with ice ornaments lining it and hanging from it.

"Here it is," Eilis says, crossing her arms. She glances at Ravven. "You ready to do yer magic?"

Ravven stretches his fingers and rests the tips of them on the wall. He holds still for a long moment before nodding. "I will be able to lower the ward, however, I will not be able to make it look like it was not tampered with."

Eilis shrugs. "What does it matter if it does? He'll know that we were here the second that he finds his antler gone, but what will he be able to do about it then?"

"A fair enough point," Ravven says as he presses both his hands against the wall. The space in the doorway shimmers a translucent dark blue and there is a cracking sound.

"Go, and do be quick about it!" Ravven snaps, his tone strained. White frost trails up his fingertips from where his hands are pressed against the wall, but then it melts dripping down to the icy floor below his boots. "The ward is designed to turn anyone who crosses the threshold without permission to ice and I cannot hold it off forever."

Eilis and I both hurry into the room. I turn in a circle, taking in the icy surfaces of everything. So sharp, so cold, so reflective. I can't find it in myself to be surprised.

Eilis is at a small chest, picking the lock and swinging it open and I throw myself on top of his lavish bed, checking underneath his pillow and patting down the mattress.

"Do you want us all to turn to ice?" Ravven demands. "Be faster!"

I shoot a desperate glance over my shoulder to where I can just make out his silhouette, Eilis has moved to a table. I'm about to join her when I spot something out of the corner of my eye. A faint glow. I shove my hand down into the space between the bed and the wall and find an open space, a small cubbyhole carved into the ice. My hand wraps around a smooth item and I yank it out.

The antler!

"I've got it!" I cry.

"Not so loud," Eilis hisses, rushing to my side and grasping my arm. She yanks me off of the bed and out of the room.

The ice is now all the way to Ravven's elbows even though it is still melting. There's a veritable pool at his feet.

As soon as we are out, Ravven releases a wounded cry and stumbles back, slumping down to the ground.

"Ravven!" I drop to my knees next to him. I reach out to touch his shoulder, but then I yelp and pull back. Touching him stings and reminds me of the Winter Queen's touch. "Are you okay?"

"I will survive," he rasps, as he braces his hand against his knee and stands unsteadily. "Accursed iron." He squeezes his fingers shut around the bandage on his palm as bits of ice break off of his arm and land tinkling on the ground. "I should have handled that well enough, but this wound has weakened me."

I stand, eyeing him suspiciously. He looks like he might pass out any second now. "But you'll get your full strength back soon enough, right?"

Ravven straightens, adjusting his cuff. "Of course I shall," he says shortly. "Have some faith. As if I am going to let a little iron cut get me down."

Eilis inhales a short-surprised breath. "Ye've been cut by iron?"

Ravven nods, though somewhat hesitantly.

"And it entered yer bloodstream?"

He snorts. "I don't see how this conversation even matters?"

"When did this happen?" she demands.

Ravven is silent.

"Last night," I answer since Ravven doesn't appear to want to.

"And yer still standin'?" Eilis says with a huff. "I'm impressed."

"I am quite impressive. I believe it's high time people and faeries alike began accepting that fact, but enough of me."

My eyebrows shoot up. That's something I never thought I would hear come from the great and vain Ravven Crowe.

Well, I suppose that I'm just full of surprises, love.

I'm even more surprised until Ravven starts talking, and I realize he didn't say that. I need to stop hearing Ravven's voice in my head. It is obviously not a good sign at all. "We need to get out of here before the Winter Court returns. It will not take Cliodhna long to punish that Seelie faerie and when she does, undoubtedly her court will want her to return to her rooms."

Eilis nods. "Of course. Let's go."

I don't know if I breathe fully until we make it to the Autumn Wing of the court. Even when we are out of the Winter Court, I still don't feel safe.

Ravven also seems to sigh. He runs a hand through his hair. I see now in the light that he's slightly wan.

"Are you sure you're okay?"

He shoots me an annoyed look. "I'm hardly the one who will die if I am frightened, now am I? Stop being a pest and go get ready."

"Ready?" I ask, tilting my head.

Ravven's eyes lock on the antler still clutch in my hand. "We will want to deliver this to the Summer King as soon as possible to avoid having it stolen from us. And you can't very well come into the Summer King's presence looking like that, now can you?"

I very well can, but I don't bother saying it. Instead, with a huff I hand Ravven the antler and go into my room.

Eilis follows me in to help me change into a dark green dress that I chose out of spite for its plainness. It only has a few extra embellishments and no precious gems sewn in.

When I step out of the room, Ravven is tossing the antler in the air leaning against the wall. He smirks when he sees me. "Are you ready to go, my hideous beauty?"

Hideous beauty? That's a first. It's also an oxymoron, but I'm too tired to even care anymore. The Starlight Water is beginning to wear off and I just want to crawl into a bed, any bed, even just pillows will work, and sleep for a year.

I glance at Eilis. "Are you coming?"

She shakes her head and steps back. "No. I do not wish to become more involved than I already am."

"Thank you for your help," I say. "I hope it hasn't been too much trouble."

She holds up her hands. "If the Winter Court is angry with me, it is from things that I did in the past, not from this."

"The Summer King should still be at the ball," Ravven says, tucking the antler into his vest. "The Tuatha De Danan may be not quite as wild as the Sidhe race, but they are never ones to leave a party early."

"Are you feeling better?" I ask, eyeing his complexion. It's still not quite as golden as it usually is.

Ravven stiffens. "Of course I am," he huffs, obviously offended. "You must think me extremely weak if you think that a simple charm like that could harm me."

Well, I did see the great Ravven Crowe collapse at my feet.

Instead of pressing the point I force a smile. "We're halfway done, Ravven. Tell me, did you think we would make it this far?"

He looks at me, amusement flickering in his eyes. "We've completed the easy half. Tomorrow the Winter Court tests us. Believe me, the worst is still yet to come."

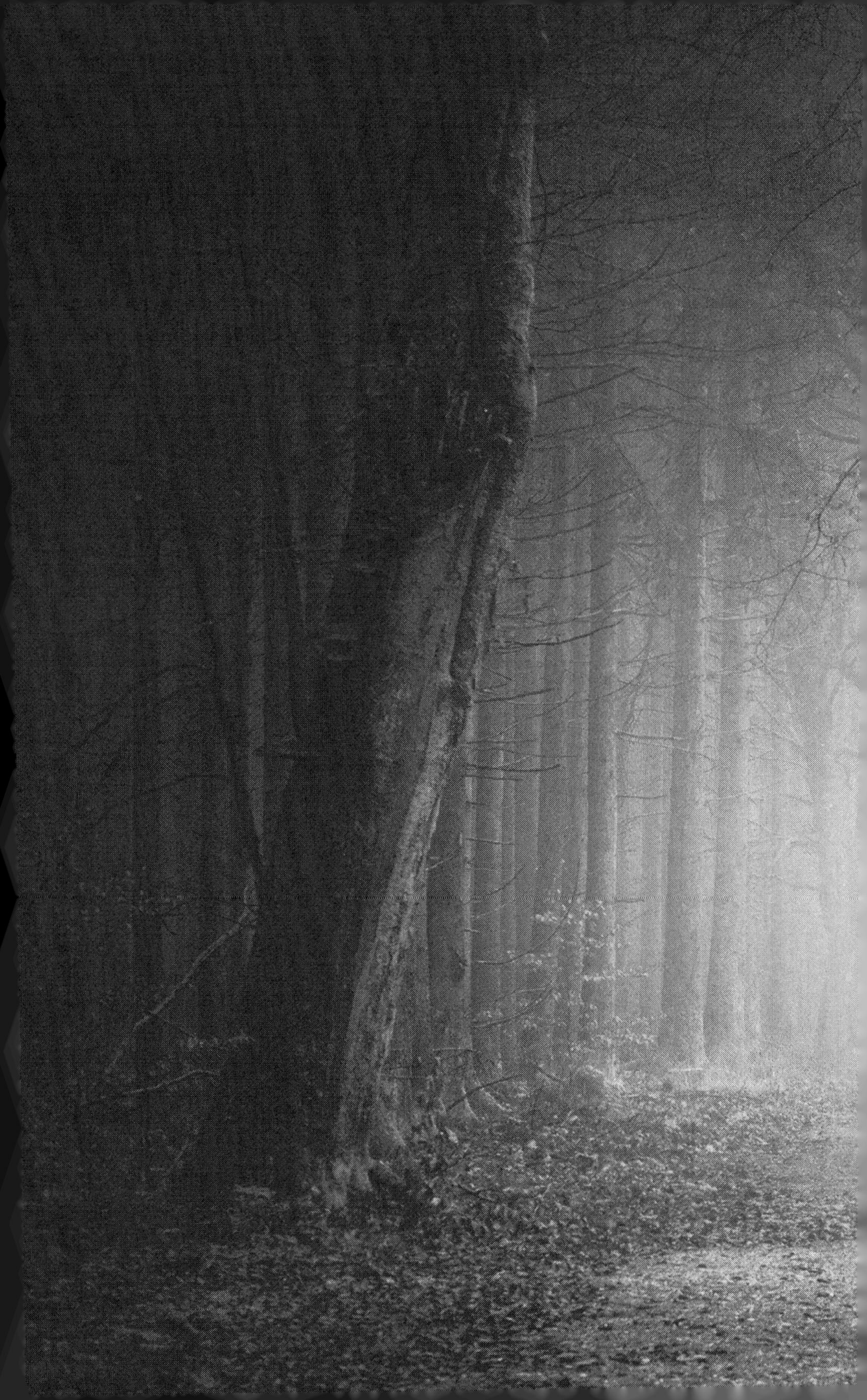

CHAPTER THIRTY-FOUR

Ravven's words haunt me for the rest of the night. So that now as we are standing outside the Winter Court's giant ice doors, I am not only burdened by lack of sleep, but also by a heavy dread.

These faeries want me dead.

The faeries of the Summer Court and the Undersea Court hadn't really cared what happened to me, but I want to kill the Winter Queen's own sister. When I complete my tasks, I *will* kill the queen's own sister, no matter how squeamish the thought makes me. And I have not kept those sentiments a secret. These faeries have every right to wish me dead. They will not want me to succeed. So what sort of test could they possibly give to me?

Ravven glances at me and frowns. "Try not to wear your emotions so clearly on your face."

I swallow and try to neutralize my features. "There. Is this better?"

His frown deepens. "Not really."

"Then what would you suggest I do?" I hiss.

He straightens and dusts an invisible speck from his midnight blue outfit. I am wearing a matching midnight blue tunic and pants. "Don't do anything that might get us killed."

Oh sure, that is so easy.

The doors choose that moment to swing open. How different it is when they open freely instead of us having to sneak in here with a stolen key. They are so grand, magnificent even. My boot slips slightly as I take my first step onto the ice floor, but I manage to steady myself before I can fall. How can these faeries all walk around on it so easily?

The circular chamber looks completely different during Highmoon and filled with occupants. Light filters through the ice ceiling as the faeries, many of which I recognize from the ball, line the crystalline walls. The Winter Queen sits on a throne carved of ice in the middle and on either side of her are Iorwerth and

Aoibheann. I spot Riagan standing in the back of the room with his giant black beast, Blackie. But I don't really care about anyone else in the throne room once I see Aoibheann. Thomas isn't with her; I have no idea where he might be. My heart is filled with hate and I no longer have to worry about them seeing my emotions written across my face because I have only one emotion and that is rage. And I don't care if they see it. This entire accursed court should know what is coming for them.

"Greetings," the Winter Queen says mildly.

Ravven tilts his head. I don't curtsy, I simply stand there glaring. Ravven shoots me a frustrated look out of the corner of his eye. I don't care. What does it matter if I anger her or disrespect her? She is already not going to give us a test we can easily pass, no matter what I do. We stand stiffly in front of the queen waiting for her decree.

"Congratulations on making it so far," Cliodnha says, not sounding very happy for me at all. "I must say, I was quite surprised that you had not died already."

"Well, I really am very sorry to disappoint you," I say, blinking twice when Ravven glances at me startled. He smiles and some of the tension in his muscles relax. I feel a shot of thrill for having made him so happy by using our code. But then I smother that. I should have no reason to feel so pleased over Ravven's smile.

The queen however, looks confused before she finally laughs a small tinkling sound like a bell. "How interesting it is that you lie over such inconsequential things."

Oh yeah sure, I lie over inconsequential things all the time. I just *love* to lie over inconsequential things. I refrain from trying to explain sarcasm to her. It didn't work out that well with Ravven and frankly I don't care enough to try.

"I believe that you had a test for us," Ravven says, drawing the Winter Queen's attention back at him. I'm thankful. Just her gaze gives me shivers. My tunic has long sleeves that extend to my wrist. I wore it not only for the cold, but also to hide that horrid handprint and the memory of it. Of a time when the Winter Queen had me so completely in her power.

It feels like so much has changed since last I was in a throne room with her. And yet it also feels like nothing has changed at all. I'm still the weak powerless mortal girl I always have been. For some odd reason, I want to hold Ravven's hand. For comfort. For support. To remind myself that there is still warmth in this world.

But I don't dare allow myself that moment of weakness, least of all one that the Winter Queen would witness. I glance at Ravven out of the corner of my eyes and he smiles slightly as if sensing my need for support.

"Indeed, I do," the Winter Queen says, interrupting our shared moment and pulling both of our gazes to her. "I have a bit of a problem, and I fear I have had this problem for some time." Her gaze moves from us to the faeries gathered around us and I get the feeling that she isn't really speaking to us anymore as she raises her voice. "A member of my court has betrayed us to our enemy the Summer King."

Gasps fill the room, but I just stand stock still.

"We have a traitor in our midst," she continues, a deep frown marring her face. "Someone who somehow aided these two in completing their task for the Summer Court."

"You know that the Fair Law prohibits any other faerie from helping Jaye—the mortal in her tasks," Ravven says quickly, his eyes remaining doggedly fixed on Cliodnha. Does he know about Riagan? He wasn't there when Riagan helped, but he seems to know more about Riagan and Eilis than I do. And Eilis had helped us. If he knew the connection between the two of them...

"And yet you still had aid from my court," the queen says simply. Iorwerth looks almost unrecognizable, and then I realize what it is. His syrupy sweet charming smile is gone, in its place is cold hard fury. "I have long known that a member of my court has been spying on me. Unfortunately, I cannot trust the word of my court or this spy. They have managed to hide from me all of these years, despite the Fair Law binding them to always speak the truth." Her gaze lands on me.

I shift uncomfortably.

"Find me the spy," she finishes. "And your task is complete."

I freeze. I'm frozen. I'm ice.

Riagan.

She wants me to turn Riagan in.

I am thankful that I am frozen because otherwise my gaze would have flown right to him and betrayed him then and there. I swallow nervously and finally glance around the court, taking in every person, not letting my gaze linger on Riagan as I pass. He's still as nonchalant as can be, not betraying that they are talking about him in the least. He hasn't even stiffened.

I quickly return my gaze to the queen.

"I understand that this would be a difficult task for you," she says. She raises her frozen gaze. "Given how this person obviously aided you in your task for the Summer Court," she sneers at the name. "So in order to ensure that you do indeed turn in your ally and if your lives are not enough, I have added another incentive. Another mortal's life is at risk. Every hour you tarry shall be punishment upon your friend so keep that in mind."

My heart stills. If she has done anything to Thomas...

I cannot let him be hurt just because I don't want to betray a faerie. But Riagan's only crime is that he helped me. He has only ever helped me.

I keep having to betray my conscience to get ahead and I don't know how much longer I can keep it up. Is this how all these faeries ended up as they are now? Did they start out as decent sorts and then this accursed world formed them into the unfeeling monsters they are now?

The queen dismisses us with a careless flick of her hand as if we are gnats. I don't immediately move. Ravven has to grasp my arm and pull me away from the queen whom I am staring at in horror. Aoibheann chuckles and I want to rip out her vocal cords. I want to kill every single Unseelie faerie in the room.

I reach to grab my dagger, but Ravven somehow anticipates my move and grasps my other hand. He practically drags me toward the door. I don't move to follow him, but the slick ice does not give me the traction that I need to fight against his pull. "Patience, pest," he murmurs in my hair. "He is not dead and nor will he be."

"Oh," The Winter Queen calls after us just as we reach the door. Her voice freezes every muscle in my body as if it is coating it over with ice. "And do not bring me the wrong person. Else you will have failed the test. Your lives will be forfeit and so will the life of your mortal friend."

Then the doors slam shut behind us. I sag in Ravven's arms. This is an impossible choice.

Every pathetic human sentiment in me tells me that I cannot turn in Riagan. I don't even know when I started to consider him a friend, but now I realize that I do.

And yet how can I not when not only my life is on the line, but also Ravven's and Thomas's?

I don't realize that I'm shivering until Ravven wraps his arms around me and starts rubbing my arms. "We will figure out something to do," he says, his hand moving up to stroke my hair.

Does he know that the spy is Riagan?

Maybe he thinks that my breakdown is due to stress over not knowing how to find out who this traitor is. But I know. I already know. Oh, goodness how I wish that I didn't.

I straighten and look at Ravven as he pulls away with a frown.

I can't tell him; Ravven will turn Riagan in. What does he care about what happens to Riagan?

But then a niggling voice asks, *why should I?*

He is just a faerie after all. But I'm starting to believe that faerie doesn't mean that they have no decency or ability to love. Just like being human doesn't mean that *I* have it.

I can't just abandon Riagan to a fate that would be my fault because I turned him in. I'm not that selfish. But how can I truly be that selfless and give up everything for him?

I'm not quite sure how we reach the Autumn Court, I was walking in a haze. Ravven turns to me. He runs a hand over his jaw. "You stay here."

"Where are you going?" I ask, stepping after him.

Ravven looks at me. He hesitates. "I'm going to go talk to Eilis about this."

I stare after him as he leaves. Does this mean that he knows that the traitor is Riagan? She's the most important person to him, that much is apparent even to me. And maybe she's the one who will lose the most if I were to turn him in. She tries to hide it behind her callous exterior but I think that she actually cares about Riagan.

Or maybe he just went to talk with Eilis because she might be able to help him locate the spy.

I shake my head as I sink down on the pillows.

But then I hear a buzz, like a fly whizzing past. I lift my head just as a glowing yellow creature stops in front of my face. I nearly scream, but bite down on my lip to keep from doing so. It's just a messenger pixie. It tilts its head, large black eyes staring straight into my soul. Then it flies forward, moving aside my hair. I hold perfectly still as it breathes next to my ear.

It whispers two words, "Sprite's Toadstool," and then it is gone, zipping off into the darkness of Highmoon.

I spring to my feet and race toward the door. I don't know who sent me the messenger pixie. Was it Ravven? He's only been gone a few minutes, besides, he was never who I met in that dilapidated building. But maybe it's Eilis or Riagan who want to talk to me about this newest development.

I check my boot for my iron dagger, just in case this person who sent the message turns out to be someone who wants to kill me, then I pull the latch.

"Where are you going?" Keane asks, suddenly materializing in the hall beside me.

I pause at the stairs that will lead down to the exit and glance back at him. It's unsettling how he's watching me like I'm doing something bad. "I hardly think that's any of your business."

Daithi huffs from inside his room. It's an extremely loud huff.

"Why are you leaving?" he asks again.

I shift my weight, edging toward the stairs. "I have somewhere to be. Is there something wrong with that? Am I not supposed to go anywhere?"

Keane's eyes flick to the door that leads out of the rest of the Court of Dreams and Nightmares.

I stiffen. "Did Ravven tell you not to let me leave?"

Keane shakes his head. "He just wanted me to keep an eye on you."

"I don't need a babysitter," I snap.

"No, you do not," Keane says, stepping back. I turn back to the stairs, but his words stop me. "Be careful with him."

I whirl back at him, confused. "Who?"

"My son," Keane says softly. "He is meant for so much more than he even knows. Do not break him."

"I won't," I say with a snort. As if anyone could break Ravven. He's unbreakable, immortal, invulnerable. I'm the weak human here. I'm the one with all of the weaknesses.

With a shake of my head, I turn back to the stairs and begin hurrying down them. *What an odd thing for someone to say.*

I wrap my arms around myself as I walk past the spot where Ravven and I first teleported here. Where it had seemed as if he would kiss me. I hadn't thought anything of it then. Just my imagination getting ahead of me. But now he *has* kissed me. It is painfully obvious that I have feelings for him, albeit unwelcome ones. And I think he feels something toward me, even if that something is just concern.

I shake those thoughts from my head. I have no time for them now. I pause outside the door. I glance around to make certain that no one is around, there isn't. The faeries it seems don't really mingle in the hall during the day... or Highmoon or whatever. They stay in their courts, only coming out at Nethermoon, to party.

I wonder if it is because they hate each other, or because they fear what any faerie would do to them if they are caught out alone and unawares.

I slip out into the dark forest, the silver light of the moon illuminating my path. I miss the sun more than I dare to admit. Here everything is dark, everything is enshrouded in shadows, everything is cool. I shiver and turn my focus to my feet. I've only walked the path twice. Once to the shack and once back, so I sincerely hope that I don't end up lost.

Finally I spot the dark shack up ahead as I near it, dread settles more and more heavily over my shoulders. Maybe I should not have come.

Even if it is Riagan who invited me to come, how do I know that he doesn't want to kill me to ensure that I cannot share his secret. Every step that I take, that possibility becomes more and more likely.

I swallow down my panic. Maybe he wants to come up with a strategy.

He is a spymaster; strategy is what he does. I'm training to be an assassin, killing is what I do. But what if Riagan attacks me? I don't know if I would be able to kill him if it came to that.

When I hear a loud bark as I reach the door, I nearly turn and flee. I had forgotten to take the mangy mutt of his into consideration. The pooka is as large as a bear, and just as capable of transforming into one if it doesn't wish to rip me to shreds in the shape of a dog. I whirl, but then Riagan is there smiling widely. "Thank me magic you came, and so quickly at that."

Every muscle in my body goes rigid as I take in his mussed hair and his strained smile.

"What is it that you wanted to say to me?" I ask, barely managing to push the words past my locked lips. I should have told Ravven everything. He will gloat over my dead body.

Riagan looks over my face once and then slumps against the wall. "Why don't we just abandon the pretenses seeing as the act is especially painful for the both of us?"

I have no reply because my voice box ran off into the dark forest, fleeing for safety.

Riagan releases a heavy breath and runs his hand down the length of his face. "The Winter Queen has Eilis."

I stiffen. That wasn't what I had been expecting him to say. "What?"

"She's the mortal who the Winter Queen threatened to harm until you bring her me name." He grimaces, as if just imagining what Eilis is going through is enough to give him pain. He rubs at his forearms. "They must have taken her last night."

"How—how do you know?" I demand, shocked. "Did the queen tell you?"

"No," Riagan spits. "She must suspect me at least a little bit to keep me in the dark about this. I suspect that only she, Aoibheann, Iorwerth, and her most trusted guards know."

"Then how do you know?"

Riagan opens his mouth, seems to reconsider what he was going to say and then closes it before finally opening it again. "Eilis and I were supposed to meet and she never arrived. The Winter Queen must have taken her."

I back away, running my shaky hands down my face. "What am I supposed to do?"

"That much is simple enough," Riagan says with a humorless chuckle. "You do as the Winter Queen demands."

I shake my head. "But that would mean I would have to tell them that you are the traitor."

"Do you think I care about that when Eilis's life is on the line? The spying, the Seelie and Unseelie, that is all just a game. Eilis is what truly matters." He shakes his head. "She has more good in a strand of her hair than I have in my entire body. There had never been a question as to who should be the one to live between the two of us."

I shake my head. "But—"

He shakes his head. "No, do not argue with me on this. This is better for everyone involved. If ye fail, not only would Eilis die, but also you and Crowe. I am not worth that. Don't give up your chance to become the Fair Assassin for the sake of a spymaster who played his cards wrong."

I rub my temples at the reminder that this isn't just about me. Or even Eilis. Ravven and Thomas lie in the balance as well. Why did everything have to go and get so complicated? "Okay fine. I'll do it. I just need to speak to Ravven and then we can—"

"Do not waste any time. Do it now," Riagan demands, his composure cracking as his voice does. His eyes are wide with panic. He inhales a deep breath and straightens, seeming to gain control of himself. "Every moment that we wait is another moment that Eilis is trapped in their clutches."

I lick my lips and nod. "Of course. But... Riagan?"

He looks at me. "Yes, young one?"

"Are you certain about this?"

He smiles and pats my shoulder. "I appreciate yer concern, but I can handle meself. And I cannot lie so you know that is the truth."

"All right then." I exhale a heavy breath. "We had better go."

It is so cold at the Winter Court that I feel my lips become chapped. I sense the lack of Ravven's presence acutely.

I stare at the Winter Queen, noting Riagan as he strides forward nonchalantly, his pooka at his heels.

"What brings you so soon back to my court?"

"I have your traitor," I say, holding up my chin.

"Well then..." the queen says smiling, then she sits there watching me as if waiting for me to continue. I don't. Instead I place my hands on my hips.

"Your friend is waiting," she says.

"I want to see her."

She heaves a heavy sigh and waves her finger. One of the side doors bursts open and a few minutes later two dark haired guards drag a manacled Eilis through. She's dressed in the same outfit she wore last night, her hair hanging in matted tangles around her face. Blood smears the side of her face, and her forearms.

"The Undersea Court will not stand for this," Eilis spits as soon as she sees the Winter Queen.

The Winter Queen waves aside her words with a cheery little laugh. "The Undersea Court does not want war." Her eyes land on me. "As you can see, she is still very much alive. But I cannot say that will continue to be the case if you try my patience. Who is the traitor?"

Eilis freezes when she sees me. "Jaye... you wouldn't."

I swallow. "When I tell you, you will free her?"

"Of course. I have no more need with Ursulle's plaything."

"Give me your word," I say.

"Jaye!" Eilis cries.

"I swear by my magic and my immortality that I shall release your mortal friend when I have the spy in my grasp," Cliodnha says, her tone bored. She doesn't care about me. She doesn't care about me at all, or Eilis. She doesn't think I'm a threat to her sister. Maybe she doesn't care about her sister. Or maybe... maybe she doesn't think that she has anything to fear from a mortal like me, Fair Assassin or not.

I swallow. I'll prove her wrong. They'll all realize how wrong they were to underestimate me, but by then it will be too late. "No, you will release her when you know who the spy is. That is all you required of me. A name, nothing more."

"Very well."

"Jaye," Eilis says again. She lurches forward, her gaze flying around the room until it lands on Riagan who is watching her with a grim face. They stare at each other, seeming to have some form of silent conversation before she whips her head to me. "Jaye, don't do it!"

I squeeze my eyes shut to block out the panic in her tone. Would I rather remain here to be tortured if our places were reversed and it were Ravven who would suffer from my salvation? Somehow, I can't find it in myself to want Ravven to pay for my freedom. The thought is disgusting to me. Since when did I get to the point where I would choose him over myself?

I can't ask myself that. This isn't about me and Ravven. This is about Eilis and Riagan.

"The spy is Riagan," I spit, not allowing myself a chance to back down. My eyes meet the queen's as the entire court stills. I have turned them all into ice sculptures now. I smile slightly; that smile is more of a lie than anything I have ever said. "Didn't you hear me? I said that Riagan is the spy."

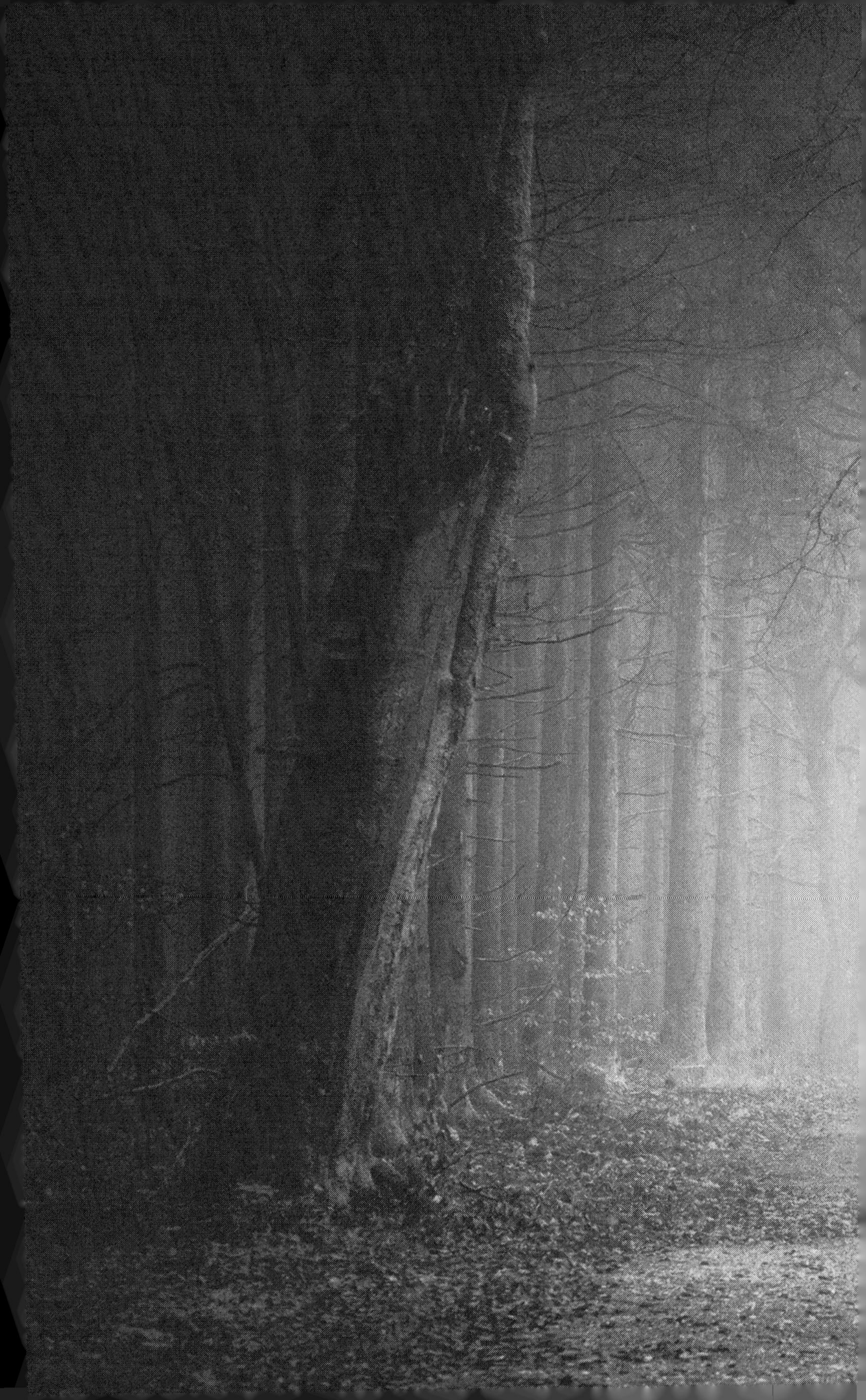

CHAPTER THIRTY-FIVE

The stillness lasts for only a few more seconds before it cracks and shatters like glass.

The courtiers let out startled cries and move away from Riagan as if he has been infected with some disease. A disease that would make him betray his court.

The Winter Queen shoots from her throne like someone set it on fire. She whirls on Riagan, seething. "Is this accusation true, spymaster?"

Riagan looks down at his nails, ignoring everyone—the seething queen, the aghast courtiers, Eilis as she shakes her head back and forth, her mouth moving but no words leaving her lips. And me, standing here, sick to my stomach, wondering what I just did.

"Are you the traitor?" Cliodnha demands. "Answer me!"

Riagan bows his head. "I always loyally serve my court, my queen," he says humbly.

The queen pulls back, her eyes darting to Iorwerth's. He hadn't actually answered yes or no.

Riagan straightens. "With that said. I will at last admit that the court I serve is not yours. The mortal bird is correct. I am your spy."

Eilis slumps against the tiles and buries her face in her bloodied hands.

"Seize him!" the queen screams. Several of the guards step toward Riagan but then Blackie lunges between them, baring his teeth. He snaps at the nearest faerie, forcing him to pull back.

Riagan grins. "You must accept my humblest apologies, but it appears that I must leave very quickly. Do not miss my company too much."

With those words, he hurtles past the stunned courtiers and the guards, held at bay with Blackie's vicious snarls. He rushes past me in a blur of wind and out of the Winter Court. As soon as he is out of sight, Blackie chases after him with the guards clamoring on his heels.

For the second time that day, the Winter Court is completely still. Everyone is still staring out the door after Riagan and the pooka and the guards. Then I turn to the queen, raising my chin and doing my best to be brave despite my stomach wobbling and sloshing.

"Our bargain?" I prompt, causing all eyes to turn to me.

Cliodnha holds my gaze, she's gritting her teeth so hard that if she were truly made of ice she would shatter. Perhaps she sees me as more of a threat than she had originally let show. "Very well, mortal," she spits. "As is required by the Fair Law, you have the support of the Winter Court. Take your fellow corpse and leave."

I keep my chin up as I stride across the floor and grasp Eilis's arms. She has tears in her eyes, but she regards the queen coolly. "You will not have heard the last of this."

"And you have not heard the last of me," the queen says.

I shoot Aoibheann a scathing look. "Might as well give up now. After tomorrow I will be the Fair Assassin."

"After tomorrow, you will probably be dead," Aoibheann says, blinking innocently. "And then so will your brother. He doesn't have much longer."

Her words slice deeper into my chest than I wish they would have.

I try to suppress my wince, but when I see Iorwerth's cold smile, I know that I haven't succeeded.

Neither Eilis nor I look back as we support each other out of the carved pale blue doors. If we did then the entire court would see the tears on our faces.

The doors slam shut and I wince. Tears drip off of my numb chin and onto the fabric of my tunic. "I'm sorry," I say to Eilis, though I don't know what exactly I am apologizing for.

For involving her? For getting her tortured? For turning Riagan in?

She shakes her head mutely, staring down the hall with a lost gaze. I know that she is thinking about Riagan. If I ever had any doubts that she cared about him, they are gone.

My own heart lurches. Was that the last I will ever see of Riagan? The one truly selfless faerie I have ever met.

I sincerely hope not, but I don't see how I could. I have no doubt that if anyone from the Winter Court ever sees him again, they will try to kill him on sight. If he hasn't left the Court of Dreams and Nightmares already then he is probably dead. Or captured. In a faerie world, I'm not entirely sure which is worse.

I inhale a shaky breath and look Eilis over. Her scratches look pretty bad. "What happened to you? What did this?" I ask, my hand hovering over the marks. They look almost like claw marks.

"I did," Eilis whispers, staring down at her blood crusted fingernails. "Filthy faeries enscorcelled me into... they didn't even have to raise a hand against me."

She shoots me a side glance. "Yer an ideal candidate for the position as the Fair Assassin. Any other mortal would probably be dead or a faerie's slave by now, but ye stand strong. Yer gift protects ye from the worst the faeries can bring, a blessing not even I have." She whirls on me and grips my shoulders. "Ye have ta win this. Don't let his sacrifice be in vain."

His sacrifice.

Those words hurt more than they should.

A faerie, someone I barely know and didn't trust at all yesterday, sacrificed himself for me, and for Eilis, and for this stupid deadly contest. My face crumbles and several tears leak from my eyes. Where is the justice in all of this?

Footsteps pound down the hall and I force myself to be alert. Who is running over here? Is it Riagan? Guards? An enemy?

I begin to crouch, my fingers reaching for my iron dagger when Ravven rounds the corner, his hair tousled.

He freezes when he looks us over. His eyes scan me urgently. I stare at him, unsure of what to say.

It all went horribly bad.

Or.

Congrats, we only have the Spring Court left.

I feel like he would prefer the latter, but I can't find it in myself to say it because this test cost me one of my only allies.

"Are you all right?" Ravven finally asks breathlessly.

I blink and nod. "Of course. What, did you think I would be dead or mauled?"

"It's just... you were upset," Ravven says.

I rub at my temples. "Yeah. It has been one heck of a day—wait, how did you know that I was upset?"

I raise my head, but Ravven is no longer looking at me. His gaze is on Eilis and he is horrified. "What happened?" he demands.

Eilis shakes her head before inhaling a deep breath as if fortifying herself. The tears are gone like they never existed. "Riagan has left."

Ravven's eyebrows draw together.

"I finished the Winter Court's test," I clarify.

Ravven blinks. "But..." he turns to me surprised. "You told them?"

I'm shocked for a second. Ravven did know. Ravven who I didn't tell because I was afraid that he would do exactly what I just did. I thought he would tell, when really, I did.

I lift my chin. "He wanted me to. They had Eilis. He came to me, Ravven. He asked me to do it," I say again, as if repeating it makes it any better. Assuages my guilt. Did I do it because he asked me to or because it was the easiest path? Riagan was correct—it was the way that ended with the fewest deaths. I was at a crossroads and I hope that I chose correctly.

"You did," Ravven mutters, rubbing at his chin.

I shoot him a surprised look, but then Eilis steps away, drawing my attention back to her. "I need to clean myself up."

"I don't think it's wise for you to go anywhere alone," I say, stepping after her. I grasp her upper arm. She glances over her shoulder. "I have survived in this world for more years than you have lived. For more years than Crowe has lived."

Ravven shifts uncomfortably as if the thought of a world without him makes him upset.

She shakes my hand off. "I think I can manage."

"But I can't," I say, shooting her a steadying look. "I can't have you being used as a pawn against me anymore."

Eilis opens her mouth as if to argue, but then she leans forward, her shoulders slumping. "I will be quite safe once I reach the Undersea Court. They snatched me on my way there."

"Then we will make sure that you make it there in one piece," I say.

"And I shall have words with my father," Ravven says almost to himself as he turns.

His words awaken my frustration and I hurry to catch up. "Excuse me, but what exactly were you thinking when you told your dad to keep an eye on me?"

Ravven glances back at me. "I was thinking that you would get yourself in trouble. I was right."

I roll my eyes. "I'm clearly still in one piece and I don't even have a nick so I don't know what you're talking about."

Ravven turns back around. "Jaye, you forced yourself to betray someone you cared about. I may not know you that well, but I am learning. And I know that loyalty is one quality that you treasure above any others. And that a breach of such a thing is something that you will never forgive. Even if it is you who does it. Do not say that you are in one piece. I know full well that you are not."

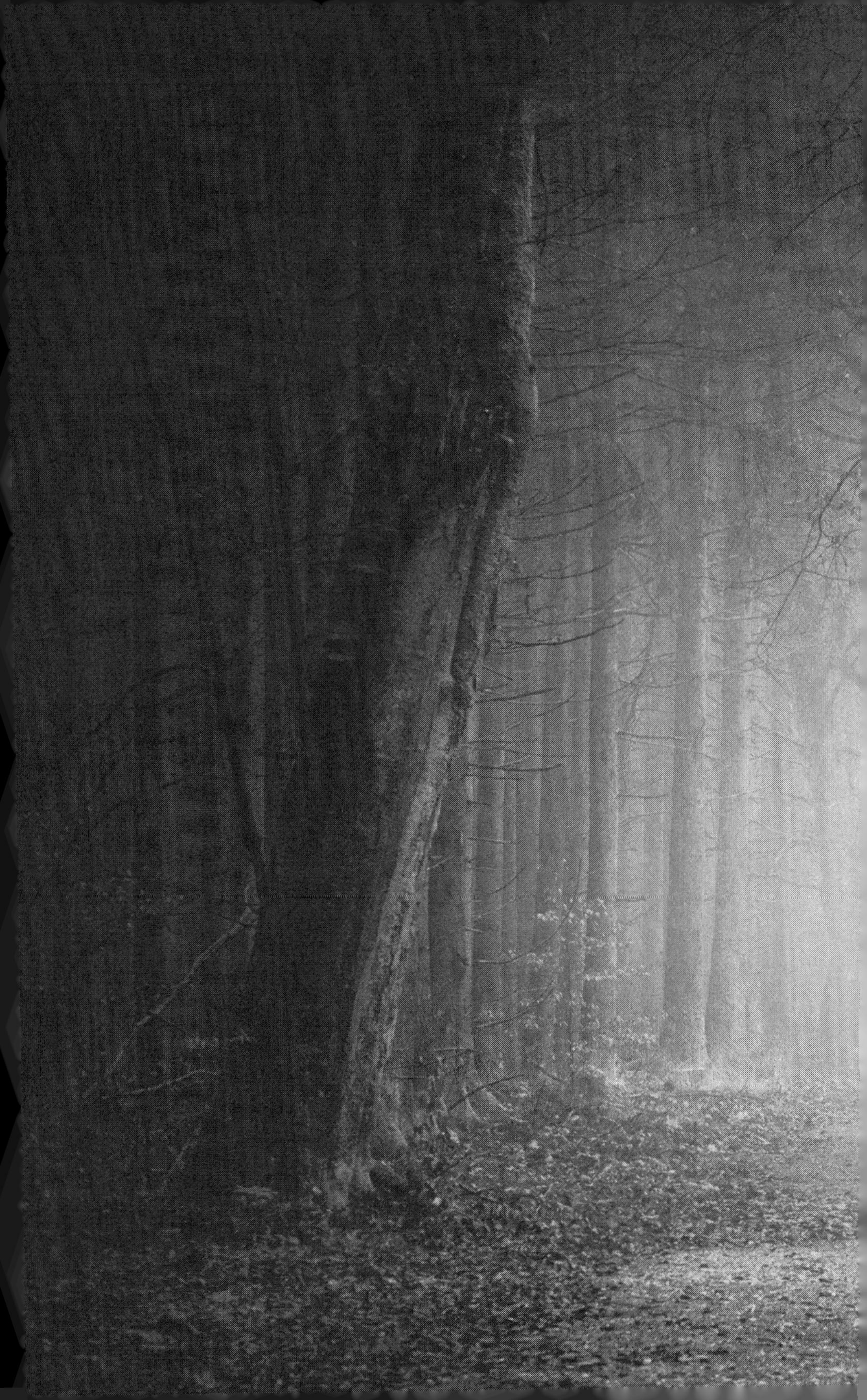

CHAPTER THIRTY-SIX

I am not ready to face the world of faeries, but if Eilis can do it after she was tortured, then I sure as heck can as well.

The air of the ballroom is different than it was on the previous night. More excited, more nervous. I don't think the faeries were expecting me to make it this far, to make it past the Winter Court. I only have one more court. One more day.

And then I'm the Fair Assassin.

I feel like I'm in a dream. Not even a week ago I had no desire whatsoever for this thing that I have spent the past days risking my neck to achieve. And now I'm counting down the days.

Only the Spring Court left.

Ravven's court.

I glance at him out of the corner of my eye. He's dressed in a dark red coat, the color of blood. His black hair combed across his honey toned forehead. He looks every bit the Solitary faerie of the Autumn Court. Until you realize that his complexion is too golden. His face too beautiful.

Then you start to notice the beautiful Sidhe faeries and despite his dark looks and his tendency to scowl more than he smiles, you can see that he belongs there as well.

They will not want us to succeed either. They already sent an assassin to try to kill me. I am pretty sure that Cinaed knows what I will do with my title as Fair Assassin. What Ravven will have me do.

But I had thought the same of the Winter Court, and yet they had not sent me on any dangerous missions. Sure, their task was the hardest of all, even, even harder than when I had a Lake Dragon trying to eat me, but I still completed it.

What will the Spring Court have in store for us?

And if I win?

Well, then that will be that. I have to save Thomas, no matter how distasteful I find the thought of killing anyone, even a heartless Leanhaun Shee like Aoibheann. I am trying to become a flipping assassin for crying out loud.

And then I have to keep my word with Ravven and kill Cinaed too. It makes my stomach churn, the thought of having to kill someone, and not for self-defense or defense of someone I love either. Simply because someone told me to. I know that's sort of the idea of being an assassin, but once I have Thomas, it's not like I ever planned on sticking around to finish a few jobs.

I remind myself that this man killed Ravven's entire family. He has a right to want him dead, heck, he didn't even kill my family and I half want him dead myself. I just... I guess I just don't want to be the one to kill him.

I'd never considered myself someone who had an innocent conscience, I always thought that I would be perfectly willing to do whatever needed to be done. That I wouldn't be one to balk at how terrible the act is and simply get it done. I always thought that when everything was said and done, I would move on and never look back. That I wouldn't care. But I suppose that I was wrong, because my conscience is bothered. My stomach is weak. And my heart feels very, very soft.

I shake my head. Enough worrying about this. First, I have to survive. What use is it to worry about how I will manage to kill someone when it is very likely that they will kill me first?

I spot Eilis standing near the Undersea Queen and King. Neither of them looks desperately relieved to see her and it makes me wonder how much she really means to them. If they would have made the same sacrifice that Riagan did, had it been them there instead of him?

I stare out over the crowd. I'm feeling far too heart sore for anything today. And it seems that no matter what I do, I'm overthinking things. It must be the stress. I never overthink. I live in the moment and I don't worry about the future or think about the past.

Ravven rests his hand on my arm and I glance at him, confused. He rarely ever sticks around this long at my side. Normally he slinks off to some corner to hide, or he doesn't come altogether like Keane and Daithi.

"What?" I ask, my voice coming out too harsh. I'm not angry at him specifically. It's not his fault that I'm in this mess. I'm not even sure if it is my own. It was just one unfortunate circumstance after another that led to this trial.

"I was going to ask if you wanted to dance with me, but now I am starting to think that such a question would be hazardous to my health."

"Oh, don't be ridiculous," I snap, "I don't dance with faeries."

"Come now, you know you can't be ensorcelled. What would be the harm?"

He has a point, I guess there isn't any harm. And this will probably be the only chance I ever get to dance with Ravven. I don't know why it suddenly seems so important that I do, but I find myself nodding.

He grasps my elbow and takes my hand in his other one. He touches me gently like I'm fragile and might break if too much pressure is applied. Maybe I am. I certainly feel fragile right now.

We start to sway gently and I look up at Ravven, studying his features. Trying to memorize them, although I'm unsure why I would want to. I shake my head, ripping my gaze away from his strong brows and straight nose. "I need a distraction so I hope that you're one heck of a conversationalist."

Ravven clears his throat. "I think you know that I am not. Solitary faerie and all that. But if you wish to hear my voice, I would be more than happy to comply."

"Fair enough," I say with a shrug. I must be truly desperate for a distraction if I'm relieved just to hear Ravven talk about himself. "You can talk about anything but this Fair Assassin thing."

Ravven nods once. "Very well then, what is it that you plan to do?"

"Plan to do?"

"When you get home," Ravven prompts. "When this is all over, what will you do?"

I trip in surprise.

His hands steady me and he looks down at me with those deep purple eyes. "What is it?" he asks, his voice nothing more than a rough whisper.

"Nothing," I reply breathlessly. "I'm just a little surprised is all." I clear my throat and straighten so that I'm no longer standing so near him. "I thought you would say something about yourself."

"You have a very low opinion of me," he mutters darkly.

"Only because you have such a high opinion of yourself," I reply with a teasing smile as I smooth out a wrinkle in his jacket.

He rolls his eyes. "Are you going to answer my question or would you rather make the conversation about me? I will happily comply."

I sigh. "All right, fine. I'll answer your question. I guess the first thing I do when I get home is kiss my parents, then I'll take a shower, eat some pizza. Watch TV and listen to my favorite songs..." They'll sound like trash compared to the soothing melody playing here, but I suppose I'll just have to survive.

"But after that?"

I press my lips together as I think. It's something I should know, considering I'll be doing it in only a few short days. "I don't know? Catch up on my homework?" I'll train, but for what? Just to patrol a border created by a one-sided treaty? What had once seemed like the grandest adventure ever is now a dull task. I fear that once I leave this world, I'll never come back. Not because I will not want to, but because if I did, I doubt I would ever leave. And then I will end up like Eilis, a lost human in a world not my own.

I never thought about it but... I will miss this. I will miss this world. I will miss the adventure, maybe not the danger, but the thrill. I will miss the strange and otherworldly creatures around me. And most of all I will miss *him*. It scares me when I realize how much I will miss him.

"And I'll live happily ever after," I say jokingly, shoving that idea so far away. "At least I hope so."

"How do you plan to do that?" he asks so earnestly that it scares me. Because he wants an answer, and it's not something that I have an answer to.

"Why do you care?" I demand instead, trying to cover up my swirling thoughts and empty heart.

"I'm curious," he replies. "I don't know much about the human world. It's been more than a hundred years since I had any sort of contact with it. Your world is always changing, *you* are always changing."

"Careful," I say in a tone that was supposed to be light but comes out sounding far too serious. "Or you might just sound jealous of us humans."

Ravven shakes his head. "I'm not jealous. I just don't understand how much you can change in such a short period of time. In the blink of an eye you are different and I... I am always the same."

I can't argue. It's the truth. I've changed so much in just the short few days I've been in this world.

"Will you miss me, Jaye?" Ravven asks, suddenly drawing to a halt.

I freeze as well, afraid to give him the answer. Afraid that it will be the wrong answer.

Afraid that there are no right answers.

The memory of the kiss weighs heavily on my shoulders. He's standing so close that I want to kiss him. I *could* kiss him. But I can't. In only days I will leave. I won't look back. I *can't*. There is nothing for us.

Apparently a lot of harm can come from one dance. Who knew?

I snort and pull away. "You were just saying that humans always change."

"That is true," Ravven says. "But it is not an answer to my question."

"What does it matter if I answer your question? I could always lie." Oh, why did I say that? That means that I have a reason to hide my answer. I should have just said no and made a big joke of it.

"Just tell me anyway," Ravven says, leaning closer. I just have to lift my chin a little bit and I will kiss him. I *want* to kiss him. But there are so, so many reasons why I cannot kiss him, least of which him being a faerie and me being a human and us both being surrounded by a bunch of other faeries. "Will you miss me?"

"Only until I forget you," I whisper. It's the truth, but it's also a lie. Because I will never forget him.

Ravven exhales a long sigh, it blows my hairs across my face. I notice that we aren't dancing anymore. We are probably creating a scene, starting some scandal. I'm about to move to step away when Ravven says, "Jaye, there is something that I must tell you."

I raise my eyes and meet his gaze. I'm surprised to see that his eyes have gone from a deep purple to crimson.

"What?" I ask with a frown.

He shakes his head quickly. "Nothing," he says, the crimson morphing to black almost as quickly as it had changed from the purple.

"No really," I say. "What was it?"

"It's nothing of importance. Just something... unimportant." He grimaces, though I don't know why. He looks away, but not before the black of his eyes melts into a blue so dark that it matches the sky above the Forest of Night. "It appears that we have stopped dancing," he states solemnly.

"You're only just now realizing that?"

Ravven begins to sway gently. "I'm just not used to this issue. Whenever a faerie dances with a human it usually goes on forever, the human unable to break away. But when I dance with you, well it appears that you dictate the rules of the dance. When we start, when we stop, whether we go on forever." His eyes hold mine.

It's almost like an invitation, but to what, I have no idea.

Before I can ask, Ravven stiffens.

"What?" I ask, craning my neck to see over my shoulder. "Or are you going to refrain from telling me that as well?"

"Iorwerth is watching us," Ravven says, staring with an unfeeling expression on his face.

"Why is that such a concern?" I ask, turning.

Ravven moves his hands to my shoulders. "Jaye—" he begins, but it is too late. Because I've already turned to see Iorwerth. Aoibheann is standing next to him, sipping the red faerie drink from a glass, her lips stained crimson. And standing next to her, almost completely devoid of all color, is my brother. Other than his auburn hair which doesn't even seem to have its usual sheen, he's colorless. If not for his height, he could be confused for a Fear Gorta. He's positively skeletal, only skin and bones and not a bit of color to his face.

"Thomas," I whisper. I sag against Ravven, feeling almost as weak as my brother looks.

Tears flood my eyes. Aoibheann was right; he obviously doesn't have much time left.

I only have one last test left, but that might be too late.

Ravven wraps a steadying arm around my shoulder and pulls me back as I try to take a step toward him. "There's nothing you can do for him right now," he whispers, burying his face in my hair.

"But—" I say, still half struggling to pull out of his grasp.

"A confrontation will only make things worse for him, and bring Iorwerth and Aoibheann pleasure. Come, Jaye, do not give them what they desire."

I don't protest any more as Ravven pulls me away and toward a staircase in the back of the room. It leads up to the back wall and a doorway that reveals the dark sky beyond. He leads me up and out through the doorway onto a balcony.

I didn't even know that a balcony existed here. Cool night air washes over my face, stinging the tears coursing down my face. I slip out of Ravven's hold and slide down the wall to sit, gazing out at the starless sky.

Ravven sits down beside me, but he doesn't say anything as the tears leak from my eyes. What would happen to Thomas if he were to die while under Aoibheann's control? I think I've heard something about her enslaving his soul, which will be held captive for all eternity. I don't know if I'm right, or even how that is possible, and frankly I am too scared to ask Ravven.

He shifts his position. "Jaye... I'm sorry," he says at last.

I sniff and turn to him, wiping at my cheeks. "It's not your fault," I mumble.

Don't sound so sure.

I shake that thought out of my head. I don't even know where it came from. Ravven may be a faerie. He may have kept my gift from me, but I guess I haven't really doubted him since he saved me from that faerie assassin and finally opened up about his past.

Which shows how foolish you are.

Shut up cynical voice in my head that ironically sounds like Ravven.

Never trust a faerie.

I shake my head and massage my temples. I glance at Ravven out of the corner of my eye, but he is staring off into the night with his brows drawn close together, deep in thought. I clear my throat. "So, I think we should discuss our strategy of what should happen tomorrow."

Ravven turns to glance at me and arches his eyebrow.

"I don't care if it doesn't actually do us any good," I hurriedly rush to say. "But I need to know how close we are. I need to talk about it. It'll make me feel better."

Ravven nods. "We only have the Spring Court left. As the High Lord of the Spring Court, Cinaed will be the one choosing our task. Which is unfortunate, because he has much to lose if you succeed and he knows it."

I shake my head. "Why does the Spring Court not have a king or queen? Why does it have a High Lord?"

"Because the line of the throne is questionable," Ravven replies after a moment's hesitation. "You see the inheritance of royalty is very tricky and very specific due to the restraints of the Fair Law. Only the next in line can rule, and Cinaed is not the next in line. He cannot inherit the throne. The true heir left the Spring Court long ago and that is why Cinaed is only the High Lord. But that doesn't matter. What matters is that he is the High Lord and that he will be deciding our task."

I'm staring at Ravven, watching him but his face is impassive now and gives nothing away. "Ravven, where is the true king of the Spring Court?"

I think you know that already.

"I'm not really involved in politics," he replies. "I haven't been for some time. That does not change the fact that Cinaed hates me." He twists at his finger and then leans toward me, holding out his hand. "I want you to have this."

I frown and hold out my hand as he drops a small ring into my palm. It's a simple band with the Celtic knot engraved around a ruby sitting in the center and a deer carved on either side. It's his ring. I hold it up, but no light in this sunless, moonless little world reflects off it. "Why do you want me to have this?"

"That is my item of immortality," Ravven says in the barest of whispers.

I nearly drop the ring. I stare down at it, lying in my palm. It's warm, probably since Ravven had just been wearing it, and weighs heavily against my palm. It seems like such an inconspicuous thing, and yet this thing is what keeps Ravven alive. It is the equivalent of if Ravven had given me his still beating heart. I close my fingers around the ring, feeling such an intense surge of protection toward it. Like my life depends on the survival of this ring.

"Why would you give it to me?" I choke out, but instead of giving it to him, I clutch my hand to my chest as if I can shield it with my own body.

Ravven's smile is but a ghost. "Cinaed knows me too well. I'm afraid that if he were to see me wearing this ring that he would realize its importance. My mother had it forged for me when I was born, as it is the custom for your parent to create your item of immortality. But Cinaed knows that I do not have much left from my past life. That ring would give it all away. I cannot however simply leave it lying around."

"Don't give it to me," I hiss, tightening my fingers around the ring. "Give it to someone else who won't be part of the test. Like your father."

"I trust you, pest," Ravven says, and then he leans forward and brushes his lips against my forehead. I freeze, too warm to be ice or marble, but too hard and immovable to be truly alive. "And only you."

I don't know how to reply as he pulls away, his hand still cradling the side of my face. Though my brain is laughing maniacally at that cynical part of my brain who had told me only minutes ago that I couldn't trust him. And now I am holding his item of immortality so tightly that my pulse seems to give it a heartbeat.

Ravven leans toward me again and I tilt my chin up. Forget the consequences. Forget the future. Forget everything but this. The here and now. Me and him. Nothing else matters.

His lips brush mine once, twice, my pulse picks up. I lean closer to him, desperate for more, but then Ravven quickly jerks away. In a second, he is on his feet and I'm sitting there blinking and stunned. Ravven turns as a dark silhouette steps into the doorway. The light from the ballroom reflects off her fiery hair.

"I thought I saw ye come up here," she says, her tone strained, and I wonder how much she saw.

Ravven dips his head. "I was actually just leaving so why don't you keep Jaye company?"

Before either of us can reply he's gone, disappearing out the door and heading for the stairs that will take him back to the ball.

"I hope you aren't mad at me," I say quickly to Eilis who hasn't moved. I'm desperate to keep the conversation off of what just happened. If she asks for an explanation, I will not have one to give.

Eilis pulls her gaze from Ravven's retreating form and then to me. She arches a brow. "Mad at ye?"

"About Riagan."

"Oh," she says. Only that word. Her shoulders slump slightly and she releases a heavy sigh as she comes over and takes Ravven's place by my side.

"Eilis, did I do the right thing?"

Eilis shrugs. "As much as I dislike the options we are left with, I see that it was the only choice. Riagan knows what he is doing, he has lived too long to have not learned how to survive."

"Do you know where he will go?" I ask.

"I'll know sooner or later," she replies somewhat ominously. As soon as the words are out of her mouth, a small creature flies past her head.

Her hand shoots out and grabs it, trapping it between her fingers like they are bars to a prison. "If you would like to see me, make an appointment with me secretary," the little creature says, perching in her hand.

Eilis stares down at the creature, her mouth twisting to the side. "Messenger pixies are very hard to come by. First ye have to catch them, then ye have ta train them to deliver the message, and even if ye train them well, there's still always the chance that they won't return unless given a message. They will sense their freedom and fly off into the night. Riagan hoards them like a dragon hoards gold," she says with a small little laugh. "I'm surprised that he spared one."

I shift my position uncomfortably. I didn't give the yellow messenger pixie that Riagan used to summon me a message, the sprite probably flew off as fast as it could, never returning.

Eilis opens her hand enough to reveal the pixie sitting placidly inside. It is a blue pixie with longish hair or fur or whatever it is on its head.

"If you would like to see me, make an appointment with me secretary," the little pixie repeats.

Eilis chuckles and leans forward. "Tell Riagan that if he dies, I will kill him and make O'Clonnel clean up the mess."

She opens her hand and releases the pixie. It flies off into the night. I stare after it and then glance at her. "What was all that about?"

She shakes her head. "Nothin', he was letting me know where he was."

I shake my head. "You must have some form of code."

"It wasn't a code," she says with a small laugh. "Riagan went to stay with his old secretary O'Clonnel, who is a leprechaun. He's in the Autumn Court now, where he was always meant to be. Riagan is a Solitary faerie, but when the courts were created, he forced himself to go where he felt he was most needed, not where he would be most comfortable. He and O'Clonnel had a bit of a falling out over that."

She stares down at the dark trees below the balcony, her eyes crinkles. While she reflects, I turn my attention once again to the ring.

I still can't believe that he gave it to me. I just can't believe it. This is his item of immortality. Quite literally, his life is in my hands.

"What is goin' on between ye and Ravven?" Eilis asks suddenly.

I look up, quickly tightening my fingers around the ring. "You know what is happening between us. We are partners."

"Are ye sure there isn't more than that?" she asks mildly.

"Like what?" I ask, struggling to keep my voice light. I want to say that there is nothing between us. That we are only what we appear, because isn't that what we are? That is what I would think we are, except for those kisses. Those kisses change something. Because I think I might actually be falling in love with him, and that isn't nothing.

As if sensing my thoughts, Eilis sighs. "Love between a mortal and a faerie is never a wise thing." A small smile pulls at her lips, but it is tainted with the sadness of a hundred years. "The faeries would have you believe that they are incapable of love, but they are only disinclined toward it. Just like death, it is more difficult to achieve but not altogether impossible."

I clear my throat. "I hardly think that anything will change when in only a few days I will be back to the human world with Thomas, and I don't plan on ever coming back. I'll be dead before Ravven knows it."

"Will you be?" Eilis asks, she traces her finger across the swirls on her skirt.

"What is that question supposed to mean?" I ask, shifting my position uncomfortably.

Eilis turns to me, her gaze serious. "My friend, I must ask you a difficult question, but... are you bonded with Crowe?"

I choke on the air in my lungs. "What?" I splutter.

Eilis tilts her head. "It is hardly as if bonding between a human and a faerie has never happened before. It is uncommon, yes, even more uncommon than bonding at all. Most faeries are not willing to love another more than themselves, but even the ones that do consider humans lesser beings."

I shake my head. "So then why are you bringing this up?"

"Because Crowe does not view you as a lesser being."

I snort and look away, ignoring the weight of the ring in my hand and his words *I only trust you.* "Believe me, Ravven does not see me in any sort of way like that."

"He views you as if you are his whole world."

"*He* is *his own* world," I snap. I turn to her. "To him, I am nothing but a hideous mortal who might be sometimes amusing, but is too much trouble to be at all useful."

"Hideous?" Eilis asks, sounding amused.

"He has said so himself," I reply bitterly. It was his first words to me.

Eilis stares at me for a long moment. "He has? Well, that is very interesting."

"Oh, extremely," I say, turning to stare straight ahead. "So, as you can clearly see. We are not bonded."

"Bonding is not a conscious effort," Eilis says, her voice hard. "It happens without you even realizing it. When a faerie is meant to be a soul mate with another, the bond begins forming the second they meet, finally snapping into place during a monumental event in their lives. After that moment, they are joined by mind and soul. They can share thoughts and they know one another's pain."

"How do you even know so much about bonding," I say grudgingly, wrapping my arms around myself.

Eilis smirks. "I have spent more of my life in this world than my own. I know many things."

But already my face is starting to tingle and I think I'm going into shock. I think about those random thoughts that came from nowhere that sounded like Ravven's voice in my head. I had thought that I was losing myself to hopeless infatuation, but now I am not so sure. And when Ravven had killed the faerie assassin and cut his hand, I felt a pain in my hand. A hand that is unharmed.

I stare down at the palm of my hand, unblemished pale skin meets my gaze, but still I can feel a faint throbbing.

After the attack, he had asked me if I could breathe, when I already know that he doesn't understand well how human bodies work.

My breath leaves my lungs. Are we truly bonded?

Eilis is watching me for a long moment. "I suspected it since this afternoon when Ravven came to find you when you were upset, clearly thinking that you were in trouble. He must have sensed it."

I half wonder if Ravven will come find me now. Because I am feeling very upset. But I don't know how reliable this bond is. If this thing even exists because obviously I don't feel everything that he does and I don't think everything that he does and... I have a headache.

Eilis's laugh fills the air, just as dark as the world around us. "So, no, I do not believe that you will be dead before Ravven knows it. If you are indeed bonded, he will know every little thing that kills you because he will feel it. A faerie can live even as their soul mate dies, but it is not a pleasant experience and they will never find another."

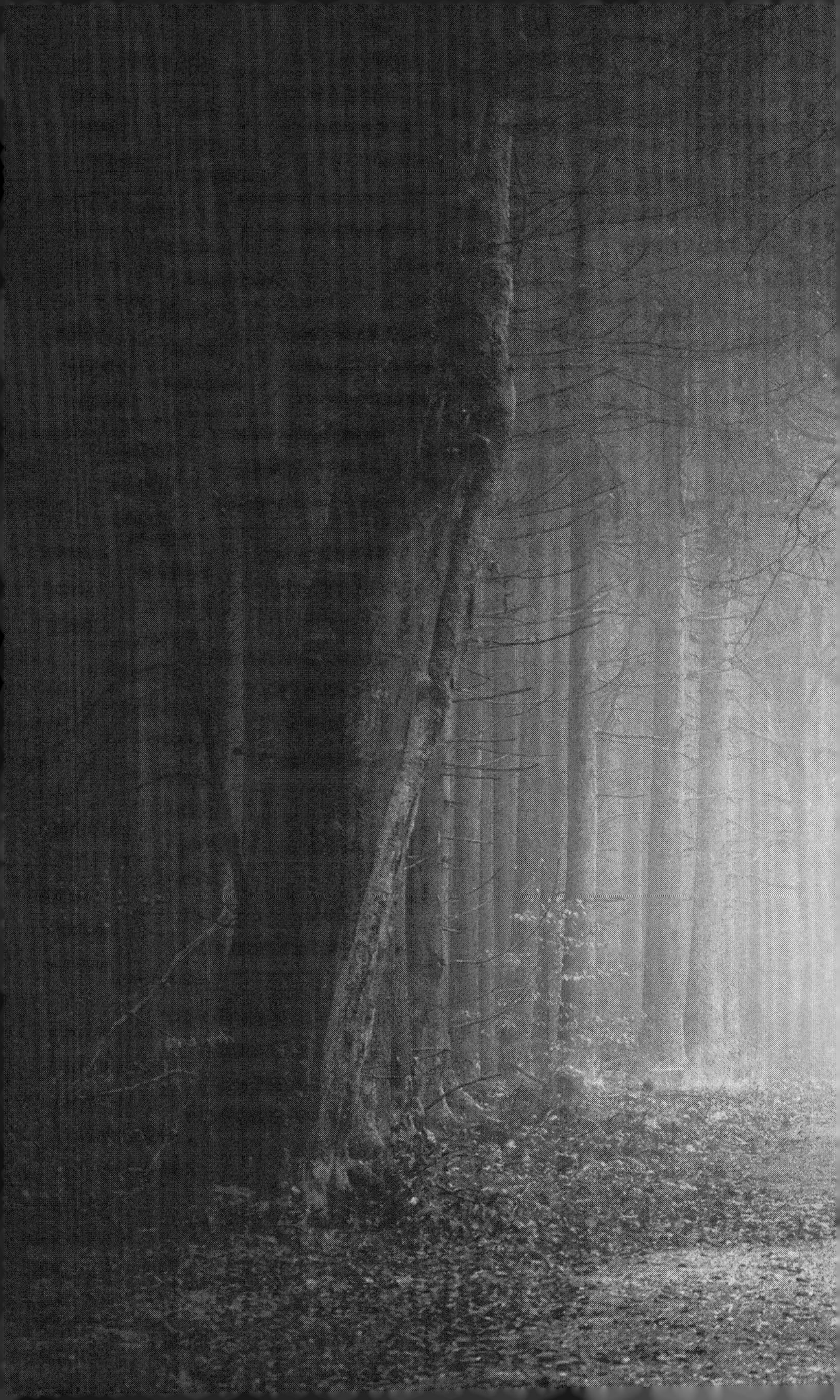

CHAPTER THIRTY-SEVEN

I really need to talk to Ravven. I have no idea what the heck I'm going to say to him, but I need to have one regular conversation with him. A moment where I can recollect my thoughts and assure myself that Eilis is completely wrong and I am simply seeing things that aren't there.

Because there is no way that I could have somehow accidentally bonded my soul to Ravven Crowe. No. That is impossible. It's ridiculous. It's disastrous.

Eilis has left to join her Undersea Court and I'm stuck wandering through the throngs of faeries, trying to remain unnoticed while still keeping an eye out for Ravven. I step forward, but am hindered by a familiar smiling face and devilish dark eyes.

I draw to a halt, unsure of what I should do. I didn't like Cinaed before, but I certainly don't trust him or even want to be in the same room as him after having heard what Ravven said about him killing his entire family.

"Ah, the young mortal warrior," Cinaed says, bowing slightly. His little human slave isn't here. I wonder whatever happened to her. "I had wished to run into you. There is something that I want to tell you."

I stiffen, Ravven's item of immortality weighs awkwardly in the pocket of my dress, reminding me of its fragility. "And what is that?"

I spot Ravven making his way through the crowd to us and breathe a sigh of relief. The relief is quickly transformed with wonder at how he would know that I needed him. I shove that thought quickly aside as Cinaed studies me. Ravven probably just saw Cinaed cut me off.

Cinaed smiles when he sees Ravven. "I see that my cousin desires to join us. Very well, I shall wait to say what needs to be said because this concerns him as well."

I swallow as Ravven comes to a stop next to me. He reaches out for me, but then drops his arm just as his fingers brush the back of my hand. "What are you doing here, Cinaed?"

"I did not realize that it was a crime to speak to our mortal warrior," Cinaed says with a laugh.

"She's not *your* anything," Ravven growls.

"But she is yours," Cinaed says, his voice sobering. "Your champion. Your pawn."

Ravven stiffens until I'm almost afraid that he has turned into a statue.

Cinaed's eyes are blacker than Ravven's have ever been. "Keep in mind, Ravven, that anyone can use a human; you are not the only one capable of such a thing."

I cross my arms tightly. "Excuse me, but I'm no one's pawn."

"So you say," Cinaed says with a laugh as Ravven growls. "That is not what I wanted to say, I came to give you your test." He waves his arm in a sweeping gesture. "I thought that you would prefer an early start, and seeing as this event is the perfect setting for it, I figured I would be kind enough to help you this once."

Unease rolls off of Ravven in waves. I swallow, my stomach churning.

"What is the test?" I ask. Not because I want to do it, but because I need to, and the sooner I can get it done, the sooner Thomas is free of that witch's clutches.

"My task for you is simple really." Cinaed pulls a small vial from his cloak and holds it out. When Ravven doesn't move to accept it, I take it. I hold it up to look at it. The torchlight filters through the empty vial.

"I wish for you to fill that vial with the blood of one of the rulers of the courts and bring it to me," Cinaed continues giving Ravven a meaningful look. He smirks. "You should not find that too difficult, now should you, cousin?"

Ravven doesn't reply, he's too busy clenching his jaw, staring at Cinaed who is looking quite triumphant. "You have until the next ball to complete your task or I will consider it forfeit."

"A thousand curses on him," Ravven mutters, running his hand through his hair, finally snapping back into motion the second Cinaed is gone.

I turn to him, holding up the vial. "We need to work fast," I say, scanning the crowd for the nearest royal. My gaze lands on the Summer King. I don't care what kind of bargain I will have to make with him, probably to assassinate someone, but I'm so close. I'm so close to saving Thomas, I have to do it. I just have to.

I move to step toward him, but Ravven's hand wrapping around my upper arm draws me short.

"No," Ravven says, pulling me into an alcove so that we are no longer pressed from every side by nosy faeries. "Stop and listen to me, pest. I swear, your recklessness will be the death of us yet."

"Ravven, we're so close," I state, craning my neck trying to keep an eye on the Summer King.

Ravven grasps my arms and turns me around, a scowl darkening his features. "Did you hear me when I said death? Because I can assure you that I meant it."

I cross my arms. "What is the matter with you?"

"You," he replies.

I throw my arms up into the air. Honestly, I don't even know why I ever thought that it was remotely possible that we could have been bonded or anything. We can't stand each other. We can't even discourse civilly.

Ravven shakes his head, pressing his dull red eyes shut. "You don't seem to understand that trying to get the blood of any of the royal family is suicide. It would be easier to break into Iorwerth's chamber than do this."

I toss the vial into the air and catch it, holding his gaze. "If you don't think that we can get one of rulers who like us to give us a drop of their blood then we'll just sidle up next to Cliodnha and stab her or something." I wouldn't be able to use iron, sure, but other things can break a faerie's skin. Iron is just what will kill them.

Ravven shakes his head. "You don't get it. Our blood binds us to our words. If someone were to get a vial of any faerie's blood, they could make them agree to any Blood Bargain, against their will. No faerie will allow that to happen to them. Least of all a royal."

"Then what do you suggest we do?" I demand. "We are too close to give up just because your jerk of a cousin gave you a task that intimidates you."

"It doesn't intimidate me," Ravven replies quietly. "But it would condemn me."

I shake my head. "You're not making any sense!"

Ravven steps away, pinching at the bridge of his nose. "I just—I need time to think this through." With those words, he promptly turns and leaves me standing alone in the alcove. Easy for him to say, he's only ever had time, but my brother is dying *right now*. I'm all out of time.

I watch as he disappears into the crowd before I finally yank my eyes away. I scan the rest of the ball. I'm not sure what exactly I am looking for until my eyes land on her. Queen Cliodnha.

Maybe I don't want to risk angering the Summer King and the Undersea Queen, but Cliodnha is already my enemy.

With a deep breath I begin striding across the hall to her. I try to figure out what best approach I should take. I need a plan because pretty much what I have right now is hit and run. I clutch the vial tightly in my fist. And if I try to run in this dress I will probably trip and fall before I make it to my destination.

I think of Ravven's face and how defeated he looked when Cinaed gave him the mission, and Thomas's worn face. And how Riagan had to leave. So many people are suffering. And I have one task left. I need that blood and I'm going to get that blood if I have to intimidate the entire ballroom into letting me have it.

Cliodhna has her back to me. I drop to a crouch, hoping that no one else is paying any attention to me. She is wearing an almost transparent dress comprised of ice spikes. Perfect.

I reach out and snag the nearest ice spike and snap it off. This is pointy enough that it should break skin. But how am I supposed to get her to stay still long enough to get her blood in the vial. I should have probably thought of that before I got myself in this position.

"My queen, look out behind you!" Iorwerth cries.

Cliodhna whirls and her eyes widen when she sees me crouched behind her. She stumbles back a step, at the same time swinging her hand around. It collides with my chest with the force of an icy train.

Cold pierces my lungs and I fly backward, landing in a heap on the ballroom floor in a spot which had previously been filled with skirts and feet but was quickly vacated as the faeries scurried away, leaving a wide berth for me and my knife. I sit up and glance wide eyed at where it had fallen out of the pocket of my dress where I had been forced to keep it while wearing this ridiculous contraption that the faeries called shoes. It very inconveniently lands next to the vial making this look way worse than it actually was.

I quickly check my other pocket, but Ravven's item of immortality is still safely secured.

"You," Cliodhna gasps, her eyes wide. She flung an accusing finger at me. "She tried to wield iron against me. And she is no Fair Assassin yet. She has broken the Fair Law!"

I struggle to sit up, but my chest is still a block of ice. I gasp for breath. "I didn't!"

The queen gestures with her hand and Iorwerth steps forward with a smirk on his face, but darkness is in his eyes. And a flash of something. Maybe regret. Perhaps he truly did care for me, as a pet that is. He kneels in front of me. "You just had to keep trying, ignoring the fact that you are a mortal. How shall I do it, my little bird?"

Painlessly is what I want to say, but then Ravven bursts into the circle, his hair tousled. "Wait!"

Oddly enough, Iorwerth does. Cliodnha turns to him. "Why should I? You have no power in this situation. You should have clipped your bird's wings before she flew too close to the danger."

Ravven smiles, but it's one with a ghost of pain. He kneels down and picks up the vial and then my dagger. He holds them up. "You see, that is what your problem is. You think that a creature needs to be weakened to be kept safe. But what if I simply give my little bird talons of her own?"

Before anyone can react, Ravven slides the dagger against the palm of his hand, grimacing.

The entire court gasps in such a mix of horror and awe at seeing a faerie actually wield iron against himself. Has that ever even happened before?

Fire stabs my hand, mixing with ice and acid and every stinging and painful sensation there is, as it laces up my elbow. I gasp in pain and clutch my unblemished hand to my chest. I would scream from the pain, but it seems that I am so completely in shock that I can't find it in myself to do it.

Ravven holds his hand over the vial and squeezes until the blood trickles out, filling the vial and staining the sides. He holds himself stiffly as he turns and hands the vial to his cousin who has stepped up right behind him. Cinaed smiles like a cat who just found an entire den of mice.

"The last task is completed," Ravven says, his voice husky. He won't turn to meet my gaze. "Jaye MacCullagh is now the Fair Assassin."

The faeries begin cheering after a long moment of silent shock, but I can't join in. Because I now know the truth.

Ravven and I are truly bonded, or else I would not have felt his pain just then.

And Ravven is the Spring King.

I wish neither of them were true.

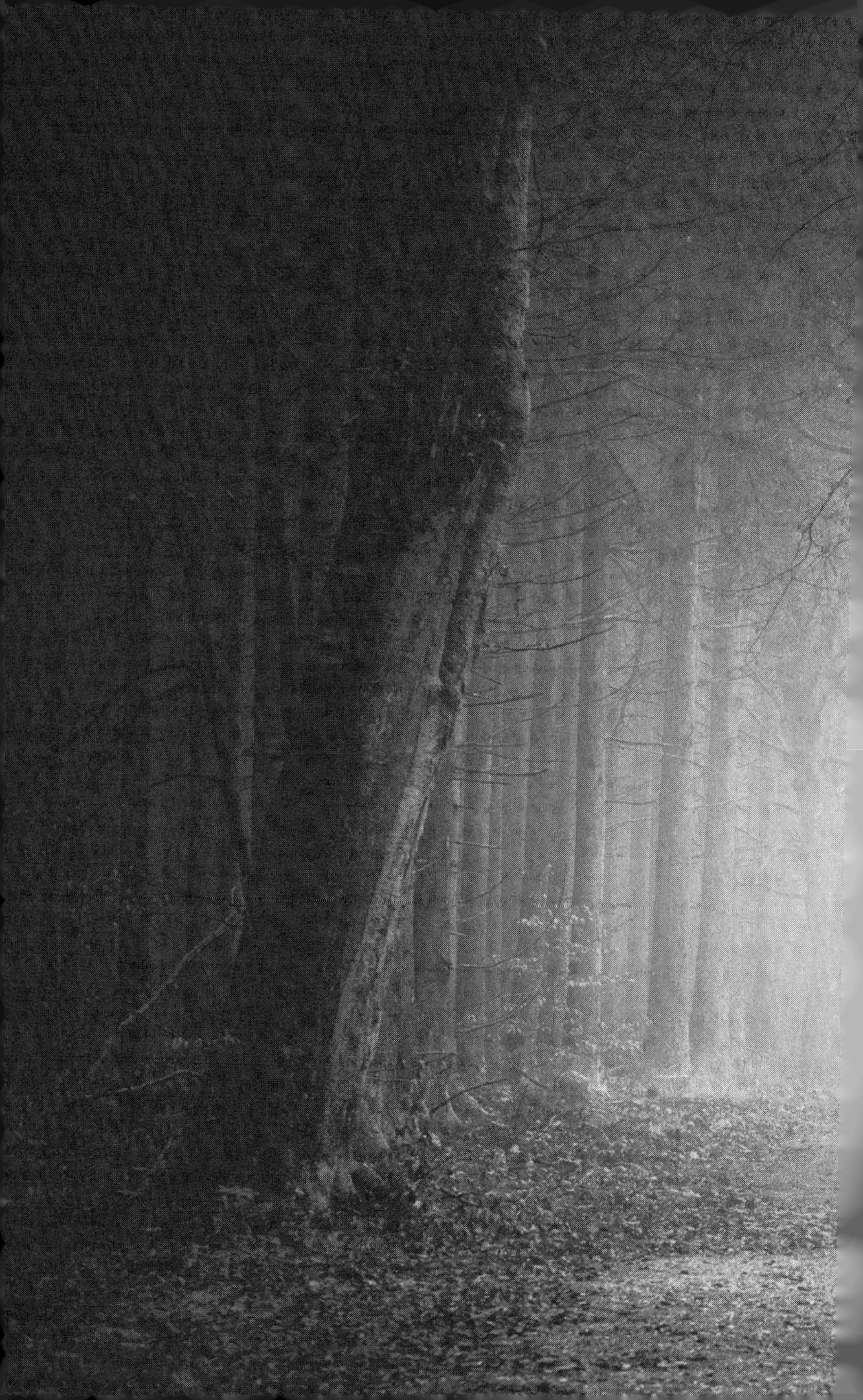

CHAPTER THIRTY-EIGHT

I'm numb with shock as I'm pulled to my feet and am jostled around to the front of the room. I'm dragged to the platform where Ravven had stood when he first introduced the idea of me becoming the Fair Assassin.

Only when I stand on it, the platform doesn't rise up from underneath me on antlers.

The thrones stand sentinel in front of me. The Summer King and the Undersea Queen are already sitting on theirs. Cliodnha primly and elegantly makes her way to her throne and sits down on it, shooting me a scathing look.

But my attention is barely on her as I watch Cinaed take his place behind the Spring Throne. Behind *Ravven's* throne.

"Mortal, you have passed the tests required of you," the Summer King says. "And as such, we rulers of the courts now name you the Fair Assassin."

I pull my gaze away, briefly my eyes flit around looking for Ravven, but I don't know where he is. He's disappeared, taking the answers to all of my questions with him. My hand still throbs painfully. I clench it, trying to ignore the bitter reminder of how this all went wrong.

I am bonded with the Spring King.

And he kept both of these facts from me.

A small figure steps up to me, holding a bundle clutched to her chest. It takes me a moment to recognize her. It's Sarah, the human girl who had been with Cinaed. She is dressed in what appears to be giant rose petals melded together.

She winks at me and I suddenly feel very uncomfortable. My fingers tingle as I reach out and grasp the hilt protruding from the bundle of cloth, glinting a dull gold. I pull it toward me and with a grate the sword slides out of the sheath. I step back and hold it up. The iron glints in the light and as one all of the faeries pressing in around me draw back.

The Blade of Gold and Iron.

My heart jolts in my chest. I can't believe it. I am the Fair Assassin. After all this time, so much has happened and so much has changed, it's surprising that my goal is still the same.

I inhale a shaky breath through my nose, trying not to think about anything right now. I tighten my fingers around the sword and lower it.

A loud cheer or cry or whatever it is, echoes up through the still air and suddenly the faeries are rushing around and out the door to the right.

I frown as I watch them go and Sarah grasps my arm. I startle and look down at her. "Come," she says with a mischievous smile. She tilts her head slightly, her eyes sparkling.

I follow her, wondering what exactly it is that I'm supposed to do. As we walk, I glance at her. "Are you all right?" I ask.

She turns to me inquiringly and I clear my throat. "I mean, are you happy to be here? Or are you... not?"

"You mean to ask me if I am Cinaed's slave as your brother is Aoibheann's?" she asks lightly.

I nod and shrug. "I guess so."

Sarah shakes her head. "No, of course not. I am happy to remain with Cinaed." A dreamy smile crosses her face. "He is going to help me become a faerie so that I can remain in this world forever."

So, I suppose my first impression about Cinaed was wrong. Apparently Sarah isn't enslaved by him, at least unwillingly so. Though why Sarah would ever choose to become a faerie, I will never understand.

I shake my head, but then freeze when I see Aoibheann standing stiffly off to the side alone except for Thomas.

I move away from Sarah's hold and step toward them.

Aoibheann tilts her head as she watches me approach. Her shrill laughter fills the now empty ballroom. "And what have you come to do little mortal? Finally kill me? Or will you balk?" She is trying to hide it, but I can tell that she is frightened.

"I don't have to kill you," I say, trying to keep my voice steady and my hand as well, but I'm failing. I'm terrified too. "Let Thomas go and I shall allow you to go free."

Aoibheann laughs again. "Your brother is mine and so he shall remain for all eternity."

Thomas winces behind her and sways as if he will collapse.

"Please just free him!" I cry, feeling a lump form in my throat. "Don't make me do this."

Aoibheann smiles. "I cannot, because you cannot do it. Weak little mortal, you are not even capable of slaying your enemy."

I shake my head repeatedly. I blink and a tear slips out.

Aoibheann doesn't understand it. I don't want to kill her, but I came too far, betrayed too many people and went through too much to stop now. I squeeze my eyes shut and thrust the sword forward. Her shriek meets my ears, but I keep my eyes squeezed shut even as a weight pulls the sword downward and the scream turns into a gurgle. Blindly, I pull the sword toward me, freeing it from her body. I feel small droplets splatter against my skirt.

Finally, I peel my eyes open, though I refrain from staring down at her lifeless form. It is almost enough to destroy me to see the silver, gold, and crimson blood dripping from my blade and pooling around my skirts.

I raise my gaze to the faeries who had not yet entered the other room, staring at me in shock and horror. I struggle to swallow past the lump in my throat.

But then arms wrap around me and I'm engulfed in a familiar scent. I turn into it and a few tears leak out as I inhale a shaky breath. "Thomas."

"I can't believe that you did it, Jaye," he whispers, his hand rubbing up and down my shoulder blade. His voice is gravely and his hands are bony enough that they make my bones seem soft. I press my forehead into the cavity of his chest underneath his chin.

"I had to," I whisper. "I had to. I had to. I had to." I don't know how many times I have to say it before I start believing myself. Before I stop feeling like a murderer.

"I know," Thomas whispers and his tone is just as broken. "I'm... I'm, so, so sorry, Jaye." He pulls back and I see that there are tears in his eyes too. "I'm the older brother, I'm supposed to protect you. Not force you to do... *this*."

I smile up at him weakly. "We're siblings, Thomas, we take care of each other."

"I hate to interrupt such a touching display of human sentiment, but the faeries will begin the banquet soon and they will not be pleased if the guest of honor does not arrive."

I raise my head to see Sarah standing anxiously to the side. She waves her arms urgently toward the door.

With a frown and making certain that I do not release Thomas's hand, I move to follow her through the door that all of the other faeries disappeared through.

Sarah wasn't wrong when she said that the faeries were beginning a banquet. The faeries don't seem to care that it is the middle of the night... or the Nethermoon or whatever. Because they seem to expect everyone to eat right now.

There is one long table in the middle of the room and adorning it are stacks and stacks of food, liquids cascade from an invisible point in the air down to evaporate before reaching the table.

Thomas shakes his head beside me. "I can't believe this world."

He sits down against the wall and I hurry to get him some food. Thomas accepts it, reluctantly staring at some form of creature's meat that could very well have been a dragon. "I cannot wait until we get home."

I slide down the wall next to him. "Neither can I."

The sooner I leave this cunning world of half-truths and deceptions and false beauty, the sooner I will be freed from the hold it has over me.

Not long after sitting down, Thomas begins sagging. I wrap my arms around him and push to my feet. The faeries have all become so intoxicated that none of them seem to notice as I slip away.

Once I'm out in the ballroom, I'm having a hard time dragging him and my sword. I went through too much trouble to get it to just leave it here, but I can't carry Thomas with only one arm.

"Allow me," Ravven says, suddenly at my side.

I startle and am about to demand how he got here, but then I faintly recall a crow flying down from the ceiling. It only reminds me of everything he lied about. When we first met, he led me to believe that he was only a Far Darrig. No one of importance. Only for me to learn that not only is he a Sidhe, but their king.

I eye him up suspiciously. "I've got this."

"Don't lie just because you can," Ravven says as he steps up to me.

Thomas pushes away from me and sags into Ravven's arm. Obviously ready to no longer tax his sister even if it means trusting another faerie. "Glad to see you again, grumpy," he says with a wan smile. "Thanks for... you know, everything. I can't believe that you came through."

"Do not thank me," Ravven says, but his eyes are on me and not Thomas.

Thomas follows his gaze. "Guess you were right about this one, Jaye. Leave it to you to find the only noble faerie in this world."

Ravven huffs a laugh that pretty much sums up how I'm feeling. Bitter but still amused because everything around me, including who I am... it's a lie. And that's funny, because if there was one person that I was supposed to trust here, it was me.

Turns out, I was the worst of them all.

Neither of us says anything the rest of the time that it takes to get back to the Autumn Court. I leave the room as Ravven lays Thomas out on my bed. I turn my attention to a tapestry, it depicts a hunt, several faeries chasing after a large white stag. It reminds me of the Summer Court's test. Of everything that happened before and after that. All of the tests that we barely survived including that final test.

Not that I needed the reminder.

I know the exact moment he shows up behind me. I don't hear him but somehow, I know.

"When exactly were you planning on telling me?" I demand.

Ravven, for once, is silent.

I whirl on him. "You're the King of Spring. Were you ever planning on telling me that?"

Ravven shifts slightly and then sits down on one of the red and gold embroidered cushions. His face is an ashy shade. I know that his hand is paining him because I can feel it in my own palm. "Never."

I nod and turn back to the tapestry. Fair enough. It's just added to the long list of things he never told me. Like about my gift, how I was immune to faerie curses. But instead he played along and pretended that he could give me a boon that would protect me. All for what?

What could he possibly gain from not telling me?

"How is your hand?" I ask, even though I know full well how his hand is doing. I can feel it myself. I turn back to him and cross my arms.

He presses his lips together and his eyes stray down to his hand. I notice that he has wrapped it in a cloth. Maybe even one of the bandages that I made for him out of his torn shirt. "I think I will survive."

"Why did you do it?" I demand. The anger and shame and frustration coursing through my veins makes me feel lightheaded. We had the rule for a reason. *Never trust a faerie.* And I broke that rule, these are only the consequences of my actions. I should have known that Ravven would in some way betray me.

And yet, he also saved me.

He's lied to me, kept so, so many secrets from me. But he saved me. And now because of me he is beholden to Cinaed. The man who killed his whole family.

"What do you mean, why did I do it? It's hardly as if you left me with any choice. They would have killed you if I did not."

"As if you would have cared," I say with a scornful laugh.

"Of course I would have cared," Ravven says. "Considering that they would have executed me after my champion died."

"And was that the only reason you did it?" I demand. "Was that the only reason you helped me?"

"Of course," he says.

"You had another reason."

His eyebrows rise. "Was self-preservation not a convincing enough motivation?"

I cross my arms tightly. "No. And don't try to pretend that you don't care about me. I know that you do. Your actions speak louder than your words, Ravven Crowe."

"What actions?" he demands.

"How about we start with that kiss."

"I was using you! I got what I wanted. That doesn't mean that I care about you."

"Except you do." I step toward him. "You do and I know it."

His eyes are red. He looks terrified, but then they fade to black till they are just two coals situated on his face. "You are living in a delusion, pest. You mean nothing to me," he says, his entire face crumpling as if it pains him to say simply that sentence.

I step back away from him, stumbling back as if his words were actually a barrier that struck me. "And I thought that faeries could not lie."

"What?" Ravven asks, his eyes fading to a dark crimson again.

"I know about the bond, Ravven," I spit. I watch the shock and then horror cross his features before I turn on my heel and stalk out of the room.

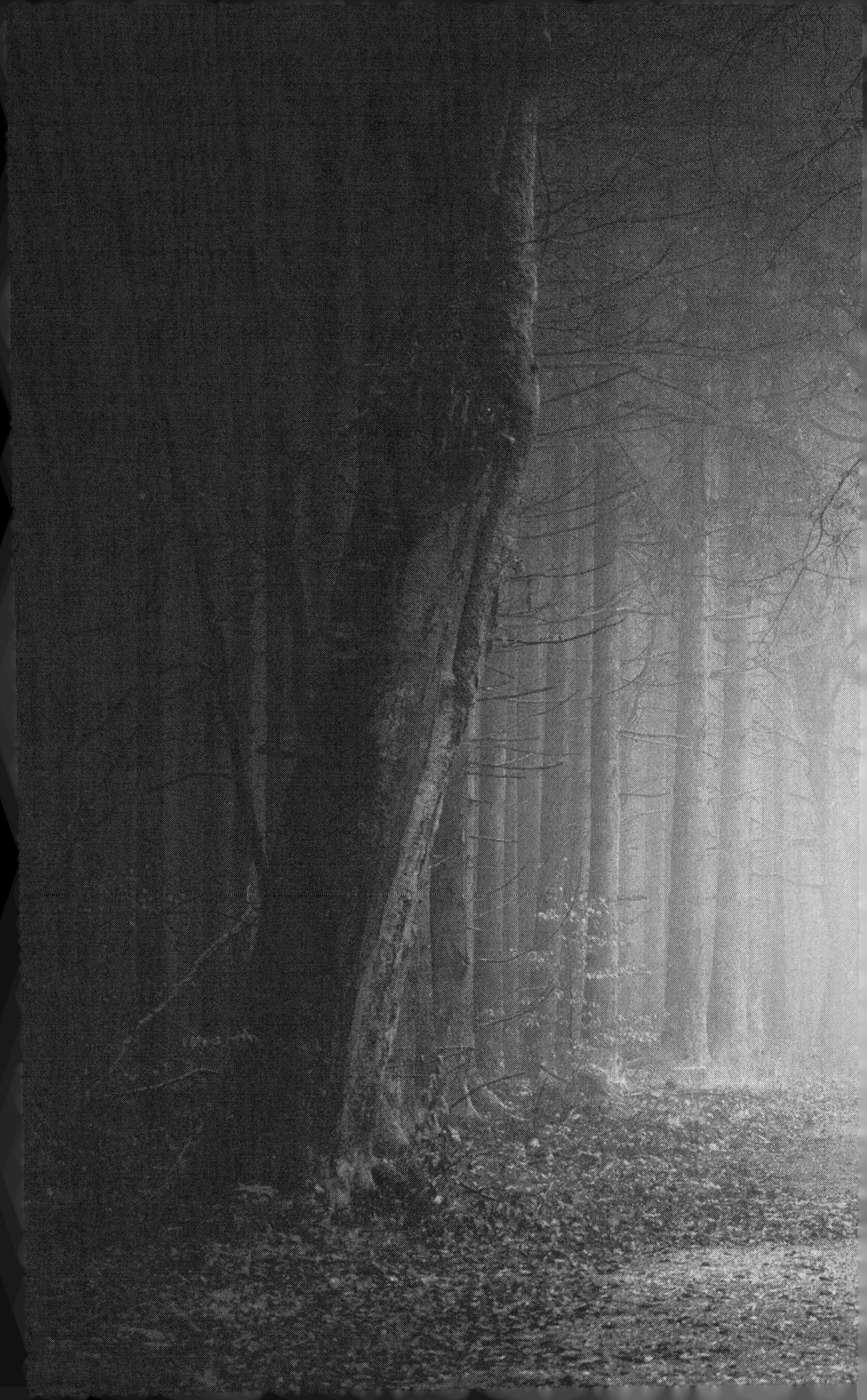

CHAPTER THIRTY-NINE

I never knew the world could be so dark, but then I've never been outside during Nethermoon either. I inhale a shaky breath, closing my eyes as the chill clean air seems to penetrate my soul.

I gain some solace from the dark trees around me and the still stone of the castle to my left. I keep my hand on it so that I do not lose my way as I plunge into the dark world.

I want to run and leave all of this behind, but I cannot. I would get lost in the never-ending darkness. Besides I can't leave Thomas, and my blood bargain with Ravven binds me here.

But if I remained another moment within those confining stone walls, I had feared that I would suffocate. So that was how I found myself outside with the darkness just as suffocating and the clean cool air. Goosebumps cover my arm and I wish that I had changed out of the light material of my dress that is really more flowers than material.

My foot snags on some unseen obstacle and I pitch forward only to find that the area ahead of me is lit. I remove my hand from the wall and step toward the light, relieved for something other than the darkness and my oppressive thoughts to keep my company. I find myself standing in some sort of garden. Hedges wrap around me with pale roses twisting around their leaves. Torches protrude from the green, burning steadily as if they would not possibly set this whole garden on fire.

I continue deeper until I enter an open expanse in the garden. Flowers twine around my ankles, growing out of a stone ground. Steps lead down from an open door, leading back into the Court of Dreams and Nightmares.

I wrap my arms around myself, trying to focus on the scent of the flowers and nothing else.

"Oh dear, you look quite gloomy for a victor. Is there trouble in paradise, my sweet?" I startle and whirl, wishing that I hadn't left my Blade of Gold and Iron in my room. It had been covered in blood and I hadn't the heart to keep carrying it around. Not when I thought of the faerie that I had killed. I reach for my dagger but then I remember that the last time I had seen it, Ravven had been holding it right before he cut himself, I don't know what happened to it afterwards. I am defenseless without the one weapon I can actually use.

Ravven had said that Fair Assassins didn't last long, often ending up assassinated themselves.

Of course though, Ravven had said a lot of things.

Cinaed smiles and holds up his hands as if trying to pacify me. It does little to comfort me. With a flick of his wrist and he could have these flowers wrapping themselves around my neck. "I thought that I would save you the trouble and come to you."

"Pardon?" I ask, eyeing the flowers suspiciously, but they don't move.

"My cousin has been waiting a hundred and thirty years for his revenge. I would be a fool to think that he wouldn't strike now, when he has an opportunity to finally kill me."

I grit my teeth. How blithely he speaks of his own death and Ravven's pain. And my part in this, like I'm nothing more than a weapon at Ravven's disposal.

Cinaed's eyes take in my face, not missing anything. "But you are no one's to command, I see that. So, tell me, how exactly did my cousin manage just that?"

I swallow and glance away. A blood bargain. One I cannot break. But that was the only way I could save Thomas, and Ravven did keep his end of the bargain. Thomas is safe now.

"We have an arrangement."

"How convenient, don't you think?"

He chuckles as he strides toward me, his arms outspread. "Go ahead. Strike me down. If I know my cousin, he has probably been planning this meeting for a very long time. A way for his wayward cousin to die by mortal hands in the most humiliating way possible. I'm surprised that he isn't here now. Where is Crowe?"

I swallow, not comfortable in telling him that Ravven has no idea where I am. Instead I decide to keep him talking. "What do you mean, he's been planning this? There's no way he could have known that it would end this way?"

Cinaed harrumphs to himself. "You underestimate my cousin if you do not think that he did not plan every step of your journey to get you to stand here. Ravven is many things, but above all he is manipulative."

I open my mouth to argue, but it seems as if my voice has died. Ravven has kept a lot of things from me, but it wasn't his plan for me to take him captive or for us to both be captured by the Winter Court. That blood bargain we made was a spur of the moment decision and so was everything after that.

"You know his story, I am sure," Cinaed says. "The story of the poor broken king. But you never stopped to ask me mine."

He moves two steps toward me and I don't move away. My eyes are locked on his black ones as they flicker to the faintest blue.

"Our mothers were sisters. Ravven's the oldest and mine the second. Ravven's mother had been born of our grandfather and one of his human slaves. It was my mother who was the true heir. She was the one who should have inherited, but since her sister was older the throne would pass to her, mixed blood or not. That was the Fair Law. Unfortunately, his mother did not care that her battle was already won. She was desperately jealous of my mother and her pure bloodline, until finally she killed her own sister by destroying her item of immortality. Did he tell you that part? How his filthy mongrel mother killed mine."

No, he had not. The image of the beautiful kind woman I had always imagined, the woman who had the love of two Solitary faeries began to shift. But then something else Cinaed had said clicks in my mind.

"Wait," I say, rubbing at my temples. "Are you saying that Ravven is part human?"

"A quarter human, yes. It isn't enough human blood for him to not have magic, but it is enough that he has a higher tolerance to iron than other faeries. And it means that he can lie, though he was always terrible at it. His faerie magic fights against it, but it never stopped him. He considers it a great privilege to be able to do so, a special power. Even though it pains him every time he does."

I stumble back several steps, nearly tripping over the hem of my skirt. Cinaed's eyes are black again, but his face does not twist with pain the way that Ravven's always did when his eyes were black.

Ravven's eyes were black when he told me I meant nothing to him. I knew he was lying; I just hadn't known how he could.

My heart stutters in my chest and then a sharp pain pierces it. The first time I ever saw Ravven, his eyes were black as tar. He told me I was ugly. He grimaced.

He was lying.

Eilis's words from earlier filter back to me. *He looks at you as if you are his whole world...*

But I hadn't believed her, I had been blinded by the security I felt knowing that faeries couldn't lie. I never once considered the fact that Ravven wasn't fully faerie. If he lied about something so inconsequential as my appearance then what else did he lie about?

My mind races back to that fateful night with the clumps of dirt lying strewn all around us as he tells me that he wasn't the one to destroy the faerie ring. His eyes had been black then. He had grimaced as if in physical pain.

He had been lying.

My heart is tearing to shreds. Tears blur my vision and I clench at my chest, but there is nothing there but a dark void of pain and unhappiness. Black as Ravven's eyes always seem to be at crucial moments of my life.

Cinaed doesn't seem to care for my pain as he continues talking about his own twisted past as if my present is not twisted enough. "I finally got revenge on my family, determined that I would be the one to rule just as it should always have been. Of course Ravven was already gone. Upon learning of his heritage, he fled the court, taking a human slave with him. He went to live in the Autumn Court, but curse his every breath, he was still the rightful heir. I could not ascend the throne while he lived."

"Why are you telling me all this?" I demand. I keep my hand firmly over my heart as if trying to somehow hold my heart together.

Cinaed languidly spreads his hands out. "To show you that I am not the villain. I never have been."

Perhaps not by faerie standards.

Cinaed takes another step toward me, the petals of a rose crunching under his booted heel. "I believe that we can make a bargain that could be beneficial to us both. I have put revenge behind me, unlike Crowe. I just want to rule. Also, unlike Crowe. You see, Crowe fled his responsibilities and his people when he joined the Autumn Court. He was supposed to be our king and now our people suffer without a ruler. The Spring Court suffers." Cinaed looks at me pleadingly. "I just want to end my people's suffering."

"And what do you think I can do about it?" I demand.

Cinaed smiles. "You see, this is somewhere my cousin and I differ. He thinks of mortals as his pawns. I see them for what they truly are. Invaluable. A queen. Just ask my Sarah. He will use your kind; I do not make the mistake of underestimating you so."

"What do you want from me?" I ask again.

"I want Crowe's item of immortality. If I have it then I can claim his throne. The Spring Court will not have to suffer under a careless king."

I gasp and stumble back, my hand almost straying to my pocket. Cinaed would take it from me if he knew I had it. Take it with force if he had to. I don't know why I still feel a loyalty toward Ravven now after everything else that has been said and done. But I do.

Cinaed's dark eyes spark in the darkness. "I see that you do know what it is. I was right to think that you were the person to aid me."

I swallow hard, unable to protest. Something tells me that he would see through any lie I tried to muster.

"And I believe that I am the person to aid you. Your brother Thomas is still in a very dire condition and without magical aid, he might even die. However, my people are renowned healers. They can restore him to his former glory. Give me Crowe's item of immortality and I will heal your brother. I swear it."

"No," I say, stumbling back another step. I shake my head hard. Ravven had trusted me with his ring, not for me to give it to someone else.

"Surely you would not protect the person who put you all through this? Who did such a thing to your brother?"

"You don't know that Ravven is responsible for…" I can't even finish my sentence. For what happened to Thomas. Because if he was…

No. No, he could not be.

"And you do not know that he isn't. You are wasting your loyalty on the wrong individual. I think that if you should have learned one thing during your time in our world, it is that there is only ever one person you should be loyal to. And it is not Crowe. It is not me. It is yourself and only yourself. Why hold onto a loyalty to Crowe, a faerie who lies, when you can save your own brother?"

My thoughts are swirling through my head, telling me to do it then screaming at me not to. Thomas or Ravven? Which should I choose? But who is to say that I have to choose anyone? Perhaps Ravven would have to live a life bowing to Cinaed's whims to hope that his immortal item is not destroyed, but if he is responsible for everything that happened to me since coming to the Otherworld then perhaps he deserves it.

But this is Ravven, my heart screams at me. *Ravven who you worked with. Ravven who helped you. Saved you.*

You are broken, my head tells my heart, *how can you know what is right or not?*

Ravven or Cinaed? Who should I trust when I cannot trust either?

"Think about what I said," Cinaed says with a devilish smirk and then he disappears into the dark hedges of the garden. I'm staring after him, wondering why he left so soon when I hear a footfall behind me. I turn to see Ravven step hesitantly up to me.

He stares at me for a long moment, not speaking. I don't know why he sought me out. Maybe he felt the pain tearing my heart to pieces. Or maybe he simply wants to explain himself. But then he doesn't say anything. He only stands there watching me. I feel his own guilt, the weight of a thousand tons weighing at our joined souls.

"Tell me about the bond," I say, surprised by how cold my voice is.

Ravven bows his head, a lock of his hair covering his eyes. "What is there to say? Obviously it is a mistake."

"And is there any way to reverse this mistake?"

"I—I don't know of any. As soon as I felt the bond snap into place, I asked my father if he knew anything. He did not. I believe the best cure for our... *malady* is distance."

"And you were never going to tell me? Never?"

Ravven finally raises his gaze, he looks me straight in the eye. "Never."

"How could you have kept something so monumental from me? Our souls were bonded, don't you think I deserved the right to know?"

"What difference would my telling you have made? Our bond does not change anything. It does not mean anything." He grimaces and my heart picks up speed, even though it is too dark to see the color of his eyes.

"You're lying," I whisper.

"I'm not though. Think, pest. Is it truly going to change anything? This knowledge that you now have. Is it really? Is it going to mean that you don't leave?"

I press my lips together. Does he want me to stay?

"I didn't think so," Ravven says, his tone bitter. "As I said. It's a mistake. Our destinies are leading us in different directions."

He's right. They are. So how did we end up spending so much time together, if it wasn't planned? If someone did not forcibly manipulate our lives and make our destinies cross paths?

The one scene keeps playing over and over. His dark eyes. His grimace. He lied to me when he said that he wasn't the reason I was trapped in the Otherworld. Ravven was our guide, he could have led us to where the Winter Court could trap us. After that, it was a simple matter of using Thomas against me to force me into this position.

No, no, no, my heart screams. *This can't be true.*

Only because I don't think I will survive it being true.

But what I want does not change the facts.

"Ravven," Cinaed says, stepping back into view. "Just who I wanted to see. You have been quite busy manipulating this poor mortal."

Ravven shoots me a look filled with dread. He opens his mouth as if to speak but then closes it again.

"And all for what? Revenge? Well, before you have it, allow me to at least have one last say." He pulls something out of his pocket. We both stiffen when we see the vial of blood. "It is a pity that this can only make you do so much, or I would demand your throne or perhaps your true name. But since I cannot demand that, then I demand the truth for this poor mortal." He unscrews the lid and dumps out the liquid on the flowers at his feet. He smiles at us with such vicious cruelty for a second he looks hideous. "By your blood you are bound."

I whip my gaze to Ravven who looks to be in physical pain. More than just the pain in his hand. I shake my head. "Don't say it." I don't want to know. I don't want to hear it.

"I can't stop myself, pest. Besides, I—you deserve the right to know."

I step toward him and Ravven doesn't back away. I grasp the lapels of his coat, yanking him down and pressing my lips against his.

I kiss him with a frenzy, with every emotion that I have ever felt.

The kiss is a hello. A goodbye. A declaration of love. The venom of hate.

But most of all, it is a betrayal.

A betrayal to myself, to him, and to a fledgling of a bond that never should have existed.

A lie to cover a truth that I don't want to hear.

I stand on my tiptoes, deepening the kiss, but then he pulls away. "I lied to you," he says, shoving me away. I let go of his lapels and allow him to put some distance between us. "I never told you to trust me," he says quietly. He is now standing in a circle of light from a torch. His eyes are a darker blue than the ocean's deep. "I didn't even try to make it easy for you to trust me."

"But I did trust you," I say, tears brimming my eyes. I curse myself, telling myself not to cry in front of him, but I'm sure he can feel my pain through our bond anyway. What's the use of hiding it? He hurt me.

I broke the first rule for him.

And I guess that a broken heart is my consequence. A half dead brother. And a faerie that I love but also hate.

Ravven bows his head. "And I'm sorry for that. It seems we were both played the fool. And all by me."

I stare at him, trying to reconcile this knowledge of everything that has happened. Of everything that has passed between us. "You did this all, you lured me to your world, you destroyed the faerie ring. You led us to be captured by the Winter Court, all so that you could turn me into a killer. So that you could have me kill Cinaed."

Ravven ducks his head. "It is as you say. I have been plotting this for a hundred and thirty years. Waiting for the perfect human to force into this. Then you were born with your unique gift and I knew it had to be you." He lifts his head. "I had already made the plan long before I met you. I simply had to put the pieces into motion. I allowed myself to become captured by the Winter Court, but I was not in league with them. I was just using them."

"Like you apparently use everyone."

"I don't know what to say... I'm sorry. I did not know you then, Jaye. I only cared about revenge."

"You were responsible for Thomas's captivity," I spit. "Maybe I could forgive anything that you did to me, but not to him. You hurt my brother."

"I suppose you have made up your mind then?" Cinaed asks smugly.

I turn away from Ravven, unable to witness the guilt written across his face or the twisting of his beautiful features. I close the distance between me and Cinaed and then I yank the ring out of my pocket. I toss it into his hand, before my common sense has a chance to catch up to my rage.

"I agree to our bargain." I say softly, watching the ring sit in the palm of his golden fingers. It seems wrong.

Everything in me screams at me to take it back, instead I step away.

"You can't trust him!" Ravven cries, his voice breaking.

"I can't trust you," I reply softly.

I squeeze my eyes shut.

This isn't just for me. This isn't to hurt Ravven. This is for Thomas who needs a healer. This is for the Spring Court who hasn't had a king in a hundred and thirty years.

Cinaed chuckles. "It appears you have nowhere to turn then, poor little mortal. But I thank you for this ring." He clutches the ring more tightly and pink light flares out from between his fingers.

Ravven cries out as a stabbing pain pierces my chest. "What are you doing?" I demand.

"I am finally finishing what I started all those years ago. I'm killing my family."

"No!" I cry. I grimace as more pain shoots up my chest. "You said that you would convince him to give up his throne."

"No, I said I would take his throne. Over his dead body. Pay attention, little mortal, to what a faerie says or else you will forever be bamboozled."

He tightens his hand and the light flashes out between his fingers with ever increasing brightness until it is practically blinding. I lunge for him, but I can't see anymore and I grasp at empty air. Ravven cries out in pain just as it hits me.

The pain I had felt earlier was nothing. The void was comfortable, this is a gaping maw wanting to consume anything that could possibly fill it.

I clutch my chest and lurch blindly toward Ravven, to where his screams are echoing from. My foot catches on something, it must be a flower and I collapse in a bed of petals. I don't bother to get up, I can't even try. I exist in a world where everything is pain and torment. There is nothing else. Then finally bit by bit it subsides. I draw in a ragged breath, blinking trying to clear my blurred vision, staring at a large pink rose.

My hand is lying extended toward Ravven, my fingers only inches away from his own. But there's something wrong with the picture. His fingers are a chalky gray and motionless. He is motionless.

"Ravven?" I croak, pushing to my elbows. I drag myself toward him even though every movement is torturous. Not as torturous as the pounding of my broken heart. I rest a trembling hand on his chest. There is no warmth. There is no flutter of movement.

"Ravven?" I shake him, but he doesn't stir. His face is expressionless with his eyes staring blankly at the sky. "Ravven!" I scream, slapping my hands against his chest. He has to wake up. He has to blink. To scold me. To tell me that I ruined his life.

To do anything but lie there so, so still under my murderous touch.

Cinaed's laugh echoes into my panicked thoughts. "I cannot believe this! You were bonded to my unfortunate cousin and yet you still betrayed him? Oh, that is rich. But never fear, mortal. I will keep my bargain. Even now, my court is collecting your brother."

There is a threat in his words. His people have Thomas. I can't hurt him, or make him pay for tricking me, without risking harm befalling my brother. Why do I keep making bargains with faeries?

I bury my face into my hands and sob over the empty form of my lifeless lover.

Ravven was right all along. I'm an idiot. He may have put this into motion, but the final move is mine. I made a very grave mistake. And now he's gone and I don't know what to do.

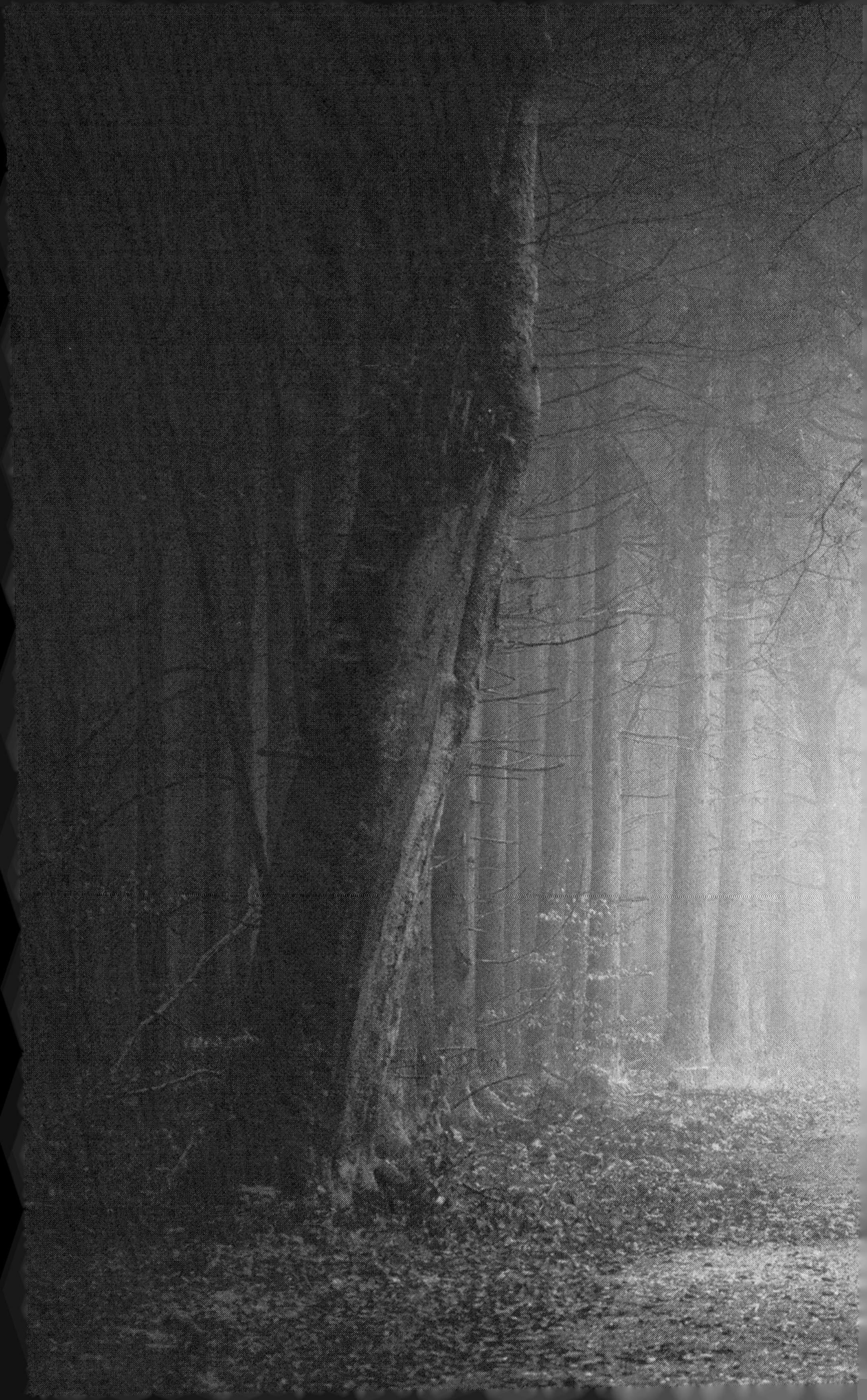

CHAPTER FORTY

It's been two days since we left the Court of Dreams and Nightmares. Two days since my dreams stopped and the nightmare began.

At least Thomas is better, regaining color and his weight, though I do watch the food the Sidhe faeries bring him like a hawk. I don't trust a single faerie in this whole blasted court.

I don't trust anyone. Not the new King of Spring. Not Thomas to not somehow end up hurt again. And certainly not myself.

I wrap my arms around myself, the unfamiliar slick material of the pale pink shirt I am wearing slipping against my arms.

I guess I should have known Cinaed's plan from the start. I had thought that perhaps my new position as the Fair Assassin would somehow protect me. Surely he would not anger someone who could so easily kill him. But when he agreed to help my brother, he gained for himself a bargaining piece.

I'm starting to worry that he isn't afraid of me, but rather that he wants to use me. To be the court with the Fair Assassin at his disposal. That when everything is said and done and Thomas has finally recovered, he won't let us go.

At least not that easily.

I should never have made a bargain with a faerie. What was I even thinking to consider myself capable of that? No matter what, they will always, always come out on top.

Not always, love. Sometimes we die instead. It's a dangerous game, for both sides.

Of course, it is a deadly game. And I'm still just a pawn. The problem is that, idiot that I am, I've killed my king. The game was lost before it even started.

Don't expect me to feel pity for you. You deserve whatever comes next.

I hiss and clutch the side of my head, breathing in and out as I focus on the flowers twining up the dirt walls in front of me. I count them, count their petals, focus every bit of my attention on those flowers.

I had been so relieved to see the sun again, up until I was brought into Cinaed's rath here under a hill with no sunlight except for the areas where a window has been cut into the earth around us.

The air is suffocating and earthy and filled with the deathly sweet smell of the flowers, which only makes me think of another patch of flowers. And a lifeless form slumped on top of them.

No!

I clamp my hands over my ears as if that will somehow keep the memories away. I have to stop thinking about it. Reliving those screams and the pain over and over. What I have done is in the past. There's nothing I can do but move on.

I need to move on.

Or I'm afraid that I will be yet another human that the faerie world has claimed for its own. A hollow husk with empty eyes and an even more empty smile like every slave that I pass in the halls, enthralled out of their minds, thinking that they are happy.

Already it's driving me insane. I keep hearing the voice, *his* voice in my head. I suppose to make certain that I never forget what I did to him.

Why do I have to remind you of that unpleasant matter when you won't let yourself forget?

Ravven's voice is as painful as the rose thorns that dig into my hand when I slam it against the wall. But one pain does not rid me of the other, and I fear that I will always be faced with this haunting voice in my head. Come back to torment me from the grave. I suppose I deserve every bit of it. I did kill him after all.

Yes, you did.

It might have been Cinaed who destroyed the ring, but I was the one who gave him the power to do so. I gave him the ring that Ravven had entrusted to me.

I can tell you which one hurt worse.

He had said that I was the only person he trusted.

What a foolish statement.

I grit my teeth and squeeze my eyes shut. I had sworn myself that I would not think of it again and yet I had already broken my word countless times. Every word from the voice is an agonizing reminder of everything that I lost. Everything that I destroyed. And the fact that I will never hear Ravven mock me out loud again.

Oh, you poor foolish soul. Do you really think that you have rid yourself of me? Have you learned nothing? We are forever twined, pest.

My eyes flutter open and I stare at the dirt wall in front of me, the weight of The Blade of Gold and Iron at my waist, the only thing grounding me to this world. "Ravven?" I whisper into the darkness of the solitude of the Spring Court.

But it can't truly be him. He's dead. I saw him die. I *killed* him.
He isn't coming back.

Your faith in that fact is about to be tested. Because I am *coming. For you. I hope that you're ready for when I find you.*

To be continued in book two:
Of Stars and Shadows

Nicki is a twenty-something author of clean YA speculative fiction. She has been writing since she was eleven years old, and has published several works including portal fantasies such as *A Week of Werewolves, Faeries, and Fancy Dresses* and *A Certain Sort of Madness*; as well as *Winter Cursed* a dark fantasy Snow White retelling. Nicki lives in Ohio where she spends far too much time watching TV and sleeping. She listens to music basically all the time, and adores obsessing over mythologies, her shows, and her slew of fictional boyfriends. When not writing, she can usually be found at her desk with either a paintbrush or a pen in her hand.

To my amazing support system. AKA my family.

To my publisher. AKA my dad.

To the person who taught me how to read and write. AKA my mom.

To everyone who read this story in its earliest forms and still enjoyed it. AKA my beta readers: Skye, Grace, Hannah, Faith, and Katrina

To my editor: AKA Deborah

To everyone who got excited when I announced I was publishing this book. AKA my readers.

To the furbabies who snuggled me as I tried to write. AKA my dogs.

To my Lord and Savior. AKA Jesus.

Made in the USA
Columbia, SC
08 March 2023